Praise for *Blood's Echo*

"Maldonado has crafted a top-notch thriller that will have police procedural junkies and thrill-seekers turning page after page ... "

 —Maegan Beaumont, award-winning author of *Carved in Darkness*

"Isabella Maldonado is off to a great start, giving us a tense thriller with a strong sense of place and an insider's look at some of the most dangerous work in law enforcement. This first Veranda Cruz novel will leave readers eagerly awaiting her next adventure."

 —Jan Burke, *New York Times* bestselling author

PHOENIX BURNING

THE BATTLE BETWEEN
VERANDA CRUZ AND THE VILLALOBOS
CARTEL TURNS PHOENIX INTO A WAR ZONE

ISABELLA MALDONADO

MIDNIGHT INK
WOODBURY, MINNESOTA
MIDNIGHT
INK

First Edition
First Printing, 2018

Book format by Bob Gaul
Cover design by Ellen Lawson
Cover illustration by Dominick Finelle / The July Group
Editing by Nicole Nugent

Midnight Ink, an imprint of Llewellyn Worldwide Ltd.

This is a work of fiction. Names, characters, places, and incidents are either the product of the author's imagination or are used fictitiously, and any resemblance to actual persons, living or dead, business establishments, events, or locales is entirely coincidental.

Library of Congress Cataloging-in-Publication Data
Names: Maldonado, Isabella, author.
Title: Phoenix burning / Isabella Maldonado.
Description: First edition. | Woodbury, Minnesota: Midnight Ink, [2018] |
    Series: A Verando Cruz mystery; #2
Identifiers: LCCN 2017043124 (print) | LCCN 2017046365 (ebook) | ISBN
    9780738753935 | ISBN 9780738751023 (alk. paper)
Subjects: LCSH: Policewomen—Fiction. | Women detectives—Fiction. | Drug
    traffic—Fiction. | GSAFD: Suspense fiction.
Classification: LCC PS3613.A434 (ebook) | LCC PS3613.A434 P48 2018 (print) |
    DDC 813/.6—dc23
LC record available at https://lccn.loc.gov/2017043124

Midnight Ink
Llewellyn Worldwide Ltd.
2143 Woodale Drive
Woodbury, MN 55125-2989
www.midnightinkbooks.com

Printed in the United States of America

For Max.
Each day, you show me the world through your eyes.
How privileged I am.

DETECTIVE VERANDA CRUZ SENSED the trap but couldn't see it. She adjusted her visor to block the midday glare and scanned the blighted South Phoenix street as she gave the Chevy Impala some gas. She tightened her seatbelt, crushing her ballistic vest against her body, and glanced at the dash clock. Two minutes until meeting time.

If Castillo kept his word. If he didn't, nothing she could do would save him. She'd spent more than two years investigating the Villalobos cartel and had never gotten an opportunity like this. So why were her instincts blaring a warning? She turned to her partner. Sam Stark's legendary skills were one of the reasons Veranda had been paired with him when she was transferred to the Phoenix Police Homicide Unit six weeks ago. She knew he would read the atmosphere too.

"Sam, you feel it?"

"My pucker factor's at about a nine." He slid a glance her way. "Yeah, I'm feeling it."

Eyes constantly assessing, Veranda continued toward the location where they were supposed to meet Raymond Castillo. Each street bore witness to the unfulfilled promise of regentrification. "This part of the city took it hard when the recession hit," she said, passing a row of abandoned storefronts.

"We're in the badlands." Sam peered out from under his bushy brows. "Bars in the windows, bail bonds offices, and pawn shops."

"You think Castillo's already there?"

Sam grunted. "I would be. I'd watch us drive in to be sure we're alone."

"I don't think he's that smart."

She rounded the corner onto Dalton Street. Castillo stood on a cracked sidewalk at the far end of the block, shoulder against a street-light, tattooed arms crossed against his chest. Clad in a white tank top and faded jeans, he looked more like a street punk than an aspiring crime boss.

"Why is he out in the open like this in broad daylight?" Sam said.

Veranda followed Sam's gaze. "He's a sitting—"

Wham!

A black Escalade with dark tinted windows had barreled out from a side street and smashed into the Impala's left front quarter panel. Veranda's upper body flew to the right, rebounded against the seat-belt, then slammed against the driver's door. With a deafening metallic crunch, the Cadillac SUV plowed forward until it scraped free of the Chevy sedan's front bumper. Veranda yanked the steering wheel, struggling to regain control as the car spun in a complete circle, coming to rest on the sidewalk facing Castillo. Locking eyes through the cracked windshield, Veranda returned his shocked expression.

The Escalade glided toward Castillo.

She tore off her seatbelt, snatched her Glock from its holster, and shoved at the bent driver's door. Stuck. She mashed the window's power button, but it stopped halfway down. She lifted her foot and kicked at her door, denting the inside handle. Cursing, she thrust her gun through the open top half of the car window and took aim with her left hand. She had to try.

Sam threw his door open, knelt on the sidewalk, and raised his gun over the Impala's hood, bellowing commands at the Escalade's driver.

She yelled at Castillo. "Run!"

The black SUV slowed next to Castillo, who stood rooted to the spot. The passenger window buzzed down and a rifle barrel poked out.

Veranda's pulse thudded in her ears. Time expanded, then contracted. She fired, aware it would do no good. Rounds pinged off the Escalade's armor plating and bulletproof glass.

Too late, the sound of gunfire spurred Castillo to action. He reached for his waistband as the staccato burst of four rapid-fire shots cracked the air.

Castillo jerked when bullets from the rifle drilled into his chest. A spray of blood exploded across his white tank top as the high-powered rounds tore straight through his upper body. Arms flung wide, he crumpled to the ground.

The Escalade peeled out, dark smoke billowing up from its shrieking tires.

Sam stood and took a step toward Castillo's inert form.

She shoved her gun back in its holster. "Get in the car, Sam!"

Sam swiveled and angled his head through the open car window. "What about Castillo?"

"Four shots center mass with a rifle." She shook her head. "I'm not letting those bastards get away when Castillo's got zero chance. Advise rescue and let's go."

Sam bristled. "We've got a victim over there who—"

She cut him off. Sam was the most senior Homicide detective on the department, but he didn't have her background in drug enforcement, or her knowledge of the enemy. "That's a Villalobos cartel battle cruiser lined with steel plating. The windows and rear tire flaps are bulletproof. It's got enough fire power to destroy downtown Phoenix. And that's where it's heading."

"Shit." Sam hooked a hand on the door frame and swung into the passenger's seat. He grabbed the mic from the radio mounted in front of the center console.

Sam delivered instructions to the dispatcher and responding police personnel while she mentally ran through options. The PPD had a BearCat equipped to stop an armored vehicle, but she had to keep the Escalade in sight in order to make that happen. She took her foot off the brake and pinned the accelerator to the floor.

Sam clutched the dashboard as they lurched forward. "Rescue's direct on Castillo. ETA four minutes."

"Mark us in pursuit, and tell dispatch to make sure everyone knows the Escalade is armored."

Sam advised the dispatcher of a 9-0-6 and she refocused on her quarry. The Impala was faster and more maneuverable than the top-heavy SUV, allowing her to whip around corners as Sam gave rapid-fire updates into the mic.

They headed out of the low-end district with abandoned store-fronts and into the busy downtown area. Lunchtime on a Thursday, the streets would be crowded with pedestrians and cars. Her stomach knotted with apprehension.

4

After crossing the bridge into the business district, the Escalade screeched to a stop. Close on their tail, Veranda stomped on the brakes, forcing the car into a sideways skid that left her partially exposed. A figure leaned out of the front passenger window and glared at her.

"Roberto Bernal," she breathed. A low-level enforcer with the Villalobos cartel, Roberto had obviously been sent to silence Castillo.

She barely had time to register his identity before Roberto pointed a rifle directly at her. Automatic weapon fire strafed the Impala. She ducked under the dashboard, seeking cover behind the engine block. Crouched beneath the steering wheel, she jammed the car into reverse and pushed the gas pedal with her knee. Steering blindly, she yanked the wheel in a circle to spin the Impala around, popped up into the driver's seat, and fishtailed around a corner.

Maneuvering through parallel streets, shef swerved back in behind the SUV, this time at a safer distance. A marked patrol car, lights flashing and siren blaring, pulled up next to her. Another cruiser slid in from the opposite side, flanking the Impala. The cavalry had arrived. Still, she couldn't break off her pursuit. She let the road dogs take the lead but stayed close. When this ended, she would be there to arrest and interrogate Roberto and whoever was driving him in the Escalade.

As the bizarre cavalcade sped down Mariposa Avenue, two muzzles jutted from the Cadillac SUV and a barrage of gunfire spewed in every direction, the suspects firing wildly. Motorists drove up onto sidewalks, pedestrians dove for cover, and bullets ricocheted off building fronts.

Veranda careened the Impala around a corner onto Camelback Road. They arrived at a high-end business district, heading toward the Arcadia Fashion Center, an upscale shopping mall renowned for its lush palm trees and posh retail stores.

Her pulse beat faster as they drew closer to the mall. "We can't let them get to the shopping center. It'll be packed in there."

A patrol supervisor came on their radio frequency, took command of the pursuit, and directed responding units to set up bull's-eye perimeters. The police helicopter announced its arrival and began a hover pattern over the area.

She slapped a palm against the steering wheel in frustration. "The supervisor's trying to box them in. But Roberto will get to the mall first."

The black Escalade veered to the far-left lane, the driver lining up for a sharp turn into the shopping center's multilevel parking deck.

"That Caddy's a tank with all the extra weight from the armor plating," Sam said. "Can't maneuver in tight spaces. What the hell is Roberto thinking?"

She jerked the steering wheel, trailing the Escalade and patrol cars into the shopping center parking lot. The SUV driver attempted a hard left into the garage next to one of the main entrances, lost control, and slammed head-on into a concrete pylon.

Veranda jammed on the brakes and the hood of the Impala dipped down as the car skidded on the cement. Smoke billowed from the tires of the patrol cars in front of her as they screeched to a halt, momentarily obscuring her view.

The Escalade burst into flames.

Sam unbuckled his seatbelt. "What were they carrying? The thing's going up like tinder." He opened his door and slid out in a crouched position.

Veranda jerked her sidearm from its holster, clambered across the console to Sam's seat, and rolled out of the Impala. Squinting through the haze, she spotted Roberto jumping from the passenger side a split second before he hoisted an AK-47 with an extended magazine and sprayed bullets all over the garage.

Rounds pinged on parked cars and cement pillars. Veranda, Sam, and the patrol officers dove behind their vehicles as they returned fire.

She popped up to get a peek at Roberto's position so she wouldn't waste ammunition. She'd already changed her magazine once and only had one more to spare.

Sam turned to her. "Did you see where Roberto went? Do we have a second gunman in the garage?"

"The driver never made it out when the Escalade caught fire."

"Any chance he's still alive?"

She flicked a glance at the blackened chassis through a wall of flames. "He's extra crispy."

Dismissing the driver from her mind, she bobbed her head up over the hood just as Roberto darted to the vestibule in front of the mall entrance and pivoted to face them. He swung the rifle to his shoulder as the wide glass entry doors slid open behind him. He inched backward into the mall, laying down suppressive fire in rapid full-auto bursts in their direction until the doors closed.

A roiling mix of fear and fury burned her insides. "Shit! He's inside."

2

STANDING FROM HER POSITION of cover behind the Impala, Veranda grabbed her portable radio and rattled off an update.

A heartbeat of silence followed before the dispatcher announced the radio channel would be split, dedicating their frequency to the critical incident and transmitting a single long tone.

Veranda's pulse always quickened at the sound of the emergency signal. From her earliest days as a booter, she stopped whatever she was doing and listened to the next radio traffic. Like an action movie in freeze frame, every officer halted, ears pricked to take in information, then zoomed ahead at high speed, scrambling to respond.

The dispatcher announced the situation had changed to an active shooter in the mall. A flurry of radio traffic blasted through Veranda's portable. As more patrol cars sped into the garage, some of them sliding in sideways, Veranda tapped Sam's elbow and rushed over to the two patrol officers who had joined their pursuit first.

"Active shooter scenario," she said, motioning toward the mall entrance. "Let's go." Without a word, the two uniforms raced after Veranda and Sam toward the wide glass automatic doors.

Veranda knew they would follow. All Phoenix Police officers train for active shooters. The first four officers at any scene, regardless of assignment, take immediate action to preserve life. In such a situation, there is no time to stage and wait for a tactical team to respond. Seconds count.

The ad hoc response team gathered into a tight diamond formation. Both patrol officers had microphones clipped to their uniform shirts. The short blond one pressed the transmit button to inform the dispatcher they were about to enter the mall at the east side food court entrance.

Another foursome pounded up behind them, all patrol officers. Veranda raised her hand to signal the other group, who were performing a cursory check of their equipment before heading inside.

She addressed the most senior officer. "We'll make entry together and split into two teams. Search the second level as soon as you can find a way up. We'll cover the main floor. Are you direct on the suspect description?" He gave her a curt nod.

Veranda paused a moment longer for the second team to relay their status to the dispatcher, then she and her group approached the entrance as a single unit. Veranda took point, the two patrol officers secured flank positions, and Sam acted as rear guard, watching their backs, Glock in low-ready position. Crouched in a tactical stance, they covered ground at roughly the speed of a jog with the second team on their heels.

When the automatic glass doors slid open, utter chaos greeted Veranda. She made a quick assessment of the situation. Hundreds of people scattered in every direction, eyes wild with terror, their shrieks reverberating through the cavernous space. Tables and chairs lay strewn around the food court, overturned or knocked down by fleeing patrons desperate to escape. The heavy scent of overcooked Chinese food, charred pizza, and hamburger grease filled the air. A group of teenagers sprinted past her toward the entrance. Other shoppers ran in the opposite direction, scurrying into stores and vanishing down corridors.

Veranda searched for the epicenter of the disturbance. If the crowd ran one way, she could assume they were heading away from Roberto, which would help pinpoint his location. Unfortunately, the shoppers were a panicked sea of humanity, surging in multidirectional waves.

A gunshot rang out over the din, inciting a fresh onslaught of screams from the shoppers. She whirled to see Roberto on the far side of the food court. He raised his weapon and fired into the air a second time. She swung her Glock up to take aim, but couldn't get a clear shot. More than fifteen yards away, he scurried behind a display of potted palm trees before she could battle her way through the masses to get to him.

She used her free hand to snatch the portable from her waist. "Charlie thirty-four, advise incident commander the shooter may blend in with the crowd to leave the mall. Separate all exiting shoppers. I can ID the suspect if they detain anyone matching the description."

She started toward Roberto's last position. "Let's go." The response team only made it five steps before a horde of shoppers stampeded straight at them. The officers struggled to hold formation as they were buffeted by bodies crashing into them from all sides.

She kept pushing forward, stopping short when a middle-aged woman clutching an oversized shopping bag jabbed an accusatory finger at her. "She's got a gun!" the woman shrieked.

More screams erupted as shoppers changed directions like a school of fish, now rushing away from her team.

A whistle's shrill blast cut through the cacophony.

"Sam … Sam Stark!" A man with sparse gray hair wearing a mall security uniform elbowed his way toward them. A silver whistle dangling from a lanyard attached to an epaulette on his shirt.

Sam did a double take then addressed the security officer. "Leo, any sightings of the active shooter?"

Leo pointed to a brick-sized radio clipped to his thick leather belt. "Last report I got was a Hispanic male subject with a rifle in the east food court area." He surveyed the rapidly emptying space. "Thought you'd need help. Got here as fast as I could."

The blond patrol officer to Veranda's left quirked a brow at the mall cop, skepticism tingeing his words. "We've got this, sir."

The security officer's jaw tightened. "I've had the same training as you, only more of it."

When the young officer opened his mouth to retort, Sam intervened. "This is Leo Garland. He's retired from the job.."

The blond officer addressed his comments to Sam. "I appreciate that he's had the same training and all, but we need to clear this floor. We've wasted too much time already. The shooter went down that corridor."

Leo straightened. "And I know where that corridor leads, how to access shortcuts behind the stores to intercept him, the location of every exit, and where the best hidey holes are in this mall." He leaned forward. "Do you?"

Out of patience, Veranda cut in. "Point taken." She shot a quelling look at the blond officer before turning back to the guard. "You don't have a gun, so we'll put you in the middle of the diamond formation. Is that a ballistic vest under your shirt?"

"Never without it." He raised his chin. "Ready when you are."

The mall seemed eerily empty as the group scuttled past storefront windows featuring sparkling jewels on plush velvet cushions and mannequins adorned in the latest styles.

"We've lost him," Sam muttered.

"Turn into that alcove to your right," Leo said from his position behind Veranda. "There's an access point to the corridors behind the stores."

She opened the service door and led the team through. In stark contrast to the gleaming polished tile in the main area, the network of passageways connecting the delivery doors and employee entrances to the back of the stores had a grimy cement floor. The walls were bare cinder block and industrial fans hung from the ceiling between the exposed ductwork. Intermittently spaced bare bulbs provided the only light in the gloom as they moved ahead.

The blond officer sounded annoyed when he asked, "What are we doing back here?"

Leo gave him a terse response. "We're taking a shortcut to the security office. I can pull up video and we'll see where the shooter went in about two minutes. A lot quicker than going on foot through two hundred thousand square feet of retail space."

Veranda analyzed their situation. Leo's plan made sense. "The shooter ghosted on us," she said. "This is our best chance."

After another six turns through the labyrinth of hallways, they stepped through a glass partition to a foyer with a clean blue industrial-grade carpet and a metal reinforced door equipped with a Cypher lock.

Leo punched in a code and pushed open the security office door.

"Where is everyone?" Sam asked.

"We were instructed to evacuate the customers and leave the premises." He frowned. "Screw that. Unlike the rest of the security staff here, I was on the force. Knew I could help."

Veranda kept them on task. "Where's the video monitoring station?"

"Over here." Leo led them to an elaborate array of thirty-two video screens, each flicking between different angles inside the mall and parking lot. Flashing emergency lights caught Veranda's eye and she grimaced at the cluster of police and rescue vehicles in the far corner of the east parking lot.

Leo plopped down in a worn swivel chair. "I'll pull up the food court cameras and reverse them. Stop me when you see the shooter."

He typed commands on a keyboard, isolating footage from the food court on a large screen directly in front of them. Veranda watched as the images began to move in reverse.

She held her breath as people ran backward, mouths open in silent screams.

"Stop!" She pointed at the screen. "There he is. Back up a bit more, then go forward."

With growing dread, Veranda watched Roberto shoot his rifle in the air twice and duck behind the palm trees lining the food court. Another camera picked up his movement as he whipped down an adjacent corridor, looked over his shoulder, and shoved the rifle into a trash can. After a furtive glance around, he joined the throng bolting toward the nearest exit. A final switch of cameras confirmed her worst fear. Roberto had blended in with the terrified shoppers and surged outside with the crowd.

3

Two hours later, Veranda stood at the back of the raised stage in the police headquarters media briefing room. She checked her watch. The news conference would begin any moment. She cast her eyes around at the sea of reporters jockeying for position as they waited to sink their teeth into the PPD chief. Her attention locked on a petite redhead, Kiki Lowell, the local television reporter famous for her fluff pieces. Dressed in a clingy canary yellow skirt and teetering on five-inch stilettos, Kiki looked out of place next to her less colorful colleagues.

Kiki raised a microphone to her collagen-enhanced lips, peered at the camera perched on a tripod in front of her and said, "Phoenix in fear." After these words, she furrowed her brows in a grim expression and continued in a dramatic voice. "It's now day seven of a brutal new crime wave. Warring cartels from south of the border have brought a new level of violence to the nation's fifth-largest city. The death toll now stands at three, with thirty-nine injured."

Veranda did a mental body count. The past week had seen escalating violence between the SSS gang and the Villalobos cartel, resulting in bloodshed on both sides. The first murder had drawn her into the investigation, and she'd been chasing her tail ever since.

This afternoon, the mayor had called a news conference to address public fear after the fiasco at the city's largest shopping mall. The general public mostly ignored crime on the south side, but this new spate of violence had now spilled into the downtown area. And on a scale Phoenix had never seen.

The unprecedented street war drew coverage from national and international news outlets. Veranda caught snippets of commentary as reporters faced their cameras. One network correspondent intoned, "Phoenix is under siege," while another announced, "The savage and bloody cartel war has reached the US."

She clenched her jaw. The public's reaction was worse than she'd expected. People were scared and angry. And, not surprisingly, the media hype wasn't helping.

She stood silently next to Sam, shoulder-to-shoulder, along with ranking officials from the department. The line of police personnel stretched across the back of the wide platform to provide a backdrop for the mayor and police chief to speak at a lectern bristling with microphones near the front of the dais.

She stifled the urge to fidget. The conference should have started five minutes ago. Every second they delayed, she overheard reporters trading rumors and circulating theories.

Feet shuffled behind her and she inched closer to Sam to make way for the chief, Steven Tobias, and the mayor, Umberto "Bertie" Benitez, to pass.

The jostling gaggle of reporters quieted as Chief Tobias stepped to the bank of microphones. "Today's incident at the Arcadia Fashion

Center represents a deplorable situation I will not tolerate in our city." He glanced down at his notes. "Detectives from our Homicide Unit were attempting to meet with a person of interest when the subject of the interview was killed in front of them in a drive-by shooting. The detectives were unable to stop the fleeing suspects, who drove an armored vehicle. Unfortunately, this led to a pursuit through downtown Phoenix in which shots were exchanged. The situation ended with the suspect driver deceased and a gunman evading capture by fleeing into the Arcadia Fashion Mall and blending in with shoppers as they dispersed before perimeter containment was established."

When the chief paused to take a breath, a tall, lean man with dazzling white teeth, perfectly windswept hair, and pancake makeup shouted a question. "Can you confirm that the escaped shooter is from a Mexican drug cartel?" Veranda recognized the correspondent from the nightly evening news out of New York.

Chief Tobias looked up from his prepared statement. "The suspect has been identified as Roberto Bernal, who has ties to the Villalobos organization. We've secured arrest warrants, and we are hopeful he will be taken into custody without incident. A full description and photograph of Bernal are in your press kits."

When several reporters called out at once, Tobias pointed at various individuals, forcing them to take turns.

A dark-haired man in a pinstripe suit got first dibs, his accent bearing the distinctive tones of Guatemala. "Mario Duarte from *Noticias Centroamericana*. What are you doing to find Roberto Bernal?"

"In order to prevent further evasion on the part of the suspect, we cannot disclose our methods. The public should rest assured, however, that we are utilizing all available resources to capture him."

A local print reporter spoke up next. "Why wasn't the initial pursuit called off once it reached the downtown business district?" His eyes moved down as he flicked back a page of his notepad. "Last estimate was thirty-nine injured, mostly in minor vehicle crashes and running away from automatic gunfire. No figures yet on property damage … Is this in compliance with your pursuit policy, Chief?"

Tobias answered in a measured tone, a slight twitch of his jaw muscles the only indication he didn't appreciate the question. "In a word, yes. Every scenario is unique. In each case, officers are trained to assess the threat to public safety posed by pursuing a fleeing suspect versus the potential harm if we let him escape without an effort to make immediate apprehension. In this case, due to the extreme violence of the murder committed in the detectives' presence in a public place, along with the use of a fully automatic assault rifle, my officers decided to pursue." His knuckles whitened as he gripped the edges of the lectern. "And I support that decision."

"When the initial pursuit started, why didn't you have a police helicopter take over?" the reporter followed up. "Don't you have something like ten helicopters?"

"The Phoenix Police Department has seven helicopters in our air fleet, but only one is usually up at any given time. The on-duty air unit was approximately six minutes away when the pursuit began. It did, however, reach the area and lend air support." Apparently trying to shift the discussion, Tobias gestured to a different reporter.

"Why did the police return fire in a crowded area? Why not just follow the vehicle at a safe distance?"

"Responding officers had to use lethal force to stop the suspects each time they fired on pedestrians and other officers. Due to their efforts, no bystanders were shot downtown or in the mall. I am, however, very concerned that people were injured trying to avoid gunfire."

Kiki Lowell waved frantically. With an air of resignation, Tobias pointed at her. She smiled brightly. "Why didn't they just shoot the tires out to stop the vehicle?"

A pained expression flitted across the chief's face before he suppressed it. "Shooting from inside a moving car while swerving to avoid traffic, and aiming at the tires of another moving automobile that is also going all over the road at varying speeds, is extremely difficult. We also had information that not only was the Escalade armorplated, but there were bulletproof flaps shielding the tires."

Undeterred, Kiki followed up. "Then why didn't they ram the car to end the pursuit?"

"The vehicle involved was a full-sized, steel-plated Cadillac Escalade, which is much heavier than our squad cars. Additionally, with a gunman shooting an assault rifle at them, the officers couldn't get close enough to make contact. Several police vehicles sustained multiple gunshots. Fortunately, no officers were injured or killed."

One of the older reporters standing next to her looked like he wanted to elbow Kiki when she blurted another question. "Why didn't they shoot the suspect after he got out of the Escalade before he ran inside the mall?"

Tobias tensed, his back ramrod straight. "As the shooter exited the vehicle, he continued to lay down suppression fire while he retreated into the mall. The math is simple. He had an assault rifle capable of firing six hundred rounds a minute and our officers had handguns and shotguns, which can only fire one round at a time."

The older reporter stepped in front of Kiki, preventing more followups from her, as he posed his question. "Chief, are you saying you're outgunned? Has Phoenix become like some cities south of the border where innocent citizens are victims of drug wars and cartel violence?"

Mayor Benitez edged next to Tobias, who took the cue and stepped aside.

Sam bent to whisper in Veranda's ear, "I wouldn't be the police chief for love or money."

The mayor centered himself in front of the cluster of microphones and a hush fell over the sea of reporters. "Let me reassure you that I will not let our city suffer at the hands of criminals. The police have all the necessary resources at their disposal to handle any situation. In this case the department's investigation indicates the factions involved in the recent wave of violence over the past few days are a cartel and a local drug gang."

He let his words sink in a moment as he looked around the room. "Chief Tobias and I have developed a new strategy to deal with this situation."

Benitez paused before his next proclamation. "I am announcing the formation of a new temporary task force, consisting of local and federal agencies, which will be housed at a satellite location we will refer to as the Phoenix Fusion Center. The task force's mission is to end the immediate threat posed by these two groups."

The mayor nodded to one of his staff, who slid a dark cloth from a display board at the front of the stage, revealing an organizational chart. "The name of the operation is Scorpion Sting, and the objective is to arrest and prosecute major players within each organization plaguing our city."

Sam leaned down to Veranda. "Is it written somewhere that any group of three or more people in law enforcement requires a code name and an org chart?"

Veranda suppressed a grin.

Benitez indicated the second tier of boxes on the chart. "The task force includes agents from the FBI, DEA, the US Marshal's Office, and

Homeland Security. In addition, two agents from the Ministerial Federal Police in Mexico are flying in to join our team and lend their expertise. As you can see, we are bringing pressure to bear on the criminals perpetrating these heinous acts, and we expect quick results."

A query bubbled up from the pool of reporters. "With the alphabet soup of agencies involved, who's in charge of Operation Scorpion Sting?"

The consummate politician, Benitez waited until every eye was on him. "I want to make it very clear," his voice rumbled in a low, clear tone, "the task force will be under the direction of the Phoenix Police Department. This is our city, and we will take the necessary steps to ensure public safety. Other agencies are assisting, but this is a Phoenix-based operation and our police department is more than capable of leading it."

"How's this going to work?" the network correspondent asked. "Don't the Feds have greater authority?"

Benitez stepped back. "I'll allow the chief to explain law enforcement protocol."

Tobias returned to the microphones. Camera lights glinted off his gold badge as he spoke. "All homicides committed in relation to this investigation occurred inside Phoenix boundaries by local residents who are not foreign nationals. In short, the Phoenix Police Department has jurisdiction."

As a cacophony of reporters began to fire questions, he held up his hand. "This is not a law enforcement turf war. We leave that sort of thing to the drug dealers." A slight chuckle went around the room, breaking the tension. "Every federal agency listed on the org chart has made it clear they prefer a support role. They have access to the best intelligence and technology available, and can augment our investigation as they have done on many prior operations."

"If the PPD is running the operation, who have you put in charge?"

Tobias swung an arm out to indicate the command staff on his left. "Responsibility for the overall operation will fall to Assistant Chief Alexander Delcore."

Veranda hadn't seen Delcore since he had forced her out of her position as a narcotics detective. Not a happy memory.

Tobias signaled the next person over. "Under Chief Delcore, Commander Nathan Webster, who runs the Violent Crimes Bureau, will receive twice-daily briefings and make regular visits to the facility."

Tobias continued down the line. "Day-to-day operations will be supervised onsite by our new Homicide lieutenant." The chief's expression darkened. "I have just filled a vacancy in that position."

The mood in the room shifted. A hush fell over media and law enforcement representatives alike as Tobias continued. "I am taking this opportunity to announce the selection for this critical assignment."

For over a month, rumors had swirled throughout the department about who might take the coveted slot. Veranda had watched a stream of lieutenants traipse through the second floor on their way to her commander's office for interviews.

She had to crane her neck to see who the chief was about to introduce. The stage was packed with so many police personnel that some had been forced into the background. The row of officers parted as the chief announced the name.

"Lieutenant Richard Diaz."

Veranda's jaw dropped. Sam nudged her and she snapped her mouth shut.

Tall and athletically built, with tan skin and eyes so dark they appeared black, Diaz inclined his head briefly before he melded back into the line of police spanning the stage.

She couldn't believe Commander Webster had chosen Diaz as the new Homicide lieutenant. In his position as a sergeant in the Professional Standards Bureau, Diaz had been a constant thorn in her side. His zeal for rules and regulations had made it almost impossible for her to do her job, especially the last few weeks. Now she would be under his command.

Furious about Diaz's appointment, Veranda momentarily forgot her trepidation about the chief's next announcement.

"The most critical position," Tobias said, "is the individual who will lead the investigation itself." The unease roiling just beneath the surface of her thoughts all morning flooded back as the chief cleared his throat.

An hour ago, Tobias had tapped her to lead the investigation. When she objected, he waved away her concerns about mixed reactions from the media. Their coverage of her recent run-in with the Villalobos cartel still rankled her. She'd landed on her feet, but not before paying a steep price. Now her face would be back on television. Accompanied by questions about her suitability to lead the task force. She wanted to step backward and slip behind the row of blue uniforms, but she lifted her chin and steeled herself as Tobias continued.

"For that assignment, I chose someone who has intimate knowledge of cartels, their history, methods of operation, and major players. In short, I appointed a Homicide detective who also has a strong background in narcotics enforcement." He swiveled in her direction. "I designated Detective Veranda Cruz as lead investigator on the task force."

A scald crept up the back of Veranda's neck when a shocked silence ensued. Every eye turned to her as she stepped forward, gave a curt nod, and tried to lose herself in the line of detectives next to Sam.

Questions ricocheted around the room until a print reporter with a deep, booming voice gained the chief's attention. "Detective Cruz was recently ousted from the Drug Enforcement Bureau under questionable circumstances. Why would you put her in such a crucial position?"

A hot wave of shame blasted her at the memory of her expulsion from DEB, a public spectacle. When her face was plastered all over the news, her career as an undercover narc had abruptly ended.

Tobias had a ready response. "An internal investigation exonerated Detective Cruz. In her capacity as a narcotics detective, she led a task force that included several federal agencies, and therefore has a proven track record of leading this type of team. She played an integral role in making the largest busts in the history of our department. Her work was exemplary, and the circumstances of her departure from DEB were beyond her control."

The reporter kept gnawing the bone. "Detective Cruz's informant was exposed and murdered by the cartel. Can she be trusted to safeguard sensitive information?"

"The Professional Standards Bureau conducted a thorough investigation into the facts surrounding the unfortunate death of her confidential informant. She was cleared."

"Wasn't Detective Cruz just recently transferred to Homicide? Shouldn't someone more experienced lead the investigation?"

Her cheeks warmed. The reporter had voiced her other concern. Despite her investigative experience in property crimes and narcotics, she'd only recently transferred to Homicide.

Tobias appeared unfazed. "She won't work alone. Her fellow squad members are among our most seasoned detectives. Detective Cruz is partnered with Detective Sam Stark, who many of you know by reputation as our most senior Homicide investigator."

A male reporter standing next to Kiki Lowell started to pose a question, then yelped, hopping on one foot. Kiki glanced at him, then down at her five-inch spiked stilettos. "Oops." She gave a disingenuous smile before directing her gaze at the chief. "Could this announcement cause the cartel to put a bounty on Detective Cruz?"

The chief's face reddened. "No. And that kind of speculation is completely irresponsible. This news conference is over. All information released here is in your press kits." He stepped back from the microphones, pivoted, and stalked toward a rear exit from the stage, the mayor in his wake.

Behind their retreating backs, several reporters called out to Veranda for a comment. Lieutenant Diaz appeared and moved in front of her to intervene, directing questions to Public Affairs as she turned and left the stage.

Once in the hallway, which was cut off from the media by heavy double doors, she spun and confronted Diaz, launching into her area of greatest concern. "Why are you running day-to-day operations at the Fusion Center?"

A sardonic smile raised one corner of his mouth. "Well, Detective, it's a pleasure to work with you again too."

She put a hand on her hip. "Will you work *with* me ... or against me, like before?"

Sam, who had halted next to her, interrupted. "Lieutenant." He proffered a hand. "Congratulations on your promotion, and welcome to Homicide."

Diaz shook Sam's hand. "Thank you, Detective." He turned his dark gaze on Veranda. "We'll all get used to our new situations. Meanwhile, I've arranged for the computer forensics team to help get the Fusion Center ready. They'll work through the night to set up equipment. You two swing by this evening and check out the facility to see if there's anything else we need. The computer geeks won't get there for another hour. You can grab a bite before you head over."

"Yes, sir." She laced the last word with contempt.

He stepped closer, invading her space. "You heard the media out there. A lot of people are questioning your leadership of this operation. The chief and mayor put their faith in you. As your supervisor, it falls to me to make sure they don't regret it." He angled his head down to her ear and lowered his voice. "Know that I'll be watching every step you take."

She refused to give him the last word. "You and everyone else."

4

Villalobos family
compound, Mexico

ADOLFO VILLALOBOS OCCUPIED ONE of five chairs surrounding the ornately carved conference table in his father's opulent office. Sweat trickled between his shoulder blades as he caught a glint of afternoon sunlight reflecting from the crystal water decanter. His eyes traced the beam over the mahogany-paneled walls. He fought to keep his expression calm as anxiety coursed through him. During his flight to Mexico on the family jet, he'd rehearsed his speech. Now, in *El Lobo*'s presence, the words dried in his mouth like dust in the desert.

His father, Hector Villalobos, had designated everyone's place at the table as soon as his children came of age. As the family's leader, he sat at the head. His firstborn son, Adolfo, was directly to his right. The chair to Adolfo's right stood empty. Hector's second son, Bartolo, used to claim that seat. Its vacancy still left a palpable sense of loss among the family in the room.

His youngest siblings, Carlos and Daria, occupied the two chairs across from Adolfo. Hector left the foot of the table vacant so everyone had an unobstructed view of the massive flat-screen television, now dark, affixed to the wall.

Adolfo squirmed in the plush leather chair, awaiting his father's judgment.

"I am disappointed in you, *mi'jo*," Hector finally said.

The twitching muscle in Hector's jaw told Adolfo his father was livid. In refined Spanish, Hector spoke softly—another indication of his fury. Other men shouted and hurled objects when angered, but *El Lobo* grew quiet.

His father had just clicked off the live satellite newsfeed from Phoenix Police headquarters. Immediately after Roberto Bernal's fiasco at the mall, Adolfo, Carlos, and Daria had been summoned to the palatial Mexican estate. They were wheels up in the family jet within the hour, arriving from Phoenix at the private airstrip on the family compound before the news conference began. Now, watching the media coverage, the enormity of Adolfo's failure pressed down on his shoulders.

He salvaged what he could. "At least Raymond Castillo didn't get to the police. We only knew about his plans because of me."

Hector's eyes narrowed to obsidian slits. "You mean because of Nacho."

Adolfo barely managed to hide his shock. His father had referred to his computer expert, Ignacio Vasquez, by his nickname. While people named Ignacio were commonly called Nacho, Adolfo knew his father's comment conveyed a veiled threat. *He has an informant in my camp. And wants me to know it.* The realization troubled Adolfo on many levels.

He tried for a businesslike air. "Yes, Nacho acted on my orders. I promised you weeks ago I would hack into the Phoenix Police Department server, and I did."

Adolfo dreaded Daria's inevitable interjection. She found her opportunity and pounced. "Yes, yes." She rolled her eyes. "We all remember you crowing about reading Veranda Cruz's case files."

Four days ago, an SSS gang member shot one of Adolfo's dealers while stealing his heroin shipment. No one had dared to cross the cartel before, and Daria laid the blame at Adolfo's feet. According to her, his weakness invited attack.

He held his anger in check. "I wasn't bragging. Without information from our hacks, we would never have known Castillo planned to turn state's evidence." He shook his head, considering the breach of his family's operation. The one piece of the puzzle he hadn't found. "I still have no idea how Castillo got into our supply line."

"I do." Hector ran his fingers along the lapel of his white linen suit. "And I have already taken steps to correct the problem at its source in South America. Still, Castillo had to be silenced before he could talk to Veranda Cruz."

Again schooling his features to hide his surprise, Adolfo reinforced his point. "Which is why I had him killed."

Instead of smiling on his eldest son, Hector scowled. "Castillo could not have contacted Detective Cruz if you had already killed her." The planes of his face hardened into stone. "I recall your vow to eliminate her. But instead she now leads a task force to hunt us down."

Adolfo cast his eyes around the table at his siblings, seeking support. None came. "As I said before, her death is part of a plan I've already set in motion. Soon I'll have everything in place. We have to act carefully now. Every eye is on us."

Daria crossed her legs, a smug expression crossing her beautiful face. "And whose fault is that?"

Adolfo's blood boiled as he slowly turned to confront his sister. Her smirk told him she intended to undermine his leadership at every turn. He struggled for composure. "I sent Roberto Bernal in to perform a critical task. All he had to do was eliminate Castillo, but he screwed up." He turned back to his father. "I promise you, *Papá*, he will pay for his mistake."

Hector picked up a second remote from the table's polished surface and pressed a button. "I have no doubt he will." As his father spoke, Adolfo heard the mechanism of a wooden panel the size of a single-car garage door sliding to one side. Crafted to match the woodwork in the wall, the panel was undetectable until opened.

Adolfo's stomach lurched as the panel slowly retracted to reveal a glass wall. The transparent partition formed one side of a small room. Adolfo had witnessed atrocities committed in that chamber many times. He knew the glass wall facing the office was bulletproof and the side walls were plastic-coated for easy cleaning. His father often arranged to have special punishments meted out as designated individuals watched.

El Lobo disciplined his employees and his enemies in a manner calculated for maximum impact. Adolfo recalled being forced to observe killings, maimings, and beatings from his early childhood. His father always explained who had been sentenced, who was to administer the punishment, and why. Each aspect carried significance. Adolfo hated to watch the brutality, but his siblings seemed to relish the spectacle.

He strove to appear calm as Carlos and Daria swiveled their leather office chairs completely around so they could have a front-row seat for the show. Hot bile rose into his throat as he recognized the man strapped to a metal folding chair in the center of the viewing room.

Roberto Bernal's eyes, filled with terror, stared at them as he worked his jaws frantically under two thick strips of silver duct tape. Adolfo was certain the muffled gurgles he heard were Roberto pleading for his life, but knew it would do no good. Failure on such a grand scale had sealed his fate. Adolfo would have seen to the execution back in Phoenix, but he would have ordered one of his men to perform the task and dump the body into one of the hundreds of empty mineshafts that dotted the desert outside the city.

For a full minute, nothing happened. Dawning horror crept into Adolfo's throat as he realized his father meant for *him* to carry out the execution. *El Lobo* knew his oldest son abhorred the sight of blood. Knew the gore and wails of agony from a condemned prisoner repulsed him. He was also aware his father wanted him to perform such acts to show his resolve to rule their empire with an iron fist.

Resigned, Adolfo got to his feet. A narrow door inside the chamber opened. Adolfo slumped back down in his chair in surprise when Salazar strode into the viewing room to stand directly behind Roberto.

Adolfo's sharp intake of breath matched that of his siblings. He had no idea *El Matador* had returned to Mexico. His roiling stomach iced over.

Salazar was handsome, intelligent, and, as far as Adolfo could tell, without conscience. After Salazar had proven himself both capable and lethal in cartel operations, *El Lobo* had taken him under his wing, treating him as a protégé and trusted "fixer." Because of that bond, Adolfo viewed Salazar as a threat and prevailed upon his father to place him in charge of the various Villalobos grow operations in Colombia. Adolfo applauded his own cleverness when his father agreed and sent Salazar away to South America. Secretly, Adolfo hoped one of the vicious rival Colombian cartels would exterminate Salazar, but the man had proved to be not only an excellent businessman, extracting more product from the farmers than ever, but also ruthless at eradicating threats.

Now he was back in Mexico. Why? His appearance on the scene when things were going badly did not bode well for Adolfo. He stole a quick glance at his father, who touched his fingertips to his forehead in silent salute to Salazar inside the enclosure.

Adolfo tore his gaze away from his father and looked back to Roberto. Salazar inclined his head toward *El Lobo* and reached inside his suit jacket. Unlike his father, who favored white Armani suits, Salazar always wore solid black. The color matched his hair, eyes, goatee, and, Adolfo suspected, his soul.

Salazar slid a Sig Sauer pistol out of a shoulder holster under the tailored jacket. Trained with guns from early childhood, Adolfo recognized this was not Salazar's customary matte black .50-caliber Desert Eagle. Clearly not wanting to test the limits of the ballistic glass, he assumed Salazar had chosen a 9mm handgun from his personal arsenal for today's wet work.

Adolfo's heart pounded as Salazar raised the pistol behind Roberto. Carlos leaned forward in his chair, eyes riveted to the scene. Daria licked her lips and bared her teeth in a feral smile.

Salazar placed the muzzle of the gun against the back of Roberto's head. Roberto squeezed his eyes shut and let out a muffled scream through the duct tape.

Adolfo held his breath. As if in slow motion, he saw Salazar's finger tighten on the trigger. A split second later, Roberto's face exploded. Adolfo flinched as a crimson plume spattered the glass in front of him. His gorge rose when he peered through streaks of brain matter oozing down the clear panel to see Salazar calmly slide his gun back into its holster. The reinforced glass had stopped the round, which left a pea-sized impact crater in the smooth surface.

Adolfo let out his breath in a long sigh. Too late, he recollected himself and cut his eyes to his father, who watched him with overt disdain. In that moment, Adolfo understood that he had orchestrated this entire performance as a chastisement. Roberto had been punished for his failures but, as always, the circumstances of the execution conveyed a message. Adolfo had been forced to watch on the sidelines while a more capable member of the cartel carried out the death sentence. Furthermore, the rest of the family would see that someone else had been called in to correct the mistake while they also witnessed Adolfo's aversion to violence, contributing to the perception that he was weak and further undermining his efforts to gain control of the cartel as future leader of the family.

Suffused with impotent rage, he had no time to recover before the main door of the office opened and the butler ushered in Salazar, quietly shutting the door behind him. Relaxed, Salazar ambled across the room and took the empty chair to Adolfo's right at the table. No one had used Bartolo's chair since his death. Adolfo sensed his father had arranged this unprecedented incursion into their inner sanctum in advance, but why?

Carlos and Daria rotated their chairs to face Adolfo and Salazar across the table. All four turned to *El Lobo*, who steepled his fingers.

"That particular problem has been dealt with," he said. "Unfortunately, Roberto Bernal left us a mess to clean up." His father jerked his chin toward a grayish-pink slimy clump oozing down the glass. Adolfo, whose seat faced the wide clear panel, caught the double entendre. Roberto's failure to quietly silence Castillo left the Villalobos family in the crosshairs of every law enforcement agency in the US. Even Mexican authorities were involved in the investigation.

Despising the pleading note in his voice, Adolfo felt compelled to speak. "We can still stay ahead of the police by monitoring their emails and reading their case files."

Daria snorted. "How? Won't their remote location have a new computer system?"

"Doesn't matter, if they use the same server," Adolfo countered. "We can still access their database."

Hector stroked his black and silver goatee. "I thought you said you were working on a way to clone their cell phones. Now that would impress me. We could have real-time information."

Adolfo seized his chance to deliver positive news. "Nacho has found a way. He says he's within hours of being able to clone Detective Cruz's mobile phone."

Hector splayed his hands on the table, eyes riveted on Adolfo. "Explain."

"Almost all cellular telephones worldwide use a program called Signaling System Number Seven, or SS7, to transmit and receive calls and messages. There is a vulnerability in SS7 that allows devices to be easily cloned if you know the phone number and service provider. When we captured and killed Detective Cruz's snitch a few weeks ago, we got her number from his phone. She never changed it. We can clone her unit and any number she calls. That will give us access to the entire task force … this Scorpion Sting operation. We will be able to intercept all of their communication in real time and read their reports as well. We can also use the internal GPS software to track the movements of anyone whose phone we've cloned. We'll know where they are and what they're saying at all times."

"Why didn't Nacho do this a long time ago?" Carlos asked.

"He had to go slowly. There are anti-hacking technologies out there to source the intrusion unless he set up safeguards. The SS7 program is complex and takes sophisticated computer equipment to crack." He leaned forward. "Remember I also tasked him with breaking into the police department's server at the same time. He's been working around the clock on both projects with only one person skilled enough to help him. He breached the server recently, and now he's almost ready to clone Cruz's phone. When he gets in, he'll also need his assistant to help monitor transmissions if we're going to watch everyone."

A thin smile compressed his father's lips. "Nacho will be busy, so you will be pleased to hear I'm providing you with extra help."

Adolfo's wariness returned. "What do you mean?"

Hector inclined his head toward the chair next to Adolfo. "Salazar will accompany you back to Phoenix as your second-in-command. He's the best operative I have, which is why I brought him up from his assignment in Colombia. Things are under control there. But your operation...not so much."

Adolfo dug his nails into his palms as he tightened his fists under the table. "I don't need another supervisor for my men. I have—"

His father stood, cutting off Adolfo's protests. "What I just saw on the news tells me you *do* need more supervision in your operation. Things have gone badly, and I will not tolerate it." His tone indicated the discussion was closed.

Everyone else got to their feet. Adolfo rose and shot a venomous look at Salazar, whose expression remained inscrutable.

"Come," *El Lobo* said, starting toward the door. When Adolfo moved to follow, his father halted, speaking over his shoulder. "Not you, Adolfo." He motioned toward the glass-paneled room. "There is a mop and bucket in the hall." His lip curled in contempt. "Clean up your mess."

5

PLEASURE THRUMMED THROUGH VERANDA as her teeth sank into the soft corn tortilla.

Sitting across from her, Sam paused mid-chew when she groaned. "You need a cigarette?" he asked around a mouth full of cheese enchiladas smothered in red chili sauce.

She grinned. "*Mamá* makes the best carne asada street tacos on the planet."

Ravenous after the news conference, Veranda had insisted they stop to eat at *Casa Cruz Camión*, her uncles' food truck. Patrons carried their meals from a service window on the side of the vehicle and seated themselves at one of eight card tables scattered under a canopy of open beach umbrellas nearby.

After the family restaurant burned down as a casualty of her last investigation, her Uncles Juan and Felipe had offered their food truck as a temporary replacement during the time needed for reconstruction. Her mother's renowned classically prepared Mexico City–style cuisine lured customers to eat in the parking lot despite the lack of ambience and the early September heat in South Phoenix.

Veranda glanced at Sam. At least twenty years her senior, her partner was already in Homicide when she graduated from the academy thirteen years ago. His salt-and-pepper hair, thick silvery mustache, and penchant for dark suits gave him a distinguished air she doubted she would ever attain. Despite the difference in their ages and styles of policing, they had developed mutual, sometimes grudging, respect for each other's methodologies over the past weeks since she'd been transferred to Homicide.

Sam cut into his enchiladas with the edge of his plastic fork and peered over her shoulder to watch the men working on the construction site behind her. "Restaurant's coming along."

She turned to look. Men in hard hats trudged back and forth, thick wooden beams balanced on their shoulders. "Once the permits got through Zoning, things started moving fast. Miguel's crew will have the place rebuilt in a few months." She craned her neck and waved. "There he is now."

A stocky man with a dense shock of gray hair waved back. She admired her stepfather, Miguel Gomez, who began his career as a teenager hand-mixing mortar for brick masons at construction sites. His weather-worn skin, burnished by years toiling in the blistering Arizona sun, bore witness to his determination to build not only structures, but a good life for his family. He'd waited until he finally saved enough to start his own company after he received his general contractor's license before asking her mother to marry him seventeen years ago. Veranda was already in high school by then, so she'd always known him as Miguel. The rest of the family called him McGomez, the Mexican MacGyver, who could build anything with a paperclip, two toothpicks, and a stick of chewing gum.

Now Miguel's construction crew was rebuilding the family restaurant. A lump caught in her throat as she recalled her younger sister Gabby's frantic predawn phone call six weeks ago. Veranda had raced to the restaurant to find the whole building in flames. A total loss.

Because of her.

Her relatives had considered leaving Phoenix after it became clear the Villalobos cartel had set the fire. But after a fierce Spanglish debate, they'd agreed to stay and rebuild. During construction, her Uncles Felipe and Juan had moved their food truck from their prime downtown location to the restaurant's parking lot so her mother could maintain the customer base. Now in a true family partnership, they cut the menu, prepped some items at their nearby homes, and managed to avoid bankruptcy.

Today Veranda had delved back into the deadly underworld of the Villalobos cartel. She couldn't help but wonder if her family would pay the price. Again.

The sight of her mother brought her back to the present. Lorena Cruz-Gomez emerged from her ancient Ford Econoline van, slender arms wrapped around a plastic grocery bag containing a bush with vibrant red-orange blossoms. She spotted Veranda, rushed to the table, and put the plant down next to their paper plates.

"*Ay, mi'ja.*" Lorena bent to kiss her daughter on both cheeks. "How are you?"

She couldn't quite meet her mother's hazel eyes. "Buried in paperwork." Aware of the pain the Villalobos family had brought to her mother over the years, Veranda didn't mention the morning's encounter with the cartel. Lorena would find out soon enough from news reports. Instead, she redirected the conversation, tipping her head toward the plant. "Did you bring that from your yard?" Veranda recognized a smaller version of her mother's favorite shrub. She had helped her plant dozens all around the group of casitas where her extended family lived nearby.

Even after three decades in Arizona, her mother's slight Mexican accent wove through her speech. "I have a few at home that are doing real good. So I cut some to grow here."

"What kind of plant is it?" Sam asked.

Lorena touched a fiery petal. "It is called a Red Bird of Paradise."

"Hold on." Sam's bushy black brows drew together. "I bought my wife one of those at the florist and it didn't look anything like that."

Lorena laughed. "You bought a Bird of Paradise *flower*. This is a *Red* Bird of Paradise *bush*. These grow in the desert and the blossom is such a beautiful color." She brushed her hand over a cluster of blossoms. "Like a phoenix bird on fire. I always loved these, but now they have a special meaning." Her gaze traveled to the construction site. "Our family restaurant will rise from the ashes like a phoenix." She turned back to Veranda. "To me, it will become the *Cruz Cocina de Phoenix*. This bush will be our symbol now. I will plant them all around the restaurant."

Veranda swallowed the lump in her throat. Her family was resilient and resourceful. Catastrophes only made them stronger. A memory, laden with regret, sliced into her thoughts. "How is Gabby?"

Lines of concern creased Lorena's brow at the mention of her younger daughter. Gabriela Gomez, Veranda's fourteen-year-old half-sister, recently had a brush with the Villalobos family. The physical wounds had healed, but her emotional trauma persisted.

"She still has nightmares," Lorena said.

Reassurances died on Veranda's lips. Everything her little sister endured was due to her vendetta against the Villalobos family. In the dark recesses of her mind, Veranda knew she couldn't give in. Couldn't stop pursuing her quarry. She felt an itching sensation under her skin. What price would be too high?

Her mother's words interrupted her self-recrimination. "At least Gabby is still excited about her *quinceañera*. When she speaks of it, she's herself again. I want to make it real special. Did you get her the present we talked about?"

"I've got it all lined up, don't worry," Veranda assured her.

"It is this Saturday." Lorena crossed her arms. "The day after to-morrow. I do not care what is going on with your work. You will be there for Gabby."

When faced with a determined Latina mother, only one answer would do. "Of course, *Mamá*."

Sam put his plastic fork down. "I've never been to a *quinceañera*. What goes on?"

Veranda jumped at the chance to turn from her mother's glare. "In our community, when a girl turns fifteen, her family recognizes her transition to womanhood with a special party. Many cultures celebrate rites of passage, and this one is particularly beautiful."

Sam looked intrigued. "What was yours like?"

Veranda smiled, recalling her own fifteenth birthday. It had been quite modest compared to what Gabby planned, but it was a favorite memory nonetheless. "Depends on what country the family is from but, in our tradition, there are several steps."

"The most important part," Lorena cut in, "is going to Mass at the church. That comes first, before the party. Father Ramirez will bless Gabriela and she will leave a doll at the altar to the *Virgen de Guadalupe*." Lorena's eyes gleamed. "She has a very special one she picked out just for this ceremony." She glanced at Veranda. "And your *tía* Juana got her a tiara." She circled the air above her head with her finger.

"A tiara?" Sam's eyes widened.

"It's formal," Veranda said. "Gabby's gown would put most debutantes to shame." At Sam's incredulous look, she added, "And then there's the *damas* and *chambelanes*."

"The who and what?"

Veranda chuckled. "The English words are 'dames' and 'chamberlains,' but it's really like bridesmaids and groomsmen. She'll have seven girls and seven boys plus a boy to escort her in the entourage. Everyone dressed in gowns and tuxes."

"All this for a birthday?"

"Not just any birthday—the planning goes on for months. She'll be viewed as a woman in the eyes of our community after this. That's why there's the changing of the shoes."

Sam leaned back. "Okay, I'll bite. What's that about?"

"During the reception, Gabby's father takes off whatever shoes she's wearing, then replaces them with her first pair of high heels. She'll wear them as she leaves."

Sam's gray eyes crinkled at the corners, a smile lighting his face. "What a great tradition."

Touched by his reaction, she went on. "The reception will be at our family property. That's where everyone cuts loose. We'll have tons of food and a live mariachi band, but Gabby will waltz with her father before everyone else hits the dance floor."

"Sounds like most weddings I've been to."

"There are similarities. Every tradition has meaning." She turned to her mother. "I'm glad Gabby's ready to go out into the world again. She's got to reclaim her life." Veranda looked at the restaurant construction going on behind them. "Our whole family has to."

Lorena nodded, a knowing expression in her eyes. "I must plant this and get into the food truck, *mi'ja*. Your *tío* Rico is making the *masa* today."

Veranda shook her head. Her mother was a five-star general in the kitchen, overseeing the troops as they prepped the food. Lorena touted good *masa* and excellent *molé* as the secret to Mexican cooking, and she would trust no one without inspecting their work before dishes were presented to her customers.

After her mother scooped up the Red Bird of Paradise and hurried toward the food truck, Veranda scanned the construction site again, amazed at the progress. The new restaurant's interior walls were going up fast. Apparently mistaking her lingering gaze for interest, one of the construction crew winked at her as he shouldered a plank.

Sam guffawed. "I think he's in love." He forked into another bite of enchilada. "Wonder if he knows he's in danger of imminent death."

Veranda directed a quizzical look at Sam before following his gaze to the hulking blond man approaching their table from the far side of the parking lot. She broke into a smile and waved him over. "Hey, Cole. I see you got my text."

She'd crossed paths with the Phoenix Fire Department arson investigator during her last case. When they'd started dating, she put up with good-natured ribbing from her squad. Police and fire had a long-standing rivalry, and the banter included references to his beefcake appearance as well as his lamentable career choice.

Cole Anderson gave Sam a curt nod before sitting next to Veranda. "Wouldn't miss a chance to eat the best Mexican food in Arizona." His light blue eyes softened as he looked at her. "Or to see you."

Sam grimaced. "If you can stop ogling my partner for a minute, we're about to start planning for tomorrow's meeting ... Captain."

She noticed Sam had emphasized Cole's official rank, a reminder that this was a working meal. Before she could comment, her *tío* Rico trotted over, juggling a bottle of ice water and a paper plate warped under the weight of massive *burro* surrounded by black beans.

He placed the food on the table in front of Cole with a flourish. "For the brave fireman."

Cole straightened and thanked her uncle.

Sam rolled his eyes. "What, he doesn't even have to order?"

Tío Rico beamed. "We know what *el capitán* likes."

"Oh, I think everyone knows what he likes," Sam muttered under his breath.

Veranda wanted to slide under the table to hide her burning face. She was sure her mother had seen Cole arrive and fired another salvo in the family's ongoing campaign to marry her off, plying him with his favorite dish. Unlike her cohorts at work, her large, noisy, interfering family had taken a shine to Cole and actively promoted the relationship.

When her uncle left, Cole took a bite of his red chile *burro* and gave her a wink. "Mmm. Hot and spicy."

Sam rested a hand on the butt of his sidearm. "I'm about to clear leather. Only I don't know whether to shoot you or myself."

Aware her partner had no patience for on-duty flirting, she switched subjects. "Cole, I hoped you could give us a briefing. You just came from the mall, right?"

The salacious grin slid from his face, and Cole grew serious. "They called me to the scene of the car fire in the garage at the mall. I understand you two were there when it went up."

Sam leaned forward and lowered his voice. "Something wasn't right about that fire. The Escalade exploded when it hit the cement post."

"We found two containers of extra gasoline in the rear compartment." Cole rubbed his jaw. "Can't imagine what for."

A disturbing picture forced its way into her consciousness. *Did the impact kill the driver? Was he unconscious when he died?*

Cole regarded her. "You're second-guessing yourself, aren't you?" When she didn't respond, he blew out a sigh. "I examined the wreckage.

The driver was pinned in the vehicle. There's nothing you could have done to extricate him."

His statement didn't make her feel better. Her first instinct had been to catch Roberto Bernal, not to save the cartel's driver. Even if he would have died anyway, her actions revealed a side of herself she didn't want to examine too closely.

Prey drive. When a predator reflexively gives chase with laser focus on the quarry, disregarding anything else.

The relentless pursuit of the Villalobos cartel had driven her life choices from the time she turned fifteen. After her own *quinceañera*, her mother had deemed her old enough to hear what Hector Villalobos had done to her family before she was born. That day, Veranda had vowed to destroy the cartel. Her mother's story was one of the reasons she became a police officer years later. When Veranda discovered recently that her mother hadn't told her the whole truth back then, the new information only fueled her anger.

Sam seemed to sense her pensive mood and resumed the conversation with Cole. "I assume you provided a report directly to Commander Webster?"

Cole nodded. "I finished it while I watched the news conference on television." Disgust tightened his features. "Why did your department promote that prick Diaz, and why is he now in charge of your entire Homicide Unit?"

The mention of her lieutenant's name pulled Veranda from her dark musing. "Search me. That's a primo assignment. Never heard of a newbie lieutenant getting it."

Sam snorted. "When you've been around as long as me, nothing surprises you. My guess is the brass wanted someone with a PSB background in Homicide after what happened with the mole."

Veranda considered Sam's point. The Professional Standards Bureau conducted internal investigations. The recent discovery of a cartel informant in their midst had stunned and embarrassed the department. If Commander Webster wanted more oversight for his detectives, Diaz was the type to crack the whip.

Cole groaned. "Toeing the line is one thing, but Diaz is so tight he squeaks." His dense brows furrowed as he eyed Veranda. "And his interest in you is way too personal. I don't want him anywhere near you."

Sam pushed his plate away. "You should be happy Veranda will be in Diaz's chain of command then."

"Why?"

"Now that she falls under his supervision, he's strictly forbidden to have any personal relationship with her."

Cole's face split into a broad grin, dimples on full display as he happily cut another bite of his *burro*. "That's the first piece of good news I've heard all day. One less thing for me to think about since I'm flying out tomorrow morning."

"Where you headed?" Sam asked.

"BATF is hosting an advanced course on the origin and cause of fires for arson investigators. It's a two-week class, specifically targeting courtroom testimony, at the Redstone Arsenal in Huntsville, Alabama. Looks like I'll be leaving just when things are heating up again."

"Don't worry," Sam said. "Nothing could get as screwed up as the last mess."

Cole ran a hand through his sandy hair and turned to Veranda. "Which brings me to my other question after watching the news. Why are they putting you in the hot seat?"

Veranda prepared for the inevitable. "I've investigated the cartel for over two years. Led a task force with Feds on the team before too."

She shrugged. "I'm the logical choice." She knew Cole wouldn't like it. He'd become increasingly leery about the risks she took.

His blue eyes became icy slits. "I'm sure the Villalobos cartel saw the same media coverage."

She gave him a defiant stare. "Doesn't matter if they did. Someone has to lead the charge."

He dropped his fork on the paper plate. "That's supposed to make me feel better?"

"It's not about your feelings. I do my job."

Cole bristled. "Why does it have to be you? Can't someone else head up the team?"

Sam's calming baritone rumbled as he waded into the fray. "Veranda makes sense as leader."

Cole shot Sam a look. "Aren't you senior to her? Shit, to everyone? Why can't you—"

"It's got nothing to do with seniority. And it's been decided," she said.

Cole crossed his arms over his broad chest, his plate completely forgotten now. "Let me get this straight. You're going to be the public face of the fight against two different drug gangs involved in a turf war?"

Veranda fought to control her temper. She knew Cole wanted to keep her safe, but he wasn't a police officer and didn't understand the mission. At times like this, his misguided overprotectiveness set her teeth on edge.

She drew a deep breath and mentally counted to three before responding. "In a word, yes. I'm front and center."

Cole opened his mouth, but Sam spoke first. "This is different than before. There's a ton of support from the top down. We have the Feds involved too."

Cole didn't look appeased. "But it's Veranda who'll be in everyone's crosshairs."

She held her tongue. Cole and Sam didn't know her secret. Didn't understand why she would always have a target on her back. The current turf war was nothing compared to the grudge that she knew festered in *El Lobo*'s heart.

6

STANDING ON THE BONE-WHITE sidewalk bleached by the late afternoon sun, Veranda used the back of her wrist to mop a line of perspiration from her forehead. Eyes shaded with her hand, she peered up at the Grace Court School building at the corner of 8th and Adams Streets. The early-twentieth-century building made an excellent choice for an ad hoc operations center. A short walk from police headquarters and vacant for years, it could be quickly adapted for their use.

Standing next to her, Sam tilted his head back, eyes travelling up the four imposing pillars at the entry steps to the Classic Revival structure that would house the Fusion Center. "I can remember a time when this school was open."

Veranda gave him a wry smile. "You and the other kids rode here on horseback, right?" She put a finger to her lip, tapping it lightly. "Or did you all wait at the local trading post to catch a ride on a Conestoga wagon?"

His silver mustache twitched. "I didn't attend here, but I knew some who did." He turned to her. "It opened in 1911, by the way."

"Oh, so you were already out of high school then."

"Such a smart ass."

She grinned, enjoying the banter. She respected Sam's experience, was at times in awe of his accumulated knowledge, but she liked to needle him about their age gap. In turn, he gave her a hard time about having worked as a narc.

Sam trailed her up the steps to the main entrance and jerked a thumb at the parking area. "The computer tech van's in the lot, so they're already here." He stopped at the immense wooden double doors, painted white to match the trim on the windows. An electronic keypad jutted from the wall next to the doorframe. "Maybe they'll give us the entry code."

She knocked on the door.

A man in his late twenties with dark hair and black-framed glasses answered. His sallow skin and red-rimmed eyes bore witness to years toiling under fluorescent lights. The ID card dangling from a lanyard around his neck confirmed Veranda's assumption. A computer forensics detective. "Come in, Detective Cruz."

She'd started to pull out her creds, then realized everyone would have recognized her after the news conference when the detective greeted her by name.

Sam followed her in. "There must've been some renovations over the years."

The computer detective nodded. "Infrastructure looks good, and the main level has over seventeen thousand square feet of office space. More than enough. And if this grows legs, we can take over the entire second floor as well."

Used to the cramped confines of the Violent Crimes Bureau with its warren of cubicles, the vast open space in what would become the Fusion Center reminded Veranda of a furniture warehouse. The building had not served as a school for decades, and in the interim, the owners had obviously renovated it for potential office use before putting it on the market for sale. Veranda wondered what kind of arrangement the city had made with the proprietors to lease the space.

As the detective ambled away, she surveyed the space, planning workstations in her mind. She pointed an empty corner out to Sam. "We could push two or three long tables together over there to make a central briefing area. We'll need two walls for posting materials and projecting images."

Sam squinted at one of the few private offices bordering the room. "I suppose Diaz will set up shop in one of those."

The mention of her newly appointed supervisor heated her insides. The chief's announcement had blindsided her at the news conference. "Don't get me started about that *pinche* lieutenant." She'd thought about Diaz since their conversation over lunch. No one had ever gotten the coveted Homicide slot as a first assignment after being promoted to lieutenant. Despite what Sam said, she had the nagging feeling it had something to do with this investigation. And with her.

Sam regarded her. "If he makes life difficult, we'll work around him."

"He should've stayed in PSB where he could keep investigating fellow officers. It's what he's good at." In his previous assignment, he'd seemed to take particular pleasure in scrutinizing her every move. Diaz had made it clear he wanted her sidelined from investigations involving the cartel.

"To be fair, Veranda, PSB exists for a reason. I'll admit I've been known to stray outside the pasture, but there's a limit to how far." He hesitated a beat before his next words. "And we both know there are some cops out there who shouldn't be wearing a badge. It's PSB's job to ferret out the bad ones."

"Agreed, but Diaz needs to get his nose out of the Regs book long enough to see the big picture. He was all over me last time." She put a hand on her hip. "I've had pelvic exams that were less intrusive than his interrogations. And his enthusiasm for following rules damn near got me killed."

"So did your enthusiasm for breaking them."

She cocked a brow. "I don't see you wearing a Boy Scout badge."

He put his hands up in mock surrender. "We better finish looking this place over and make plans for your first day tomorrow. There's a lot at stake."

Her gut clenched at the reminder. She hadn't shared her feelings about the assignment. Not prone to bouts of self-doubt, she'd barely acknowledged them to herself. Now, alone with Sam, she let down her guard. "You know I don't back down from a fight."

He snorted. "Considering how you dealt with Bartolo, I'd say not."

She didn't mince words. "You should lead this investigation. Not me."

His brows shot up. "Why? You led a task force back when you were a narc. In fact, your sergeant pretty much let you call the shots. There were Feds on that team, too, and you guys broke records for asset seizure."

"I know I said all that stuff when Cole grilled me over lunch, but I just wanted him off my ass." She dragged a hand through her hair. "The Drug Enforcement Bureau was different. I was an experienced narcotics detective. I had an informant inside giving me intel on the Villalobos cartel." She threw her hands in the air. "Here, I'm flying blind. Working with Feds I don't know. I haven't been in Homicide very long and my inside track on the cartel is gone." A wave of remorse swept through her as she recalled her informant's grisly murder.

"Doesn't matter. Leadership skills are the same. Just run the team like you did before." He eyed her, speculation in his gaze. "Unless..." He stroked his mustache. "Is something else bothering you?"

She blew out a sigh. He'd been a detective for decades. Of course he would read her. She looked around to be sure no one could overhear. "Sam, do you remember when you gave me the envelope you took from Bartolo's body?"

Six weeks ago, Bartolo Villalobos, heir apparent to the cartel, claimed he held a DNA report identifying Veranda's biological father in a sealed envelope in his back pocket. He had taunted her, refusing to give her the results. To make matters worse, she'd been wearing a transmitter and her fellow officers and supervisors overheard the conversation. After Bartolo was fatally shot, Sam had surreptitiously slipped the envelope from his pocket before the evidence techs processed the scene.

The department brass, with Diaz leading the charge, had demanded to know where the missing DNA report had gone, but Sam never admitted taking it. Hours later, he turned it over to Veranda without breaking the seal, explaining that her father's identity was her business, not the department's. Then he left, giving her the choice to read the contents or destroy them.

Once she was alone, her fingers had trembled as she slid the documents out. The pages inside had shaken her to the core. Everything she had believed, all of her life, had been a lie.

Some on the department suspected she'd taken the envelope, but no one could prove it. Sam had never asked her about the DNA results, and she'd vowed to take the knowledge to her grave. But now

Chief Tobias had set a new chain of events in motion when he gave her this assignment. The weight of the past pressed on her.

Sam straightened and dropped his voice. "You don't need to tell me—"

"I know," she said. "I haven't told anyone. And I swore I never would, but—"

"I don't care what was in that envelope."

"I do. And everyone else would if they knew."

"Then don't tell anyone."

"But *El Lobo* knows." She grasped Sam's elbow, pulled him inside what would be Diaz's office along the wall, and closed the door. "And I'm sure he told Adolfo. Hell, probably the whole cartel knows." Bile rose in her throat at the thought. "I don't know why Adolfo hasn't leaked the info to the media yet." She swallowed hard. "One day he will though. And I'll be toast."

Sam's deep voice was neutral. "The envelope held bad news." He made it a statement.

She bowed her head, unable to look her partner in the eye. Time for her to come clean.

She drew a ragged breath before speaking in a hoarse whisper. "Hector Villalobos—*El Lobo*—is my biological father."

Her heart thudded as a silent chasm stretched between them for a full minute.

Then Sam clasped her shoulder. "I seriously considered burning the envelope without telling you I had it." Regret etched his features. "But I figured you should decide for yourself."

Her gaze raised to meet his. "If you had destroyed the DNA report in that envelope, the cartel would be the only ones who knew the truth about me. That's why I had to open it." She cast her eyes to the floor again. "I can take the blowback if word gets out. My biggest fear is the pain this could cause my mother."

He withdrew his hand. "You haven't told her?"

How could she make Sam understand? "Remember what I told you that day at the park?"

He inclined his head. "That Lorena admitted she wasn't sure who your father was."

Veranda's stomach roiled at the memory of her mother's recent confession. After hiding the truth for over thirty years, Lorena had finally broken her silence. With tears in her eyes, her mother recounted how Hector Villalobos had come to her house after murdering her husband, Ernesto Hidalgo. A slender nineteen-year-old bride, Lorena stood no chance against Hector's brute force. He had raped her.

That night, Lorena fled across the border with her five younger siblings to escape *El Lobo*'s wrath. They were granted asylum in the United States, then became citizens and created a life in Phoenix, safe from the cartel. Veranda had joined the PPD to honor her father's memory. Ernesto had been a Mexican *Federale*. A police agent. An honorable man. Now she knew her real father was his killer.

"My mother raised me hoping I was Ernesto's child, but she knew I might be Hector's. I look exactly like her, so she couldn't tell from my appearance."

Sam let her talk. His gray eyes patient.

"She's convinced herself I'm Ernesto's daughter because she loved him." Grief sliced into Veranda as she bared her soul. "That's why she kept me, you know. She thought Ernesto lived on through me." She swallowed hard. "I don't have the heart to tell her the truth. Or the rest of my family." Her voice broke on her final words. "I always felt different from my relatives. Now I know why."

Sam waited a long moment before he spoke. "Let me explain something. Everyone who wears a badge feels different. And there's a good reason for it."

"What do you mean?"

Sam stroked his mustache. "Say there's a flock of sheep out in a pasture surrounded by wolves. When the shepherd sleeps, who protects the flock?"

She recalled a friend who owned a large ranch in southern Arizona. "A dog."

"Exactly." Sam became animated. "A dog doesn't have hooves and eat grass like the sheep. A dog has fangs and claws and eats meat ... like the wolves, not the sheep. A dog is a close relative of the wolf. That's why the shepherd chooses a dog to guard the flock, because it takes a predator to understand and fight another predator."

She turned his words over in her mind as he continued.

"I knew a lot of kids growing up who could've gone either way." He lifted a shoulder. "Hell, I was one of them. We drove too fast, got in fights, even broke a few laws. Because of that we understood the criminal mindset. We were one of them. Felt the violence inside ourselves and could see it in others. The difference is that some of us mastered it instead of letting it rule us." The corner of his mouth kicked up. "That's what makes us the good guys."

She appreciated his words, but he didn't seem to understand how deeply she was tainted by her blood. "Unlike you, I haven't mastered the violence inside."

He grew serious again. "Some of the best cops I know have a hard edge. Embrace it. A dog lives with the flock but is never truly a part of it. He's a guardian. Ever vigilant and ready to lay down his life so others can be at peace and live in safety. The wolves are always out there. Ready to attack. Guardians have to be ready too."

"Dammit, Sam. You make it sound so … noble. But I didn't feel noble when I took off after Roberto Bernal while Castillo bled out. My first instinct was to abandon him and pursue Roberto." She jabbed a finger at him. "Yours was to render aid."

Sam gritted his teeth in exasperation. "You didn't force me back into the car. I got in because you were right. Castillo was a lost cause. You made a split-second decision to protect the public by trying to catch the perpetrator before he could kill again."

"But if you were driving, you'd have stopped to check on the victim. When I was locked in on Roberto, you were the one who mentioned Castillo."

Sam shook his head. "That was a reflex. I would've made the same choice you did. His entire upper body was destroyed. No chance. You made the right call." Irritation drew Sam's brows together. "And don't forget, Castillo led a violent street gang. He had plenty of blood on his hands."

"I know he was far from innocent, but I still wonder if I'd have acted differently if I … well … if … "

"If you weren't the daughter of a notorious killer?"

Her eyes slid away from his penetrating stare. "Yes."

"Well, you're also the daughter of a kind, compassionate woman who is respected and loved by her family and her community." When she didn't respond, he went on. "Hell, Veranda, when you've lived as long as I have, you'll understand people make their own choices. Sometimes fate has a hand in it, too, but mostly it's the path people *choose* that makes the difference in their lives."

The path. The journey. The words triggered a memory. When her mother recently told Veranda about the circumstances of her birth, she'd also explained the meaning behind her unusual name. Lorena had created it from two Spanish words. *Ver,* meaning "to see," and *la andadura*, meaning "path" or "journey." When Lorena chose to keep her newborn, she also decided to love the child fully and withhold judgment. She would wait to see what her daughter made of her life. Which path she took. The name Veranda had served to remind Lorena of that private vow.

"Thank you." Two simple words couldn't possibly convey her gratitude for her partner's support. He had reminded her why her mother named her, and that she amounted to more than her bloodline. "But not everyone will share your feelings if it ever gets out that *El Lobo* is my father. If Lieutenant Diaz suspects I've been hiding something, he'll be the first in line to take my badge." She met his gaze. "And if my mother learns the truth, she'll always see Hector Villalobos when she looks at me." She heard the catch in her own voice as she whispered, "I couldn't bear that."

7

AN HOUR LATER, VERANDA perched on a stool at her kitchen counter, studying the man across from her. She pushed a cold bottle toward him. He glanced down at the icy drink and rested both hands on the blue Saltillo tiles covering the countertop. Tattooed above each of his knuckles was a letter, spelling V-I-D-A on one hand and L-O-C-A on the other.

He raised a black brow pierced with a metal stud in the shape of a ball bearing. "What? No lime?"

She rolled her eyes. "Seriously, Chuy?"

"Jus' sayin." He shrugged. "Would taste better with a slice of lime."

"You've gone soft after getting out."

He narrowed his eyes. "Prison teaches you to appreciate simple things." He lifted the bottle to his lips. "Like a cold one." As he swallowed, the leering silver skull dangling from the heavy chain around his neck glinted in the light from the overhead kitchen fan.

She eyed him speculatively. "So, will you do it for me or not?"

He finished a long pull and passed a hand over his bald head, which was covered in dark tattoos ending in a point resembling a widow's peak on his forehead. "Yeah, I'll do it." He looked around. "Do you have the stuff?"

She pointed at a black nylon bag on the floor slouched against the kitchen wall. "Everything you need is in the backpack."

He nodded and took his right hand off the table. The muscles in his bare arm made the tattooed sleeve of body art ripple as he reached down into his lap.

She put her bottle down and lowered her voice. "Careful now."

He brought his hand up slowly. "You can't tell anyone about my, uh, little secret." Inch by inch, he lifted his arm higher until he revealed a tiny, tan-colored Chihuahua puppy quivering in his palm.

The pup's huge brown eyes blinked and settled on Veranda, who grinned. "You mean that you wear a black leather thong under your jeans when you ride your Harley? Because that's no secret, Chuy, everybody can tell."

He leveled a glare at her.

She pointed to his Coke bottle. "Let's see, it can't be that you've given up beer. Everyone knows that too. Hmm, what else?" She smacked her forehead. "Wait, it's a different secret. Don't tell me you sometimes don't claim all the income you get from selling choppers on your taxes?"

"Don't even joke about that, *mi'jita*, I know better than to mess with the IRS." He lifted the puppy higher and gave it a kiss on top if its apple-shaped head. Its tiny tail wagged. "My secret … is that I have a soft spot for these little guys." He looked back at her. "If word gets out, I'll lose my street cred."

Veranda reached for her cell. "That is so damned cute. I have to get a picture."

Chuy lowered the dog back onto his lap. "You may be my favorite cousin, but if I see you point that smart phone at me, I'll cut you."

She snorted. "I've heard that before. And the guys who said it are behind bars." He chuckled and petted the puppy as she laid the phone on the counter and reached out to squeeze his free hand. "Thanks for finding him for me, Chuy."

"*De nada.*" He waved dismissively. "My neighbor breeds them. There was a litter a couple of months ago and she asked me if I wanted one. Heard you were looking for a puppy for Gabby, so I checked and she still had this one."

Remorse pierced her at the mention of her kid sister's name. She wished she could take away the terror Gabby had suffered at Bartolo's hands. Her sweet, young sister had become yet another victim of her relentless pursuit of the cartel. Of the insatiable need spurring her to take them down.

Chuy interrupted her rumination. "I never heard the whole story about Gabby. All I got was bits and pieces from the news. No one in the family will talk about it." He leaned forward. "What really happened?"

"The Villalobos cartel happened." Anger tinged with shame tightened her throat. "You remember I was in narcotics investigating their cartel?"

He nodded.

"Bartolo Villalobos, the second born son, was supposed to take over their empire from his father. After two years, I finally had enough physical evidence to make a solid felony charge. Before I could move on him, Bartolo kidnapped Gabby and offered to trade her for the evidence."

Chuy loosed a stream of Spanish expletives.

She waited for the outburst to subside before continuing. "I can't go into details, but we managed to rescue Gabby before Bartolo could do her lasting physical harm. She sure as hell suffered a lot of emotional trauma though. She still has nightmares, barely eats, and doesn't leave the house unless she has to."

Chuy's dark eyes took on the hooded stare of a hardened criminal in gen pop. "It's a good thing Bartolo's dead. If he wasn't, I'd kill the motherfucker myself."

She gave him a wry grin. "And I'd look the other way."

They clicked their soda bottles together and sipped in silence.

Veranda blew out a sigh. "I set Gabby up with a victim assistance counselor. He says she's got PTSD, which is why I asked you to find her a dog."

"Gabby's wanted a puppy for ages."

"The counselor liked the idea, so I cleared it with *Mamá* too. I'm going to give it to Gabby at her *quinceañera* Saturday. She'll love it. This little guy can comfort her, and she can take care of him." Veranda tilted her head and considered the pup. "He seems like a pretty good listener."

Chuy stroked the fur on its tiny ears. "Can I at least get him a black leather collar with metal studs on it?"

She laughed. "Fine. I'm too busy to care for a puppy until the party, so I need you to bring him and meet me there." She pointed a finger at him. "But don't get too attached."

Before he could answer, the doorbell rang. Chuy got to his feet.

Not expecting a visitor, Veranda rested her hand on the grip of the gun tucked into her waistband at the small of her back, padded to the front door, and peered through the peephole. A wide expanse of chest filled the viewing portal. She grinned and yanked open the door.

61

Cole stood on her doorstep. "Hi th—," he began, then his gaze traveled up and locked onto something over her head. His smile evaporated.

Veranda turned to see Chuy standing behind her, arms crossed. He had stashed the puppy out of sight. Tension crackled in the air between the two men, and she tried to see the situation from Cole's perspective, appraising Chuy's appearance objectively.

Almost every inch of visible skin except her cousin's face was covered in biker tattoos. Indigo skulls, crosses, and gothic symbols formed a mosaic of ink that spanned his muscular arms. More body art decorated his chest, bare except for a black leather vest. Faded jeans were encased by chaps reaching down to the soles of steel-toed boots. Veranda had to admit, Chuy looked every bit the ex-con he was. Cole would wonder why she was alone in her house with him.

As the two men glowered at each other, Veranda pointed behind her. "This is my cousin Chuy," she said, then turned, sweeping her arm in Cole's direction. "And this is Captain Cole Anderson with the Phoenix Fire Department. He's my … uh … friend." She grimaced at the lame description of their relationship.

Cole was definitely more than a friend, but she didn't want word spreading around the family about their current status. Her mother tended to get overexcited. Veranda winced inwardly as she recalled a previous boyfriend. After three dates, her mother had started thumbing through wedding magazines. In front of him. He hadn't called her again.

Cole's demeanor stiffened, stance wide, jaw rigid. She wasn't sure if he was more irritated by Chuy's presence or her hesitance to acknowledge their relationship.

From his position behind her, Chuy directed a challenge over her head at Cole. "You got a problem?" His voice dripped venom. Her cousin had used the mad-dogging technique he'd learned in prison. Meant to intimidate, it was a show of force, staking a claim to his space.

Cole brought himself to his full, and considerable, height. He scowled back at Chuy. "No. You?"

She sensed that her cousin had taken offense at Cole's tacit judgment. And Chuy wouldn't tolerate disrespect. Without intervention on her part, things would escalate.

She spun to face her cousin. "Chuy, you have everything you need. I'll see you later." She made it a statement instead of asking him to leave.

Chuy tore his gaze away from Cole and tramped to the kitchen, boots thudding on the tile floor. He scooped up the backpack and bent over the dining chair with his back to them. From her vantage point, she could see him lift something and slip it inside his vest. When he pivoted around, only a slight bulge indicated where the puppy nestled against his chest.

Chuy directed a menacing glare at Cole. "I'm done here."

Veranda tugged Cole inside to let her cousin pass and closed the door.

Cole's eyes, frosted blue chips of ice, met hers. "What the hell, Veranda?"

She didn't appreciate his attitude toward a member of her family. "Don't be so quick to judge, Cole." She stalked back to the kitchen as Chuy's Harley roared to life in her driveway.

Cole trailed her. "Family or not, I can tell a criminal when I see one."

"He's an ex-con, but he's out of the life now."

"Really." The word oozed sarcasm.

She tamped down a spike of indignation. How could Cole know what Chuy meant to her? "When he was younger, he did heavy drugs.

Stole cars to support his habit. After his last stretch, he got involved with a volunteer program and got clean."

She didn't add that she'd visited him in prison regularly. "Chuy's been sober going on five years. He earns an honest living now as a mechanic. Even managed to set up his own garage a few months back."

"What was he doing here?"

"Family stuff." She changed the subject. Thoughts of Gabby were too painful. "Why did you come?"

"Wanted to say goodbye before I leave for training in the morning. You've got to work on your presentation for tomorrow, so I won't stay long."

"Ah." The reminder of her impending leadership role clawed at her raw nerves.

Cole shook his head. "I still can't believe Diaz is in charge. He's got no business running the operation."

"Maybe he'll just hang out in his office and read reports. Either way, I plan to keep my distance."

"Good." He snagged a finger on her belt loop, pulling her close. "Because it doesn't matter what the rules say about fraternizing with subordinates, I don't like the way he looks at you."

She traced the stubble along his jaw with her nose, nuzzling him. "You mean like he doesn't trust me?"

"No, like he doesn't trust himself around you."

She pushed away, rolling her eyes. "We've been through this. He doesn't want me like that. He thinks I'm a loose cannon, so he keeps an eye on me." She opened the fridge, pulled out a Coke, and handed it to him.

"That's your take." Cole twisted the top off. "Mine is that he's overprotective and jealous whenever you're around."

"It adds up to the same thing. He's going to scrutinize everything I do. If he finds any excuse, he'll pull me off the case and reassign me."

"To be honest, I wouldn't mind you investigating something else. A nice safe serial killer or ax murderer. Anything but that damned cartel." He took a swig. "Diaz may be technically in charge of the operation, but your chief made it clear you'll be the lead detective. That puts an even bigger target on your back."

They'd been over this ground before, but Cole would never accept her self-imposed mission. "I'll go after the Villalobos cartel until they're all behind bars."

He thumped his bottle on the counter. "That entire family's nothing but murderers, sociopaths, and degenerates. I swear, there's something defective in their gene pool. Not one of them is normal."

His words seared her heart. He had just expressed her worst fear. Said what everyone would think of her—what *he* would think of her—if word got out about her parentage. She blinked away a hot stinging behind her eyes and glanced down, unable to face him. "I'm getting a headache. And I've got a lot of prep work for the briefing tomorrow morning. I'll catch up with you after you come back to Phoenix."

His shoulders sagged, concern crossing his features. "Can I get you something for your headache?" He reached for her.

"No." She took a step back. At his hurt expression, she softened her tone. "Like you said, everyone's looking to me. And I've only got a few hours to come up with a plan."

This time when he approached, she didn't stop him. His hands circled her waist before he slid a large palm up her back and tightened his arm, pressing her body against his. She wrapped her arms around his neck and allowed herself the comfort of a brief embrace. She felt like a thief of the heart, stealing tender moments on a false pretense. Gathering herself, she gently pushed away. She must not get too attached to this man. He had revealed his true beliefs. He could never accept her for who she was. She didn't blame him.

She couldn't either.

8

THE COFFEE IN THE paper cup next to Veranda's fingertips had grown cold. She had arrived in the Fusion Center early in the morning, an hour before the scheduled meeting, to set up the room. She'd pushed four rectangular tables together to make one large conference area in a corner of the vast open space. Her plan was to brief everyone as a group, then dole out assignments and separate the tables so each team could work independently.

Some bleary-eyed computer techs helped her with power strips, cords, and chairs. She had them connect her laptop to the projection equipment they had installed overnight so she could brief the team with the PowerPoint she'd created before going to bed.

She sat at one end of the elongated table to confer with Sam about her plan.

"I've got one question." His deep baritone rumbled as he spoke. "How drunk were you when you came up with this scheme?"

"I know it's a bit … bold, but it's sound. I've led similar operations in the past, just not on this scale and within this time frame." She lowered her voice. "I need your support, Sam, I've got to—"

He raised a finger and looked over her shoulder toward the far door. "Here they come."

She stood as Chief Tobias strode in, Assistant Chief Delcore, Commander Webster, Lieutenant Diaz, and Sergeant Jackson in his wake. Behind the procession of police brass, a line of people wearing dark suits, ID cards clipped to lanyards around their necks, filed in.

She recognized two of them. *Feds.*

Had they just come from a private meeting before entering the Fusion Center? Unease rippled through her as she speculated about what they might have discussed behind her back. Chief Tobias had supported her in the past, but the shit storm he'd weathered at the news conference could have changed his mind about her.

Everyone else in the Fusion Center had gotten to their feet as well. A gaggle of computer techs clustered in the far corner where they had set up an array of equipment, Veranda's Homicide squad clutched Styrofoam cups of rot-gut coffee in the middle of the room, and Gang Unit detectives leaned against the back wall.

"Good morning," Chief Tobias said, stopping next to the make-shift jumbo conference table. "A special thank you to everyone who worked through the night so we could hit the ground running today. This is the most critical situation Phoenix has faced since I've been in law enforcement. We're all hands on deck."

A beat of silence added weight to the declaration as Tobias's piercing green eyes swept the room. "As I stated at the news conference yesterday, Assistant Chief Delcore will be at the top of the chain of command for the Fusion Center and will provide daily briefings to me. Lieutenant Diaz will oversee the day-to-day operations and will keep management apprised of all developments." The chief turned to his right. "Assisting us are several Federal partners."

He started with a tall, slender woman in a navy pantsuit. She surveyed the room with a reserved expression as the chief introduced her. Her ebony hair was cut in a smooth chin-length bob tucked behind one ear, exposing a pearl stud earring that contrasted with her dark skin. "This is Special Agent Gwen Gates from the FBI. She'll be transferring to the Charlotte Field Office after this investigation. Accompanying her is Special Agent James Tanner. The Phoenix Field Office is his first assignment out of Quantico."

Tanner's blond curly hair, freckles, and pale blue eyes gave him a boyish appearance. His fair skin revealed a flush that betrayed nervousness, making her question whether the task force was also his very first investigation.

"Looks like we'll be breaking that one in," Sam muttered so only Veranda could hear.

She knew the next person in line. "Special Agent Craig Wallace from the DEA regularly coordinates with detectives in our own Drug Enforcement Bureau."

She had also worked with the man standing to Wallace's right. "Deputy US Marshal Tim Fitzhugh has been on task forces with our detectives for several years."

Pleased to see two friendlies among the suits, she relaxed a bit. Two years ago, Fitz had arranged to deputize Veranda and her fellow narcotics detectives as federal officers so they had law enforcement powers beyond Phoenix city boundaries. She could parlay their prior working relationship into an alliance if necessary. Given the scope of her plan, she needed every ally should could muster.

The chief had gotten to the next person in the row of agents. "Special Agent Nicholas Flag is with Homeland Security. Since our operation will have international ramifications and we're partnering with foreign nationals, we need communication and cooperation from all sides. He works with ICE agents regularly since they're under the same umbrella."

Sam nudged her and leaned down. "If that guy's not a spook, I'll eat my shoe."

She looked at Special Agent Flag. In his late thirties, he wore his light brown hair in a flat top. Tension practically vibrated through his body as he assessed the room.

"Which agency?" she whispered.

"It'll be the CIA, NSA, something like that," Sam said quietly. "With international and national security involvement, the intelligence community's going to want Oxfords on the ground."

She studied Flag. His cobalt eyes darted in every direction, as if he expected an armed assault at any moment. *Sam's probably right.*

Chief Tobias smiled as he indicated the last two men at the end of the row. "We are very fortunate to have two agents from the Ministerial Federal Police in Mexico. These gentlemen just flew into Sky Harbor Airport this morning. For those of you not familiar with law enforcement south of the border, the Ministerial Federal Police are similar in function to the FBI. They have broad powers and are the main investigative arm of the Mexican Attorney General."

Tobias inclined his head toward the older of the pair. "Agent Esteban Lopez has over thirty-two years of experience and is a subject matter expert on the Villalobos cartel. He's also familiar with many other notorious criminal organizations throughout Central and South America."

Lopez's thick silver hair swept straight back from his forehead. A narrow gray mustache tapered down both sides of his mouth, blending into a neatly trimmed goatee. His suit, dress shirt, and tie were a monochromatic black. Wry amusement tipped up the corners of Veranda's lips. Lopez was Sam's Mexican counterpart.

Chief Tobias continued to the last person in line. "Agent Manuel Rios is his partner. He's been working closely with Agent Lopez for several months and has a background in special ops."

To Veranda's practiced eye, Rios certainly looked like he had tactical experience. About her age, she could tell he was ripped, even in his suit. His military-style haircut completed the mission-ready effect. She realized she'd been staring at Rios when he cast an appreciative glance her way and gave her a slow smile.

As her face heated with embarrassment, the chief's next words dragged her mind back to the task force.

"Lieutenant Diaz will participate directly in all meetings and activities," Tobias said, "but Detective Cruz is the lead investigator." He glanced at his fellow command staff officers. "We'll take our leave so you all can get to work. I expect results." He turned a sharp gaze on Veranda. "Soon."

With that, the brass filed out of the room.

Veranda noted fifteen detectives, agents, and supervisors assigned to the main task force, not including support personnel and other investigative bureaus, remained in the Fusion Center. She decided to have her Homicide team sit at the extra-large table with the Feds while the computer and Gang detectives listened from their workstations.

Diaz cleared his throat. "We'll start with an overview so we all have the same base level of information to work from. Detective Cruz will run the meeting."

All eyes turned to Veranda, who pulled out a blank sheet of paper. "Please write out your contact information on this sheet." She handed it to Special Agent Fitzgerald, who stood to her right. She'd given dozens of briefings over the years, but this one felt different. Her highly controversial plan was sure to draw fire.

Aware she would be dealing with Feds, she had donned a charcoal gray tailored business suit this morning and twisted her long, thick hair up into a sleek chignon. Striving to project professionalism and competence, she pointed at the main table. "Please take a seat."

Sam slipped into the chair immediately to her right before Diaz, who had started in that direction, could get there. Diaz's mouth pressed into a hard, flat line and he sat farther down the table.

Veranda remained standing as the rest of the group jockeyed for position. Her entire squad was there, and she wanted to put them on par with the agents.

"Before we start the briefing, some background on PPD Homicide," she said. "Over fifty detectives are in the Homicide Unit, which contains the Cold Case squad and five Homicide squads, each with a sergeant and five to ten detectives."

As her mentor, Sam was effectively her partner, but she wanted the Feds to understand how the squad functioned as a group. "We get called out together, and work cases as a team." Under intense pressure from the relentless pace and scrutiny of several high-profile investigations, the crew had bonded over the past few weeks. "Chief Tobias introduced all of you. I'll do the same for my squad."

She glanced to her right. "Sam Stark. Senior detective." She went down the row. "Marci Blane." Agent Tanner gave Marci a second look. Her long blond hair, flawless skin, and lithe figure under fitted clothes always turned men's heads. Veranda smiled to herself. If Tanner made a play for Marci, he was in for a disappointment.

She motioned across the table to a dark-haired, slender man with horn-rimmed glasses. "Doc Malloy." Detective Malloy had earned his nickname from attending too many autopsies. His unofficial medical expertise was highly useful, but such intimate knowledge of human physiology came at a price—hypochondria. For Doc, every bump was a tumor, every twinge, a fatal illness, every cold, pneumonia.

She inclined her head at the next seat down. "Frank Fujiyama." Doc's opposite in many ways, Frank's skin had bronzed from hiking desert mountain ranges throughout Phoenix in all weather. An avid outdoorsman and introvert, Frank often ventured on solitary wilderness camping trips.

She indicated the last member of her squad. "Tony Sanchez." A proud Puerto Rican raised in New York City, Tony had joined the NYPD right out of college but was among hundreds of officers laid off during budget cuts early in his career. He'd moved west to the PPD and flourished, eventually earning a coveted detective slot. Despite living in Arizona for over two decades, Tony had never acclimated. Complaints about the blistering heat, peppered with expletives in a heavy Brooklyn accent, emanated from his cubicle all summer long.

Introductions out of the way, Veranda lifted a remote from the table next to her laptop. "The Villalobos cartel is one of the largest and most sophisticated criminal organizations in the world. They feed their growing empire with money from drugs, sex, weapons, explosives, fraud, smuggling, and murder. I'll explain their methods shortly, but first, we all need to be on the same page about why we're sitting here today."

She tapped the remote lightly against her open palm. "Let me start by briefing everyone on our current situation. Speak up if you have questions." To explain the sequence of events bringing them to this point, she started with the first domino to fall. "Six days ago, a dope slinger from a gang called the South Side *Soldados* expanded his business onto Villalobos cartel turf. The Villalobos enforcers responded."

She raised the remote, aiming at the smooth wall opposite her. She clicked a button, and all eyes turned to see the image of a patient in a hospital bed projected in vivid detail. Swathed in white bandages with tubes protruding from every visible orifice, the man looked like a disjointed lump of pulverized flesh.

Tanner's mouth dropped open. "Who are the South Side *Soldados*?"

"*Soldados* is the Spanish word for soldiers," she clicked the remote again. An image of three interlocking S-shaped snakes replaced the grisly hospital photo. "They go by SSS. Strictly local drug dealers out of South Phoenix, but their supply chain leads to a cartel in Colombia that's at war with the Villalobos family."

Veranda flashed back over her two years in the Drug Enforcement Bureau before transferring to Homicide. Her experience as the leader of an inter-agency task force targeting the notorious Villalobos cartel had provided ample opportunity to research the frequent coups and skirmishes among various cartels in South and Central America.

When her audience stopped scribbling, she continued. "After the attack on their dealer, SSS retaliated. Three days ago, a mid-level distributor for the Villalobos cartel was gunned down." She pressed again, displaying a crime scene photo of a body splayed in a pool of blood on the stoop in front of an apartment building. "His stash went missing." She inclined her head to her squad supervisor. "Sergeant Jackson assigned the case to me as my first lead."

Jackson adjusted his rimless glasses. "The victim had a black wolf's head tattooed on his chest, so we knew he was with the Villalobos cartel. Because of Detective Cruz's experience as a narc, I gave her the lead." He seemed anxious to justify his decision.

"Did you make headway?" Agent Wallace asked the sergeant.

Jackson was quick to answer. "We began with the premise that the shooting was retaliation against the cartel for attacking an SSS dealer.

Detective Cruz arranged for her former DEB squad to stage a buy-bust the next day. When the bust went down, the narcs found the stolen Villalobos cartel stash being cut for sale by SSS distributors. They even found the wolf logo on the discarded heroin packaging. The narcs arrested four SSS members, who all pointed to their leader, Raymond Castillo, as the shot-caller." He spread his hands. "We swore out a warrant for Castillo within forty-eight hours of the murder."

Jackson had taken a risk by giving her a lead spot after only six weeks in Homicide, and he clearly wanted to show she'd been an asset to the investigation. Her success or failure directly reflected on him.

"How did you locate Castillo?" Agent Gates asked.

Sam spoke for the first time. "He ghosted on us. Couldn't catch him at his residence. That's when Veranda came up with a plan." He looked over at her, giving her the floor.

"In my experience, you don't find drug dealers at their listed addresses. There's three places they go. She counted off on her fingers. "Girlfriend's house, Mama's house, and their gangbanger hangout—in that order." She had offered the sanitized version of the investigative technique she'd learned when she first became a narc years ago. One of the senior detectives in the Unit had told her how to track down informants by checking the most likely places. "Maslow's Hierarchy for street punks. Get laid, get fed, and get paid."

Veranda continued. "But Castillo couldn't lay low in any of those places. The Villalobos cartel was after him, and his own SSS crew had sold him out to the cops." She shrugged. "He was a dead man, and he knew it. He only had one play left, and he reached out to turn himself in. Offered to provide intel on his suppliers in exchange for a deal. He named the time and place for the meet."

Tanner's eyes widened. "So you just went where he told you to go?" A note of censure edged his question.

She clenched her fists, unsure if she was more annoyed with Tanner or herself. "No one knew about the meeting. I still can't figure out how Roberto Bernal got there right when we did."

The mystery had gnawed at her. How had the Villalobos cartel known where and when to deploy their urban assault vehicle? Castillo had been taken out with the precision of a surgical strike. What she couldn't understand, she couldn't prevent happening again.

Diaz glanced at her tightened hands and interjected. "Perhaps you should go over the structure of the cartel, Detective Cruz."

Blowing out a frustrated sigh, she exited the file and clicked open a different part of her PowerPoint program. She understood why, but the lieutenant had messed up the flow of her presentation.

Flicking through the first few images, she found the section she wanted. "The public believes this is all about warring narcotics trafficking organizations, but this goes much deeper than drug dealing. It's about the Villalobos empire." She inclined her head to the Mexican agents. "Jump in if you have updated information as I go through the cartel hierarchy."

She pressed the remote, and an image of Hector Villalobos glowered at the group. Cold dark eyes peered out above an angular nose and cruel mouth framed by a trim black goatee with a silver stripe down the middle of the chin.

Revulsion and fury fired her core as she gazed upon her birth father's countenance. This man had caused untold suffering and death for over thirty years. He had no mercy, no allegiance, no creed other than a lust for power. The trail of destruction in his wake proved he would stop at nothing.

She swallowed the lump that had formed in her throat. To be associated with such a person was beyond shameful. Tantamount to guilt. If the truth came out, she knew Sam would understand, but her colleagues would label her a threat and suspect her motives. And the department would never allow her to investigate the cartel again. Unthinkable.

She made an effort to pull her thoughts together. "*El Lobo* means 'the wolf.' That's what Hector Villalobos calls himself. The name comes from his surname, which means 'village of wolves' or 'city of wolves.' Since the family coat of arms features two black wolves, he's turned it into his logo. The cartel stamps a wolf head on bundles of narcotics, personal weapons, and vehicles. Loyal members of the cartel have a black wolf's head tattooed over their hearts, and enemies are branded with a wolf-shaped iron." She suppressed a shudder, remembering photos she'd seen in the past.

"*El Lobo* patterned his cartel's organizational structure as a cross between a paramilitary organization and a wolf pack," she said. "And he's the alpha."

She clicked again, and an aerial view of a sprawling group of buildings in an isolated area replaced Hector's picture. "This is a satellite image of the Villalobos family compound in Mexico. The structures include living quarters, a private airstrip, airplane and helicopter hangars, a landing pad, an outdoor auditorium, servants' quarters, and a huge covered building we haven't been able to identify yet."

Lopez, the senior Mexican Federal Police agent, cleared his throat. "I believe we can help with that," he said in accented English. At Veranda's encouraging nod, he continued. "We've been able to get intelligence from people we have arrested. What you are looking at is an indoor shooting range."

A murmur went around the room. Veranda digested this before posing her question. "What else can you tell us about the compound?"

Lopez stood, skirted the table, and walked to the projected image on the wall. "Hector's private property covers about twenty square kilometers. There are guard stations around a two-kilometer perimeter, and another internal ring of sentries about half a kilometer out from the compound. This way, he has multiple layers of protection."

Lopez pointed to a central structure. "This is the main living area. We have had one report of a dungeon underground where he tortures prisoners or holds them for execution." He hesitated. "We have also heard that some of the executions take place in the indoor shooting range, and others occur in the outdoor auditorium."

Doc looked appalled. "You mean like gladiators in a Roman coliseum?"

Lopez nodded. "We are told the killings serve both as an example and as entertainment. Of course, we cannot prove this, or *El Lobo* would be in prison." He returned to his seat. "Our problem is that we've never been able to turn anyone from the cartel. They are all scared for themselves as well as for their families. We've sent in undercover agents, but ... " He trailed off, a bleak expression clouding his face. "They died ... badly. But we will keep trying." He lifted his chin. "One day, we will succeed."

Veranda thought about the brave Mexican agents who had gone deep undercover in the cartel, never to be heard from again. All over the world, it seemed, the Villalobos family kept a step ahead of law enforcement.

Lopez dropped his gaze. "Over the years, *El Lobo* sent spies inside our agency. We have uncovered moles and arrested corrupt officials taking bribes for information. We are still cleaning up."

Veranda appreciated his candor. Rumors of corruption and infiltration in Mexican law enforcement made some of her colleagues wary of their inclusion in the Fusion Center, but she had no such reservations. She'd worked with Mexican officials during her days in

DEB and respected their determination to prosecute criminals despite threats, assassinations, abductions, and other forms of intimidation.

"Thank you," she said. "We'll add your information to our database." She touched the remote again. A picture of Bartolo Villalobos appeared, the word DECEASED stamped in red letters above his head. "Bartolo was Hector's second-born son."

Veranda's stomach tightened. This man had systematically terrorized her entire family. Bartolo had broken into her home, burned her family's restaurant to the ground, and abducted her sister. Before he died, he'd inflicted deep wounds causing lasting damage for two of them. Especially Gabby.

Agent Wallace with the DEA furrowed his brows. "That bastard certainly gave us enough trouble over the years."

Veranda had planned to lay out the structure of the cartel at this point in her presentation. Thanks to media coverage, everyone would have seen pictures of Hector and Bartolo, but she guessed some agents may not recognize the rest of the Villalobos family or understand their business model.

"If you include Bartolo, *El Lobo* has three sons and one daughter, all adults," she said. "They visit the family compound in Mexico often using the family jet, but they mostly live in their Phoenix area homes. Hector made sure all four of his children were born in the States, so they're citizens and can travel freely across the border."

She emphasized an important aspect of the Villalobos family, which was more formidable due to its leader's careful planning. "Hector grew up poor, but his children have advantages he never did. They got the best of everything, including top schools. They're not your average lowlife crime family. They're well-educated, disciplined, and strategic."

She tapped the remote and an organizational chart flashed up on the wall. Every rectangle contained a name and photograph. "Each child has a specific area of responsibility in the cartel. It's a key to the Villalobos family's power. Like any Fortune500 company, they've diversified."

She picked up her pen and used it to point to the top box. "Hector, head of the family, named his children alphabetically by birth order." She swept the pen along a row one level down from the top. Four squares formed a tier directly below Hector. "Bartolo is the second born, after Adolfo. I mentioned Bartolo first because, until recently, he was the heir apparent to the entire business. He was the *comandante* in charge of narcotics trafficking, the lifeblood of their operation. He lived in the Phoenix area, which is the cartel's main US distribution hub. Bartolo's death six weeks ago disrupted the drug market here."

Tanner raised a hand. "You're saying this whole situation we're in was caused by one man's death?"

She nodded. "While the Villalobos cartel scrambled to reorganize their second echelon, SSS picked up the slack on the streets of Phoenix."

"I can confirm that," Agent Wallace said. "SSS is supplied by a cartel from the Andean region in Colombia. They've had a few dust-ups with the Villalobos organization, which also has some grow operations in South America. A few firebombs here, some mass graves there, and both sides pretty much carved out their territory and settled down to grow their dope without bothering each other too much."

"Except the truce collapsed because of this man." Veranda used her pen to point to the photo of a slender, dark-haired man in an Armani suit occupying the square next to Bartolo. "Adolfo Villalobos is the firstborn son and the cartel's CFO. He's responsible for money laundering, gambling, loan sharking, collections, and payroll. When Bartolo died, he tried to step up and take over drug sales as well. Looks like he's making a play to be named *El Lobo*'s successor. Problem is, others in the underworld don't take him seriously, so they poached on Villalobos turf. Never would have happened while Bartolo was alive—"

This time, Agent Gates interrupted. "How does this manifest itself within the family dynamic?" She seemed to rethink her words. "That is, how does this play out inside the cartel?"

Veranda didn't mince words. "Adolfo must crush any opposition, whether internal or external, to show he can be the next alpha in the wolf pack. Adolfo is especially dangerous because he's an insecure leader trying to gain respect."

She indicated the next sibling on the chart. "The youngest brother, Carlos, runs a team of coyotes in a human-trafficking operation with a network of drop houses and brothels with sex slaves in several border states. We've managed to shut down a few in Phoenix, but we haven't gathered enough evidence to prosecute Carlos."

She ran the end of her pen along her jaw, considering the last photo in the chart's second row. "Daria is Hector's only dau—" She broke off, face flaming.

Her mind balked at the fresh reminder of the change the DNA results brought to her life. She flicked a glance at Sam, who gave her an encouraging nod.

Drawing a deep breath, she rephrased the comment. "Daria is the youngest sibling." All eyes studied the image of a willowy woman in her twenties. With liquid brown eyes set in a smooth face, Daria would be beautiful if not for a harsh set to her lips that reminded Veranda of *El Lobo*. "Her team smuggles US weapons into Mexico to feed the ongoing battles between the cartels and the police. We don't have much intel on her. She flies below the radar compared to the rest of the family."

Agent Flag with Homeland spoke up. "We've heard she's building a weapons and munitions manufacturing plant, but we can't confirm it yet. We know there's an armory at the Villalobos family compound that's used to modify and repair firearms and ammo."

Now certain Flag was affiliated with some sort of covert intelligence organization, Veranda thanked him before wrapping up the briefing. "That's an overview of the situation as it stands."

She shut her laptop. "Has everyone listed their cell phone and email on this page?"

"We didn't put our information down," Lopez said. "Our orders were to keep our participation secret for the safety of our families."

Veranda nodded. "We'll loan you burner phones and use code names." She signaled one of the techs working at a terminal across the room. "Can you hook them up now?"

A heavyset man in a rumpled button-down shirt nodded his assent as he ambled over. He looked like he'd pulled an all-nighter to get the workspace ready. She pressed a thumb drive into his palm. "Please add the two extra phones before you download this file and send it as an attachment to everybody on this list, including me." She quickly jotted her contact info and thrust the paper at him. "As a second attachment, create a spreadsheet with everyone's cell phone and email so we can reach each other quickly." She peered at his bleary eyes. "When you're done, go home and get some rest."

Veranda watched him slouch off before she started again. "This is one of the two documents I asked him to send you." She held up a second sheet of paper. The room grew still. "It's a preliminary ops plan."

The moment had arrived for her bold strategy.

9

FOURTEEN-YEAR-OLD SOFIA PACHECO'S SLIM fingers danced over the keyboard. She hunched forward, staring at the computer screen. If she didn't take this chance, she might not get another. Holed up in a cramped room in the two-story house, she'd lost track of the days.

The Villalobos coyotes had lied when they brought her, along with her mother and twin sister, from Mexico. Instead of changing her family's lives for the better, they made her an indentured servant to the young man they called Nacho.

She'd learned that Nacho, American by birth, had grown up playing with computers. Judging by the way Señor Adolfo favored him, his advanced hacking skills made him valuable. Nacho's appearance told her he was probably in his late teens, much younger than the rest of the cartel's men. Despite their similarity in age, or perhaps because of it, Nacho insisted she call him "sir" in English as a sign of respect.

Cutting into the silence, Nacho blurted a torrent of expletives in English. She jumped, eyes darting to her overseer, who sat at a scarred wooden desk facing hers. Having learned English in school and by watching TV, she didn't understand some of the more colorful words, but got the gist from his reddened face and harsh, guttural grunt as he glared at his screen and pounded the desk's surface with his fist.

The day after she arrived, he'd set up two computer stations to double their productivity, forcing her to help him as he tried to hack into an American federal agency's database. Judging by his outburst, she assumed he'd been snagged in a honeypot or bounced out by another anti-hacking measure. The corner of her mouth angled up. Bad news for Nacho was good news for her.

She returned her attention to the screen in front of her, concentrating on her own agenda. She dragged the mouse down, highlighting several lines of text, checked to make sure Nacho wasn't looking, then hit the delete key.

Sweat beaded on her forehead as she selected the print command. Raising her chin to look at him above her monitor, she cleared her throat. When he lifted narrowed eyes to meet hers, she pointed to a card table set up in the corner of the room. "Sir, you should check the printer."

Nacho huffed out an exasperated sigh at the interruption. "What's so important?"

The line of perspiration had trickled from her forehead down her temples, sliding past her jaw. "You told me to watch Detective Cruz's email. She got a message with two attachments." Sofia found it easy to look unsure of herself. "I think one of them is a list of the task force people. The other attachment looks like a list of addresses and some other stuff."

Nacho shot out of his chair and stalked to the printer that had spit out two sheets of paper. He snatched them from the tray and quickly scoured each page, eyes widening as he read. Face drained of color, he glanced back to Sofia. "Tell no one about this."

She chewed her lip, fear creeping down her spine. *What have I done?* "I won't, sir."

He spun on his heel and barreled out the door clutching the papers.

After he left, Sofia crossed herself and wrung her hands before clasping them in prayer. Certain Nacho would take the documents straight to Señor Adolfo, she stole a glance at Nacho's unattended laptop. Would she have enough time to cover her tracks?

If he caught her sitting at his desk, she would have no explanation. No excuse. He would call in the horrible coyotes and they would beat her until she confessed. Then they would kill her. Probably her mother and sister too.

No, she couldn't chance it. She'd risked enough already. She would have to hope Nacho would be so busy he wouldn't do a cross-check. If her plan worked, she and her family would be free soon. If it didn't, they would be dead even sooner.

10

VERANDA SAW THE TECH in the rumpled shirt give her a thumbs-up from his computer station across the Fusion Center. She acknowledged him with a nod, slid a small stack of papers from a manila folder lying next to her laptop, and handed them to Sam. "Everybody take one." As each member of the task force pulled a page from the top and passed it on, she continued. "This is a hard copy of the attachment the admin just sent to all of us by email." She turned to Lopez. "They're loading your burner phones with the same information right now. They'll be ready by the time we're through."

Anticipating push-back from the Feds, she'd worked out a strategy to introduce her plan. A form of psychological gamesmanship to gain support—she would get preliminary agreement before pitching the most controversial part. Sizing up the group, she decided to start with the agency likely to have the most opposition.

She swung an arm out to encompass Agents Gates and Tanner. "The FBI is known for coordinating federal agencies on long-term investigations. With this tactic, they've gotten the most successful large-scale prosecutions in US history."

She waited until both agents nodded in silent assent. Gates looked wary, but Veranda plowed on. "I'm using the same approach, tweaking it to fit our current situation. We can work with the intel we have, add a bit more through surveillance, and gather enough probable cause to get search warrants for multiple locations."

Tanner interrupted her. "A search warrant requires cause to believe evidence of a crime can be found in a particular location."

For several seconds, no one spoke. Even Marci, normally quick with an acerbic comment, stared with a slackened jaw. A newly minted agent, fresh out of Quantico, had spouted a textbook definition of basic search and seizure rules to a group of senior law enforcement professionals, some of whom had been on the job before he was born.

Veranda's gaze slid to Agent Gates. As Tanner's superior, she should be the one to deal with him. Veranda thought she saw the senior FBI agent's left eye twitch. Apparently fighting an inner battle, Gates said nothing.

Finally, Det. Tony Sanchez from Veranda's Homicide squad delivered the obligatory verbal smack-down. He rubbed his thumb and forefinger along his stubbled jaw, tilted his head, and widened his eyes in an exaggerated look of wonder. "No shit." He endowed the words with his heaviest Brooklyn inflection.

Tanner's face reddened as several people around the table turned snorts of laughter into coughs. Doc banged Agent Wallace on the back as he choked on his coffee.

Veranda moved the discussion forward. "It takes months, if not years, to get solid evidence against upper-echelon distribution operations like cartels, or even organized local gangs. We don't have that kind of time. Our mission is specific and we need quick results. This isn't a lengthy white-collar investigation." She kept any semblance of judgment out of her voice. "People are dying, the city's in a state of panic, and the media's stoking the fire."

"And that's why search warrants should be our main tool?" Agent Flag asked. "To speed up the process?"

In her comfort zone from her experience as a narc, Veranda elaborated. "Search warrants, if executed when certain people are on the premises, let us make key arrests on the spot if we find contraband. It's a double shot. We gather intel from the scene, interrogate anyone found in possession, and file further charges as we go. We can build from the initial cases on the fly."

As her fellow task force members mulled her words, she pressed her point. "To prevent suspects in the first site we hit from destroying evidence and alerting the following locations, we need to execute all warrants at the same time."

Diaz, who had been typing into his iPad on a portable keyboard, looked concerned. "Detective Cruz, you've explained the theory, now describe the plan."

She straightened, took a deep breath, and used her most professional language. "I propose we conduct simultaneous operations at known SSS locations and Villalobos cartel properties, including their front companies. That way, both organizations get shut down. Even if they regroup—and the cartel definitely will—it halts the current war." She spread her hands. "We accomplish our objective."

Diaz raised an eyebrow. "And where do we get evidence to justify requesting these search warrants?"

An answer was ready on her lips. "Detectives from our police department's Gang Unit and Drug Enforcement Bureau can concentrate on the SSS sites. They already know some target locations and can do increased surveillance, maybe a couple of undercover buys. They can also pump their confidential informants for more."

"That's going to take coordination through chain-of-command." He angled his head, regarding her. "I can brief Commander Webster this afternoon. He can reach out to Commander Montoya from DEB—"

Bureaucratic wrangling set her teeth on edge. She cut him off. "I've already asked the Gang Unit and my former DEB team to work with what we have so far. The narcs are planning an operation tonight."

A ruddy scald crept up Diaz's neck. "You violated protocol." His furious gaze traveled across the room to the DEB and Gang detectives listening from nearby tables.

She indicated the cluster of detectives. "They work late hours. It made sense for me to call them last night." She arranged her features to appear contrite. "I wanted to be efficient."

One of her former DEB teammates winked after Diaz turned back to her. Sam stifled a chuckle, and Doc buried his nose in his notes.

Diaz's glare told her he hadn't bought her act. "In the future, you'll go through channels. Is that clear, Detective Cruz?"

She nodded, preferring to ask for forgiveness rather than permission.

Diaz switched topics. "That takes care of SSS, but how will you get PC for the Villalobos searches?"

To her surprise, Diaz had turned out to be her biggest obstacle. "Before he was killed a few weeks back, my CI provided good intel about the cartel's Phoenix operation. Federal databases will fill in some gaps once we compare notes." She worked to hide her irritation with her new supervisor. "We don't need proof, Lieutenant, just probable cause."

Diaz crossed his arms. "I'm asking a lot of questions because it sounds like you're loading up the bait and tackle."

Her patience cracked at the provocation. "*You* might call it a fishing expedition," she shot back, "but I call it good police work." Damned if she would let Diaz's skepticism taint the others. This was her best chance to strike at the heart of the Villalobos family and she intended to take it. "If we get enough evidence during the raids, we might even be able to arrest Adolfo. A serious hit to the cartel."

Before Diaz could respond, Agent Wallace from the DEA came to her defense. "I like the plan. Look at it this way, a mass high-profile warrant service would interrupt their routine operations at the very least. Guaranteed we seize a lot of dope, cash, and weapons on both sides. If we also make a bunch of arrests"—he shrugged—"icing."

Gates looked thoughtful. "When are we supposed to execute this simultaneous warrant service?"

Veranda relaxed. The task force was gradually climbing on board. "With luck, we can get what we need within a couple of weeks."

"What?" Agent Gates's pen dropped from her hand and clattered to the table. "This sort of operation takes months, if not years, to plan and execute properly."

Veranda drew a clear distinction between Gates's field experience and their current operation. "That's what it takes for methodical FBI investigations. The Bureau gets convictions. But that's because you spend years on a case before an arrest is made. Everything's wrapped up with a bow on it."

Gates snatched up her pen and pursed her lips. "Because that's what *I* call good police work."

Veranda realized she had inadvertently offended the senior FBI agent. She softened her tone. "The city is in lockdown right now. Everyone is scared Phoenix is becoming like some of those cities in Mexico where innocent citizens have been slaughtered by cartels dividing the country among themselves." She regretted the words the instant they left her mouth. She slowly turned to the two Mexican agents. Now she'd probably alienated them as well. "I apologize if I—"

Agent Lopez held up a hand. "No." His voice was grave. "You are correct. We have spent many years under attack from criminal organizations. Officials who dared to stand up to them got killed or disappeared. Judges, police chiefs, politicians, community leaders, even priests." He shook his head. "I wish we could go back in time and stop the cartels before they grew so powerful." He looked around. "There is a price on my head, and there is a good chance I will not live to retire. But I will never stop until they are gone from my country." He directed his final comment to Gates. "Don't let them get stronger in yours."

A wave of gratitude washed through her, and Veranda let Lopez's words linger before she spoke. "Agent Gates, we don't have time for a standard investigation. My proposal is the fastest way to put the SSS gang and the Villalobos cartel out of business with minimal risks." She perused the room. "Does anyone have a better alternative?"

Agent Flag from Homeland Security spoke for the first time. "I support Detective Cruz's plan."

Deputy US Marshal Fitzhugh lifted his index finger as if voting. "Me too."

"You don't even have to ask us." Marci indicated the Homicide squad with a sweep of her hand. "We're on board."

A murmur of agreement went around the room.

Diaz sat in stony silence.

Gates gave a resigned sigh. "You've got a majority, Detective."

Veranda flashed a brief smile before she picked up her copy of the papers she'd circulated around the table earlier. "You all should have a copy of this document." While the others skimmed through their copies, she explained the contents. "It's a preliminary ops plan including known Villalobos locations I'd like to hit. We need to confirm these places and get more SSS sites. This version of the plan is a starting point. We'll all refine and update it as we go."

Veranda spent the next hour laying out the details of her strategy. She illustrated with examples of successful operations she'd led as a detective in DEB. In the end, she felt she'd gained everyone's support, albeit begrudgingly in the case of the two FBI agents and Lieutenant Diaz.

At the end of the meeting, she got cell phones for Lopez and Rios before pairing detectives from her Homicide squad with Federal agents. Each team would gather information from ongoing investigations including narcotics, theft, assault, and other criminal activity. She directed the teams to write affidavits sufficient to convince a Superior Court judge to sign search warrants.

Veranda and Sam would take the Mexican officials to their hotel after first stopping by the police academy to speak with Sergeant Grigg, leader of the PPD tactical team. She wanted Agents Lopez and Rios with her to provide details about defenses they encountered at Villalobos strongholds in Mexico. Since Sergeant Grigg and his team were at the academy for a SWAT training exercise, they could modify operational tactics based on any new information.

As she started toward the exit with Sam and the two Mexican agents, Lieutenant Diaz stepped into her path. "I have an update about lodgings for our ... " He paused, looking first at Lopez, then Rios. "Guests," he finished, gaze lingering on the younger agent with an air of dislike before returning to Veranda. "I forwarded an email to you before the briefing. It's a verification form vouching for two unarmed representatives from Mexican law enforcement here on official business. They qualify for a discounted government rate at the downtown Hyatt Regency. You'll need to show your creds and the form when they check in."

"Great location," she said. "Close to my house so it's convenient for me to pick them up." She turned to Agent Lopez. "And a four-star hotel. Not bad."

She started for the door again, but Diaz touched her elbow. "Detective Cruz, a word."

Annoyed, she tossed Sam her car keys. "Go ahead. I'll be right there."

Sam caught the ring of keys, shot a dark look at Diaz, and led the agents out.

She pivoted to confront her lieutenant, but he was gone. Brow wrinkled, she glimpsed him striding into his private office. She blew out a frustrated sigh and stalked across the room. When he closed the door with a distinct *snick*, she braced herself for trouble.

He frowned down at her. "How long do you think it'll take for this to blow up in your face, Detective?"

Shocked by his intensity and his question, she stepped back. "What are you talking about?"

He moved closer, invading her space. "Why didn't you tell the group about the missing DNA results?"

His words hit her like a punch to the gut. She clamped down her physical reaction, meeting his hard stare. "Because it's not important."

"Bartolo Villalobos waved an envelope around claiming it contained your paternity information." He put his hands on his hips. "But the envelope went missing. Very convenient for you."

Reeling, she fought for composure. Diaz might as well have accused her of taking the lab report from Bartolo's body after he died.

She squared her shoulders and returned Diaz's glare. "I couldn't possibly have smuggled anything out of that crime scene." Her cheeks flamed at the memory. She couldn't have concealed the envelope because she'd been in the company of about twenty people—including Diaz. And she'd been completely naked.

He tensed. "I remember why you couldn't have hidden the envelope, but I find the whole situation suspicious." He lowered his voice. "Too many people on the department know there's a question about your parentage. Eventually, word will get out to the rest of the task force and they'll want the truth about your relationship to the cartel. The team should hear about the missing DNA results from you before that happens."

"I barely got a consensus on my strategy this morning. Do you want to undermine me right now?" She tested the water to see how much credibility Diaz put in Bartolo's claim. "Especially when the whole DNA thing is probably bullshit Bartolo made up."

"Maybe so. But if it turns out you *are* Hector Villalobos's daughter and you're the lead detective on a high-profile task force designed to take his business down—"

"I've proven my loyalty." Lieutenant or no, she wouldn't stand for this.

Anger radiated from him. "So have I, Detective. I don't want any nasty surprises during this investigation. It's too important. I didn't bring it up in front of the others … yet. But I will inform the team if you don't."

This time, she stepped forward. They were almost nose to nose. Pulse pounding in her ears, she spoke in deliberate, measured tones. "I'll tell the task force about Bartolo's insane rant if and when it becomes relevant to the investigation."

He didn't back down. "There's something you'd better understand, Veranda." It was one of the few times he'd used her first name.

"What is that?"

"Secrets are like landmines. When you least expect it, they blow up in your face."

Unable to tell if his words were meant as advice or a threat, she spun on her heel, opened the door, and marched out, hiding her turmoil behind a mask of calm.

11

ADOLFO GROUND HIS TEETH as he clenched the pages in his fist. He'd dismissed Nacho immediately after his hacker had given him two sheets of paper that changed everything. He would rise to this test of his leadership. "Ten of our facilities are compromised." His eyes slid from Salazar to Carlos. "How?"

The three men sat in the living room of the two-story house in South Phoenix, a recent rental their human traffickers used as a drop house. Carlos leaned back against the heavy blue fabric of a recliner. "The police have a lot of resources." He shrugged. "They pool information."

The flippant remark infuriated Adolfo. Didn't Carlos understand that they had to identify their weaknesses to avoid future problems? He suspected his playboy younger brother only concerned himself with his own part of the business. Especially the women involved in his sex trade. Disgusted, Adolfo turned to Salazar.

"We can figure out how the police knew about your locations later," Salazar said in Spanish. He spoke English, but not as well as the Villalobos siblings, who had been raised bilingually and sent to expensive private schools in the US. "Right now, we need a strategy."

Adolfo switched to Spanish. "Nacho gave me Cruz's email five minutes ago." He raised the papers in his hand to eye level. "How could I have come up with a response already?" Salazar always made him feel incompetent. He didn't want the man's impudence to spread to his brother. "I've got an idea how to turn this"—he shook the rumpled pages open to glance at the wording—"multiple warrant service to our advantage, but I need time to figure out the details."

Salazar's lip curled. "While you're working on your … details, there's something I have to do. It's about the *federales* who flew in from Mexico this morning. The other email Nacho intercepted said they're staying at the Hyatt in downtown Phoenix."

Always alert for danger, Adolfo's internal radar pinged on a disturbance. What was Salazar up to? "They're only listed as two agents from the *Policía Federal Ministerial* in the email attachment. No names or other information were included in Cruz's memo. Why are you interested if you don't know who they are?"

Salazar shot him an insolent look. "It's because I don't know who they are that I'm interested." When Adolfo continued to stare at him in silence, Salazar sighed as if it pained him to explain himself. "When I came back from South America last month, your father told me about a PFM agent he's been trying to recruit. So far, he's had no luck, but I want to know if it's the same man."

Adolfo bristled. His father hadn't told him anything about this. He wondered what else Salazar knew that he didn't. "What is the PFM agent's name?"

"*El Lobo* chose not to tell me. That's another reason I have to get a look at the two agents in person."

Careful to appear unfazed, Adolfo chipped at the unseen iceberg he sensed beneath the dark water. "How do you propose to do that?"

"Unlike you, no one in Phoenix knows who I am. I've never been to the States before, so there's no reason for anyone to be looking for me here."

"You plan to just go up and shake their hands?"

"Not quite." A fleeting look of contempt crossed Salazar's features. "I plan to stake out the Hyatt Regency."

"That's an upscale hotel. They have private security."

"I won't be doing anything illegal. I'll walk around outside. Maybe stroll through the lobby." He lifted a shoulder. "It's a business open to the public. Again, no one knows me. Just another tourist taking pictures."

Adolfo couldn't conceal his surprise. "You want to get a picture of them?"

"And send it to your father. He can identify them." He slid a thumb and forefinger along his jaw. "I can also see this detective, Veranda Cruz."

Adolfo tensed. "I'm the one responsible for keeping my father informed."

A slow smile curved Salazar's mouth. "Actually, that's my job too."

White hot anger shot through Adolfo. Why had his father sent a viper into his tent? Salazar's arrogance enraged him further. Other men in the cartel were cowed in his presence, but not *El Matador*. Mind racing, Adolfo latched onto a flaw in the plan. "You don't have a car or a license."

"That's why you'll have someone drive me." Condescension laced Salazar's words.

As usual, Carlos was no help. His younger brother sat impassively in the recliner, apparently unconcerned that someone outside the family dared speak to a Villalobos this way.

Adolfo jabbed a finger at Salazar. "You'd better show some resp—"

Nacho burst into the room, his face contorted with anger. "That little bitch!"

Adolfo had never seen him so upset. Already thrown by Salazar's thinly veiled mockery, he decided to overlook the unannounced interruption. "Nacho, what happened?"

Quivering and red-faced, his computer expert waved a sheet of paper. "*This* is the task force's real plan." He slapped the page on the table in front of Adolfo.

Adolfo put down the wrinkled papers he'd been holding and picked up Nacho's sheet. "Explain."

"That *puta* you assigned to help me monitor the police emails just tried to sabotage us. She changed the plan before bringing it to me. Nacho pointed at the paper Adolfo had previously been holding. "This doesn't show all the places they want to search." He balled his fists. "That whore deleted half of them to make sure we got caught with contraband on Villalobos property."

Salazar looked from Adolfo to Nacho and frowned. "What is this about?"

Adolfo drew a breath and turned to Salazar. "Six weeks ago, the coyotes brought a group over the border and took them to a drop house on the other side of Phoenix. A mother and her twin fourteen-year-old daughters were among them. My brother Bartolo wanted some ... companionship and forced their mother to choose which of her two girls he would have. He enjoyed watching the woman beg for her daughters."

Adolfo had seen—and experienced firsthand—Bartolo's cruel streak. The women were chattel, but he didn't relish tormenting them the way Bartolo had. "In the end, the mother gave him Mia." He didn't hide his disdain. "The girl was almost dead when Bartolo finished with her. Apparently, she wouldn't cooperate without ... persuasion."

Something squirmed inside Adolfo's stomach. Bartolo's perverse appetites reflected on the rest of the family. He struggled to identify the uncomfortable feeling. Slowly, a single word bubbled to the surface of his mind. *Shame.*

Salazar narrowed his eyes, scrutinizing Adolfo. "There's a point to this story?"

When Adolfo didn't respond, Carlos picked up the thread. "The mother had a reason for choosing one girl over the other. Turns out it was the same reason she brought them to Phoenix in the first place. The family is from the barrios of Mexico City. Sofia qualified for a program for inner-city youth to take advanced computer classes in the US for six months. The non-profit group would pay for Sofia, but not for anyone else. The mother, who obviously isn't as bright as her daughter, contacted my coyotes."

"I don't understand," Salazar said. "Why did she need you?"

Carlos smirked. "Because she wanted to come with Sofia and bring Mia along as well. Thought they'd be safer traveling in a strange country together." He shook his head as if the notion was beyond stupid. "When I heard about a girl with computer skills, I thought of Nacho and told the mother she could bring both girls for one transport fee. I assured her they could clean houses to pay for room and board while Sofia studied."

Salazar's heavy black brows went up. "The mother fell for that?"

Recovered from his epiphany, Adolfo answered. "She was so desperate to make a better life for her girls, she'd believe anything. When they arrived, we turned Sofia over to Nacho, who trained her to hack. And now, apparently, she's betrayed us."

All eyes turned to Nacho, who blurted his excuse. "When Sofia printed out Cruz's plan, I didn't take extra time to review the steps. The info looked urgent, so I gave it to you right away."

Nacho's red-rimmed eyes darted from one man to the next. He bore the pleading look of a dog who expected punishment. "After I got back to my desk, I read through it again carefully and noticed an extra line space. I got suspicious and searched for the same document in other team members' emails. When I compared them, I discovered Sofia deleted ten of the twenty Villalobos locations on the original plan." He hung his head. "I asked one of the coyotes to watch her and came to you immediately."

Adolfo's simmering fury broke over Nacho. "She is your responsibility. You should be watching her!"

Nacho winced and kept his head bowed, his response directed at the floor. "I do, *señor*. That's why she couldn't fix every copy. She only had time to change one and must have gambled I wouldn't go back and check."

Adolfo's nails bit into his palms as he clenched his fists. "One little girl almost brought us down."

Carlos shot to his feet. "She must be punished." He unbuckled his belt. "She will understand that the Villalobos family owns her now." He slid the thick leather through the loops on his pants and wrapped it around his wrist. His free hand snaked out to thump the back of Nacho's head. "Bring her here."

"Wait." Salazar held up a hand. "You need to have her healthy and properly motivated, yes?"

Carlos let the belt dangle from his hand. "We do."

Soft menace sharpened Salazar's next words. "Where is her twin sister?"

Adolfo motioned to Carlos, who gave Salazar an assessing look as he answered. "Mia is cleaning toilets and changing sheets in the bedrooms upstairs. She hasn't recovered from Bartolo's beating enough to entertain male clients yet, so she's on housekeeping duty."

"Perfect." Salazar's feral grin exposed straight white teeth. "Bring both girls here. I'll be back." He headed toward the kitchen.

Two minutes later, a coyote shoved Sofia into the living room. As she stumbled, the man leaned forward to grasp her hair, holding her upright. Her gaunt body trembled as she stood before Adolfo and Carlos.

A loud grunt, followed by the slap of bare flesh and a stifled yelp reverberated into the room from the hallway. Another coyote dragged Sofia's twin sister behind him. Gripping Mia's stick-thin upper arm until his fingers dug into her skin, he yanked her roughly around to stand next to Sofia.

Adolfo could tell Mia's nose had been broken recently without being properly set, something he recognized when he looked in the mirror. Bartolo had smashed Adolfo's nose when they were children. True to form, his father had left it crooked as a constant reminder of the consequences of weakness.

Unlike her sister's, Mia's eyes blazed with fury. Her hair tumbled down from a messy knot tied at the nape of her neck, her T-shirt drenched in sweat from hours of rigorous housework.

Salazar strode into the living room, concealing something behind his back. His hooded gaze swept both girls before he addressed Sofia.

"You chose to defy us." He stepped closer, looming over her. "But you were caught." He used his free hand to snatch hers and lifted it up to eye level. "I should get a hammer and pulverize every one of your fingers so you can never use a keyboard again." Sofia gasped as he guided her fingertips along the edge of his dark goatee. "But that's not an option, because we need your skills." He inclined his head toward Mia, still held in place by the coyote who had dragged her in. His voice dropped to a whisper. "Instead, your sister must pay for your crime."

Sofia's eyes rounded in stark terror. "No!"

Salazar dropped Sofia's hand and pivoted to Mia. Cold, calculated wrath radiated from Salazar as he grasped Mia's sweat-soaked shirt and ripped it off. He flung it on the floor, then tore away the thin white bra she wore underneath, exposing her upper body completely.

"Hold her still," he commanded.

The coyote used one hand to pin the girl's wrists behind her, while his brawny arm wrapped around her waist, pulling her back against his large frame. Salazar swung a long metal rod out from behind his back. Adolfo recognized the glowing hot branding iron instantly. The stylized shape of a wolf's head at the end of the rod seared the cartel's logo on their heroin shipments. Or over the hearts of their prisoners.

Both girls screamed and thrashed against their captors.

Eyes boring into Sofia, Salazar spoke over the clamor. "Every time you defy us in any way, your sister will be punished."

As Salazar approached Mia, all traces of her defiance evaporated. Her anguished shrieks became hysterical, and Adolfo averted his eyes. He knew Salazar's brutality would assure Sofia's compliance. He was also aware that Mia had already been forced to pay a heavy price in lieu of her twin for their entry into the US. She was the expendable one.

He understood what it was to be considered less important than a sibling. How deep such wounds went. Much deeper than the burn she was about to endure. It was this awareness that forced his gaze away.

12

ATTENTION DRAWN BY A dark flicker passing over her, Veranda squinted up to see a magnificent red-tailed hawk soaring above the police academy grounds. The bird was in for a shock if it lingered over the shooting range. The raptor glided high in the turquoise sky, riding thermals as it searched the desert ground for prey. Dipping a russet wing, it banked to the left, flying over the crest of South Mountain, its shadow grazed the rocky soil, silently sliding over the corrugated metal roof of the building at the base of the mountainside.

"Fire in the hole!"

Sergeant Grigg's bellowed warning, muffled by her ear protection, brought her attention back to the tableau in front of her. Eight men, outfitted in black SWAT gear, lined up beside a steel security door. The first tactical operator angled the adapted muzzle of a 12-gauge breaching shotgun beside the lock and fired. Even from her vantage point twenty feet away, the concussion rumbled through her sternum as the blast shook the ground beneath her.

The breaching officer pumped a second round in and peeled away while the second operator raised a booted foot. The door crashed open with one powerful kick.

Veranda's pulse quickened, catching the excitement as she watched Sergeant Grigg and his SAU team rush inside the Shoot House. She'd been on enough operations with them to know they were fanning out, clearing each room as they went, with a tail gunner to watch their six. Live fire training always ratcheted her adrenalin, even though this time she only observed the exercise.

"Clear!" Grigg's shout echoed from within the cinder block walls. Scenario concluded, he appeared from the interior gloom, his bulk filling the empty doorway. He stepped over the broken metal door, which dangled from its lower hinge, and treaded in her direction.

"Where's everyone else?" she called out to him. The eight-man group practicing the door breach was only a small fraction of the entire SAU team. Her question was answered when a wave of black-clad tactical personnel poured through the heavy gate separating the range from the Shoot House.

Sergeant Grigg lifted the helmet from his head, revealing a dark buzz cut glistening with sweat as he continued his approach. Easily the tallest man on the team, he towered over her when he halted, the toes of his boots almost touching hers. His cobalt blue eyes bore into her.

She'd seen hardened criminals wet themselves when he glowered down at them with that expression, but she refused to be intimidated. She crossed her arms, tilted her head back to meet his gaze, and waited him out.

The silence grew awkward. Sam, Rios, and Lopez shifted on either side of her, but said nothing. Apparently, they didn't understand the relationship Veranda had with Grigg, who had been on countless operations with her in a tactical support role when she was a narc. Over time, they'd come to trust each other. In truth, the crusty SAU team leader was her favorite sergeant on the department. She suspected he had a soft spot for her too—if such a thing was possible. This ritual dance was one they had engaged in many times before.

Grigg thrust the helmet under his arm, freeing his hand to poke a finger at her. "I can't believe you're laying this steaming pile on my doorstep," he finally said in his deep, gruff voice. "Why do you always do this shit to me?"

She raised a brow. "You're not up for it?"

He waved the question away. "Don't blow smoke up my skirt, Cruz. I don't care how good we are, this kind of turnaround time for a major tactical operation is insane. Even for you."

"There's more." She braced herself for his reaction. "I can't guarantee how much lead time we'll have. If there's another fiasco like the one at the mall, we might have to execute the op even sooner."

Grigg snorted. "Peachy." He ran a meaty hand over his damp hair and eyed the two Mexican agents standing next to her. "Can the *federales* offer any intel?"

Sam grimaced. "*Federales*. Is that okay to say?"

Agent Lopez chuckled. "It's like when people call American police officers 'cops.' And it's easier than saying we're agents from the *Policía Federal Ministerial*." He grew serious as he turned to Grigg. "In Mexico, when the Villalobos cartel sets up a long-term location, they build hidden escapes, like tunnels. They also have countersurveillance." He inclined his head toward his younger counterpart. "Agent Rios can tell you more. He was on our SWAT team until a few months ago."

Rios straightened. "I went on some raids at Villalobos strongholds." His gaze traveled to the Shoot House and a wistful expression crossed his features. "I miss the action."

Veranda had thought Rios seemed physically fit when she met him, but now she noted his calloused hands, the wary set to his eyes, and a faint scar just above his left brow. Signs of battle.

Grigg gave Rios a nod. "Bet you had more than the fifteen minutes Cruz is giving me to plan your ops."

"Sure." A dimple creased Rios's cheek. "We had at least twenty minutes."

Grigg guffawed, then turned to Veranda. "I'll need to coordinate with outside agencies to pull this off. Even though our unit is good-sized, hitting that many sites at once is manpower intensive."

Grigg had switched from belligerent to strategic, and now concerned himself with how to accomplish the objective. Despite his bluster, he always came through. She grinned up at him. "Your group occasionally trains with other SWAT teams in the region, right?"

"Of course. I'll reach out to DPS, Scottsdale, Tempe, Mesa, and the Maricopa County Sheriff's Office. See who's up for it." He threw her another scowl, but it was halfhearted. "I don't look forward to explaining why we should do this when I think it's a clusterfuck myself."

Veranda had no doubt he would get everyone on board. Grigg was well-respected in the tactical arena. His excellent reputation would go a long way to garner support.

He hooked a thumb in his tactical belt. "How many places did you say you wanted to hit?"

"I'm not certain yet. The rest of the team will finalize the list for the search warrants. Since SSS is strictly a local gang, they should only have two or three locations. The cartel will take up most of our resources. Our list of potential front companies, warehouses, residences, and drop houses contains about twenty sites around the city. We can't get warrants for all of those. We'll narrow it down to the top twelve places most likely to yield arrests and contraband."

"So I should plan to execute about fifteen simultaneous warrant services?"

"Should cover it."

Grigg grunted. "All right, Cruz. I'll start pulling teams together and running through scenarios. I'm going to need that final list of locations from you ASAP."

"Deal."

"Also, I want to set up a practice run before we go live on this." He nodded toward the Shoot House behind him. "Right here."

She extended her hand. "Thanks, Sarge."

His hand engulfed hers in a firm grip. "Just remember to have a backup plan for that thing."

She mentally reviewed her ops plan for a flaw. "What thing?"

"The thing you never see coming." He released his hold. "The one that fucks up all your plans."

13

VERANDA RAISED HER GLASS of beige liquid and rotated it slightly, watching a droplet of condensation course down the smooth side to drip on her finger.

Sam tilted his head. "What the hell is *horchata* anyway?"

She chuckled. "A cold drink made from rice milk, cinnamon, and vanilla. My mother also uses almonds when she makes it. Sweet and delicious. Everyone loves it."

After leaving the Shoot House, Veranda had driven Sam and the *federales* to the Hyatt Regency downtown. After checking Rios and Lopez in at the front desk, they had all agreed to eat lunch at the hotel café upstairs in the mezzanine.

Lopez nodded. "My mother always used almonds too. She used to make homemade *horchata* ice cream when I was a boy." He chuckled. "Of course, that was many years ago."

Rios picked up a white ceramic mug. "I like coffee." He took a long sip. "This is good, but when I brew my own at home, I add pure cocoa powder and some agave nectar." His eyes slid to Veranda. "Because things taste better when they're hot, and a just little bit sweet."

Veranda choked on her drink, unable to miss the innuendo.

Lopez gave his younger counterpart a sidelong glance and spoke into the awkward silence as Veranda dabbed her chin with a white linen napkin. "The world has Mexico to thank for inventing chocolate," he said. "We put it in a lot of things."

Moving to safer conversational ground, Sam picked up on Lopez's lead. "Good to see they have *horchata* on the menu at such an elegant hotel."

Veranda put down her napkin. "I'd prefer a mimosa, but I'm on duty."

"A mimosa?" Sam snorted. "That's not a cop's drink."

She raised a brow. "I suppose you drink straight whiskey from a dirty shot glass? Is that what you guys did back in the day after your patrol shift was over? I'm sure it gave your horses a chance to rest before the long ride to the homestead."

Sam looked at Lopez. "Can you believe how she talks to a senior detective?" His tone was full of mock outrage.

"Emphasis on *senior*," Veranda said.

Lopez laughed. "It's the same where I work. I've been there over thirty years. They call me *El Viejo*, the Old Man." He shook his head. "No respect."

"It's this generation." Sam tipped his head toward Veranda and Rios. "They don't appreciate that it takes years to develop the skills we have. They were in diapers when we started our careers."

Veranda couldn't resist the opening. "And you're going to be in diapers before you finally pull the plug and retire. When are you going into DROP, Sam?"

"What is DROP?" Rios asked.

Veranda heaved an exaggerated sigh. "Die Right On Premises. It's a scheme the old guys cooked up to stay on the job until they're wheeled out of their offices in a body bag."

A smile played under Sam's heavy mustache. "You're lucky I like you, Veranda." He turned to Lopez. "It actually stands for Deferred Retirement Option Plan. It's a program where you retire, but you're allowed to keep working another five years. The department keeps its most experienced officers and we get to add to our deferred comp account." His gaze traveled back to Veranda. "Your pension won't get any better, but you can build up a nest egg in case you need extra money for a motorized scooter."

"Don't let him fool you," she said. "He won't go into DROP because he knows they'll kick him out after five years. It'll ruin his plan for leaving his cubicle toes up."

Sam straightened and took on a dignified air. "I haven't done it yet because there's no one ready to take my place."

"Sounds familiar." Lopez tilted his head at the younger *federale*. "I'm supposed to be training Rios, but he's not ready yet."

Rios looked affronted. "*Ay*, that hurts." Then grinned. "And I thought I was like the son you never had."

Sam lifted his coffee to his lips. "I bet if you asked Special Agent Gates, she'd tell you Agent Tanner gives her heartburn on a regular basis."

"That's a low blow." Veranda pointed back and forth between Rios and herself. "You can't compare us to the Junior G-man."

Lopez cocked his head to one side, a thoughtful expression in his eyes, which were on Sam. "This conversation has made me realize Hector Villalobos has the same problem we do. He wants to retire and turn the business over to his children, but he thinks they are not ready."

Sam regarded Lopez, slowly nodding. "Bartolo turned out to be a disaster and Adolfo seems weak." He stroked his mustache. "Looks like he's letting Adolfo give it a try, though."

Veranda turned the concept over in her mind. Adolfo's behavior had become more erratic lately. "Adolfo's overcompensating. That's the only explanation for the increased chaos on our streets. He's *El Lobo*'s firstborn. There's a lot of pressure on him to step up."

Lopez remained pensive. "Did you know Hector Villalobos used to be a *federale*?"

Veranda and Sam exchanged glances. They both knew Hector Villalobos had started out as a law enforcement officer before turning to crime. When Sam didn't comment, Veranda understood he was deferring to her to acknowledge she was aware of Hector's history.

Veranda decided she wanted this fresh perspective on *El Lobo*'s background. "Yes." She didn't elaborate, but posed a question. "He would have been on the force about the same time you were. Did you know him?"

Lopez stirred cream into his coffee and carefully set the spoon down before he began. "I was the junior agent on his squad when I was first hired more than thirty years ago. Back in those days, our agency was called the *Policía Judicial Federal*, the Federal Judicial Police."

He gazed upward, as if to summon a distant memory. "Hector was always ambitious. He grew up in poverty and desperately wanted success. He worked hard, but advancement did not come easily to him. He was … how do you say? A bit rough. I think the breaking point came when another agent on our squad got the promotion Hector thought he would get. We didn't find out until later, but that was when Hector began taking bribes from the cartels. He was finally caught in a sting by the man who was promoted in his place, Ernesto Hidalgo."

Veranda's hand tightened around her glass. She'd believed Ernesto was her father until that damned DNA test Bartolo had done six weeks ago. Now she and Sam were the only ones outside the Villalobos cartel who knew Hector was her biological parent. What would Agent Lopez think of her if he found out? The man had spent his entire career in a dangerous battle with the cartel in Mexico. Like everyone else, he would probably feel she had tainted blood.

She didn't realize her attention had wandered until Lopez's words interrupted her thoughts.

"Hector murdered Ernesto and burned his office to the ground. All evidence against him, destroyed in the fire. But Ernesto had already informed his chain-of-command that Hector was the traitor." He absently stroked his silvery goatee. "In fact, I have often thought that is why Ernesto was killed. Someone in upper management tipped off Hector." He shook his head. "But I've never been able to figure out who."

Silence fell around the table as everyone considered Lopez's story. Veranda wondered whether someone in the highest echelon of the old Federal Judicial Police agency betrayed Ernesto. If so, why? Hector hadn't risen to power yet, so he couldn't have exerted much influence. Veranda had the sense there was much more to learn from the older *federale*, but she couldn't fathom a way to get details without divulging more about herself. And that would never happen.

Out of the corner of her eye, she caught covert movement across the expansive mezzanine floor. A Latino man held a smart phone so that its camera lens pointed in their direction.

Forgetting the mystery behind Ernesto's murder, she tapped Sam's upper arm. "Is that man taking a picture of us?"

Three pairs of eyes followed her gaze.

Lopez released a stream of expletives in Spanish, ending in one word: "Salazar."

Rios jumped to his feet, upending his chair, and sprinted toward the man. Veranda had never heard the name but deduced from the reactions of the *federales* that Salazar was a problem. Aware Rios had no law enforcement powers in the US, Veranda pushed back from the table and joined the chase.

The man Lopez had identified as Salazar stuffed the phone into his pocket and pivoted in one fluid motion, legs a blur as he bolted toward the stairs leading down to the lobby.

Veranda shot a quick glance over her shoulder as she ran. Lopez dashed toward her as Sam tossed a wad of cash onto their table and grabbed his suit jacket.

She caught up to Rios as he reached the top of the staircase. Salazar had already made it downstairs to the lobby, now only steps away from the glass main doors. From there, he could quickly blend into the downtown midday bustle and disappear.

She flew down the stairs, darted outside to the valet area in front of the hotel, and spun in every direction.

Salazar was gone.

Rios caught up to her, breathing hard. After he bit out a few colorful obscenities, Sam and Lopez pounded up behind them.

"No sign of him?" Sam asked.

Veranda shook her head and looked at Lopez. "Who the hell is Salazar?"

Lopez's dark eyes narrowed. *"El Matador."*

14

AN HOUR LATER, VERANDA stood in the Fusion Center surrounded by members of the task force. Detective Sanchez from her Homicide squad stared at her openmouthed, and she met his bemused expression with a frown. "You got a problem, Tony?"

Marci, always ready to needle her favorite target, piped up before Tony could respond. "Oh, he has lots of problems." Her eyes trailed down his body. "Where do I begin?" The pair enjoyed verbal fencing matches, but Marci's quick wit and acerbic tongue usually won out.

Refusing to take Marci's bait, Tony kept his gaze on Veranda. "What the hell happened to you?"

Veranda realized she must look very different from her appearance this morning. Loosed from its sleek chignon, her mussed hair now tumbled halfway down her back in flowing waves. She'd tossed her suit jacket over the back of her chair as soon as she entered the Center, and her silk blouse still clung to her damp skin. She could feel the flush on her face from the adrenalin rush and knew she didn't exude the image of a polished professional any longer.

She cast an appraising glance at Sam, Lopez, and Rios and stifled a groan. The men showed no sign of physical exertion. Granted, Sam and Lopez had only jogged briefly. Rios, however, had sprinted after Salazar out into the blazing midday heat. Why wasn't he sweaty and disheveled? Damned men.

She pursed her lips, answering Tony over her shoulder. "I'll explain later," she said, turning toward the center of the room, where the tables had been pushed together again for a group briefing. "For now, we'll concentrate on our plan. Scorpion Sting is a big op with a lot of moving parts."

She walked to her seat at the end of the table to reinforce her unspoken directive. Everyone else seemed to get the message and followed without asking further questions about her altered appearance.

Once the group was seated, she set the agenda. "We'll start with progress on the local gang, then cover the cartel." She turned to Special Agent Wallace. "Craig." She made it a point to address the DEA agent by his first name, emphasizing their past work history. "You've partnered with our Gang Unit and Drug Enforcement Bureau on SSS. Anything to report?"

Wallace scratched the bald spot on the back of his head. "Sergeant Fromm with DEB brought me up to speed about a high-value confidential informant his squad cultivated inside SSS. This CI can set up a buy-bust before we do our warrant services.

She had to change the plan. She could use intel from the buy for the affidavits, but arrests could alter the gang's behavior.

"Good," she said. "But could you make it a buy without the bust?"

"No problem. We'll make it a controlled buy."

She continued with Wallace. "What about other locations for SSS?"

"The CI verified two more locations. After the cartel took out Castillo, SSS moved half their product to a member's house and the rest to another warehouse. We've got addresses for both places and DEB has undercover narcs on surveillance. We can share the intel we've gathered so far."

She loved working with Wallace, a team player. No grandstanding or political gamesmanship. Hoping she'd set the tone for the other Feds, she turned her attention to the FBI team. "Did you touch base with your colleagues in the Criminal Investigative Division?"

She had directed the question toward Gates, but Tanner drew a sheaf of papers from a glossy black leather portfolio and cleared his throat. "My first objective was to enact deconfliction protocols." He looked around the room as if expecting a reaction.

Gates closed her eyes and massaged her temples.

"Wow." Marci oozed sarcasm as she gazed at Tanner with a look of wide-eyed wonderment.

Veranda interjected before Marci could go any farther. "Thank you, Agent Tanner." Everyone in the room not only knew what deconfliction protocols were, but had used them many times during their careers.

Apparently out of patience, Gates straightened and took over. "There are currently no ongoing investigations on the cartel involving any operatives. We've obviously known about the Villalobos family for years, but haven't been able to sink our teeth in." She threw a hand up in frustration. "Informants die, paper trails go cold, front companies are suddenly disbanded before we can get traction on a large-scale racketeering investigation."

Veranda could sympathize. She had investigated the cartel for over two years on a previous task force to build a case and it had blown up in her face. In the aftermath, she'd been forced to start from scratch.

"It takes years to investigate and the cooperation of many people. Leaks are inevitable, and the cartel has tentacles everywhere."

Marci arched a penciled brow. "I'd think the world's most powerful cartel would be at the top of the FBI's to-do list."

Gates gave her a cold look. "Since 9/11, we've been up to our eyeballs in counterterrorism investigations. Crime syndicates that don't support people who are actively trying to blow us up aren't on the front burner."

"I suppose not." Sam's baritone was unusually harsh. "These guys just want to destroy a whole generation of kids by selling them hard drugs and keeping them addicted. Not your concern."

DEA Agent Wallace put up a hand as Gates and Tanner opened their mouths with every appearance of starting an argument. "No one's giving up on those kind of investigations, we're just letting local law enforcement agencies take the lead when it's domestic and supporting our international partners to intervene at the source." He nodded at Lopez and Rios. "Just like the PPD, we have to allocate our resources."

"Fine." Sam tugged a pair of reading glasses from his shirt pocket and shook them open. "Let's get on with it." He flipped his notepad open.

Veranda sought out another familiar face at the table. "Fitz." She turned to the Deputy US Marshal. "What have you got?"

He grinned and jerked his chin toward Nicholas Flag from Homeland. "Nick and I've been working with your Homicide Squad to narrow down the potential Villalobos locations. We think we can get warrants for twelve sites out of the twenty you gave us. The team has already started writing affidavits."

She understood the legal hurdles in their way. As a former narc, she had plenty of experience with judges denying search warrants because they felt probable cause was lacking.

She emphasized the positive. "Good work fast-tracking the affidavits. Forward the final locations for SSS and the Villalobos cartel to me and I'll update the ops plan immediately." She addressed the group. "I'll email the new version to everyone so we can stay on the same page." A potential problem occurred to her and she turned back to Fitz. "Finish the documentation, but don't swear out the warrants until we finalize a time for the operation. We've only got seventy-two hours to execute them once they're signed." She looked around the table. "Anything else?"

"Yeah," Tony said. "Where were you guys before you got here?"

"Sam and I took Agents Lopez and Rios to see Sergeant Grigg at the academy. SAU was at the range for a live-fire training exercise. Grigg agreed to cover all of our locations using outside resources along with his team. Of course, he insisted on a practice run using the Shoot House." She glanced at Diaz. "I'm following chain-of-command this time, *sir.*" She emphasized the last word. "Grigg's lieutenant will call you to coordinate a time."

Tony looked her up and down. "If you were at the range, how come you came in here looking like you wrestled a rattlesnake?"

She described how they'd checked the Mexican agents in at the Hyatt Regency downtown and had brunch at the atrium restaurant. Diaz's eyes narrowed as he looked from her to Rios and back again, an irritated expression darkening his features.

After she relayed a brief description of the unsuccessful foot chase, she turned to Lopez. "Now that everyone's caught up, could you loop us in on this Salazar guy?"

Lopez paused as if considering where to begin. "Salazar is a dangerous man. Born and raised in Mexico City, he joined the military at seventeen and later served in the special forces. He left the army after ten years and began working as a ... what is the word ... fixer ... for the Villalobos family. When a city police commander intercepted their drug shipments and arrested their drivers, *El Lobo* sent Salazar to kill him. He also murdered the commander's wife to set an example."

"Holy shit," Tony muttered.

Grim lines etched Lopez's face as he continued. "Five months later, a judge signed an arrest warrant for one of the cartel's top heroin producers. Salazar assassinated the judge and his entire family even though they had around-the-clock security. The warrant was still active, but *El Lobo*'s attorney found a technical problem with the paperwork, so it would have to be reissued." His expression hardened. "No judge would sign the new documents."

Sam paused in the midst of scribbling on his pad. "Are there murder warrants out for Salazar now?"

"Yes, we found enough evidence to charge him, but he got away. A rival cartel in Colombia tried to cut into Villalobos profits, so *El Lobo* sent Salazar to South America to fix the problem. We believe Salazar killed at least seven more police officials in Colombia over the past five years. We notified Interpol and requested extradition from any country."

Sam slid his reading glasses halfway down his long nose. "So Salazar's banned from international travel and has outstanding warrants." He gave Agent Rios an approving nod. "Explains why you chased him at the Hyatt."

Something bothered her. "I've investigated the cartel for two years. Why haven't I heard about him?"

This time Rios answered. "He's been in South America for more than five years. You probably paid attention to their trafficking into Phoenix and US distribution network, not their grow operations in Colombia."

She nodded. "Where does he fit into their organization?"

Lopez clasped his hands together, resting them on the table's smooth surface. "Salazar has an unusual position. He reports directly to *El Lobo*, who assigns him specific tasks." Lopez stopped but seemed to be withholding something. When no one else spoke, he finally continued. "To be honest, I am most unhappy to see him in Phoenix. He is the cartel's most dangerous weapon. In the past, he's been sent to kill anyone in law enforcement who gets in the way. Officer, chief, judge." He shook his head. "It does not matter to Hector Villalobos. The fact that Salazar is here … at this time … "

Sam leaned forward, eyebrows drawn into a frown. "What are you getting at?"

"You heard me call him *El Matador*," Lopez said quietly. "Do you understand what that means?"

Sam nodded. "That's a bullfighter."

"In Spanish culture, a *matador* is much more than that." Silence pervaded the space as everyone hung on Lopez's words. "A bull faces several *toreros*—bullfighters—in the ring. Unlike the others, the *matador* stands alone at the end to deliver the fatal blow. He has only a cape and a sword, and could easily be gored or trampled. A *matador* must be brave, but also handsome, graceful, and skilled. He puts on a show for the audience before he uses his sword on the bull." Lopez seemed eager to convey a deeper meaning. "This is not shooting an animal with a gun or an arrow. The *matador* must stand right next to a raging bull to pierce its heart." Lopez surveyed the rapt faces around the table. "Salazar is called *El Matador* because he kills this way."

Veranda had never seen a bullfight, but she understood the ritual. Now that Salazar was in Phoenix, she wanted to understand her new adversary. "What exactly does he do?"

"When Salazar executes someone, he gets in close. Whether he uses a gun, knife, rope, or his bare hands, he physically touches his victim at some point. Because of his special forces training, he is a certified marksman, but I have never heard of a case where he used a long-range weapon." Lopez's eyes found hers. "And he always has some kind of contact with his targets before he kills them."

Understanding flashed through her like a bolt of lightning. "Like a *matador* swishing his cape to draw the bull in."

"Exactly."

Sam's rumbling baritone cut through the ensuing silence as he addressed Lopez. "There's still something you're not telling us."

A look passed between the two men. Finally, Lopez heaved a resigned sigh. "*El Lobo* sends Salazar to eliminate people who are a threat to the cartel. I have dealt with Hector Villalobos for many years, I know how he thinks, and I can only come to one conclusion." He looked pointedly at Veranda.

A palpable sense of foreboding swept through the room.

Unnerved, Veranda refused to show the slightest hint of concern. She crossed her arms over her chest. "You think he's here to kill me," she said, her comment a statement, not a question.

Lopez indicated the federal agents around the table. "Your police chief briefed us early this morning before our first meeting. He explained that you had personally targeted Bartolo Villalobos." His brows drew together. "Bartolo is dead, and our sources say Hector holds you responsible. Now you are leading a new task force with the goal of shutting the cartel down. *El Lobo* will make you his top priority."

"Hector would put one of his key people at risk to eliminate Detective Cruz?" Diaz asked, his tone sharp.

Lopez turned to the lieutenant. "Hector is a strategic thinker and an excellent chess player. He's the king, and his family members are major pieces. Everyone else in his organization is a pawn. Salazar, however, is a high-value piece, so Hector would only use him on a high-value target."

Gates snapped her fingers. "Like sacrificing a knight to take the opponent's queen."

Lopez inclined his head. "I see you understand chess."

Scowling, Diaz pulled out his cell phone. "I'll contact Commander Webster to request use of the safe house for Detective Cruz."

"No way!" Veranda's outburst drew all eyes to her.

Dark glare fixed on her, Diaz lowered the phone. "Not your decision, Detective."

She paused to rein in her anger and spoke with grim resolve. "I won't run and hide." She reached down to her waist, unclipped her detective shield, and thrust it at her lieutenant. "You can take my badge."

Sam closed a hand over hers, forcing her outstretched arm down. "Detective Cruz has shown she can take care of herself. Besides, she'll be working with all of us practically around the clock until the operation goes down."

"And that makes her safe?" Diaz shot back. "Keep your badge, Cruz. You can't carry your service weapon without it."

Veranda thought about her supervisor's words. Diaz seemed more upset about the potential threat than anyone else. Not for the first time, she wondered about his motives. Sam and Cole both thought he was overprotective due to hidden feelings for her. She had argued that Diaz was suspicious and overbearing, always looking for an excuse to put her on the sidelines. Either way, his attitude grated on her.

She changed the subject to distract him. "Speaking of working around the clock, it's Friday, but we'll need to work through the weekend. I have one firm commitment. Does anyone else have a schedule conflict they can't rearrange?"

No one spoke, and Veranda felt self-conscious at their questioning looks. "I need to take a few hours off tomorrow for my kid sister's fifteenth birthday party."

Agent Gates scoffed. "We're in the middle of a major investigation here. Can't you just give her your present and see her later?"

Veranda wasn't surprised Gates felt this way. Family members of those in law enforcement had to accept missed gatherings and special occasions. The job never slept. But Gates wasn't from a Latino family and her mother wasn't Lorena. Veranda would never hear the end of it if she didn't show. And, after everything her little sister had been through, she owed Gabby.

"It's not an ordinary situation," Veranda said. "It's Gabriela's *quinceañera.*" Aware everyone at the table would have read the file about the incident involving Gabby, Veranda wanted to be clear about the circumstances. "She paid a huge price for being my sister." Guilt formed a knot in her throat. "She hasn't left the house since Bartolo Villalobos kidnapped her. That was six weeks ago, and she still has nightmares."

She stopped short, the knot constricting her speech. A vision of her sweet sister, gagged and chained in a cartel stronghold, swam before her eyes. That day, Veranda had experienced the most profound rage of her life, followed by a tidal wave of remorse. "I will be there for her." She heard the edge in her voice as her final statement came out in a raspy whisper. "I have to."

Sergeant Jackson, who'd been silent for much of the discussion, cleared his throat. "It's okay, Detective. We all have our assignments and can manage without you for a few hours. We do have experience in investigations, you know." His smile eased the tension in the room.

Relief poured through Veranda when no one raised any further objections. She forced herself to regain her footing. Leading task forces in the past, she'd learned to appear strong and capable at all times, regardless of her inner turmoil. "While I'm out tomorrow, everyone can finish writing the affidavits."

"What about the operation itself?" Marci asked.

"Sergeant Grigg from SAU just sent me a text. We'll meet tomorrow night for a dry run. He set it up with SWAT teams from other agencies."

"When and where?" Agent Tanner snatched up his notepad.

"We'll be at the Shoot House. Let's meet at nineteen-thirty hours tomorrow evening at the front gate of the police academy. That gives me plenty of time to suit up after I leave my sister's party. Plus, I want to practice at dusk because the lighting's similar to conditions around dawn, which is when we'll do the real operation. I'll text everyone with the exact address and other details."

"At least we get a practice run," Agent Wallace said. "We can tweak the actual operation based on the debrief and after-action review."

"What about Agents Lopez and Rios?" Jackson angled his head in their direction. "They can't write affidavits in the US. What's their assignment for tomorrow?"

She'd considered the problem and was about to suggest they shadow one of the other teams when Lopez spoke. "Agent Rios and I should go with Detective Cruz to the *quinceañera*."

"What?" Diaz's eyebrows shot up. "Why?"

"She may take time off, but the cartel won't." Lopez's expression darkened. "Her family gathering could become a target. I wouldn't put anything past *El Lobo*."

Veranda felt the blood drain from her face. She couldn't miss the event and let Gabby down, but neither could she lead the cartel to her family's doorstep again.

Lopez's warm brown eyes softened as he turned to her. "You enjoy the party." He pointed back and forth at Rios and himself. "Let us watch for Salazar."

"I can do that," Diaz snapped. "I have full law enforcement powers in this city, and I'm already attending the party."

Veranda's mind reeled as the conversation careened in a new direction. "Wait. What?"

Diaz squared his shoulders as if bracing for a fight. "There's a young man I've been mentoring through a program for at-risk youth. He's in your sister's *quinceañera* court."

"What are you talking about?"

"One of your sister's friends is dating him." Diaz looked short on patience. "She got Gabriela to invite him. He asked me to come because he's nervous about dancing. I've already spoken to your mother about it." He waved a hand as if that settled the matter.

Thunderstruck, Veranda could barely manage a response. "You know my mother?"

"Everyone knows your mother."

She should have seen this coming. Active in church, volunteering in the community, and donating extra food from her restaurant, Lorena had woven herself into the tapestry of South Phoenix. Revered for her generosity, she was a true matriarch.

Irked at the intersection of her professional and private lives, Veranda scowled at her boss. "When were you going to tell me about this?"

"I wasn't." Diaz shrugged. "It doesn't concern you."

"When my family is involved, it definitely concerns me. In fact, you'd—"

"Excuse me." Lopez cut in, directing his comment at Diaz. "But your presence will not help. Salazar changes his appearance often. It's one of the reasons no one has caught him for so many years. Agent Rios and I are the only ones who can spot him through a disguise. We need to go too."

"Fine," Veranda said, tired of the discussion. "I'll pick you both up at the hotel at noon tomorrow."

She led the group through the rest of the meeting, explaining the particulars of the controlled buy involving SSS scheduled for that night and how it would provide the final intel for that part of the operation.

As she spoke, the dark recesses of her mind repeatedly dredged up horrific pictures of Salazar, the man Agent Lopez had referred to as *El Matador*, making an unwanted appearance at her sister's birthday party the next day.

15

ADOLFO LOOKED UP WHEN Nacho burst into the drop house living room.

"I've got her!" Nacho blurted.

For the second time, his computer expert had violated protocol by entering without knocking. Because of Nacho's work on various hacking projects, Adolfo interacted with him often. Over time, the young man had become accustomed to direct communication, and Adolfo relaxed the usual code of conduct out of convenience. Perhaps too much. He was about to admonish Nacho when Salazar stood and crossed the room in one lithe movement. His well-practiced hand shot out, latched onto Nacho's throat, and squeezed. The rest of Nacho's words became an indistinct gurgle.

Salazar leaned in close to Nacho's purpling face and whispered in Spanish, "You do not enter without permission."

Adolfo knew Salazar was enforcing order, but he resented it. Adolfo would discipline his men when and how he saw fit. He recognized the subtle undermining. Salazar's actions implied Adolfo needed assistance to control subordinates. Salazar, the interloper, exerted power effortlessly, like a matador wielded a sword. Adolfo watched the scene before him with a certain amount of detachment and realized he despised Salazar.

Finally, Nacho began to slump, the laptop slipping through his fingers to drop on the carpeted floor.

Adolfo got to his feet. "Enough. Nacho is useless to me if he's unconscious." When Salazar showed no sign of stopping, Adolfo raised his voice. "Or dead."

Salazar released his grip and Nacho fell to his knees, coughing and clutching his throat. Adolfo waited for him to pick up his laptop and stand on shaky legs.

"S-sorry," he mumbled, putting the computer on the table and opening it to face them. "Was excited." He continued in a hoarse rasp. "Wanted to show you right away." He pointed at the screen. "Look."

A two-dimensional map of downtown Phoenix with a red dot on it filled the display area. Adolfo leaned closer. The stationary dot hovered at the intersection of 8th Avenue and Adams Street.

He glanced back to Nacho. "What's this?"

Nacho appeared to regain a measure of his enthusiasm. "I cloned Detective Cruz's phone." He managed a tenuous grin. "I've accessed the internal GPS and now we can track her movements in real time. Whenever her phone gets a call or a text, I can listen in or read them as they come through. I get the outgoing stuff too." He pulled a smart phone out of his pants pocket. "This unit mirrors her phone."

Adolfo took the device from Nacho's outstretched hand. His computer tech could be cocky, sometimes bordering on disrespectful, but he was damned good at what he did. Adolfo smiled to himself. His trust in the young man had been rewarded, but he still had questions. "Can she tell we're monitoring her?"

Nacho flicked a nervous glance at Salazar before returning his attention to Adolfo. "No, *señor*. There's no way to tell it's been cloned."

Adolfo scrutinized the phone before handing it back to Nacho. "What about the rest of the task force?"

"I already have their numbers from the email Cruz sent out earlier. That's all I need. Within the hour, I'll have duplicate phones for the whole team and their supervisors. Once that's done, they can't take a shit without us smelling it." His gaze dropped to the floor.

"What is it, Nacho?" Adolfo couldn't hide the impatience in his voice. Nacho had obviously been traumatized by his near-death experience with Salazar, and his demeanor had changed dramatically, leaving him uncharacteristically cowed.

Head bent, Nacho murmured his response. "I'll need help watching all the phones, more computers, and a place to set up a workstation so we can monitor communications around the clock. I'm sure Cruz and her team will be working at all hours, and we don't want to miss anything."

"How has Sofia been acting?" Adolfo asked. "Can you use her until we get more people for you?"

"She's been very compliant since…since your last visit. I gave her a fifteen-minute break to change her sister's bandages. Keeps her in line. Reminds her to obey me."

Salazar's obsidian eyes gleamed. "Good," he said. "What have you learned from the detective's phone so far?"

Nacho trembled as he answered. "Cruz sent out an email updating the ops plan we intercepted before. It's got the final locations for the search warrants. Three are SSS and twelve are ours. There's no date or time given, but the email says the affidavits will be completed tomorrow.

There's also something about a full-scale practice exercise tomorrow night."

Adolfo's pulse picked up. "Sounds like they plan to move fast." He hadn't anticipated this. Law enforcement agencies were usually methodical and careful in their planning. He would have to adapt to their condensed schedule. He sorted through various options in his mind. Through the mental chaos, a strategy took shape, and everything clicked into place. He could turn the situation to his advantage.

"Nacho." Adolfo deliberately barked the word, causing the young man's head to pop up as if he'd been slapped. "Send out a blast text to all of our men in the Phoenix area. Tell them to stop whatever they're doing and report here immediately. I have a plan, and it's going to be a long night."

For the first time, Adolfo felt the full confidence of a man with a well-formed strategy who knew how to carry it out.

As Nacho left the room, Adolfo paused a moment to savor the prospect of his success. Veranda Cruz was totally compromised ... and she had no clue. He considered the intelligence the GPS tracker provided, factored it into his plans, and a smile played across his lips.

He owned her now.

16

THE BLADE WHISTLED THROUGH the air in a silver blur. Veranda twisted away from the knife's cutting edge as the tip thudded into the butcher's block, almost slicing her arm. "Hey, watch it!" She stepped back.

Tío Felipe grinned. "Not a lot of room to work in here, *mi'ja*. If you get in the way ... " He shrugged, hoisting the enormous meat cleaver again.

After her meeting at the Fusion Center, Veranda had driven to the food truck in search of answers about Diaz. Instead, she found herself drafted into service as her aunt and uncles helped her mother prepare for the dinner rush. Juana and Juan were outside setting up card tables and umbrellas in the parking lot, while her mother oversaw Felipe and Rico inside the truck's tiny galley.

Lorena slid a cutting board laden with vegetables in front of her. "Don't just stand there, *mi'ja*, wash your hands and get to work."

Veranda cleaned up and yanked a chopping knife from a magnetized bar bolted to the interior bulkhead. She grabbed a red bell pepper, lopped off the top, and blew out a sigh. She shouldn't have tried to interrogate her mother during dinner rush the evening before a major family event. Lorena was recruiting everyone in sight to help with the party. Some of tonight's food prep was also for tomorrow's *quinceañera*.

Tío Rico handed her a spoon to scrape seeds from inside the pepper. He cast an appraising glance in her direction. "So, are you bringing him?"

"Who?" She laid down the knife and took the proffered utensil.

"*El capitán.*" Rico waggled his brows. "Your *novio*. He is coming to the party, yes?"

She thrust the scraping spoon into the pepper with so much force it burst through the bottom. "No and no."

"What do you mean? I only asked you one question."

"No, Cole Anderson is not my boyfriend." She dragged out a clump of small white seeds. "And he's out of town, so no, he won't be coming."

Tío Felipe stopped cutting strips of beef to join the conversation. "If he is not your *novio*, then why was he kissing you in the parking lot last week?" He brandished the cleaver. "Should I have a talk with him?"

Veranda gave herself a mental forehead slap. "No, Felipe." Her family constantly interfered, especially in her love life. "You shouldn't get used to him anyway." She tried to sound casual, but she wanted to lay the groundwork in case things went badly when Cole returned. "I'm not sure where we stand right now."

Her heart constricted when she recalled Cole's parting words. He'd made it clear he thought anyone related to the Villalobos family was from a defective gene pool. What future did she have with a man who found her very existence repulsive? Whether she told him the truth or he discovered it on his own, he would spurn her in the end.

"*Ay, dios mio.*" Lorena gestured at her oldest daughter, no doubt reading the subtext. "This one will never give me grandchildren."

Veranda had grown used to her mother's endless complaints about her lack of romantic prospects. Over the years, she'd fended off more fixups than she cared to think about. Anxious to change the subject, Veranda steered the discussion to the reason she had come. "Why is Lieutenant Diaz coming to the party tomorrow?"

Lorena's hazel eyes brightened. "Ah, now there is a man I like very much." She nodded approvingly. "Richard Diaz would be good for you if the *capitán* doesn't work out."

Veranda felt her jaw go slack. The prospect was too hideous to contemplate, so she tried for more answers. "How do you even know my lieutenant?"

In the South Phoenix Latino community, many families attended the same churches and generally knew each other, but she had no idea her mother was personally acquainted with Diaz.

Rico slung a heavy pot down from its hook. "Because Lorena helped his mother through a very bad time."

At Veranda's questioning look, her mother sighed. "Although we have not been close for many years, Anita Diaz was once my dear friend. Out of respect for her, no one talks about it, so please do not repeat what I am about to tell you."

Veranda's pulse quickened at the prospect of secret information about her boss. "I won't."

Lorena's expression grew distant. "Twenty-five years ago, Richard Diaz was only ten years old. His father was dead, so he looked up to his older brother, Manny, who was sixteen at the time." Her words were suffused with sorrow. "We were all so poor back then, everyone in the neighborhood. Families helped each other, but there wasn't much anyone could do when Manny started to get in trouble."

Veranda searched her mind for details and came up blank. She would have been in second grade at the time, but she didn't remember the Diaz family at all. She waited while her mother gathered her thoughts.

"One night, the police caught Manny running with a gang." Echoes of past grief lined her mother's face. "For months, we all watched over him. Said prayers for him. Tried to talk sense to him. But he would not listen." Lorena pressed a palm to her chest. "Then one day, Manny did not come home."

Tío Rico moved to stand next to Lorena. "Someone from another gang shot Manny because he was on the wrong street." He shook his head. "Anita couldn't even have a funeral to bury her son, because the police were worried there would be more gang attacks at the service."

That explained why she had no memory of the funeral. Such a tragedy would have been marked in the community. Her heart went out to Anita Diaz, a widow whose oldest son was senselessly murdered, leaving her to raise her younger boy in poverty, without even the support of her community at the memorial service to comfort her.

"How did Anita manage?" Veranda asked.

Rico lifted a plastic carton of water from the counter. "Anita was terrified Richard would follow his older brother's path. People wanted to help her raise the boy, but Anita moved to a different neighborhood and kept everyone away. Our families grew apart, and that is why you didn't meet Richard until you were both on the police department."

"What happened to Richard after they moved?" It felt strange to use his first name.

Rico twisted off the carton's lid and began to pour water in the pot he'd gotten down earlier. "Turns out he was good at baseball. When he got to high school, his coach took an interest and helped him get a scholarship to ASU."

Her mother took up the story. "After he became a police officer, Richard and his old high school coach started a program to help boys from the neighborhood stay out of trouble. They teach them baseball, basketball, boxing, and soccer." The corner of her mouth lifted in a slight smile. "He calls them the South Phoenix Boys."

Veranda had noticed her lieutenant's athletic physique before but had figured him for a gym rat. She didn't realize he kept in shape by cross-training with a bunch of teenagers.

Never one to shy away from conversation, tío Felipe chimed in from the meat prep area. "Richard is the one who keeps those boys in line. They have to keep their grades up, volunteer in the community, and take drug tests. He works them hard." Felipe tossed a hunk of raw beef onto the butcher's block. "I think he keeps them too tired to get in trouble." His cleaver sank into the wooden surface as he spoke, severing a strip of meat. "He's the closest thing most of them have to a father."

The revelations came so fast she had trouble keeping up. "But Diaz investigated me six weeks ago, and he didn't know much about my background. He didn't even know I had a step-family." During his intense interrogation, she'd left out certain facts. If he'd known she was lying, he would have taken her badge on the spot.

Her mother gave her a patient look. "Like I said, we lost touch with his family twenty-five years ago. That was long before I met Miguel and married him. Long before Gabriela was born."

Something still didn't add up. "If you haven't spoken with him for all that time, how do you know about the South Phoenix Boys?"

Rico turned to face her, his warm brown eyes meeting hers. "Because of Chuy."

Realization flooded through her. Chuy was Rico's only son, and he'd been a criminal. "Did Diaz lock him up?"

"Yes." The word came in a soft whisper.

She saw shame and anguish in her uncle's eyes and resented Diaz more than ever. "That bastard."

"No, *mi'ja*, it's not like that." Rico waved her comment away. "Richard went to see Chuy in prison before he got out five years ago. He wanted to help him get out of the life, but Chuy was twenty-five then. Too old to be one of the South Phoenix Boys." Rico turned on the burner under the pot. "Richard's old high school coach couldn't keep up anymore, so he asked Chuy to help out with the boys. Chuy agreed, and he also talked to them about prison so they would not want to go there."

Felipe chuckled. "I think just looking at Chuy would scare the *caca* out of those kids." He shot a sheepish grin at his older brother. "Sorry Rico, but your son looks like one mean *vato*."

Rico huffed out a humorless laugh. "I know." He turned back to Veranda. "Chuy had to follow all of Richard's rules, just like the kids. He had to volunteer in the community and show up for his parole officer's drug testing. Richard was real tough on him because he was an adult."

Veranda rolled her eyes. If anyone was enough of a hard-ass to tame Chuy, it would be Diaz. He had certainly put *her* through hell. The thought gave her pause, and she reflected back on his investigation into her actions six weeks ago. Diaz had dragged her through her story repeatedly, tightening the screws each time.

She cocked her head to one side, processing the new information. Diaz had known Chuy for years by then. He must have known she was Chuy's cousin and could have asked him about her step-family. She was sure he hadn't, or Chuy would have said something. Also,

Diaz would have caught her in a lie and busted her down to permanent school crossings. Why had Diaz cut his investigation short?

Her lieutenant was an enigma and her family kept secrets. The game had changed and no one had given her the new rules. She didn't like it. "How come Chuy never told me any of this?" She looked back and forth between them. "Or you guys?"

"Richard keeps the names of people in the program secret," Rico said. "Most of them are still kids, so it's ... what is the word?" He rotated his hand in a circular motion as if flipping through a mental Rolodex. "Confidential."

She thumped her spoon on the cutting board. "But I'm family." She would give Chuy a piece of her mind the next time they were alone. He'd been holding out on her.

Her mother cut in. "I know, and that is why we are telling you now. You didn't need to know before." She regarded her daughter with suspicion. "In fact, I'm not sure why you need to know now."

"I need to know because I still don't understand why my lieutenant is coming to the party. He said something about a boy he's mentoring who's nervous about dancing. But I don't get it. Why does Diaz need to be there for a boy who's afraid to dance?"

Lorena's expression cleared. "Oh, he's talking about Joey." She gave a slight shake of her head. "The boy is scared to dance in front of others because he was born deaf. He has never heard music before and has to feel the beat through the floor. But he really wanted to go, so Richard and Chuy practiced with him for weeks. Chuy's girlfriend helped."

Yet another side of her lieutenant—and her favorite cousin—she never expected. Curiosity overwhelmed her, and a question popped out before she could stop it. "What about Diaz? Does he have a wife or girlfriend?"

Lorena grew serious again. "Richard had a fiancée, but she did not like the South Phoenix Boys. I think they scared her. A few months ago, Chuy told us she made Richard choose between her and his program. He would not give up on those kids. So, she left." Lorena's expression became calculating as she considered her oldest daughter. "Richard would do better with a very strong woman at his side."

"*Ay, Mamá.*" Veranda jutted out a hip. "Please stop whatever you're thinking. Lieutenant Richard Diaz is the last man on earth I would ever consider." She leveled her spoon at her mother. "And don't you dare pull any of your tricks at the party tomorrow."

"Fine." Lorena's eyes widened with feigned innocence. "If you don't want a handsome man with a good heart and a steady job, I'm sure somebody else's daughter will take him."

Veranda heaved a noisy sigh. How could she explain to her mother that Diaz was an overbearing, exasperating bureaucrat who scrutinized everything she did and generally made her miserable at work? Besides, she was under his command and therefore off-limits for him. *Gracias a dios* for that.

Thoughts of chain-of-command jarred her memory. She laid the spoon on the counter. "When will the reception be over?"

"We should be done by eight o'clock. Why do you ask?" Lorena scowled. "You do not think to leave early, do you?"

"Not planning to." Veranda slipped a cell phone from her pocket. "But Sergeant Jackson is in charge since Diaz and I will be at the party. I'll give him my schedule in case he needs to reach me."

She tapped the hours of the party and her mother's home address onto the screen. "Don't worry, Mamá, I'm sure nothing will come up." She pushed SEND.

17

VERANDA WOKE IN HER bed the following morning drenched in sweat. She shook her head to dissolve the image of a nightmare featuring *El Matador,* who waved a red cape in front of her before piercing her heart with his sword.

A long shower washed the last vestiges of the dream away. She took extra time on her hair and makeup, then dressed for Gabby's *quinceañera* between phone calls from Sergeant Grigg from SAU about the upcoming practice run. Working through the details meant missing Gabby's special service at church, but at least she would arrive in time for the reception at the family casitas.

She'd called Sergeant Jackson, and then Gabby to update them, receiving a hefty dose of guilt from her mother, who spoke loudly enough in the background for Veranda to make out the words, "always about her job," and "better not be late to the house." By the time she left to pick up the *federales* at the Hyatt, the asphalt shimmered under the midday sun.

Standing in the hotel parking lot in her dress, she popped the Tahoe's rear door latch so the two Mexican agents could each hoist identical black duffel bags inside the cargo hold next to hers.

She put her hands on her hips, eyeing the three bags shoved together. "Luggage says a lot about a person. Some people are into Louis Vuitton." She closed the trunk door. "Cops like black nylon."

Rios grinned. "You told us to come prepared. All we need is a place to change before the practice operation tonight." He inclined his head in her direction. "By the way, you look nice."

Veranda had put on a bright blue dress with a hem several inches above her knees. The gauzy material skimmed her slender waist and clung to her curves, and she wondered what *Mamá* would think of it. She'd pinned half of her hair up and allowed the rest to flow down her back in thick waves. A pair of high-heeled silver sandals and turquoise jewelry completed the festive outfit.

She blew out a sigh. "*Mamá* will be thrilled to see me in a dress for a change."

Rios did a slow perusal. "I can see why." He seemed to reconsider his comment when Veranda raised a brow. He backpedaled. "I mean, you look *muy guapa* ... very pretty, that is to say—"

Lopez cast a pitying look at his younger counterpart and cut in. "Where is the *quinceañera* to be held? Are we going to the church now?"

Grateful for the change in subject, she turned to the senior agent. "They already celebrated the Mass. I had to miss it because I've been on the phone with Sergeant Grigg all morning. We're good to go." She circled to the driver's door and opened it. "Commander Webster will be there personally to oversee the practice op."

Lopez shook his head as he climbed in the front passenger's seat. "I am sorry you could not go to the church service. It is quite beautiful. I remember my daughter's."

Riding a fresh wave of guilt, she pictured Gabby at the altar in her beautiful gown. Veranda deeply regretted her absence at church, but at least she'd be there for the rest of the celebration. "*Mamá* would come after me with one of her wooden spoons if I missed the reception. It's at the family property."

Lopez looked intrigued. "The family property?"

The men buckled up and she drove out of the parking lot, eyes on the road as she recounted one of her favorite stories. "Many years ago, when land cost less, my relatives scraped enough money together to buy a three-acre corner lot in South Phoenix near the mountain. My mother and her five younger brothers and sisters started in one big house. Over the years, as each of my aunts and uncles got married, they built their own casita on the land. Now there are five houses surrounding a large open space where we hold gatherings."

Lopez frowned. "You said your mother had five younger siblings. There should be six houses."

"My *tía* Maria is the only one who didn't stay in Phoenix. She moved to Sedona when she graduated from high school. She's into astrology and takes people on guided tours to the vortex areas. Totally New Age. I doubt she'll be at the party. We always invite her, but she never comes to town."

Rios leaned forward to poke his head between the two front seats. "What kind of things do you celebrate at the property?"

"Weddings, funerals, holidays, birthdays…really anything. My stepfather, Miguel Gomez, built a huge pavilion with fans, a misting system, and a fire pit so we can use it year-round. He's a licensed general contractor and owns a construction company. My mother met him when she was selling burritos at a work site when I was in high school."

"So, he is Gabriela's father, but not yours?" Lopez asked.

"Yes, Gabriela's really my half-sister, but I always call her my kid sister." An image of Gabby's luminous smile warmed her heart. "She sent me a text before I picked you up. Said she won't start the reception until I get there." Veranda glanced at her watch. She'd be a few minutes late, which—to her family—meant she'd be on time.

"Excuse me if I am too curious." Lopez hesitated before he asked, "How did your family come to live in Phoenix?"

Veranda gave him the sanitized version she provided to everyone who asked. Only Sam knew the whole story. "Many years ago, my mother arrived from Mexico with nothing but the clothes on her back and her younger siblings. She couldn't speak English, but she knew how to cook. She sold lunch food out of an old pickup truck and eventually opened a restaurant called *Casa Cruz Cocina*." She shook her head. "Before she got the restaurant she was totally unlicensed. She'd have been toast if anyone caught her, but *Mamá* did what she had to back then."

She neglected to mention certain details of her family's first years in the US. Like the Legal Aid attorney who helped Lorena file for asylum because of what he termed "imminent danger" from Hector Villalobos. And her mother reverting to her maiden name, Cruz, to make it easier to care for her younger brothers and sisters.

Lorena had endured such pain and grief. All of it at the hands of *El Lobo*. But her mother, ever the survivor, had created a new life for her family. She heard the pride in her own voice as she spoke. "They built the business over thirty years and expanded it many times." The swell of joy abruptly melted into self-recrimination, silencing her.

144

The restaurant had burned to the ground. Because of her. Because she had dared to challenge *El Lobo*, the very monster her mother had escaped. Veranda had brought the wolf back to their door.

Reverting to the present, she pulled into the long gravel driveway leading to their family grounds. Veranda found an opening wide enough to park the Tahoe among the line of cars and trucks.

She stepped down from the elevated driver's seat, landed awkwardly on high heels, and jerked her hem down over bare thighs. She cursed under her breath as Rios took in the impromptu show.

Straightening, she led the *federales* toward the pavilion. A slight breeze made the Red Bird of Paradise bushes sway. A few piles of freshly turned earth showed where her mother had removed some of her beloved plants. She remembered her mother taking them to the site of the new restaurant. A symbol of survival. Of overcoming adversity. Of hope.

Another warm rush of air brought the rich aroma of exotic spices and she breathed in the scent of treasured family recipes as she stepped onto the stone floor under the enormous pavilion at the center of the casitas. A few dozen round tables, each set for six people, clustered around the area, with overflow seating on the grass. Hot pink and jet black, Gabriela's favorite color combination, adorned every surface and stanchion.

She searched the crowd for signs of her kid sister. As her gaze roved over the throng, she realized Gabby and the honored guests would be waiting inside her mother's house to make their grand entrance. Aware they had delayed the ceremony for her arrival, she turned toward the main house to knock on the door when Chuy jogged up to her.

"I just texted Gabby that you're here." He motioned toward a table near the front. "C'mon, you're supposed to sit with me."

She followed him over to the table trailed by Lopez and Rios, who took seats on either side of her. She mentally rolled her eyes at the protective arrangement and introduced them to Chuy. She was relieved when they didn't comment on his appearance. Of course, that could have been because they were distracted by his girlfriend, who sashayed toward them in a skin-tight fluorescent pink mini-dress and patent leather pumps with the highest heels Veranda had ever seen.

Chuy nodded at the voluptuous bleach blonde, who sported almost as many tattoos as he did. "This is Tiffany," he said to Lopez and Rios.

Tiffany smiled and winked at Agent Rios, whose eyes widened when she brushed against his thigh as she wiggled into the seat next to him. Certain the intimate contact hadn't been an accident, Veranda stifled a grin. Chuy, who sat on Tiffany's other side, either didn't notice his girlfriend's blatant flirtation, or didn't care. Rios looked like he wanted to bolt. Lopez turned his laugh into a polite cough.

"Good afternoon."

Veranda recognized the deep male voice before she turned to see Diaz standing directly behind her. Chuy abruptly rose, circled around to Diaz, and pulled him into an *abrazo*, pressing their chests together and thumping each other on the back. She'd have been shocked at the customary familiar greeting between Latino men if not for her mother's story the night before. Now, the sight made her speculate about her lieutenant. What else didn't she know?

Diaz took the last empty chair, which was between Chuy and Lopez. His ebony eyes swept the table, rested on Tiffany for a moment, then darted away when she slid her tongue seductively across her upper teeth.

Veranda hid a chuckle behind her hand, enjoying Rios and Diaz's discomfort. It seemed Tiffany had a taste for Mexican, and this party was a veritable smorgasbord.

Rios looked up at the sky. "What is that?"

Veranda followed his gaze. An object about the size of a trash can lid with four propellers buzzed overhead.

"A drone," Diaz said, squinting. "What's it doing here?"

The drone circled and flew to the other side of the yard.

Chuy shrugged. "Probably one of Gabby's friends shooting a YouTube video. Seems like everyone is putting footage of their *quinceañera* on the web these days." He shook his head. "When they're not doing cat or dog videos."

Chuy's comment reminded her of Gabby's gift. She leaned across the table just as the mariachi band, in full regalia, struck up a processional tune. "Chuy," she whispered, "where's the puppy?"

He pointed at Tiffany. "She's got him."

Tiffany reached down and picked up a black leather purse. At least, Veranda thought it was a purse at first. When Tiffany turned it to one side, a tiny nose poked out through a wide fleece-lined opening. Big brown eyes and soft triangular ears followed. The bag was actually a carrier for little dogs, and the puppy seemed quite happy nestled inside.

Chuy grinned. "We put a pink bow on the carrier. Gabby gets to keep it. I also got a black leather collar for him too." He wrinkled his pierced nose. "I just hope she doesn't name him something like Foo-Foo."

She chuckled. The dog was adorable, and Chuy had obviously doted on the little guy. The pup would be thoroughly spoiled by the time Gabby finally got him today.

Agent Lopez touched her elbow. "Excuse me," he said, pointing at his cell phone. "It's my wife. She'll worry if I don't take this."

Veranda pointed toward a lattice festooned with black satin ribbons and bright pink bougainvillea. "Go over there behind the trellis. You'll be far enough away to hear your wife over the band."

She watched Lopez traipse to the lattice, thinking how nice it must be to have someone at home, when a swirl of color distracted her. A glint of pale purple caught the corner of her eye, and she swiveled in her chair to see her stepfather and mother stride slowly into the pavilion. Her mother's lavender dress fluttered in the light breeze. Face radiant, eyes sparkling, head high, in that moment, Lorena was the most beautiful woman at the party.

Next in the procession, Gabby's *padrinos*, her godparents, walked arm-in-arm down the aisle dividing the tables. Long-time friends, the older couple had attended every family function and gone to their church for decades.

The *quinceañera* court followed. Seven lovely girls wearing hot pink gowns were escorted by seven young men in black tuxedos with pink sneakers, cummerbunds, and bowties to match the dresses. Absolutely adorable.

After a long moment, the music shifted and Gabriela strode forward on her *chambelan*'s arm. Dozens of chairs scraped back as everyone stood. Veranda's heart caught in her throat when Gabby made her appearance in a floor-length traditional gown of rosy pink. Made of satin with folds of taffeta under the skirt, the dress harkened back to a bygone era. With her dark, glossy tresses piled high on her head and Lorena's silver choker with its etched cross circling her neck, Gabby looked every bit the sweet, virginal beauty she represented at this time of passage to womanhood. Veranda looked on as her mother walked to Gabby and gently placed a glittering tiara on her head.

Unexpected tears stung Veranda's eyes. She'd almost ruined this special moment. When Bartolo had captured Gabby, he'd threatened to … Veranda swallowed the bile surging in her throat and pushed the rest of the thought from her mind.

A warm hand touched her arm, and she glanced over to see Agent Rios scrutinizing her. "Are you remembering your own *quinceañera?*" he asked.

She glanced around the table. All eyes were on her rather than her sister. She had made a spectacle of herself. Her hard-won training and self-discipline often deserted her when it came to her family. The group at her table obviously thought she was having a nostalgic remembrance from her youth. They could not have been further from the truth.

Veranda waved an arm, indicating that everyone should take their seats again. She used the few moments to compose herself. When she finally answered, her words barely carried over the music. "We didn't have much money back then. I didn't have a *quinceañera* like this." She gestured to the band and elaborate decorations. "Just family at the church and a small gathering at home."

Chuy puffed out his chest. "I was her *chambelan.*" When his proclamation met with silence, he added, "I was three years younger than her, but she scared off all the guys in her class."

She wanted to slide under the table and crawl away. Chuy had shared one of her most embarrassing memories. Face flaming at the stunned looks around the table, she decided to elaborate. "When I was little, I got picked on. Like I said, we were poor back then. My clothes mostly came from the donation bin at church. For lunch, sometimes all I had in my brown bag was a cold tortilla and government cheese. Didn't make me popular. My family was always working, trying to make ends meet, so it wasn't hard to hide the bruises and scrapes I got from fighting."

She scrutinized the centerpiece, refusing to meet anyone's gaze. To witness their pity would make it all real again. She clasped her hands in her lap and went on.

"After I got a black eye, though, my uncles caught on. They took me to a local gym and asked if they could teach me kickboxing in exchange for free food at our family restaurant. I learned how to take care of myself. Then I started to stand up for other kids who were bullied. Got kind of a reputation as a fighter." She tucked a loose strand of hair behind her ear. "Guess that didn't exactly charm the boys."

Eyes still trained on the floral arrangement in the middle of the table, she heard the groan of a flimsy folding chair under the strain of a man's shifting weight as Diaz leaned toward her. "You were three years behind me in school. I was already in college before your *quinceañera*." The intensity in his voice dragged her gaze up to meet his. "Too bad ... I wouldn't have been intimidated."

The implication hung in the air. She blinked and looked away. Maybe the earth would open and swallow her. Maybe she would find a discreet way to kill Chuy and hide the body so no one would ever find it.

The band started playing again and her stepfather invited everyone to eat while the traditional ceremonies began. A long rectangular table set off to the side practically bowed under the weight of an elaborate buffet with Gabby's favorite Mexican and American delicacies.

Tucking his phone in his suit jacket pocket, Agent Lopez walked back to the table and reclaimed his chair next to Veranda. He gave her a smile and they craned their necks to watch as the crowd made a wide circle around Gabby and her father, who were in the middle of the pavilion.

The DJ's voice reverberated through the speakers set up around the yard. "And now, *la última muñeca*."

Tiffany looked at Chuy, who was engrossed in conversation with Diaz. She blew out an exasperated huff of air and signaled Veranda from across the table. "I've never been to one of these things. What's the DJ talking about?"

Veranda smiled, proud of her Latina heritage and the beautiful traditions of her culture. "It means, 'the last doll.' When a girl turns fifteen, she leaves her childhood behind and becomes a young woman. The presentation of the last doll is symbolic, so it's a miniature of Gabby."

They watched in silence as Gabby's father, Miguel, handed her a porcelain doll with dark glossy hair and a tiny tiara, its pale pink satin and taffeta gown an exact replica of Gabby's. The crowd cheered and applauded as Gabby clutched the figurine to her chest.

Miguel stood by and the audience grew quiet as a young cousin walked solemnly toward them holding a white satin pillow with a pair of pink strappy sandals resting on top.

Tiffany quirked a brow at Veranda, who leaned closer to explain the next part of the ceremony. "Now Gabby's father will take off her kid's shoes and put the first pair of high heels on her feet."

Miguel knelt in front of Gabby, who sat in a chair and tugged the flowing skirt of her gown up above her ankles, exposing a pair of hot pink Converse high tops. Her father gently unlaced the sneakers, pulled them from her feet, and slid the pink heels on in their place. He stood and extended a hand to his daughter.

"Now," Veranda continued her narrative, "is *el vals*. It means, 'the waltz.' Upon becoming a woman, a *quinceañera*'s first dance is a traditional waltz with her father, so they ... " She trailed off, impulse overtaking her. She would force Diaz out in the open. "But you know all about this, don't you, Tiffany? You helped one of the boys learn to dance?" She deliberately raised her voice to get a reaction. "Joey, right?"

At the mention of the name, Diaz and Chuy abruptly ended their conversation. She smiled. How would they talk their way out of this one?

The two men traded glances before Chuy turned to Veranda. "I love your mother, *mi'jita*, but she should keep quiet about my business."

She couldn't believe her ears. "This is what you say after keeping secrets from me for years?"

Diaz shot her a quelling look. "This isn't the time or place, Detective."

Temper stoked, she rounded on her lieutenant. "And what have *you* been hiding all this time?"

Agent Lopez placed a hand on her shoulder. "*Perdón*, but you might want to watch the dance. It has already started."

With a few quiet words and a fatherly touch, Lopez had extinguished her fire. Chastised, Veranda scooted her chair to get a better view of her sister. This was Gabby's day, and she wouldn't mar it with bickering.

The band played a Mexican-flavored waltz as father and daughter glided in a graceful arc around the center of the pavilion. Veranda allowed herself to get caught up in the beauty of the rite of passage handed down through generations.

The dance ended to more applause and the entire *quinceañera* court joined them. Miguel gave his daughter's hand to her *chambelan* and stepped away. The other seven young couples, all dressed in their pink and black finery, filled the floor in another elegant dance. She couldn't pick Joey out, which meant the boy blended in perfectly. Despite her feelings about the secrecy involved, she was happy the lessons had worked.

Absorbed in the father-daughter ceremonies, Veranda had lost track of her mother. She straightened, peering around at the partygoers, when Lorena grasped her shoulders from behind.

"*Mi'ja*." Her mother's soft accent radiated warmth. "I am so glad you are here. I missed you earlier." She indicated the table. "Will you introduce me to your guests?"

Veranda rose from her chair, looped her arm in her mother's, and turned toward the *federales*. *"Mamá* this is—"

Lorena's eyes fell on Agent Lopez. Her hand flew to her mouth. "Esteban ... " she breathed.

Lopez gasped. *"Ay, dios mio,"* he murmured, staring at her mother. "Lorena Hidalgo. I ... I thought you were dead."

18

MIA PACHECO WINCED AS her twin sister peeled back the bandage from her chest. She held Sofia's wide brown eyes with her own, saw guilt mingled with horror, and braced herself to prevent any anguish from showing on her face. She knew her sister felt responsible for angering Salazar, who didn't want her distracted from her duties. That wouldn't do.

They sat together on a lumpy, bare mattress, its frayed sheets spinning in an ancient washing machine down the hall. The tiny upstairs bedroom served as a private space for the coyotes to take Carlos's women for their amusement.

Still physically unable to entertain men, Mia kept the room clean. Revolted by wet, slimy stains when she stripped the bed, she'd touched only the corners of the threadbare fabric when she loaded the sheets inside the washer and added extra soap.

After Mia finished her cleaning duties, Nacho had ordered her sister to treat her burn with a foul-smelling ointment. She didn't think for a moment her captors wanted her to feel better. She was certain they wanted both of them to remember their lesson.

As Sofia reached for the salve, Mia braced herself and started a conversation to divert her mind from the impending pain. "Sof," she said, "you can tell me about it."

Sofia's hand tensed as she dipped her fingers in the jar. "About what?"

"I didn't sleep last night. Too much noise. I've never heard so many men in the house. And I for sure never heard so many women. Señor Adolfo was shouting at everyone. Couldn't make out the words, but he sounded mad."

"I was working at my desk next to Nacho all night. He never lets me out of his sight anymore, so I don't know what went on in the other rooms."

She wouldn't let her sister off that easily. "But you hear them talk, Sof. You know what Señor Adolfo is planning."

"I only know what Nacho tells me. I make guesses from there."

"What's Nacho got you doing now?"

"He ordered me to make a larger map and ping every cell phone from the task force. He wants color-coded dots so we know who's where at a glance." Sofia gently touched the raised red welt with the burn cream.

Mia forced herself not to flinch. "What else?" she asked through gritted teeth.

Sofia hesitated. At her sister's nod, she continued with the treatment and the information. "The men are all upset about a couple of *federales* from Mexico City. I heard Señor Adolfo and that *pendejo*, Salazar, talking to Nacho about it. Sounded like they chased Salazar out of some hotel downtown and almost caught him."

The mention of Salazar's name sent an involuntary shudder through Mia. Thoughts of him terrified her every waking minute. Then he haunted her dreams at night.

"We can't go on like this," Sofia whispered, dabbing more ointment on the raw burn. "One day, they'll kill us."

Mia sucked in sharply before schooling her features. "What choice do we have?"

"Sorry." Sofia stayed her hand. "I've got to figure out the street address where we are. I want to send that detective—Veranda Cruz—a message and tell her to come rescue us."

"You said Nacho cloned her phone and hacked her email. How can you get a message to her?"

Sofia bit her lip. "I don't know yet, but I need to ask you something really important first."

"What is it?"

"If I succeed, we'd be free and the Villalobos brothers and their coyotes would go to jail. But if I get caught again … "

Sofia's unspoken words echoed through the room as if she'd shouted them. Mia held her gaze for a long moment. She knew what her sister asked of her. It would not be Sofia's, but Mia's life on the line. While her sister waited for an answer, the bitter memory of the day *Mamá* had chosen between her twin daughters rushed back to Mia.

Both of them had taken a programming class at school, and the moment Sofia sat in front of an ancient, outdated computer monitor, she seemed to connect to the world of computers. While Mia found herself baffled by the increasingly complex coding, Sofia was in her element. Programming came easily to her sister, who rapidly expanded her skills. Unable to keep up, Mia eventually dropped out.

When Sofia qualified for an internship in the United States, the whole family celebrated the opportunity of a lifetime. The program only covered Sofia's expenses, but *Mamá* wanted both of her daughters to go. That's when *Mamá* made the mistake of contacting Villalobos coyotes, who promised her room and board and a job as a cleaning lady in a neighborhood near Sofia's school. They would even arrange for Mia to attend school as well.

Total bullshit.

Nothing could have prepared her for what came next. The day their motley group of border crossers arrived at the drop house in West Phoenix, Señor Bartolo came to inspect them. Even though she was a virgin, she recognized the heat in his deep-set eyes as they slid over her body. When he learned they were twins, the heat burst into flame. Señor Bartolo wanted both of them. Together.

When *Mamá* begged him to take her in their place, he'd laughed in her face. The sadistic bastard tormented her mother, offering to spare one of the girls if she chose between them. If *Mamá* didn't hand over one daughter, he and every one of his men would have both of them.

The moment the words left Señor Bartolo's mouth, Mia had known what her mother would do. Sofia was the shining light in the family. The beacon of hope for a better future. The one who had to be saved at all costs. Not Mia. Sure enough, her mother had finally hauled her over to Señor Bartolo and pushed her into his grasp. He had dragged her down the hallway to a back room and thrown her on the bed. When she struggled against him, he had beaten her almost to death.

After waking up in some sort of clinic covered in bandages, she'd spent the past six weeks recovering from her injuries while she cooked and cleaned for the coyotes. Señor Carlos said she'd be ready to entertain clients soon, but she still suffered from dizzy spells and blinding headaches.

Her swollen face had returned to its normal shape, except for her broken nose. Every so often, she caught Sofia looking at her with eyes full of guilt. They used to be identical, but each day the resemblance faded as their lives took divergent paths. And now the branding iron had ensured they would never be mistaken for one another again.

"Mia?" She jumped at her sister's voice. Sofia wanted an answer.

Salazar had made it clear Mia wouldn't survive another attempt by Sofia to thwart the cartel, and her sister plainly wanted do exactly that. Because Mia would pay the ultimate price, Sofia needed her permission to try again. It all came down to her. Did she have the courage?

An image of Señor Carlos sprang to mind, his large hands squeezing her flesh, checking to see if she had healed enough to start taking male clients for him. She squared her shoulders. "Sof, do whatever you can to get us out of here. If I die, it's no worse than living like this."

Sofia gave her a lingering look.

Mia set her jaw and hid all traces of fear.

Finally, Sofia nodded. "One way or another, this has to end." Her doe-brown eyes swam with tears. "You are my hero, Mia."

She clutched Sofia's hand. "And you're mine. I'm putting all my faith in you, Sof. You can do this. And if you can't … " she trailed off, then raised her voice with renewed determination. "Like I said before, I'd rather be dead than go on like this."

19

NOW SITTING AT THE circular linen-covered table, Veranda's gaze flicked from her mother to Agent Lopez. How had they known each other?

Lopez gave her mother a tentative smile. "Lorena, I cannot believe it is you." He broke into rapid Spanish. "For so long, I have wondered what happened. When I couldn't find you, I feared the worst."

Tears spilled from Lorena's eyes as she dropped her hands from her mouth and answered in her native tongue, as she always did when she wanted to be clear. "Esteban, I didn't want to be found. I changed my last name. I stopped being Lorena Hidalgo the day my Ernesto died."

Veranda knew this much. Lorena had switched back to her maiden name, Cruz, in order to protect her younger siblings, and took them with her when she fled Mexico. Using her maiden name had also helped in other ways. She had documentation when she filed for asylum in the United States and could prove she was related to the children in her care. Lorena hoped Hector Villalobos wouldn't find her in Phoenix and, until recently, *El Lobo* had left the Cruz family alone.

Agent Lopez's part in the story, however, was new to Veranda. How had he been involved and why had he searched for her mother? She sensed the growing confusion around the table and voiced the obvious question: "Could you explain?"

As they all exchanged glances in stunned silence waiting for Lopez to collect his thoughts, Tiffany pulled a packet of tissues from her purse. She slid one out and handed it to Lorena. The noise of the party seemed to recede into the background. All of Veranda's attention was directed at the man in front of her.

As Lorena dabbed at her nose, Lopez answered in English, addressing everyone at their table. "More than thirty years ago, Ernesto Hidalgo was my boss. His promotion to supervisor left an opening on the squad, and I transferred in to fill the slot. Ernesto became my mentor. I was young and single and didn't know my way around Mexico City. I looked up to Ernesto like an older brother. There were many times he knew I didn't have much food, and he invited me home for dinner after work." He gave her mother a fond smile. "I'm not surprised Lorena opened a restaurant. Even then, her cooking was so delicious it made me homesick for my *Mamá*."

Veranda hung on the older agent's words, picturing him as a young man at the beginning of his career, living alone in one of the world's biggest cities.

Lopez frowned. "After a while, Ernesto changed. He hardly spoke to me anymore and he stayed late at the office almost every night. What happened next, I only learned after he died." Lopez drew a deep breath before going on. "Ernesto figured out someone on our squad sold information to the cartels. Eventually he discovered the mole was

Hector Villalobos, and he told his superiors he would get an arrest warrant for Hector the next day."

Veranda's stomach clenched, knowing what came next.

Lopez gazed into the distance, as if he sought a clue hidden in the past. "Someone must have let Hector know, because that night he killed Ernesto at his desk and burned the office down." His voice dropped to a low rumble. "When I heard, I went to find Lorena, but her house was empty. The whole family, gone. I thought Hector had taken them away and killed them all, but I searched anyway. I had to know."

He took Lorena's hand, a pleading expression etched into the lines of his face as he spoke to her. "Once I realized someone in the highest ranks of my agency had betrayed Ernesto, I knew I couldn't use law enforcement resources to track you down. If you were still alive, Hector would have followed me straight to you.

"Lorena." He squeezed her hand, willing her to understand. "I had to stop searching, but I never forgot about you. Or about Ernesto. I vowed to bring Hector Villalobos to justice." He released his grip and Lorena's fingers slid through his. "Unfortunately, the fire destroyed the evidence Ernesto had gathered against Hector. I had to start over again to build a case against him."

A loud snap caught Veranda's attention and she looked for the source of the noise. His face a mask of thunderous rage, Chuy held two broken halves of a plastic fork in his calloused hand. Dredging up painful memories from the past caused anguish for everyone. She realized Lopez had recounted not only her mother's suffering, but also her aunts' and uncles', including Chuy's father.

"What did Hector do next?" Veranda asked, desperate for every scrap of information Lopez had.

"He left the agency immediately. His days with a badge were over and he knew it." Lopez dragged a hand through his thick, graying hair. "Instead of putting him in jail, I've spent over thirty years watching him grow richer and more powerful."

"How did he manage that?" Veranda was curious whether what she'd heard about Hector's rise to power matched background from Mexican intelligence sources.

Lopez's lip curled. "First, the ruthless *cabrón* butchered his way to the top of the cartel he had sold information to. Next, he married a rival cartel leader's daughter, killed his father-in-law, and took over. Then, he combined the two organizations to create the largest criminal enterprise in the world, and named it after himself—the Villalobos cartel." His voice grew cold. "And he became known as *El Lobo*."

She'd studied the origins of the Villalobos cartel but never interviewed anyone with direct personal knowledge of the history as it unfolded. Lopez's account filled in some blanks.

"There are times I doubt I will ever bring him down," Lopez said quietly. "Even though I am an old man, I haven't retired because I want to see Hector in jail first. But I must face facts." His shoulders drooped, a bleak expression on his careworn face. "That may not happen. So I train Agent Rios." He clapped the younger man on the shoulder. "He will carry on if I cannot."

"Passing the baton to the next generation." Veranda voiced the thought as it surfaced, unbidden, in her mind. "The same thing Hector's doing with Adolfo. Like we talked about in the café at the Hyatt over lunch."

Rios nodded. "That's right, Veranda. And it's the same thing Detective Stark is doing with you."

She recognized the truth in his words. Sam had mentioned he couldn't go into DROP until he felt the next generation was ready to take the reins. She had teased him about it, but now realized he meant *her* specifically. The changing of the guard was something they all had in common.

Lopez leaned forward. "*El Lobo* and others like him have hurt the people of our beautiful country, and now they want to do the same to yours." His eyes, tired a moment ago, gleamed with renewed energy. "It is no coincidence I am here. When I read the news reports about the Villalobos family's actions in Phoenix, I used my seniority to come here and join the task force. I thought this would be my best chance to fight the cartel. For once, I wouldn't have to worry about the Villalobos family interfering with the investigation using police informants or corrupt politicians. That's why I'm here." He turned to Lorena. "*Gracias a dios que te encuentro*. Who would believe I would find you after all this time?"

Lorena dabbed at her eyes with a tissue. "Thank you, Esteban." She had switched back to English as well.

The older agent held her mother's gaze. "Lorena, I have always wondered, what happened that night ... when you ran to the US?"

Every muscle in Veranda's body tensed. Lopez couldn't possibly know the pain his innocent question had caused. He had asked her mother about the worst night of her life. When she became a widow. When she was forced from her home. When Veranda was conceived.

All eyes turned to her mother. Voice thick with emotion, Lorena finally responded. "After he murdered my husband, Hector came to my house. You may remember, my younger brothers and sisters lived with us. But it was late, and everyone was asleep." Lorena spoke haltingly at first, clearly struggling to express herself without revealing too much. "Hector broke in and ... and ... threatened me. My brother Juan woke up from the noise. Hector was ... hurting me, and Juan hit him on the head with a pot from the kitchen." Lorena gripped the tissue with trembling fingers. "Then Hector was lying on the floor, not

163

moving. We stole his car and drove north. Crossing the border was easier in those days. We got as far as Phoenix and settled here." Her eyes drifted to Veranda. "I didn't realize I was pregnant for another two months."

Lopez's mouth fell open, his head whipping around to face Veranda. "But then … you are … Ernesto Hidalgo's daughter!" He looked to Lorena, who nodded in confirmation. He turned back to Veranda. "*Increíble!*" He clasped both of her hands in his, a look of wonder lighting his features. "I am sorry your father died before you ever knew him. He was a great man."

"Yes, he was," Lorena said, a watery smile on her lips. "And she followed his path when she joined the police department. We are all so proud of her, even though we worry about her every day." Her mother glanced from Lopez to Veranda. "She also fights the Villalobos family. You two are much alike."

"I still cannot believe Ernesto had a daughter," Lopez said, letting go of Veranda's hands. "Because of you, he lives on. And you continue his battle." His expressive face held an almost reverent look. "I am honored to know you."

Humiliation burned through Veranda. She couldn't bear the heartfelt emotion in Lopez's eyes or the pure love in her mother's. She was not Ernesto's daughter, and had no right to their admiration. She was the offspring of the man they hated above all others. If they ever learned the truth…

She stood, overwhelmed by the urge to escape.

The mariachi band had switched to a boisterous rumba, and the floor soon filled with gyrating couples. Her thoughts in shambles, Veranda practically bolted from the table toward the pavilion.

Agent Rios, who had also gotten to his feet, caught her arm. "What's the matter?"

164

"Nothing," she shot back. Then, aware she'd spoken too harshly, she smiled up at him. "The conversation got too intense. I just need to think about something else for a while."

"Then may I have this dance?" he asked her in formal Spanish, his penetrating gaze darkening as he bent at the waist and extended his hand.

Caught off guard, her head still swirling with emotions, she nodded. A broad grin dimpled his cheeks as he led her to the stone floor in front of the band. In perfect time with the music, he pulled her against him, then stepped back and spun her in a tight circle. Devoid of thought, she surrendered to the pulsating beat and joined in the sensual dance. His eyes locked with hers as they moved in rhythm, his hand occasionally touching her hip to enhance a spin or sharpen a turn. For a few moments, she let her cares melt away and lost herself in pure movement.

Diaz appeared and seized her free hand, jerking her out of the dance-induced spell as he yanked her away from Rios. "You're supposed to watch her back." He scowled at the younger *federale*. "Not grab her ass."

Rios clenched his teeth and took a step toward Diaz, nostrils flaring.

Veranda shook free of Diaz and stepped between the pair. She stretched her arms out, placing a palm against each man's chest as they squared off. She wasn't in the mood for Latino male bullshit. She didn't care for machismo in general, and certainly refused to tolerate it at Gabby's special party. Rios flirted shamelessly, but Diaz reacted as if he had a right to care. She could sense the undertow and didn't want to get pulled down into the vortex.

"Stop stamping and snorting." She shot them each a withering glare. "This isn't a bull ring. It's my sister's *quinceañera*. Show some respect." She waited for their breathing to normalize before dropping her arms. "I'm going to give my sister her present now." Still fuming over Rios and Diaz, she marched back to the table to find Chuy and Tiffany.

Everyone else had left the table, but her cousin and his girlfriend had remained seated. She squatted down between their chairs. "Can I have the puppy to give to Gabby?"

Tiffany pouted her highly glossed lips, then handed the black shoulder carrier over to Veranda. "We set up a little crate and a big box of toys for him in Gabby's bedroom after she got ready for the party." Tiffany giggled. "Gabby has no idea."

"I can't thank you enough." Veranda glanced at each of them in turn. "This present means the world to me. And to Gabby. I couldn't have pulled it off without you."

She tucked the carrier close to her body and sought out Gabriela. Her sister wasn't hard to find. Surrounded by friends in festive dresses, Gabby looked somewhat subdued. Veranda fought her way through the crowd to reach her.

Veranda took Gabby's small hand and looked at her lovely young face. "I'm so happy for you, *hermanita*. I want to give you your birth-day present now."

"You don't have to give me anything, Veranda. You were there when I needed you most, when I had lost all hope. You saved my life."

The words sank like lead weights in Veranda's stomach. *Only after I endangered it*. She pushed the thought away and forced a smile to her lips. "This is no ordinary present. It's very special. I'm giving you a fierce protector and a friend who needs you. You two can take care of each other."

Gabby furrowed her brows, blinking her confusion.

Veranda reached inside the carrier and lifted the tiny puppy out. Enor-mous brown eyes looked around inquisitively. A black leather collar with

166

silver studs contrasted with the angelic little face. With a measure of relief, Veranda noted Chuy hadn't opted for spikes on the collar.

"Awwww," Gabby cooed. "That's the cutest thing I've ever seen. Can I hold him?"

"Of course, honey. He's yours."

"Mine?" Her sister swept the quivering little dog up and held him to her cheek.

"You've been begging for a puppy for years. *Mamá* finally agreed."

"Why did you say he's a fierce protector? He's so tiny." Gabby laughed. "And he's shaking."

Veranda did her best to look serious. "Don't let his appearance fool you. They may be small, but Chihuahuas are feisty. Size isn't everything. They're proud guardians of their pack."

"But if he ever got into a fight, he'd be—"

Veranda interrupted before her sister could complete the thought. "—barking his head off before the fight even started. No one will get near you without you knowing about it." *Like Bartolo did.* "This guy is your personal alarm system."

Gabby beamed. "He's perfect, Veranda." She gave him a kiss on top of his round head. The dog's tail wagged frantically. "Thank you."

Veranda knew Gabby had understood her message. Fear was insidious. It robbed you of joy, peace, and the strength to face your enemy. Chihuahuas may not win in a fair fight, but they would not cower or back down, no matter the size of the opponent.

Veranda's cell phone vibrated in her purse. She slipped it out and tapped the screen. When Sam's name appeared on the caller ID, she walked toward her mother's house for privacy as she answered the call.

"What is it, Sam?"

His deep baritone sounded harsh. "Commander Webster ordered everyone on the task force to report to the Fusion Center immediately.

Pass it on to Lieutenant Diaz and the *federales*. You guys need to change into your gear before you get over here."

Alarm spiked her pulse. "What happened?"

Sam didn't mince words. "This whole operation just became a clusterfuck."

20

BARRELING DOWN ADAMS STREET, Veranda wove the Tahoe through traffic toward the Fusion Center. Agent Lopez clutched the door handle as she swerved to avoid a petite redheaded reporter in sky-high heels perched in the street next to a satellite truck. Veranda suppressed a groan, recognizing Kiki Lowell, who watched as a white concave dish the size of a manhole cover locked into position on the vehicle's roof.

Veranda spotted Sam, huddled with Commander Webster and someone in uniform, several paces away from the media. She careened into the Fusion Center parking lot, skidded to a stop, swung down from the Tahoe without waiting for her passengers, and stalked over to Sam and Webster. "What's going on? Why aren't we at the Shoot House?"

Webster jerked a thumb in Kiki Lowell's direction. "Someone told that freakin' reporter we're doing a dry run for a series of raids." He paced in a tight circle, gritting his teeth. "I called Hearst out to broker a deal and ordered SAU to meet us here."

When Webster moved, she recognized the uniformed officer as Sergeant Hearst from Public Affairs. Tall and distinguished in his neatly pressed blues, he could be seen regularly on local news channels as the handsome face of the PPD. With his straight white teeth and the perfect amount of silver at the temples of his jet-black hair, he looked camera-ready at all times. He tipped his head to her, pivoted, and strode toward the news van.

The Tahoe's doors slammed shut. Moments later, Lopez and Rios arrived at her side. She turned to the screech of tires as Diaz parked his Chrysler and trotted over to join the group.

She spared them a glance before she reconsidered the problem at hand, directing her question at her commander. "How is that possible?" She refused to believe anyone on the force would provide confidential information to the media. Especially when it could compromise a tactical operation. She knew leaks happened, but the idea of such disloyalty when police lives were on the line infuriated her.

"No clue," Webster said. "Ms. Lowell doesn't have a lot of details. Of course, she won't say how she found out, just said she got a tip that we were meeting here for advance prep."

Veranda clenched her jaw so hard her molars ached. A principled reporter would go to jail rather than reveal a source, but some cops ran their mouths without thinking—one of the things she learned while working undercover. "You think someone on our team looped her in?"

Webster scratched the back of his ear. "Can't rule it out, but I doubt it."

The Public Affairs sergeant broke away from the media crew and reentered the law enforcement huddle.

His face expressionless, she couldn't get a read on Hearst. "What are we supposed to do now?" she asked him. "If Kiki Lowell goes on the air tonight with this dress rehearsal story, both target organizations will bug out, and we'll get *nada* when we go in."

Hearst smoothed the front of his uniform shirt. "I cut her a deal. I can't legally prevent her from reporting what she's heard, or from shooting footage of the SWAT teams gearing up and heading out—as long as she's in a public place when she records the footage." He addressed the commander. "I did the only thing left, sir. I got her to sit on the story."

Webster massaged his temples. "For how long?"

"Until morning." Hearst spread his hands. "Best I could do."

"What?" Her voice sounded shrill to her own ears. "That's no help. We planned this for a couple of weeks from now. The whole point of doing the dry run tonight was to give us time to iron out the kinks before we go live."

"She won't wait two weeks," Sam said, speaking up for the first time since Veranda arrived. "Hell, she won't even wait two days. She's playing hardball. This operation goes down now—or never."

Webster straightened and faced Veranda. "Detective Cruz, this mess began a couple of hours ago. Once I saw how the wind was blowing, I told the detectives on the task force to go ahead and swear out the search warrants."

She closed her eyes for a long moment. Webster's move had started the clock ticking. A signed search warrant had to be served within 72 hours. After that, it was toilet paper.

"This is a full-scale practice exercise, so all the players are here," Webster said. "We'll just move the schedule up and go live tonight. We've already got paper on all the premises and we have an ops plan on file. Dispatch, helicopter, K-9, paramedics, and prisoner transport vehicles are on standby. We just need to divvy up the assignments, gear up, and head out."

She jammed her hands onto her hips. "We could be walking into a buzz saw, Commander. There aren't even UC's doing surveillance on the sites we're going to hit."

She would have positioned undercover narcs to watch the search warrant locations prior to their deployment. The UC detectives would provide current information about who was present and other details critical to their safety when the time came to move in.

"You think I don't know that?" Webster sounded testy. "I had no time thanks to this breaking story."

She flicked a glance at Sam, who nodded in silent accord with their commander. With no other viable options, she accepted the situation with a heavy sigh and motioned toward the Fusion Center. "Is everyone here?"

"Now that you've arrived, yes," Webster said, drawing a deep breath before spitting out the details rapid-fire. "While I went over the operation with the investigating officers and reviewed the warrants, Sergeant Grigg provided a tactical briefing to the SAU operators. We've already notified dispatch and secured a dedicated communication channel. We were only waiting for your group to get here."

Her mind shifted into strategic planning mode. "What's the plan of attack?"

"I went through the locations and personnel list and split everyone into teams. We'll hit a total of fifteen sites. Twelve are associated with the Villalobos cartel and the remaining three are South Side *Soldados* premises. Each address will have a designated team consisting of six SAU officers, one federal agent, and one detective from the PPD. I distributed the rosters to everyone else, and they're interacting with their counterparts on their individual raid teams to enhance communication."

Despite her trepidation, Veranda was impressed. Commander Webster had certainly handled his fair share of large-scale operations. She listened intently as he finished.

"Since we can't do a dress rehearsal, we can't plan for unexpected contingencies. We adjust on the fly."

Webster's idea was sound, and probably the only way to save the situation. But it rankled her that her meticulous planning had come to this. A last-minute scramble without proper preparation. And if it blew up, she would be held responsible.

She turned to Sergeant Hearst, hopeful for one more chance to stop the train before it left the station. "Did you explain to the reporter that her story could ruin our investigation? That both the cartel and the street gang could hide or destroy evidence before we arrive?"

Hearst gave her a wry smile. "The more I explain, the more it verifies her source, and the more leverage it gives her. She can smell our desperation to keep this quiet, and it gives her juice."

A new thought made Veranda's stomach sink. "I'll hate myself for asking, but what does she want in return for keeping this quiet until morning?"

Hearst pointed at the news crew several yards away. "See how they're prepping as if they're filming a live shot? That's part of the negotiation from their end. They're showing us they can break the story any moment if we don't put meat on the table." At everyone's questioning looks, he added, "They have an exclusive at this point, which pressures us to come up with something tempting to offer."

She narrowed her eyes. "I'm not going to like this, am I?"

"We agreed to do a major press conference first thing tomorrow morning. We'll set up tables with seized narcotics, cash, weapons, and any other contraband we snag. We'll include arrest photos and press kits." Hearst spread his hands. "The whole dog and pony show. Chief Tobias already spoke to the mayor, who liked the idea once he understood our predicament."

Unease slid down her spine. "But you just said this reporter has an exclusive. She won't agree to be part of the herd tomorrow morning if she has a scoop tonight. What else did you offer her?"

Hearst hesitated before he met her gaze. "You."

"Excuse me?" Veranda put a hand to her ear. "It's hard to hear over the sound of the revving engine."

Hearst's brows arched. "What are you talking about? The sat truck is idling."

She dropped her hand to her hip. "It's not the news van. I'm talking about the bus you just threw me under." She leaned forward and got in his personal space. "Right before you stepped on the gas."

Sam stifled a laugh, Webster became interested in his cell phone, and the two *federales* exchanged nervous glances.

"That was Kiki Lowell's price," Hearst said, his face reddening. "She wants an exclusive one-on-one with you immediately after the presser."

Veranda crossed her arms. "No. Fucking. Way."

Hearst drew himself up to his full height. "Detective, you're the lead on this task force, and this entire multiple warrant service was your idea, so I'll put it to you. Would you rather scrap the entire operation, or complete it now and talk to the reporter in the morning?"

She wanted to throttle the sergeant. The fact that he was right only fueled her temper. "I don't have much of a choice, do I?"

Sam's dark brows drew together. "You play the hand you're dealt, Veranda." A hint of irritation edged his voice as he turned a cold glare on Hearst. "And sometimes, you've got shit for cards."

21

FIVE MINUTES LATER, VERANDA pushed open the inner door to the
Fusion Center and breathed in the pre-op chaos. Others might find it
hectic, but she thrived on the industrious turmoil. Packed with personnel, the cavernous room buzzed with activity. Screens flickered on
tabletops, phones beeped, and black-clad SWAT operators pointed at
oversized maps taped to the walls as they slurped steaming coffee
from Styrofoam cups.

Glad she'd changed into tactical gear at her mother's house, she
blended seamlessly into the group as she strode to the far corner of
the room. Commander Webster, Lieutenant Diaz, Sam, and the *federales* followed in her wake. Mind still on her confrontation with Sergeant Hearst, she crashed headlong into a solid black wall in her path.
She stopped short and looked up.

Sergeant Grigg towered over her, head-to-toe body armor making
him appear even more gargantuan than usual. "Better get your head

in the game, Cruz." His rugged face twisted into a wry grin. "Or at least, pull it out of your ass."

She returned his smile. "Speaking of my ass ... why don't you pucker up, Grigg?"

Grigg guffawed and held a sheet of paper out to her. "The entry teams are listed by radio call-sign order."

She took the page and found her name near the top. Sergeant Grigg, five other SAU tactical personnel and the two FBI agents were listed under her name, forming one of fifteen entry teams. She assumed the two FBI agents were together because Tanner was new. The other Feds were dispersed among the teams. "How were these groups assigned?"

Agent Gates had walked up behind her. "I requested your team because I want to be on a high-value target. I reviewed recent activity reports with one of your vice detectives this morning while you were gone. This address looks like our best chance at Carlos Villalobos."

She wasn't sure if she detected a slight note of judgment in the senior FBI agent's tone, or if her own guilt about taking personal time during an important assignment colored her perception. Gates continued, pulling her back to the discussion.

"Two weeks ago, a dealer your PPD narcs arrested tried to work off his charges by providing the location of a brothel he claimed was run by Carlos. The informant said he witnessed Carlos inside the premises. It's a single-family home rented under a false name. Undercover detectives did surveillance there last week and confirmed the intel." Gates included her junior partner, who had appeared next to her, in her comment. "We believe Carlos will be there in person."

Veranda would have preferred to locate Adolfo, but he'd dropped from her radar recently. Still, Carlos made a good second choice. The search warrant could get them inside to look for human trafficking victims. If they found Carlos on scene, they could take him into custody, along with any of his coyotes or clients, and begin the interrogation process. The youngest Villalobos son brought a lot of cash to the cartel with prostitution rings. His coyotes smuggled workers into the US and weapons back to Mexico, doubling their profits on each run and fueling bloody wars south of the border. Shutting down that portion of the operation would not only save lives, it would seriously choke the cartel's income stream. She understood why Gates wanted to be at that address, but she had concerns about Tanner. She doubted he'd ever been on a raid before.

Veranda leaned in close and whispered to Gates. "Just keep a tight leash on your partner. I better not see Tanner with his FBI raid jacket on perp-walking Carlos in front of the cameras."

Gates gave Veranda a discreet nod.

Commander Webster raised a hand to get everyone's attention and the general chatter died out. "Has everyone received your assignments and met with your teams?"

He waited for heads to bob in agreement. "And each team has a hard copy of the search warrant for their assigned location?"

After nods all around, Webster continued. "Every warrant is no-knock, so SAU operators will make dynamic entry with the investigators immediately following them in." He jerked a thumb behind him at a digital wall clock set to military time hanging behind him. "Synchronize your watches with that clock. Simultaneous execution will occur at exactly twenty-one-hundred hours. That should give each team time to check equipment, load up, get to the location, deploy discreetly, and observe the premises for a short period of time. Some of you have longer to travel than others. Are there any final questions or issues?"

A voice called from the back, "What's our frequency?

"Channel one is dedicated to this op," Webster said. "Anything else?"

Silence.

"Then let's go."

Everyone began filing out through main door toward the parking lot.

Sergeant Grigg leaned down to her ear, speaking in an undertone. "Lucky us. We got the junior G-man."

She snorted. "Don't get me started. Just do me a favor. If Tanner tries to pry Carlos out of my cuffs, shoot him a little."

Grigg grinned. "I'll make it look like an AD."

"No good. No one would buy an accidental discharge coming from you. You'll have to think of something else to keep the Feebs from taking my prisoner." She grew serious. "All kidding aside, I want Carlos. I want him bad."

A dark scowl replaced Grigg's easy smile. "I've read the reports on that asshole and his human trafficking ring." His eyes hardened. "You and the FBI can fight over his carcass when I'm finished with him."

She appreciated the sentiment. Sergeant Grigg was a pro. He wouldn't use excessive force, but he wouldn't go out of his way to be gentle with a man in the sex slave trade. One of many things she liked about Grigg. She inclined her head toward him in tacit approval and continued to the parking lot. "At least the news van is gone. Which one is our ride?"

Grigg pointed to his right. "The BearCat. She's a beauty, right?"

"More like a beast." The midnight blue urban assault vehicle was straight out of a combat zone. She gaped up at Grigg. "People in the 'hood where we're going will shit themselves when they see this bitch coming down the street."

Grigg waved a dismissive hand. "We're not going to pull up at the driveway in front of the target address. We'll be ... what did the commander say?" He tapped his chin with a gloved index finger. "Discreet."

He winked as one of his men heaved the rear bay doors open and walked around to hoist himself into the cab in the driver's seat.

"Sure. This thing screams 'discreet.'" She rolled her eyes and climbed into the back. Four SAU members followed her. Gates and Tanner clambered inside next. Grigg hauled himself in last, banging the doors shut and taking the last seat on a thick metal bench soldered to the interior wall.

The monstrous twin-turbo diesel engine roared to life, its guttural growl thrumming through her body. As they bumped along, she checked her weapon, fitted an earpiece on, and tightened the elastic band holding her ponytail. The SWAT team pulled balaclavas over their heads before donning black helmets and goggles.

She assessed the row of tactical officers, ending with Grigg, all geared up and mission-ready. She shook her head. "They'll need to change their *chonies* after you and your band of merry men burst in."

She couldn't see Grigg's grin, but the corners of his blue eyes crinkled behind his goggles.

In the confines of the armored vehicle, she lost all sense of time. Without windows, the sense of motion rising from the floorboards under her feet was her only source of orientation. No one spoke, everyone seemingly going through a mental checklist for the final time.

When the vehicle stopped, Grigg's voice carried through her earpiece. "We're on scene." He opened the hatch and she scrambled out with the others. The sun had set, but it wasn't quite pitch dark.

She checked her watch. "We have time to get in position and watch the house for a few minutes." She squinted to see the target location several doors down. The modest two-story detached Craftsman occupied a secluded lot off a cul-de-sac at the end of the street.

Grigg pointed over his shoulder, indicating they should get behind him. "Form a line. We need to move to our recon site. I'm on point."

She sized up the SAU operators, aware the largest person would sometimes go in first during a dynamic entry to provide tactical as well as psychological advantages for the team. She figured Grigg had opted to use his overwhelming physical presence as an immediate deterrence.

The sergeant continued to give orders through her earpiece. "Brinkowski will take rear guard. I want the detectives and agents just ahead of him."

This made sense to her. Five of the SWAT operators would enter first to clear the premises. The sixth would watch their backs for anyone who might come out from hiding to attack from behind as they went through. Agents and detectives, who weren't tactically trained and equipped, would have the most protected positions.

They got in line with the sergeant in the lead and made their way toward the target house in its deep-set lot surrounded by mesquite and palo verde trees. The dense foliage hid their progress as they moved in unison, like a giant centipede, to the side wall of the house. Once in position, each person in line used their non-weapon hand to grip the shoulder of the person in front of them and waited for the cue.

Veranda heard nothing coming from inside the house but figured they couldn't possibly be asleep this early. A sense of foreboding cascaded through her as the moments stretched.

Finally, Grigg raised his hand in a silent signal to make entry. Weapon in low-ready position, she waited for Brinkowski, at the rear, to confirm he was set to go by squeezing her shoulder. After an interminable second, she felt his gloved fingers press down hard. She mashed Agent Tanner's shoulder and knew each person would repeat the motion up the line. Every muscle in her body tensed, waiting for the moment when Grigg felt the tightening of the hand resting on his shoulder and raced forward.

Time, which to Veranda had been frozen, slammed into high speed. She moved her feet quickly, taking short, rapid steps to stay in formation. They whipped around the corner to the front door and two SWAT operators peeled off to take positions on each side of the entrance. A third smashed a battering ram into the door directly below the knob.

The door flew back on its hinges and crashed against the interior wall. Sergeant Grigg's wide shoulders filled the doorway as he barreled inside. The officer breaching the door laid the battering ram down and joined in the stream of team members charging into the house yelling, "Police! Don't move!"

Guns drawn, Veranda, Gates, and Tanner trotted forward with the tactical personnel in rapid search formation, calling out "Clear!" with each room they checked.

Every time Veranda heard the word, her apprehension grew. Something wasn't right. The sound of their boots thumping against the floor echoed off bare walls. Where was the furniture? The clothing? Any sign of life at all? The place had an abandoned air.

They finished clearing the house and gathered in the living room. In the oppressive silence, all eyes swiveled in her direction.

This couldn't be happening. "We had good intel," she said, attempting to keep the pleading note from her voice. "They must have just left."

"Obviously," Tanner said, his tone acerbic.

She raised a hand to her earpiece to secure it more firmly in place before pressing the transmit button on her portable radio. Enough time had gone by for other teams to begin reporting in. As the task force leader, she should give the first update.

"Adam team is ten-four," she said into the mic. "Subjects GOA. Repeat, subjects are gone on arrival. Target location is empty."

A moment later, Sam's baritone rumbled through her earpiece. "Bravo team. Same traffic. Subjects GOA. Target location empty."

Another raid site with a deserted building.

"Charles team. Subjects GOA. Target location empty."

"David team. Same traffic."

"Edward team. Same traffic."

Each response thundered in her ears. The sense of dread coalesced into a tight knot in her belly.

"Frank team. Nine in custody. Large cache of weapons and narcotics on scene."

The knot loosened as relief washed over her. The mission wasn't a complete failure. She tugged a folded page out of a concealed flap in her ballistic vest. She checked the paper and found the assignment for the Frank team. It was one of the three SSS locations.

"George team. Twelve in custody. Narcotics located."

Another SSS location. Sweat beaded at her hairline, prickling her scalp.

"Henry team. Seven in custody. Narcotics located."

The third and final SSS address. Her heart quickened as she waited for the next report.

"India team. Subjects GOA. Target location empty."

"John team. Subjects GOA. Target location empty."

"King team. Same traffic."

"Lincoln team. Same traffic."

Her stomach plummeted as the Mary, Nora, and Ocean teams reported the same results. Every single Villalobos location had been empty. Only the SSS sites had been successfully raided.

Realization hit her like a punch to the solar plexus. In a matter of hours, she had disposed of the cartel's adversaries, giving them undisputed control of her city. She had done the work of the Villalobos family for them.

Nice going, Cruz.

22

AT EIGHT THE FOLLOWING morning, Veranda's eyes traveled over the array of weaponry on the long table positioned at the back of the PPD headquarters media briefing room. Neat rows of rifles, pistols, revolvers, improvised explosives, and exotic edged weapons covered the table's wood-laminate surface. Tagged with evidence cards, they lay beside packages of heroin, marijuana, and cocaine wrapped in tight plastic bundles of varying sizes.

The Public Affairs Bureau had gone all out for the news conference, which had just gotten underway. Chief Tobias stood at a lectern on the dais fielding questions, while she and other members of the task force lined the stage behind him.

During the pre-conference briefing in the greenroom an hour earlier, Sergeant Hearst told her the press kits he would distribute to the media covered only the positive points. The packets of information emphasized the quantity of contraband seized and number of arrests made during the operation, without mentioning any empty locations.

Hearst had looked like he'd been chewing antacids all morning. Still irritated the Public Affairs sergeant had offered her up on a platter, Veranda had little sympathy for his gastrointestinal distress.

A familiar voice drew her attention back to the present, and she spotted Kiki Lowell shouting to be heard over the din. Scores of media representatives jockeyed for position in the limited space, each vying for the chief's attention. Shorter than the others, Kiki jumped in place and waved an arm in a wide arc, almost hitting one of her colleagues with the notebook clutched in her hand. "Why are you calling Operation Scorpion Sting a success?"

Chief Tobias pointed at her to acknowledge the question before responding. "Because we arrested twenty-eight people and will be filing additional charges shortly. What's more, we seized hundreds of kilos of illegal narcotics and took over four dozen weapons off the street. I'd call that a good day."

Apparently not satisfied, Kiki followed up. "Every person listed in the news release you provided is with the SSS gang. There are no Villalobos cartel arrests." She glanced at the notebook she held. "Not one."

Veranda cut her eyes to Hearst, who stood ramrod straight in the back corner of the room next to the display tables. His face flushed and he patted his pockets, no doubt searching for another antacid.

Chief Tobias shifted uncomfortably behind the bank of microphones. "We've seriously crippled a criminal gang operating in Phoenix. Not every police action is a total success, but we made good progress and the investigation is far from over. There will be more to come."

Veranda recognized the tactic. Tobias was trying a different shade of lipstick on the proverbial pig.

A network television reporter with a tailored gray suit, Day-Glo white teeth, and overly gelled hair seemed to scent blood in the water and surfaced to take a bite. "As you just stated, you crippled one of two criminal organizations. The other was left completely untouched. Do you see this as a victory for the Villalobos cartel?"

Standing behind him, she could see the back of the chief's neck redden as he answered. "No. I do not."

"I have a follow-up," hair gel said. "Shutting down the SSS gang gave the cartel a clear field. Since the Phoenix Police Department led this operation and it appears to have backfired, are there plans to turn the investigation over to the FBI or the DEA?"

Tobias squared his shoulders. "No."

Another shark swam toward the chum, shouting his question at Tobias. "Will you change leadership on the task force?"

Veranda sucked in a breath. Her reckoning had come. The warrant service had been her idea. She owned it. And she was definitely the most junior detective in Homicide. She waited for the axe to fall.

Tobias straightened. His response consisted of one terse word: "No."

She let out a relieved breath. The chief would give her another chance. When she heard her name, thoughts of gratitude dissipated.

"Do you believe this situation occurred because of Detective Cruz's lack of experience in Homicide?"

From her position at his back, she studied her chief's posture and body language. He'd switched to short, sharp answers as the reporters lobbed questions at him. This one, however, made it personal. About her.

After a slight pause, Tobias spoke slowly and clearly, enunciating the word: "No."

The cold cereal Veranda had eaten for breakfast churned in her stomach. Under heavy fire from the media, the chief stood up for her.

Tobias had gone on record supporting her actions, and would now be associated directly with any outcome, good or bad. Another public disaster on this scale could push him into an early retirement. He had cast his lot with hers.

Chief Tobias raised his hands to stave off further questions. "That concludes our news conference. Details about the operation are in your press kits. Sergeant Hearst from Public Affairs will be available later today for further clarification."

Tobias stepped aside to join Mayor Benitez, who had opened the event and introduced the chief. The pair strode out amid a barrage of questions from reporters.

She filed out behind them along with the rest of the task force. Everyone remained silent until the heavy double doors of the greenroom adjacent to the media briefing room swung shut, cutting off the din.

Lines of fatigue imprinted every face. After last night's operation, the task force had come together to catalog each item of evidence from the SSS raids. Meanwhile, narcotics detectives from the PPD Drug Enforcement Bureau and Federal DEA agents interrogated arrestees for information about their supply line from Colombia.

She'd been up half the night, only going home for a few hours of fitful sleep before putting on a black pantsuit and picking up Agents Lopez and Rios on her way to headquarters.

Starting before sunrise, everyone had pitched in to prepare display tables for the news conference. Sergeant Hearst hoped a visual sign of progress against the drug gang would divert attention away from a complete lack of arrests involving the cartel. The strategy hadn't lasted ten minutes into the conference before Kiki Lowell started asking pointed questions.

Veranda thought back to her conversation with Chief Tobias in his office on the fourth floor earlier that morning. When she explained about the lopsided arrest tally, he'd taken the news stoically. Everyone knew the significance of the shutdown of only one side of the equation, but no one could figure out how it had happened.

Now she looked around the greenroom and prepared for the inevitable recriminations to begin.

Hearst opened the door and slipped inside to join them, his handsome face uncharacteristically haggard. "We called local news outlets yesterday evening to put a calendar hold on their schedules for this morning, but we didn't tell them why." He addressed Tobias. "Chief, those reporters couldn't have known we were holding a news conference about an operation involving the gang war."

"Maybe they guessed," Sam said. "This is the only Phoenix news story getting national attention right now."

Agent Gates leveled an angry gaze at Hearst. "Do you think the media leaked info about the news conference and Adolfo Villalobos put two and two together?" She threw her hands in the air. "How else would the cartel have known to clear out?"

"Not a chance," Hearst said without hesitation. "I know how reporters think, and they'd never leak info before the takedown. They'd lose their sources, their credentials, and their story."

Diaz shifted, wariness crossing his darkly stubbled face. "Do we have another mole on the department?"

The room grew silent. The unspoken suspicion had lurked beneath the surface all night, and now her lieutenant had dredged it up in the light of day.

She recalled the spy she'd discovered in their midst six weeks ago. The cartel, known for cultivating informants inside law enforcement agencies south of the border, had managed to turn someone on the PPD. The department still reeled from the effects of the subterfuge, even though the mole was gone.

The mere idea of a second traitor heated her blood. "Impossible." She kept her voice calm despite her fury. "I refuse to believe one of our people would ever do that again."

Agent Lopez threw her a pitying look. "I have seen too much to be shocked by anything involving *El Lobo* and his cartel."

Chief Tobias cleared his throat, breaking the tension. "Detective Cruz, we need answers. Mayor Benitez and I are backing you, but we won't be able to do so much longer if we can't determine how the cartel got wind of the raids and escaped the dragnet."

Her pulse quickened. The chief had now tied the mayor's political future as well as his own to the success of her investigation. No pressure. "I'll get to the bottom of it." She had no idea how. "But in the meantime, I want to devote our resources exclusively to the cartel investigation."

Commander Webster spoke up. "You have homicide cases involving the SSS gang to work."

Diaz interjected before she could mount an argument. "Every case where an SSS gang member is a perpetrator is closed, Commander. All suspects have been murdered, arrested, or refused to cooperate. We could intensify our work on the cartel without hindering our progress."

She couldn't fathom what Diaz was up to, but she'd take support anywhere she could get it. Slogging through lengthy SSS homicide investigations would take time from her main focus.

"I'll bring it up if no one else will," Agent Tanner said. "That reporter had a point. Perhaps it's not a bad idea to consider a change of leadership on the task force."

The room crackled with tension. The junior FBI agent had spoken out of turn, managing to insult both the police chief and the lead detective on the task force at the same time.

Gates raised her voice to cover whatever Tanner was about to say next. "Chief Tobias already publicly rejected that suggestion." She shot her subordinate a look clearly designed to silence him. "Besides, it would send the wrong message."

"There's something you need to understand about how we operate in Phoenix." Sam's gray eyes skewered Tanner. "We don't change horses midstream."

Marci stepped directly into Tanner's personal space, tilting her face up to his. "You want to be in charge?"

Tanner stepped back. "We're strictly in a support role." He spoke quickly. "The FBI didn't call the shots on this operation, which violates our standard procedures, by the way."

Sam's face darkened. "We would've had more time for proper procedure if someone hadn't seen fit to tip off that reporter."

A light rap sounded on the greenroom door.

"Speak of the devil," Sergeant Hearst said, turning to Veranda. "That will be one of my staff escorting Kiki Lowell here for your one-on-one interview."

Lieutenant Diaz interrupted the awkward silence, addressing members of the task force. "Everyone except Cruz, get down to the Fusion Center, put your heads together, and come up with a new plan. Dismissed."

She watched her team leave. Tension formed a line of knots along her spine as she stayed behind, a sacrificial offering to Kiki Lowell, who knew way too many secrets. If she could turn the tables, she would ask three questions. First, how did Kiki find out about the operation in advance? Second, how did she know the cartel search warrants yielded nothing? And finally, who the hell was her source?

23

Villalobos family compound, Mexico

A WARM RUSH FLOODED through Adolfo when his father stood and raised his crystal champagne flute. Struggling to identify the strange sensation in his body, he got to his feet. With a jolt of shock, he realized what he felt was … pride.

Chatter in the room died, every eye on *El Lobo* as his resonant voice echoed through the expansive dining hall. "A toast to Adolfo. In one stroke, he put our rival out of business, took control of Phoenix, and humiliated Detective Veranda Cruz."

He noted his father used formal Spanish. Hector Villalobos frequently used elegant speech to distance himself from his impoverished childhood in the barrios of Mexico City. The ornate surroundings reinforced the message that he had far exceeded his early circumstances.

The richly upholstered chairs scraped back from the long dining table, their occupants rising to lift glasses. "Adolfo." The name chorused around the room, which Hector had designed in classic European style. Three multi-tiered sparkling chandeliers cast a diffuse glow on tremendous oil paintings adorning the walls. The largest art piece was a full-sized portrait of his father, dressed in his customary white Armani suit and peering regally down his angular nose. The claw-footed table, decorated with intricate marquetry and draped in crisp snowy linen, seated eighteen. The meal, a luncheon, was presented with the pomp and circumstance of a royal dinner.

"I must admit," Hector said, pausing to sip the bubbling liquid in his flute, "Adolfo's cunning surprised me."

The champagne turned bitter on his tongue. His father's compliment couched an insult. *El Lobo* hadn't believed his firstborn son capable of turning an unforeseen predicament to his advantage.

When he observed the other guests, the ill-concealed scorn on Salazar's face told him he'd read the subtext perfectly. His brother and sister already knew of his father's ambivalence toward him, but the sight of so many people at the table hearing it for themselves undermined any authority he'd hoped to gain from his victory.

Hector resumed his seat and waited for the others to follow suit before he continued. "While we wait for dessert, I'd like an update from each of you. I'll start with Adolfo." His father's penetrating gaze found him. "What are your future plans?"

He emphasized the morning's success. "Detective Cruz has only felt the first cut. She'll shed more blood before I'm finished. She—"

Hector held up a hand, silencing him. "We will talk about Detective Cruz later." His father's voice dropped to a low rumble. "In private."

Senses alerted, he scrutinized his father for signs of trouble. Unlike other men, *El Lobo* grew quieter when angered. Now he saw tautness around his father's mouth, a slight flaring of his nostrils, and an almost imperceptible narrowing of the eyes. Someone who didn't know Hector extremely well would miss the telltale markers of cold rage. What had gone wrong?

Stomach churning with dread, Adolfo quickly recalibrated his report. "Our new base is up and running. We only had a small window of time to move yesterday, so we had to temporarily consolidate all operations at our emergency backup location. An abandoned warehouse in West Phoenix. Law enforcement cannot trace it back to us."

"What about revenue?" Hector asked.

Adolfo swallowed hard, hoping the droplets of perspiration gathering along his hairline wouldn't trickle down his face. "We're converting part of the space into individual rooms to be used by Carlos's stable of women. For now, we'll keep our outside customers to a minimum so authorities won't find us before we're ready to decentralize again."

Hector nodded, his gaze moving down the table. "Carlos?"

His younger brother straightened. "As Adolfo said, we're remodeling the new location so I can get my women working full-time again. They're cooking, cleaning, and servicing the men while we wait." He hesitated, as if considering whether to broach a delicate subject. "One of the girls had to be punished, but she's compliant now."

Adolfo directed a quelling look at Carlos. Didn't the fool know he should never discuss internal problems in front of the guests? Then he glanced at Salazar and realized his father had probably already heard all about the branding from his inside man.

As if to confirm his suspicions, Hector didn't press for details. Instead, he raised an eyebrow at his daughter. "What do you have to report, Daria?"

Daria, who had been observing the byplay between her older brothers with a calculating expression on her lovely features, eyed her father. "I've increased production of armor-piercing ammunition. Our last gunfight with police in Mexico City was much more successful than before." She tucked a loose strand of hair behind a delicate ear. "The rounds are expensive to produce, but my last distributor had no trouble finding buyers. Profits are strong, and I'm reinvesting back into production to supply our own personnel."

"Excellent," Hector said. "The police upgraded their body armor, so we need rounds with better penetration." He turned to his left. "Salazar?"

Tension snaked through the room as everyone waited for Salazar to speak. His words often spelled doom for an underperforming cartel member. No one wanted to be the subject of his report.

Salazar's sensuous mouth curved into an enigmatic smile. "I have nothing to add to the report I gave you earlier."

Adolfo's blood froze in his veins. What had Salazar told his father in private? He exchanged glances with Carlos and Daria, who appeared equally confused.

El Lobo looked pleased. "Ah yes, we'll get to that later. Dessert is here."

Two waiters in black tailcoats entered the dining room, bearing silver salvers with small dessert plates. As they carefully placed each plate in front of a dinner guest, they rotated the dish to display a perfectly formed flan topped with fresh strawberries. Crimson sauce dripped down the side of the flesh-colored tartlet to puddle on the bone china dish.

Adolfo curled his lip, wondering if his father had ordered the chef to make their final course resemble a crime scene. Nerves frayed, he picked up his dessert fork and hesitated. His father dug into his flan and swiped it through the strawberry sauce before placing it into his mouth and closing his eyes briefly.

"Please continue to enjoy," Hector said, dabbing his mouth with a linen napkin before he launched into a speech. "It's been a long time since we've all gathered in person." He swept a hand out to encompass his assembled guests. "I invited you here to celebrate Adolfo's success and to get a direct report from each of you." He tilted his chin at the far end of the table. "Some of you have never been here before. When I made introductions at the beginning of our luncheon, you may have noticed that each person here heads part of the Villalobos family business. Indeed, everyone at this table bears the tattoo of the black wolf over their heart, symbolizing loyalty. You have all become wealthy under my rule, and I always keep abreast of developments to ensure our continued success."

Adolfo slowly laid his fork down. His father's flowery speeches often preceded appalling brutality. The more elevated the language, the more profane the act.

El Lobo turned his dark gaze to a slender man seated near the far end of the table. "Delgado, your report?"

Adolfo had never met Delgado, who was second-in-command of the largest Villalobos grow operation in Colombia.

Adams apple bobbing, Delgado swallowed audibly before he responded. "Our farms have had record harvests since Señor Salazar arrived five years ago." He flicked a glance at Salazar, who inclined his head in acknowledgment.

Delgado resumed his report to Hector. "We haven't had interference from law enforcement or rival growers in the region since he left last week. No one knows Señor Salazar is gone yet, but we're prepared to defend ourselves when word gets out."

Adolfo noticed all eyes at the table covertly sliding to Salazar. Their gazes held respect bordering on awe. *El Matador*'s reputation alone suppressed potential threats when he was present, and his absence invited attack. Adolfo seethed. He was Adolfo Villalobos, firstborn son of *El Lobo*. All of the men should turn to *him* with admiration, not an outsider.

As his temper subsided from a full boil down to a simmer, a question crossed his mind. Jaime Cortez was in charge of the largest Colombia grow operation, not Delgado. "Where is Cortez?" he asked his father.

"Cortez couldn't make it to our luncheon," Hector said, his expression giving nothing away. "But I'm sure we will see him again soon."

Before Adolfo could fully identify the sinking feeling in his stomach, his father turned to the next man at the table. "Carrera?"

Adolfo listened in silence as the other men gave their reports on their areas of responsibility for the cartel. Instinct told him Salazar and his father shared a secret. He had to figure out what it was.

As soon as the last person provided an update, Hector stood. "Let us adjourn to the bullring."

Carlos and Daria exchanged excited glances, but Adolfo's gut roiled. His father referred to the private stadium adjacent to the main mansion, which resembled arenas where the blood sport took place, but on a smaller scale.

Adolfo trailed behind the others in their tuxedos, wondering what today's horrific spectacle would be. The entire entourage traipsed through the compound in silence until they arrived at a mammoth set of oak doors with wrought iron bars and hinges. Two burly guards hauled them open and the group followed Hector into the stadium. The click of their dress shoes echoed from the concrete floor as they made their way to the tiered rows of seats. The arena could hold over a hundred people, but he'd rarely seen more than forty spectators attending one of his father's events.

Hector led them to the front row where he settled in his custom gold-plated chair, trimmed in black leather, situated to face the center of the ring. Their seats were directly in front of a dirt-covered arena floor that included a raised stage. After everyone sat, Hector pressed a button on his right armrest.

A curtain on stage right raised to reveal an iron cage the size of a single-car garage. Inside, an immense black wolf paced the length of the enclosure. Ebony fur bristling, slavering lips curled back to reveal enormous fangs, the creature turned amber eyes toward them and snarled.

Hector beamed. *"Diablo* is my favorite pet. We normally feed him every other day, but he has not eaten for a week. And he is ravenous." He pointed at the drooling beast. "Look at his nose."

Ears flat against his head, the wolf's snout twitched as he lifted his head to scent the air. His red tongue swept his muzzle, leaving glistening strands of saliva behind.

Hector scooted forward to the edge of his seat. "I believe he smells the fear of his prey." He pressed another button and a second curtain on stage left went up to reveal an identical metal cage. This one, however, held a naked man.

"Shit," Adolfo muttered under his breath. "Cortez."

"Jaime Cortez," Hector announced, loud enough for everyone, including Cortez, to hear. "Salazar transferred supervision of the crops over to him when he left Colombia to come here. The next day, Cortez decided to expand his income by selling some of his crop to our enemy. The very enemy Salazar had worked for years to crush."

Cortez shrieked a denial of the charges leveled against him. Hector paused briefly, then continued as if the man hadn't spoken. "Because of his greed, Cortez's wife and children no longer live in a fine house. They work sixteen hours a day in the fields, and he is about to meet *Diablo*."

"Please, Señor Villalobos," Cortez pleaded, changing tactics from denial to contrition. "I will never betray you again." His hands grasped the bars, which began sinking into the floor of the stage below him. In seconds, the cage around him vanished.

Hector pressed another button. "I am quite sure you won't." This time, the cage around the wolf began its descent.

As the wolf's bars lowered, Cortez jumped off the stage, legs pumping as he hit the sandy stadium ground. A futile act of desperation.

"Fight or flight." Hector sounded like a behavioral scientist observing a field study. "At its most basic, the human mind will react in certain ways when faced with mortal peril." He stroked his goatee. "Unfortunately, running from a hungry predator only further stimulates its natural prey drive."

As soon as the bars of its cage sank low enough to clear with a leap, the wolf bounded after Cortez. The animal leaped onto the man's back, claws and fangs gouging into bare flesh. Cortez let out a sustained bleat of agony as the ferocious wolf brought him down, his face thudding into the dusty ground at the center of the bullring. Cortez rolled over, using his hands in a fruitless effort to fend off the attack. Incisors tore the man's throat apart, and his head lolled as blood spewed from the ragged wound.

Gorge rising, Adolfo turned his head, unable to watch the carnage. His gaze fell on the other spectators, where he noted the excited gleam in his younger brother's eyes, the sadistic smile on his sister's lips, and the implacable resolve in Salazar's expression. The rest of the guests gaped in abject horror. Delgado, Cortez's second-in-command, leaned over and vomited.

Over Cortez's death throes and *Diablo*'s low growls as he lay atop his prey to feed, Hector addressed the spectators. "Jaime Cortez chose unwisely. Both he and his family paid the price. Go back and tell your workers what you have seen today." He pointed at Delgado, who swiped a trembling palm across his mouth. "José Delgado, you are now in charge of my grow operation in Colombia."

Hector waited while Delgado retched with a fresh wave of nausea. Satisfied he had regained everyone's attention, he turned to the others. "Adolfo, Carlos, Daria, and Salazar, join me in my office. The rest of you will stay here until *Diablo* has eaten his fill. You must remember every detail when you tell the story."

Hector strode from the stadium. Anxiety growing, Adolfo trudged behind him. The small group reentered the main residential building and wound through the halls in silence until they reached the mahogany double doors leading into *El Lobo*'s private office. As the butler bowed them inside, Carlos slid his cell phone out of his pocket and tapped the screen.

"Excuse me," Carlos said to his father. "It's marked urgent. Better take this."

"Certainly, *mi'jo*. Business first."

Carlos put the phone to his ear and switched to English. "What is it, Nacho?"

Adolfo's apprehension grew. Why was his man reporting to Carlos? When he fished his cell phone out of his pocket and tapped the screen, his mouth went dry. Nine missed calls from Nacho. *Dammit.* He'd muted the device instead of putting it on vibrate, as Carlos must have done. Now he could only stand by helplessly to find out what emergency had prompted the repeated calls.

Hector marched to the ornate conference table at the far side of the elegant room. He took his customary seat at the head of the table. Sick with tension Adolfo sat to his right while Daria slid into the seat on his left. Salazar sauntered to the table to sit at Bartolo's unoccupied chair. Red-faced, Carlos stalked in and parked himself next to his sister.

Again, he wondered at Salazar's inclusion in the group. Previously, only family members were permitted in the inner sanctum but, since Bartolo's death, Salazar had been intruding where he didn't belong. He couldn't fathom his father's reasoning, but he knew it didn't bode well for him.

"We can speak freely now," Hector began. "I didn't want the others to hear our discussion about Phoenix. It doesn't concern them." He cut his eyes to Carlos. "Nacho's phone call upset you. What's going on? And why isn't Nacho reporting to Adolfo?"

Adolfo silently cursed himself. "I accidentally put my phone on mute." He despised the pleading note in his voice. "I apologize for my mistake."

Daria let out a contemptuous snort. Salazar shook his head in disgust.

Hector sighed heavily and turned back to Carlos. "What did Nacho tell you?"

"It's those motherfucking girls again." Carlos's fist clenched. "The smart one, Sofia, helps us monitor the task force's cell phones and emails. We need her because we don't have enough men with advanced computer skills. She's Nacho's only tech support and we can't risk him missing something if we take her offline." He dragged a hand through his thick curls. "After she tried to trick us about the warrant locations, Salazar punished her twin sister with a branding iron."

Hector gave Salazar an approving nod. "I heard."

"Only Sofia didn't learn her lesson after all." Carlos flattened his palm on the table and leaned forward. "Nacho just told me the little *puta* tried to send Detective Cruz an encrypted message through her email."

Adolfo's heart slammed inside his chest. "Did Nacho catch it in time?"

"Barely." All traces of his characteristic good humor gone, Carlos met his anxious gaze. "And Nacho double-checked to be sure this was her first attempt. We're still good."

"What did she try to tell the detective?" Salazar asked, his voice perfectly calm, as if he had inquired about the weather.

"That we've hacked their phones and emails and we're tracking their movements through GPS." Carlos threw up his hands. "She also tried to send her the coordinates of our new location, which has all our property and personnel. We'd have been fucked if that message had gone through."

Hector's response was low and full of menace. "Do you still need her?"

"Yes," Carlos and Adolfo answered in unison.

Their father drummed the table with his fingers, a rare display of agitation. "Besides her twin sister, does she have any other family with her at your location?"

"Her mother," Carlos said. "You recall she brought both of her daughters here a few weeks ago."

A calculating gleam in his pitiless eyes, Hector looked at Adolfo and Carlos in turn. "As soon as you return to Phoenix, gather the three of them together in front of everyone in a central space at your new location. Force them to say goodbye to each other, then have one of your men take the twin you don't need out into the desert and kill her. Make it ... memorable. Bring back pictures of the body to put on her sister's computer. Tell the girl her mother will be next." He shifted his gaze to the foot of the table. "And Salazar ... "

"Yes, sir?"

"Brand the mother while everyone watches. We don't want rebellion to spread."

Salazar nodded.

"A final question for you, *mi'jo*," Hector said, swiveling his chair to confront Adolfo. "Why is Veranda Cruz still alive?"

Caught off guard, he reeled at the abrupt change in subject and scrambled to formulate a response. "There's one more piece to put in place for my plan to work. I need a little more time."

His father sneered. "This is taking too long. I'm done waiting." A heavy silence settled over the room before he continued. "Salazar will execute Detective Cruz as soon as you all fly back to Phoenix this evening."

Adolfo envisioned his plans and dreams shattering. *El Lobo* had said Adolfo could never become heir apparent to the Villalobos empire until he personally killed Veranda Cruz. He looked at his father. "You promised that job to me."

"That was before," Hector said. "You may still take your place as my second if your plan succeeds, but it will be Salazar who finishes her." Adolfo opened his mouth to plead his case, but his father held up a hand. "I have my reasons."

"Please give me just one more night." He reflected on his carefully laid plan. If he made some adjustments, he could accelerate the timetable and still make it work. "Salazar can kill her tomorrow. What difference can a few hours make?"

His father's salt-and-pepper brows drew together. "That is my question to you."

"The difference is in how law enforcement will respond to her death." He tried to exude confidence. "I want the task force to disband, not simply change its mission to finding Detective Cruz's killer."

"That's why Salazar will do it," Hector said. "He knows how to deal with police."

Realization dawned. Unlike the Villalobos children, Salazar was expendable. Perhaps Hector wanted to insulate his own flesh and blood from the risk of a death sentence for murdering a police officer in the US.

"Speaking of Salazar," Daria said, cutting through his tangle of thoughts. "Carlos told me Detective Cruz and some other cops chased him through a hotel in downtown Phoenix. They'll know he's in town now, so he's blown his cover." She gave Salazar a smug smile. "In fact, it will be harder for him to cross the border since he's on every watch list."

Hector frowned at his daughter. "Salazar acted on my orders. Thanks to him, I know I'm dealing with an old enemy now."

Adolfo straightened. "What enemy?" He ached to learn what secret his father had shared with Salazar.

"Agent Esteban Lopez with the Ministerial Federal Police." Hector's face clouded. "He's harassed me for decades. Back when the agency was called the Federal Judicial Police, Lopez came to my unit when that *cabrón*, Ernesto Hidalgo, got promoted. After I left the force to pursue … other options, I tried to recruit Lopez to inform for me. I needed information from law enforcement. But Lopez idolized Hidalgo."

Hector shook his head and let out a humorless laugh. "The bastard actually had the *cojones* to try to arrest me. I barely got away. Ever since, he's used every resource to interfere with my business. I haven't bothered to kill him because I have no trouble working around him. But now he's getting involved at a higher level, and I may change my mind."

"Will you have Agent Lopez killed?" Carlos asked.

"I'll deal with Lopez when he returns to Mexico, but first, we have a more pressing problem. And Salazar can solve it."

Salazar smoothed his lapel in a way that forcibly reminded Adolfo of his father. When he spoke, Salazar's tone was perfectly modulated. Just like the man himself. "I will do it tonight when we return to Phoenix. I'll make it look like an accident."

Adolfo had to speak before his father answered. His plans for Detective Cruz hinged on one more piece falling into place. He appealed to family bonds. "*Papá*, given the circumstances, the police won't be fooled. They'll spend weeks sniffing around until they catch a whiff of foul play."

Salazar spread his hands. "Then I will make her disappear."

He vied for control of the discussion. This was his chance, and he wouldn't pass it to Salazar. "We're talking about the United States." He turned from his father to Salazar. "Whatever you may have gotten away with before, you can't just make American police officials disappear without bringing on a substantial manhunt. Especially when they're leading a high-profile task force. Your usual tricks won't work." He injected a bit of condescension as he finished. "I have a better way."

Hector leaned back, steepling his fingers. "And what is that?"

He realized any plan would have to include Salazar to gain his father's approval, so he adjusted his strategy as he went. "Salazar will be involved. In fact, he plays a critical part." He hazarded a glance at Daria and Carlos before turning back to his father. "We'll leave for Phoenix within the hour. Salazar has to come on the plane with us, there's no time to send him overland using the coyotes. He'll have to go in disguise with a fresh identity. Once we land, I'll get everything in place for tonight."

Hector touched his tented fingertips to the point of his goatee as the silence stretched. Adolfo could sense him weighing his need for revenge against his desire for his firstborn son to prove himself ready to lead.

Finally Hector appeared to come to a decision. "Give me the specifics."

"I want you to trust me." Adolfo imbued every syllable with as much determination as he could muster.

"As I told you before," Hector said, cold steel beneath his soft tone, "you will never be the head of the family empire while Detective Cruz breathes."

Again, his fate intertwined with that of Veranda Cruz.

She'd cost his family the life of his brother Bartolo and millions in intercepted drug shipments. Now her very existence threatened his honor and his future. Bitter resentment heated his blood. He would drag the *puta* to her knees, publicly humiliating her before taking her life. But first, he had to convince *El Lobo*, not known for his patience, to wait a bit longer.

He squared his shoulders and met his father's fathomless eyes. "You saw what I did with the task force's raids. Will you trust me with this task as well?" Getting no response, he plowed on. "I promise you three things."

He held up his index finger. "Tonight will be the worst night of Veranda Cruz's life."

Another finger went up. "Tomorrow she will be dead."

He raised a third finger. "And no one—not the police, not her family, not the public—will give a shit."

24

STILL FUMING FROM HER interview with Kiki Lowell, Veranda marched into the Fusion Center searching for Sam. She wanted to vent, and he was her confidant. Her mentor. Her partner. She scanned the room. Without SAU and the other tactical personnel, the quiet hum of activity filled the mostly empty space. A handful of detectives hovered near their stations. No one from her task force was in sight.

Perplexed, she asked one of the nearby computer forensics investigators where she could find Sam.

The pale detective tore his eyes away from his computer screen to blink at up at her. "He's in the break room with the Homicide squad, the Feds, and the muckety-mucks. I heard shouting." He grimaced, turning back to his work. "Not going anywhere near there."

She left the main area and traversed a short hallway toward a makeshift cantina in the back of the building. She heard Sam's resonant baritone before she got within ten yards of the doorway. Giving in to curiosity, she stopped in the hall to listen.

"That's where you're wrong," Sam said. "We have serious resources here right now. We've got to keep up the pressure."

"But the stated purpose of Operation Scorpion Sting was to end the gang war," Agent Gates said, sounding exasperated. "And it's over now. There's no war when only one side is left. We should stand down the Fusion Center immediately."

Veranda's anger from her interview with the reporter morphed into humiliation. She was responsible for the partial failure of the operation... and the total success of the Villalobos family. Thanks to the operation, Adolfo had no competition in Phoenix, the cartel's US distribution hub.

"And what message would that send?" Marci's question dripped sarcasm. "That we're okay with a Mexican drug cartel running Phoenix?"

Agent Tanner's retort carried down the hall. "Isn't that what they've been doing for years?"

Everyone shouted at once, and she couldn't make out any particular words, other than some choice expletives. If the young FBI agent was correct, she'd already lost the battle. Maybe even the war. She gritted her teeth and forced her racing thoughts to stop. She would retrench, find a new strategy, and forge ahead.

Still standing outside the door, she recognized DEA Agent Craig Wallace's voice. "Look, we're at a disadvantage now, that's all. I've worked with Detective Cruz when she was in the Drug Enforcement Bureau. She won't let a setback stop her. Let's hear what her next plan is before we throw in the towel."

"Who decides when we're finished here?" Tanner asked.

"Do you two have someplace else you need to be?" Irritation sharpened Sam's tone. "Because I'm sure we can manage without the FBI."

"We're staying," Gates said. "But how long can our Mexican counterparts continue with us?"

Agent Lopez's slightly accented words were forceful. "We were not given a time limit. We can stay as long as the Fusion Center is open."

Agent Flag from Homeland chimed in. "Same here."

Not wanting to eavesdrop any longer, Veranda let her shoes strike the tiled floor loudly the rest of the way down the hall and through the open break room door. Everyone turned.

"Detective Cruz." Agent Gates's overenthusiastic greeting had the air of someone who had been talking behind her back. "How did your interview go?"

"Fabulous." Veranda scowled. "The reporter promised I'd be the lead story at five. She seemed genuinely shocked I wasn't overjoyed about it."

Sam looked sympathetic. "We were…discussing our next move. Now you're here, I'm sure we all want to hear your thoughts."

She lifted her chin. "We sink our teeth into the Villalobos cartel. We've got them on the run. Now we'll press our advantage. If we can keep them off balance, they're more likely to screw up."

"I agree," Lieutenant Diaz said. "But how?"

"Everyone not directly involved in the SSS investigations will gather intel. Adolfo Villalobos needs money, so he'll have to bring in some product to sell. The suspected brothel locations run by Carlos were also empty, so we'll try to find out what happened to his women. They'll probably have to advertise for new clientele in the sex trade underground."

Meeting several skeptical expressions, she spoke from her experience in narcotics enforcement. "Bottom line is they can't run the cartel in a vacuum. Money is their lifeblood, and they need customers to get it. Whether it's dope, sex, guns, or gambling, they've got to get the word out." She clapped her hands together. "That's their weak point, so that's what we target."

Gates quirked a brow. "This sounds like a routine organized crime case, not an investigation in need of a Fusion Center and full-time task force."

"Let's give it some time." Tim Fitzhugh from the US Marshal's Office eyed Veranda as he spoke to Gates. "If we don't gain any traction, we'll know soon enough."

Diaz addressed the team. "The chief and mayor have expressed their support of Detective Cruz. She stays in charge of the investigation until further notice." He added with a note of finality, "We'll follow her lead."

She looked at his chiseled profile, unsure why her lieutenant had been so uncharacteristically willing to take her side.

Tanner snorted. "Because that's been working so well."

Tony Sanchez from her Homicide squad got in Tanner's face. "If you weren't a federal agent, I'd punch you in the mouth."

Marci's upper lip curled into a sneer. "I think I'll do it anyway."

"Enough," Diaz said, stepping between his detectives and the agents. "We're on the same side." He rested a hand on his hip and blew out a sigh. "No one got much sleep last night and we're all tired. I'm ordering everyone to go home, see your families, eat something, rest."

He called out to the group as they turned to leave. "All of you will report to the lounge in the Hyatt Regency downtown at nineteen hundred hours this evening. That's not a request."

She had no idea what her supervisor was up to, and she read confusion on the faces of her companions as well. She looked at Diaz over her shoulder. "Why?"

"We'll do a little team-building. Relax and unwind together. Then we come in first thing tomorrow morning and start fresh—working as a cohesive unit." He paused for emphasis. "No more bickering."

Now she understood. Management 101. Create an opportunity to bond on neutral turf in a social setting. As she walked out, she doubted any amount of socializing would bring the group together.

25

VERANDA INHALED THE SCENT of fresh cilantro garnishing the *menudo* as she gently laid the paper bowl on the card table and sat down next to Sam. "I have this nagging feeling we're missing something. The cartel is always one step ahead of us."

She had invited her partner to share a quick bite at the family food truck before going to their respective homes for some rest prior to Diaz's mandatory love-in downtown. Anxious to share her concerns, she needed a private moment to confide in her most trusted ally.

"Let's talk it through." Sam scouted the other card tables scattered throughout the restaurant parking lot. None of the other customers paid them any attention. "What was the first sign of trouble?"

She paused to consider, spooning a bit of fragrant red broth into her mouth. "When Roberto Bernal took out Castillo before we could meet."

Sam nodded. "There's no way they should've known that meeting was even happening, much less when and where."

"Exactly." The tripe and garlic from her mother's *menudo* churned in her stomach as she forced herself to confront the truth. "I didn't want to admit it back at the Fusion Center, but the evidence does point to a leak." When Sam offered no response, she leaned toward him and voiced her worst fear. "The traitor would have to be on our department because the Feds weren't involved in the investigation when the Castillo shooting went down."

Sam pushed his half-finished plate of enchiladas away. "What else?"

"The cartel knew about the search warrants ahead of time. Sergeant Hearst and the others from Public Affairs don't think so, but what if Adolfo was the one who tipped off that reporter about the op?"

"Why would he do that?" He quirked a brow. "It would shorten the amount of time he had to relocate."

"Hear me out." A glimmer of understanding floated just out of sight, like an indistinct shape drifting in a heavy fog. "Adolfo's in charge, so I need to think like him. He wants to take over the family empire someday. He's the eldest son, but no one takes him seriously. He's viewed as weak by rival cartels and even by his own family." Her words quickened as her thoughts coalesced. "But I don't believe he's weak at all. He's brainy. Doesn't like to get his hands bloody, but thinks tactically, like his father."

"So he has some sort of strategy that's getting the cartel ahead of us."

"Yes." Her confidence grew as she mulled it over. "But what strategy could it be? Adolfo's stealthy. He never leaves fingerprints."

Sam rubbed the back of his neck. "None of your insight matters if you can't figure out how he's getting the inside track on our investigations."

"You're right." Her shoulders slumped. "Without a mole, how would he know what we're up to?"

They lapsed into silence.

"Listening devices?" she offered with a half-hearted shrug.

Sam shook his head. "Techs swept the Fusion Center before we moved in. And there's no way they could plant bugs at HQ."

"I'm grasping at straws here." She spooned up a slice of onion from the *menudo*. "It's frustrating when I don't have enough information to get the full picture."

Her mother and her *tío* Rico stepped down the retractable folding steps from the food truck. Sam waved them over. "Rico, what do you put in these *frijoles* to make them taste so good?"

He grinned. "Lard."

Sam clutched his chest. "Oh hell, I can feel my arteries clogging now. Wish I hadn't asked."

Grateful he'd lightened the mood, Veranda teased her partner. "Don't worry about the lard. I have relatives who are over a hundred years old, and they eat this food every day."

"Must be my *gringo* genes. I'd be huge if I ate like this all the time."

"It is not your genes." Veranda's mother leaned down conspiratorially. "I will tell you our family secret."

Sam's eyebrows shot up. "I'll bite, what is it?"

Lorena stood tall as if delivering a proclamation. "Stop eating as soon as you are satisfied, but before you are full." She drew her brows together. "Do not look at me that way, Detective Stark, I speak the truth." She swept a hand out to encompass herself and her brother. "We are about your age, and we are healthy." She shrugged. "We also work sixteen hours a day, mostly on our feet."

Sam scooped up some beans with his fork, holding them at eye level. "Okay, so you make this food so delicious it's more addictive than crack, then you tell me I have to push away from the table?"

Lorena flushed at the compliment to her cooking. "Yes, you do."

Veranda tilted her head as she considered Sam. "I don't know why you're worrying, Sam. You're in great shape. Especially for a man of your advanced years. Hell, you could be in a Geritol commercial."

Sam shifted his gaze to Lorena. "Do you know your daughter shows no respect for her elders?"

Lorena chuckled softly. "I know my daughter not only respects you, but likes you very much. I can tell by how much she teases you."

Tío Rico nodded. "It is the way of our family. We tease the ones we love, the others we ignore. They are not worth our time."

Sam stroked his mustache as if giving the matter deep thought. "So I should be flattered by her digs about my age because it means she thinks I'm all that and a bag of tortillas."

Lorena laughed. "Exactly, Detective."

Veranda gave them a sardonic look. "You three go ahead and talk about me like I'm not even here."

Sam spread his hands. "Hey, I'll take any opportunity to get dirt on my partner, especially if she's taking shots at me." He smiled. "But I'm not ignoring you. In fact, I'll answer your comment about my physical condition." He indicated his body. "I have a secret to keeping this dapper appearance."

She widened her eyes and leaned forward. "Fly fishing? Walker races? No wait, what is it the old people do in the park at sunrise? Oh yeah, Tai Chi?" Her impishness was rewarded when Sam gave her a rare laugh.

"Yoga. I do a minimum of twenty minutes every day, and my wife and I go to classes three times a week.

He had caught her by surprise. "Sam Stark, grizzled Homicide detective, in yoga pants and a tank top?"

"You can do yoga in your skivvies, you don't need fancy clothes." He glanced up at Lorena and Rico again. "You see what I mean?"

"I see appreciation and friendship in her eyes when she looks at you," Lorena said. "You are very special to her."

She let her mother's words speak for her.

When Sam turned back to her, his gray eyes had softened. "I suppose I'll keep her as my partner. Don't know who else could handle the abuse."

Veranda, uncomfortable with overt displays of sentiment, changed the subject back to safer territory. "Speaking of fitness, I'm heading to the gym this afternoon for some therapeutic kickboxing. Nothing like beating the crap out of Jake to relax me." She tapped her chin, thinking about her instructor. "Of course, this could be one of those days he beats the crap out of me."

"*Ay, mi'jita.*" Tío Rico rolled his eyes. "Only you could relax by fighting."

Lorena shifted her weight, jutting out a hip. "This is why my oldest daughter has no husband." She jabbed a finger at Veranda. "And why I still have no grandchildren."

"*Mamá*, I told you. I'll settle down when I'm ready. I have … things to do first."

"Yes, yes, I know." Her mother crossed herself. "That horrible Villalobos cartel."

Like an evil incantation, the mention of the name cast a pall over the group, dissipating all traces of humor from their conversation.

Guilt tugged at her and she lowered her gaze. "Someone has to stop them."

"Let it be someone else." Lorena's gentle hazel eyes grew moist. "Look at Agent Esteban Lopez. I remember when he was a young man. So shy and kind. He made to fight against Hector, and you see what happened? More than thirty years later, he is still trying to arrest him. And all that time, Hector has grown stronger and richer." Her voice trembled. "It is because Hector is … is … evil."

She heard the fear in her mother's voice and wanted to take it away. "No *Mamá*, it's because Hector finds ways to cheat justice."

"I am so scared for you, Veranda." Lorena gave her a watery smile. "But I'm also proud."

She was taken aback. "Proud?"

Lorena nodded. "What you said about Hector is true. But I know he cheats justice by killing those who stand in his way. He has no mercy. No soul." Lorena had switched to Spanish, something she would never normally do around Sam. Veranda waited for her mother's next words, aware she would have a compelling reason to exclude someone from a conversation.

Her mother cupped Veranda's chin. "That is how I know you are truly Ernesto Hidalgo's daughter. No child of Hector Villalobos could act with honor as you do. My heart overflows when I see you because I know Ernesto is still alive inside you, my daughter."

Tears spilled down Lorena's cheeks as she finished speaking. She pulled Veranda up from her chair and into a tight embrace.

As she hugged her mother, the tainted blood rushing through her veins boiled hot with shame. Her mother didn't know about the DNA test, and had come to believe Veranda was Ernesto's daughter.

She saw the sparkle in her mother's eyes as she looked at her with a heart full of love. And knew her mother must never find out the truth.

VERANDA HADN'T SEEN FIT to dress up for her outing with the team at the Hyatt. After coming home from the gym and showering, she'd thrown on blue jeans and a red stretchy T-shirt. Choosing comfort over style, she'd completed the outfit with her favorite shoes, black tactical boots. Not as stylish as Marci's Manolo Blahniks, but she wasn't out to impress. Her muscles ached and she would have fresh bruises tomorrow, but the kickboxing session with Jake had left her physically exhausted and mentally drained. Exactly what she needed.

When she first arrived in the Hyatt lounge, Diaz had tried to grab the seat next to hers, but Marci beat him to the spot, an ingenuous smile on her bright red lips that deceived no one. Sam sat to her other side, and she stifled her laughter at the comment he muttered under his breath for her benefit.

Surrounded by her Homicide squad for the past half hour, Veranda had scarcely spoken to the Federal agents at the other end of the long row of high-top bar tables. She pushed the half-empty glass across the glossy black-lacquered tabletop. "That's a phenomenal prickly pear margarita, Marci, but I'd better not finish it. Still have to drive home."

Tony swigged his beer and banged it down next to hers with a loud *thunk*. "You could always get a room here." He craned his neck to take in the swanky bar area. "Hell, we could all get smashed and get a room."

Marci sidled closer to him and placed her martini glass next to his pilsner. "This place is a bit high rent for you, Tony." Her voice dropped to a soft purr. "There aren't any hookers in the lobby and they don't rent rooms by the hour."

Veranda chuckled. Marci and Tony loved to spar. It occurred to her that many cops enjoyed banter when among their own. Probably a side effect of the job. Constant exposure to the worst humanity had to offer caused an odd comradery that included dark humor and permitted only the most oblique compliments.

"Why are you always busting my balls, Marci?" Tony exaggerated his Brooklyn accent and tried to look offended, but he couldn't hide his amusement.

Marci looked over the length of his body. "As Stormin' Norman Schwarzkopf used to say, you 'present a target-rich environment.'"

Everyone at Veranda's end of their section joined in the laughter.

Doc returned from the bar clutching a beer. "What did I miss?"

"Some good-natured ribbing," Sam said. "We're supposed to be relaxing, remember?"

Tony rolled his eyes. "Lieutenant Diaz referred to this little gathering as 'team-building.'" He sketched air quotes. "But I call it blowing off steam after a fucking fiasco of a day."

Veranda agreed. She still felt the sting of the tense exchange at the Fusion Center that morning. Her Homicide squad had defended her while others in the break room, especially Tanner, the junior FBI agent, questioned her tactics, her leadership, and ultimately, her competence. Self-recrimination had gnawed at her all day.

Their mandatory get-together in the Hyatt lounge had started off well enough, despite the separation between the PPD and the Feds. Lieutenant Diaz, Sergeant Jackson, and the Mexican agents seemed to be trying to bridge the gap, sitting at a bar table between the two groups.

DEA Agent Wallace's words carried to Veranda above the background murmur of conversation as he spoke to his fellow Feds. "I've been part of both types of operations, and this one's too critical to take it slow." He rubbed the fine stubble on his shaved head with the palm of his hand. "There's a body count and the public is demanding results. They want to know someone from the Villalobos cartel is going to prison."

Tanner grew animated. "But the immediate battle will stop now because the turf war is over, thanks to Detective Cruz." His tone held judgment. "There's only one side left now, right?"

At the mention of her name, she slid off her barstool and sauntered down the row of tables to the Feds. If they were going to talk about her, they would damn well do it to her face. The Homicide squad trailed her.

"Problem is," Wallace said as they approached, "taking down a major criminal enterprise leaves a vacuum. And somebody's always ready to fill the void." Ice clinked in his glass as he tilted it. "Somebody worse. That's how the largest cartels formed. Cobbled together from what was left of organizations we took down over the years."

Agent Flag from Homeland addressed the group, which now included the entire task force. "The same is true of governments.

Whenever a despot falls, there's a violent struggle for power, and often someone worse ends up in charge."

Agent Gates crossed her arms. "So we should leave Hector Villalobos to run his empire?"

Sam raised his whiskey in mock salute. "Sure. We'll leave *El Lobo* to it." He let out a derisive snort. "Please."

Wallace held up a calming hand. "It's true about the power vacuum, but I'm not saying we give up. Exactly the opposite. We need to maintain constant pressure on the cartel ... keeping in mind our actions will have unintended consequences." He cut his eyes to Veranda. "Like what happened this morning."

She held his gaze. *"El Lobo* uses spies, and he murders or terrorizes anyone who gets in his way. He's taught his children to do the same from the time they were born." She put a hand on her hip. "And I'll be damned if I'm going to let Adolfo run Phoenix the way Hector runs every place else."

Agent Rios inserted himself into the discussion. "The cartel already has a hold on parts of Mexico." He exchanged a knowing look with Lopez. "Trust us. You should stop them before they gain more power in the US."

Marci tipped her head toward him. "My thoughts exactly."

Lopez appeared to weigh his words, then drew in a deep breath. "Do all of you know the expression, *plata o plomo?*"

Veranda and some of the others nodded, while the rest looked nonplussed.

Lopez's grip tightened around the glass of bourbon in his hand. "When a cartel recruits someone to work for them, they ask, '*Plata o plomo?*' In English, it means, 'silver or lead.'"

His eyes hardened and, for the first time, Veranda discerned icy determination behind Lopez's warm exterior. "More than thirty years ago, *El Lobo* approached me with an offer. I could take his money or take his bullet."

Tension suffused the room as she waited with the others for Lopez to continue.

"Right after Ernesto Hidalgo's funeral, I left the graveside and went home. Hector was waiting for me. I walked into my apartment to find him alone, in the dark, sitting in my favorite chair." Lopez shook his head. "I am sure he waited for that moment to approach me. He must have thought seeing the man I loved like a brother murdered would make me afraid. But Hector was wrong." He looked directly at Veranda. "I told him to go to hell."

Aware Agent Lopez believed Ernesto was her father, she sucked in a breath. Heart pounding, she listened in silence as he continued.

"I attacked Hector and we fought like animals. I would have killed him with my bare hands, but he pulled out a knife." Lopez unbuttoned his cuff and rolled up his shirtsleeve, revealing two jagged scars from wrist to elbow. "I have marks like these all over my body." His mouth twisted. "I locked my gun in my car before coming up to my apartment—a mistake I have never made since."

"Fuck," Tony breathed, summing up Veranda's feelings.

"I woke up later in a hospital bed. To this day, I do not know why Hector spared my life." He opened his hands, palms up. "Perhaps he thought I would change my mind and come to him out of fear, or maybe he had other plans for me." He shrugged. "I didn't care. I went in to headquarters the next day and got warrants to arrest Hector." Lopez lowered his eyes. "Not that it mattered. He is still free. Still powerful. Still rich with possessions. But he knows he will never own me." His voice dropped to an almost imperceptible whisper. "I would rather take his bullet."

Her phone buzzed in her pocket, breaking the spell. She pulled it out and glanced at the screen. CAPT. COLE ANDERSON, PFD. She tapped the icon and heard the strain in his husky voice. "Can we talk?"

She turned her back to the others and walked to an empty corner of the room. "What is it, Cole?"

"I saw a clip of the press conference on television this morning. You made national news." She waited through a long pause before he finished. "I've had it with this whole task force thing."

"What's that supposed to mean?" Nerves already frayed, she heard the bite in her tone.

"You led multiple raids against a street gang and a drug cartel. You were directly in the line of fire. How am I supposed to deal with that on a regular basis?"

After the recriminations she'd endured all day, Cole's overprotectiveness was the last straw. "You want a woman who will stay at home in the kitchen?" She didn't hide her anger. "I'm not that woman, Cole, and you knew that before we got involved. Don't ask me to change who I am."

"Dammit, Veranda, I'm on your side."

"Yeah, I'm overwhelmed by your support."

"Can we talk this out when I get back?"

"I have a splitting headache from too much talking already." She noticed Marci next to her and ended the argument. "Goodbye, Cole." She disconnected.

"Judging by the way you ended that call with your fireman boyfriend," Marci said, "he's acting like an ass."

Too exhausted to put on a front, she went with the truth. "I went five rounds kickboxing with Jake this afternoon, and that conversation hit me harder than any punch." She closed her eyes for a long moment.

Marci stepped closer. "Have I ever told you why I took up karate, Veranda?"

"Actually, you haven't."

"I learned to defend myself because people refused to accept me for who I am." Marci raised her chin. "I was a teenager when I realized I was a lesbian. Didn't make me popular in high school, especially because I don't fit the stereotype. The other kids thought a girly-girl who likes makeup and fashion had to be into boys. A few of the jocks thought I was playing hard-to-get. So when I turned them down for dates, a couple of them decided to force the issue."

"*Ay, dios mío*, Marci, that's horrible." She pictured Marci as a lovely teen girl, alone, terrified, subjected to a ruthless attack. Her heart lurched.

"Get that look off your face. I'm not telling you this to get your sympathy. In fact, if I detect the slightest trace of pity, I'll kick your ass so hard you'll think Jake was giving you a gentle massage."

Veranda held up her hands in surrender. "Okay, it's a no-pity zone. But you wouldn't be telling me this without a good reason."

"Exactly." Marci pointed at her. "People will always judge you without knowing all the facts. Whether it's personally or professionally, they will second-guess you every step of the way." She narrowed her eyes. "Get used to it, Cruz."

Marci couldn't have known how close to home her story had hit. Acceptance was the core issue. Would Cole accept her job? Would the task force accept her as leader? From the deep well of thoughts she preferred not to examine too closely, a question bubbled to the surface: Would her mother accept her if she knew the truth?

Agent Rios came up beside her. "Everything okay?"

Completely drained and in no mood for polite conversation, she said, "I'm out of here."

Lieutenant Diaz materialized at her other side. "I can drive you home."

Rios touched her elbow with his fingertips. "You can stay in our room here if you're not comfortable driving." After an awkward pause he added, "There's an extra bed."

Diaz looked over her head, directing a venomous glare at the younger *federale*. "No way in hell am I going to let that happen."

"She doesn't need help from either of you." Sam had joined the group. "She's fine to drive home. Only had half a drink." He glowered at Diaz and Rios in turn. "You two need to dial it back."

"I've had it." Veranda jammed a wad of cash into Sam's hand. "That should cover the margarita." She leaned around him to give the rest of the team a quick wave. "See you all tomorrow morning at the Fusion Center." The sound of Rios and Diaz's raised voices carried to her ears as she stalked out without another word.

Driving the short distance to her house, she replayed her short argument with Cole. She knew he'd prefer her to be in a less dangerous line of work. In moments alone together, he'd made his stance on relationships clear. If they got serious, especially if they had children, he would expect her to stay home. The idea of a traditional happy family life felt so abstract that she couldn't decide how she felt about that.

She swung into her driveway and parked the Tahoe in the carport. Opening the rear hatch, she tugged out her black nylon tactical bag. Shoulders aching after her session at the gym, she hoisted the duffel and wearily trudged to the front door. As soon as she twisted the knob and pulled, an alert tone sounded. Once the door was opened, she had fifteen seconds to deactivate the alarm before it began to wail.

She felt a vibration at her waist and shifted her bag to her other arm to yank out her cell phone. She glanced down. UNKNOWN NUMBER appeared on the small screen. Wrinkling her brow, she touched the display as she slipped inside her house and began to enter the alarm code on the wall panel.

"Detective Cruz, Homicide," she said automatically, scrunching her shoulder to trap the phone under her ear so she could speak while she finished tapping in the code.

Silence.

"Hello?"

Nothing.

"Damn." Figuring she'd inadvertently disconnected the call as she juggled the bag and deactivated the alarm, she snatched the phone from her shoulder and bent her head to peer at the screen while she stood in the open doorway.

Weary and distracted by her bag, the alarm code, and the phone call, she was a gazelle mindlessly grazing on the savannah. She did not hear the predator stalking, smell his musky scent, or see his form silently emerge behind her.

Two hundred pounds of savage male slammed into her at full force, knocking her to the floor inside her living room. The phone flew from her hand and skittered away into the kitchen. Her duffel hit the carpet by her feet as she landed on her stomach with a thud. Before she could react, a strong hand grabbed a fistful of her hair and yanked her head around, flipping her onto her back.

Winded and stunned, she struggled to marshal her thoughts. Realization hit her with the force of another blow. The phone call had been a setup, distracting her until she entered her alarm code. Someone had ambushed her. But who? She blinked rapidly as her nightmare came to life.

Salazar's feral eyes bored into hers as he pushed himself into a kneeling position astride her hips, pinning her arms against her sides with his knees. His hands free, he pulled a slim black case out of a cargo pocket on the side of his pants, dug into it, and removed a syringe.

She opened her mouth and shouted. "Hel—!"

Salazar silenced her instantly with a powerful open-handed slap to the side of her head. She recognized the technique. A palm-strike to the temple, properly delivered, was nonlethal but left the victim disoriented for up to a full minute. Bright spots burst in front of her eyes and her vision swam.

Fight! her kickboxing coach's voice echoed in her head. She commanded her lethargic body to react, but Salazar's full weight rested over her abdomen, and his knees completely immobilized her arms, limiting her options. She struggled to draw her legs up, hoping to buck him off. A malicious grin lit his face as he leaned forward, lowering the length of his body down to cover hers. When he shifted position, her arms were freed for a split second. Taking full advantage, she made a fist and aimed for the bridge of his nose. With expert timing, he angled his head and her knuckles smashed into his rock-hard jaw instead. She readied her other hand but, lying on her back directly underneath him, she didn't have enough space to throw a decent punch.

His strong hand, encased in a black leather glove, shot out and clutched her fist, squeezing it until she arched her back in pain. Still reeling from the blow to her temple, she formed a claw with her free hand in a desperate attempt to gouge his eyes. He dropped the needle and caught her wrist before she reached his face.

A part of her mind remembered Salazar had extensive military training and could counteract her strikes. If he'd researched her background, he knew she'd been taught to fight as well, and had devised a way to catch her off guard. The element of surprise served him well. He had her at a complete disadvantage.

She felt his muscles ripple with tension as he dragged both of her arms above her head. She struggled to pull free, but he jammed her wrists together, wrapping one large hand around both of them with bone-crushing force. Now he had effectively restrained her, with one hand free to pick up the dropped needle.

She considered screaming again. Someone might hear beyond the partly open front door. Then she dismissed the idea. He would use his free hand to knock her unconscious this time, and she couldn't allow that. She had to stay alert and wait for another opportunity to strike.

They both heaved ragged breaths for a moment, then he brought one gloved hand down to caress her face. He trailed his fingers languidly down her jawline to the side of her neck. His lips curved into a smile as he pressed his fingertips on the spot where her pulse raced. She felt the smooth leather covering his thumb as he slid it over to encircle the front of her throat.

She read his intention in an instant. Compressing her carotid arteries and pinching off her airway would render her unconscious in a matter of seconds. If he continued to constrict the flow long enough, she would die. If he released the pressure, she would regain consciousness quickly, but he would have several seconds to inject her with whatever was in that syringe.

Rage seethed through her. She fought savagely, twisting her body, writhing under his solid weight.

His fingers pushed down harder and he lowered his head until she could feel his hot breath against her lips. "You are at my mercy now," he whispered in heavily accented English.

She gnashed her teeth and thrashed with all her remaining strength.

His final words drifted to her ears as her vision constricted to a pinprick and darkness engulfed her completely.

"Too bad for you ... I have none."

27

SALAZAR INHALED THE INTOXICATING scent of feminine fear. The instinctive fight for survival always left a residual trace his nose could detect if he was close enough to his prey. Their intimate position, with the length of his body pressed down on hers, gave him a particularly potent rush. She had been a worthy adversary, but he had won, and now she would pay the price for her failure.

After her struggles subsided, he released his hold on her neck and reached out to pluck the syringe from the carpeted floor. He had to hurry. She would come around soon now that blood was flowing unrestricted to her brain again.

Reaching down to tug the leg of her blue jeans up from her boots, he exposed her smooth calf. He jammed the sharp point of the needle deep into her muscle and pressed the plunger down. She moaned and her eyes fluttered open.

Returning his gaze to her face, he pulled out the syringe and waited. Her pupils dilated and her body slackened as the customized ketamine-based cocktail rushed into her system. She would be fully compliant within seconds. Planting his hands on either side of her, he pushed himself up to his feet, went to the front door, and looked outside. Reassured no one had heard the brief scream before he silenced her, he shut the door.

He slid his phone out, tapped a saved number, and spoke in his native tongue. "I'm ready." He disconnected and squatted next to the woman. After regarding her for a moment, he leaned forward, grasped the hem of the fitted red shirt near her waist, and yanked it over her lolling head.

He tossed the garment to the floor and reached toward her again when a light rap on the door interrupted him. He opened it to Omar, who held a leather satchel.

Salazar searched the immediate area for a place to restrain her. His gaze settled on the kitchen table. Well-lit. Good height. It would do.

When he removed her bra, he caught Omar staring. "We have work to do." He jerked his chin toward the kitchen. "Put your bag on the counter and help me carry her to that table. We'll turn on the light and you can get a good look before we get started."

Wordlessly, Omar put the satchel down and came back to the living room. Salazar grasped the woman's limp form under her shoulders, gloved fingers digging into her armpits as he lifted her. Omar wrapped his hands around the ankles of her boots and straightened.

Hanging between the two men, she groaned. He backed toward the table and hoisted her onto its hard surface.

Omar released her legs and stepped back to turn the overhead light on. "She's fucking hot," he said.

He agreed. Veranda Cruz was indeed a lovely woman. Stripped to the waist, her supple caramel skin and silky black hair glistened in the harsh light. But he had to keep Omar on task. Admiring their captive wasn't on the agenda.

"She's out of it, but not unconscious. Can still react to pain, even though she won't feel much."

He ran a thumb and forefinger along his goatee as he scrutinized her. She must have no visible signs of restraint, although it appeared fresh bruises were blooming all over her upper body. He'd learned she kickboxed during his research, and the GPS tracker showed her at the gym this afternoon, which would play perfectly into his plans. Any marks from their scuffle would be written off as sparring injuries. He continued to peruse her body. Her boots would cushion her ankles from rope burns, but the soft skin of her slender wrists would show abrasions.

He decided on a course of action and motioned to Omar. "We can tie her ankles to the table legs, but I'll have to hold her arms down to keep her still."

Omar pulled two nylon ropes from his bag and held them out. "I'll do the left side."

Salazar took one of the ropes and coiled it around her right ankle. He dragged her foot to the edge of the table, lashed the other end of the rope around the table leg, and tightened the cord. He checked Omar's knots on the left side to be sure they were secure before he glanced back at the satchel on the kitchen counter. "Did you bring plastic sheeting to put under her?"

"Yes. I brought everything we need." Loud *snaps* echoed off the Saltillo tiles as Omar pulled on latex gloves.

Salazar sat in a wooden ladder backed chair at the end of the table near Veranda's head. He picked up her wrists and maneuvered them until her hands were crossed behind her neck, pillowing the back of her skull. He leaned forward, trapping her bent elbows beneath his biceps. His face brushed against her cheek, and her soft moan caressed his ear. He splayed his hands across the smooth skin of her rib cage, anchoring her torso firmly in place. Veranda was beautiful in repose, lips parted, eyes closed, breathing steady.

He pressed his mouth against her delicate ear and whispered a promise. "When I am finished tonight, you will never be the same again."

He looked up at Omar, who stood holding the equipment, and nodded. "You may begin."

28

VERANDA RACED THROUGH DENSE underbrush in the forest, sharp branches scraping her bare flesh. She chanced a glance over her shoulder to see the black wolf gaining on her. Its massive paws pounded the ground behind her. Lungs burning, she tried to run faster. The thudding of the beast's feet grew louder, thundering in her ears. Its hot breath blasted the nape of her neck. She braced for the impact of claws raking her back.

Gasping, she shot bolt upright in her bed as the sound of fists hammering on her door woke her from the nightmare. The dream had recurred many times over the past week, but it was far more vivid this time.

Bleary-eyed, dry-mouthed, and sweat-soaked, she glanced at the sunlit curtains, then turned to the digital clock on the nightstand. 9:03. How had she overslept? As she shook the cobwebs from her head, a deep, muffled male voice boomed, "Open the door!"

She jumped up from the bed and almost passed out when the room spun. Clutching the edge of the nightstand to steady herself, she called back. "I'll be there in a minute."

The pounding on her front door stopped, and she assumed whoever it was had heard her. She was nude, which was odd because she typically wore an oversized T-shirt to sleep in. She lurched to the bathroom, grabbed the satin robe dangling from its hook, and pulled it on, the smooth fabric clinging to her clammy skin. Her disheveled hair cascaded almost to her waist, forming a dark curtain around her upper body. Whoever was knocking would be in for a fright.

When she stumbled to the front door, bolts of pain shot through her body. She ached everywhere. Obviously, she'd gone one too many rounds with Jake. Still confused and disoriented, she peered through the peephole. A gold police badge took up the entire view space. Sighing, she unlocked the deadbolt and opened the door.

Lieutenant Diaz barged in without asking permission, Sam in his wake. Diaz laid his briefcase on the coffee table in front of her sofa. She closed the door and followed them into her living room on unsteady feet.

Radiating anger, Diaz rounded on her after giving the room a cursory look. "Are you alone?"

She lifted a brow. Odd question. Even stranger than the wrath on his face as he asked it. "Of course. I live by myself." She looked at Sam. "What the hell's going on?"

Sam said nothing, his face inscrutable.

Diaz stepped toward her. "Open your robe." At her look of outrage, he added, "Just the top."

She wrapped her arms around herself. "You can go f—"

Sam cut her off, stepping in front of her to face Diaz. "Lieutenant or not I'll cold-cock you if you don't let me do the talking."

Still bristling, Diaz crossed his arms, stepped back, and nodded.

Sam pivoted toward her, turning his back to Diaz. "Please sit down, Veranda." He motioned to her sofa.

Leery, she padded a few steps to the couch and perched on the edge of the cushion. The men took seats in the two armchairs across from her.

Sam's eyes searched her face. "What happened after you left the hotel last night?"

When she tried to recall, disjointed hazy images and dark voids came to her. "I'm not sure." She shook her head. "I don't remember coming home, but I only drank half a margarita. I think."

"Do you feel okay?"

"I feel like shit. Every part of my body hurts and I'm queasy."

"Do you feel pain in any specific area?"

She did a quick inventory of her body. Dull aches throbbed everywhere, but when she focused her attention, a sharper sensation registered in a specific place. She touched the area and winced.

She pushed her hair behind her shoulders, so only thin satin fabric covered her. Something wasn't right. With trembling hands, she pulled the edge of the robe away from her neckline and gasped when she exposed her upper left chest. "*Dios mío.*"

A five-inch-wide tattoo of a black wolf's head had been inked just above her breast. Astonished, she looked at the two men facing her. "How did this happen?"

Diaz's eyes traveled up from her gaping robe to lock with hers. "Why don't you tell us?"

Sam's bushy brows furrowed. "Are you saying you had no idea the tattoo was there?"

She turned to him. "That's exactly what I'm saying." She strained to remember details from last night. Nothing came. No longer concerned with modesty, she opened her robe wider, letting the top slide down to expose her bare shoulders and most of her chest. "Look, it's fresh." She pointed at the reddened skin around the edges of the design. She allowed the men to lean forward and examine the tattoo before she tugged her robe closed.

Mind still stuck in low gear, she hadn't thought to ask the most basic question. She looked at each of her visitors in turn. "What are you two doing here?"

Sam tipped his head toward Diaz's briefcase. "She needs to know what's going on."

Diaz popped open the briefcase on the coffee table in front of the sofa. He slid out an iPad and set it up in front of her, then touched an icon on the desktop to open a saved video file.

With a sinking feeling in her stomach, she recognized Kiki Lowell, the redheaded reporter, clutching a microphone. The banner above her read, TRAITOR IN THE PPD? With a dramatic flair, Kiki narrowed her eyes. "Early this morning, every media outlet in Phoenix received an email from an unknown source. The email contained images that shed new light on yesterday's Operation Scorpion Sting debacle."

Kiki swiveled to another camera, and the screen split with a photo image on the left. "This is one of three files attached to the mysterious email. This picture shows members of the notorious Villalobos family sitting at a conference table in an office. Hector Villalobos, known as *El Lobo*, reputed leader of the world's largest cartel, is at the head of the table. Adolfo, his oldest son, sits to his immediate right. His other two children, Carlos and Daria, are on the left. In the chair directly to Adolfo's right is Detective Veranda Cruz of the Phoenix Police Department."

Her befuddled brain couldn't process what she was seeing. In the photograph, she had on the turquoise blue dress she wore to the *quinceañera.* Her head throbbed with the effort of trying to understand something that made no sense.

Kiki continued her exposé, breathless with excitement. "We must warn viewers that the next image is graphic." Another picture replaced the first.

Veranda reared back so hard her shoulders hit the sofa cushion behind her. Eyes wide with shock, she took in a scene that defied all reason and made her question her sanity. On the screen, she was naked from the waist up, her breasts pixilated over her nipples, sitting on the edge of her own bed. The loopy smile on her face made her look drunk.

"This image depicts a partially clothed Detective Cruz." A salacious glint crept into Kiki's eyes as the camera zoomed in for a tight shot of the tattoo. "A close-up of the body art just above her left breast shows a Villalobos cartel tattoo worn by those who have devoted their lives to the service of the infamous criminal organization."

The camera zoomed in again, the image filling the screen as Kiki continued her voiceover. "A closer look reveals the most disturbing detail of all. About an inch above the wolf's head is the letter V. This addition to the standard tattoo is reserved for Villalobos family members. Our sources confirm that an identical design was noted on Bartolo Villalobos's official autopsy report after his recent death."

Veranda's hand flew to her mouth. Dread sluiced through her as she waited to see what would come next.

"The final attachment contained in the email was a document." An official-looking paper took up the entire screen as Kiki narrated. "This is a copy of a DNA report from a paternity test performed at a laboratory in Mexico. Members of our news staff translated the document, which indicates Detective Cruz is the biological daughter of Hector Villalobos."

The screen cut back to a close shot of Kiki, who seemed to be vibrating with barely contained excitement. "We contacted the Phoenix Police Public Affairs Bureau for a comment. They confirmed Detective Cruz has never been on an undercover assignment with the cartel, and could not have been involved in a department-sanctioned activity when she met with the Villalobos family."

Kiki swiveled to face the first camera again. "The PPD claimed to have no knowledge of the tattoo on Detective Cruz's body or the paternity test. They declined any further comment, citing the need to launch an official investigation."

A graphic of a Phoenix police badge materialized in the lower right corner of the screen as Kiki continued. "We remind viewers that this information was supplied through an unknown source. We have not been able to corroborate all allegations, however, since the same email was given to all Phoenix media outlets, this breaking story is being widely reported. Stay tuned for further developments."

A photo of Chief Tobias appeared to Kiki's right, above the gold shield. "Such serious accusations certainly demand a response from the chief and the mayor. The task force, led by Detective Cruz, conducted a recent series of raids. This operation, dubbed Scorpion Sting, eliminated a rival drug gang that encroached on Villalobos cartel territory. Did Detective Cruz arrange to have her family's business not only spared, but actually profit from the task force's actions? We will have more as this story unfolds."

Diaz tapped the screen and closed the iPad cover.

She felt paralyzed. A dull roar thrummed in her ears. The air in her lungs seemed to condense, making it hard to breathe.

After a long pause, Sam spoke softly. "This is bad, Veranda."

"No shit." Her hand trembled as she pushed a stray tendril of hair from her face. This could not be real. Her wolf nightmare must have morphed into this hellish scene. She willed herself to wake up.

"What aren't you telling us?" Diaz asked.

She latched onto the first coherent thought that came to her addled brain. "You were there," she said to Diaz. "I wore that blue dress to Gabby's *quinceañera*."

"I don't see your point." He furrowed his brows. "You also could have worn it to a meeting with the cartel."

"No, I couldn't. I bought it last week for Gabby's party, and that was the first time I put it on." Her eyes darted desperately from one man to the other. "I've never been in that office, never joined the Villalobos family around a table. The picture had to be Photoshopped. Someone's setting me up."

Diaz looked skeptical. "And the DNA test results? I recall Bartolo waving around a copy of the test in an envelope." He didn't hide the accusation in his next words. "Which went missing after he died."

Feeling cornered, she lashed out. "I didn't take those lab results."

Diaz edged forward, eyes blazing. "Are you *El Lobo*'s daughter or not?"

"Don't answer that, Veranda," Sam said. "These are serious allegations." He shot an angry glare at Diaz before turning back to her. "You need legal representation."

Diaz seemed to recollect himself. "Before we talk to you any further, I'll Mirandize you and give you an NOI."

"Why?" Veranda struggled to keep up as the conversation took another shocking turn. A Notice of Investigation meant the department had opened an official inquiry. Miranda warnings applied when the allegation was criminal in nature. Her head, which had only just stopped spinning, began to throb again.

She sat, heart hammering, as Diaz opened his briefcase and pulled several sheets of paper from a manila folder. Her thoughts a jumble of impossible theories, she initialed each paragraph as Diaz read the Miranda form, signing the bottom when he finished.

"I want an attorney," she said, her voice a hoarse whisper. "And a union rep."

Diaz tucked the paperwork back into the folder, leaving a copy for her. "That is your right, and we won't ask you any further questions until you have retained legal counsel. In the meantime, I hereby relieve you from duty."

"What?" Some part of her brain understood this stage of the procedure, but she'd never been forced to give up her badge. She was the job. Losing this part of her identity felt like an amputation.

Diaz held out his hand, palm up. "Give me your badge, credentials, cell phone, duty weapon, and extra clips with ammunition. Detective Stark will drive your city car back to headquarters. You are to remain at home where you can be reached at all times."

As if in a trance, Veranda stood and retrieved her go-bag from the floor nearby. Something nagged at her. What was her duffel doing there? She always kept it in her closet. Murky images swam just out of view, then disappeared.

She handed the bag to Diaz. "Take it. Everything's there."

He rested the duffel on the coffee table to unzip it. Following proper procedure, he inventoried each specified item. When he finished, he handed her the empty bag and a property receipt. "Let me make this perfectly clear," Diaz said, his expression hard as stone. "As of now, you have no police powers."

Clutching the proffered paper in clammy hands, she wondered if she would ever see her gun and badge again. As she looked into her lieutenant's cold, dark eyes, the true nature of her predicament sank in. She was under investigation for a felony.

She swallowed a lump in her throat, wondering if she would go to prison while Adolfo went free.

29

MIA STOOD IN THE main room of the West Phoenix warehouse, her small body shaking with fear as Señor Adolfo glared down his crooked nose at her.

"You have your twin sister to thank for this," he said. "Now tell your family goodbye."

By her side, her mother wailed with grief and pain, her tattered blouse lying on the concrete floor. Mia and her sister had been forced to watch the coyotes brand their mother's chest. As the acrid scent of charred flesh lingered, her mother doubled over, clutched Mia's arm, and sobbed.

"Goodbye." Tears streamed down Mia's face as she uttered the word.

Her sister Sofia, the smart one, the hope of the family, sank to her knees and howled her anguish.

Mia couldn't bear it. Everything she had endured since this journey into hell had not come close to preparing her for this torment.

The final farewell to her family and all the other women was breaking her heart.

Her sister's plan had failed. The secret message to Veranda Cruz had been intercepted before it ever went out. The hope they had kindled with their last desperate bid for freedom had been extinguished.

Señor Adolfo signaled Salazar, the one they called *El Matador*. Nothing terrified her more than that man. He was a demon. Her knees trembled so hard they knocked together as he drew near. She backed away, but his hand latched onto her slender arm like a vise. He shook her so hard her teeth rattled. Panic overtook her, and she tried to pull free.

"Be still."

She froze.

Still grasping her, Salazar turned to Señor Adolfo. "We have much to do. I cannot attend to this errand myself. Who do you have that would make sure this one"—he gave her another shake—"suffers before she dies?"

She watched as Señor Adolfo considered the group of fourteen men gathered at the back of the building. The coyotes had made sure every woman stood in front to witness what happened to those who defied the Villalobos family.

She saw his eyes settle on a particularly brutish man with deep scars along his pockmarked face and a cruel set to his mouth. She shuddered. Easily the largest of Carlos's coyotes, his bulging arms could snap her in half.

Señor Adolfo signaled the man. "Felix, take her."

Felix pushed away from the wall and strode over to her.

Salazar shoved her into Felix's expansive barrel chest. "Take her out into the desert. Do whatever you like with her before you kill her, but don't take too long. We have more work for you here."

Felix's face split into a wide grin, showing a gold tooth and black gums.

Her mother and sister wailed louder than ever.

Ignoring the histrionics, Felix wrapped a meaty hand around her upper arm. As he dragged her toward the door, she turned to see her mother and Sofia for the last time. She held her composure until she left the warehouse, then succumbed to tears.

Felix cuffed the side of her head. "Shut up." He twisted her arm, forcing her toward a black sedan parked in the shade of the building. Earlier that morning, Sofia told her exactly where they were, explaining how this part of the industrial district was full of abandoned warehouses.

As she surveyed her surroundings, she knew Sofia had been correct. No one was around to see her. If she screamed, Felix would simply hit her, so she remained silent as he wrenched open the front passenger door and shoved her inside.

Felix pulled a zip tie from his jeans pocket and looped it around her wrists. He pulled it tight, the closure making a ripping sound as the plastic teeth ground into a locked position. When he leaned forward to buckle her seatbelt, she recoiled as the armpit stains of his grimy T-shirts released a repulsive stench of body odor, stale beer, and cheap cigarettes. She supposed he didn't secure her out of concern for her safety, but a desire to restrict her movement inside the car.

He cast a threatening glare at her. "I want you up front where I can keep an eye on you. If you're quiet, I might go easy on you when we get out of the city." He chuckled. "Who knows? Maybe you'll like it."

He slammed her door shut, then lumbered around the vehicle to the driver's door, angled his bulk to fit behind the wheel, and rechecked her seatbelt.

She took in his greasy hair, filthy clothes, and soot-blackened hands, which she imagined groping her bare skin. A wave of nausea overtook her, and she fought down the urge to retch, saying nothing as he pulled out into the street.

Felix pulled onto a wide thoroughfare. She considered her situation and saw no way out. No chance of rescue. As the car glided relentlessly toward their destination, she accepted the truth. Her life was about to end.

Her hands reddened as the plastic ties cut into her wrists, compressing them together painfully. The discomfort gathered her scattered thoughts to a focal point. She had nothing to lose. She could either go to her death meekly after Felix was finished with her, or try one last time to change her fate.

She looked around the car. Felix had no weapon she could see, although she imagined he would at least have a knife somewhere to kill her. She winced at the mere thought. Or maybe he intended to strangle her.

Choking back a sob of fear, she forced herself to think. Aware every passing second brought her closer to death, she reexamined the car, looking for any means of escape. The door latch was missing, so she couldn't open it. When she discreetly tried to power down the window, nothing happened.

Felix drove into what she guessed must be the downtown area. Traffic grew heavier and more people strolled the sidewalks. She turned her head away so Felix couldn't see her, and mouthed the word "help" to passersby. She made frantic faces to other drivers, hoping they would at least call the police to investigate. But no one reacted. Apparently, nobody could see her through the dark-tinted glass, so she didn't bother trying to wave at anyone to show them her bound hands. When she made her move, it had to count. A weak attempt to attract attention, like tapping on her window, would just piss her captor off, and waste her only chance at surprising him.

She remained quiet, hoping to lull Felix into thinking she had no fight left in her. All the while, she studied the streets as they passed, praying for an opportunity. After a few minutes, the spaces between high-rise buildings widened. Before long, she figured they'd be out of the city. She had to do something now.

As the sedan approached an intersection, the light turned yellow. Cursing, Felix stomped the gas pedal. She had a flash of inspiration. Her idea was reckless and dangerous, but she would die anyway if she did nothing.

She flicked a glance at Felix. As they reached the middle of the intersection, his eyes locked on the still-yellow traffic signal, his foot mashing the accelerator to the floor.

Now or never.

She lunged to her left, grabbed the steering wheel with both hands, and yanked as hard as she could, aiming the car at a metal light pole on the corner. As other drivers blasted their horns and fishtailed out of the way, their sedan rammed straight into the pole at full speed. Without time to react, Felix had never moved his foot to the brake pedal.

Mia had a final thought before darkness enveloped her. This one aspect of her life, the Villalobos family would not control. She would die on her own terms.

30

AFTER SAM AND DIAZ left, Veranda sat on the sofa in a state of shock for several minutes. In a near catatonic stupor, she stared straight ahead until her gaze landed on a black-and-white photograph in a pewter frame resting on the end table. The picture, a photo of her mother she had taken last year, was her favorite. Lorena sat on the bench in the gathering space under the pavilion between the casitas at the family property, her head thrown back, mouth wide, and eyes crinkled with mirth. The years had not dimmed her beauty.

Emerging from her trance, Veranda realized one person would be suffering from the devastating news reports even more than she was. A sick feeling clawed at her insides. She shot to her feet, darted to the kitchen, and used her landline to call her mother's cell phone. She assumed Lorena had already arrived at the food truck, and prayed she hadn't seen any television.

Listening to ringing at the other end, she gripped the receiver so hard her knuckles whitened. Desperate to reach her mother and warn her about the news story, she chewed her lip during the interminable wait before her uncle picked up the phone.

"Tío Rico, I need to speak to my mother." Her words spilled out in a breathless rush.

After a long pause, Rico answered. "Lorena gave me her phone." She could hear the strain in his voice. "She has gone home." The bleakness in her uncle's words tore at her heart. "She will not speak to anyone."

"I'm going over there … " she began, the empty promise dying on her lips. Even if she weren't on de facto house arrest, the department had taken her city car, and her personally owned beater was currently up on a pneumatic lift at Chuy's garage with its guts spread over the oil-stained floor.

"Don't, Veranda."

She sensed a chill in her uncle's tone that had never been there before. Like her mother, Rico had known she might be *El Lobo*'s daughter. Because he had been there. Seventeen years old at the time, Rico had been the one to hit Hector over the head during the attack. Rico had witnessed the brutish, violent act that had brought Veranda into existence.

No wonder none of them wanted to speak to her now. Bitter despair mixed with bile in her throat, burning a path down to the pit of her stomach.

Her uncle cut into her thoughts. "Veranda, we are closing the food truck for the day. We must care for Lorena. I will call you when she is ready to see you again." He hung up.

She slumped against the wall. Her knees buckled and she slid down to sit on the tile floor. As moisture pooled in the corners of her eyes, she noticed a small detail. Her uncle had not called her *mi'jita*—his usual term of endearment—as he always had. As of now, she was simply Veranda. Like she wasn't family. Wasn't flesh and blood. Wasn't welcome.

Deeper than her own pain, she felt the torment her mother undoubtedly experienced at this moment. She knew Lorena would assume people believed she'd voluntarily slept with Hector Villalobos. Worse yet, her mother had been married to Ernesto Hidalgo when she became pregnant with Veranda. Conservative and Catholic to her core, Lorena would expect her community to scorn her as an unfaithful wife. And the community meant everything to her, so she was hiding herself away out of shame. Her mother deserved better, and Veranda cursed herself for not being what her mother desperately wanted—Ernesto's child..

Soul-wrenching pain tormented her. Veranda had lost her family, her career, and finally, her self-respect. By the time the investigation ended, she might also lose her freedom. She would be reviled as a traitor to her country. Her own department would work with prosecutors to send her to prison for the rest of her life.

Somehow, the Villalobos family had done this to her. The thought ignited a spark deep in the very marrow of her bones. As the heat built, her agony burned away, and she stoked the flames into a raging fire. Done grieving what she could not change, she was ready to fight.

She scrambled to her feet and stormed into the bathroom. Chest heaving, she stood in front of the mirror over her sink and tore off her satin robe. The tattoo was a livid wound on her chest. The letter V above it, a dark stain over her heart.

Biting back angry tears, she turned on the shower and stepped under the hot water. With all her might, she tried to piece together what had happened the night before. She remembered leaving the hotel, and she didn't have the tattoo then. She recalled getting in her car, but not arriving at her house. What had happened next?

Her background in narcotics told her some drugs not only rendered a person compliant, but permanently deleted several hours from conscious memory. She needed a blood test to reveal traces of any chemicals in her system. She also needed a lawyer, and she'd better find one before Diaz sent a uniform to collect her and take her to headquarters for a highly unpleasant interrogation.

Stepping out of the shower and toweling off, she formulated a course of action. Much better than sitting on the kitchen floor drowning under a tidal wave of guilt. First, she had to be ready when an officer arrived. She dressed quickly in a pale gray pantsuit and walked into her living room in search of her briefcase. Over the years, she'd received business cards from countless criminal defense attorneys. Her experience in the courtroom told her which ones were the best. In her wildest nightmares, she never imagined needing their services as a client.

As she opened the briefcase to retrieve a stack of business cards, her home phone rang. Eager to hear from her mother, she raced to the kitchen and snatched up the receiver. "Hello?"

Lieutenant Diaz's voice jarred her. "I'm on my way to pick you up, Detective. Be ready to leave in five minutes."

Although grateful she'd already showered and dressed, she didn't understand why he hadn't sent a uniform to take her to an interview room. "I can ride to your location with an area patrol unit." She had no desire to be in a car with Diaz.

"I'm not taking you to be interrogated."

"What's going on?"

"A young girl, looks like a teenager, just arrived at Phoenix General's ER in an ambulance."

"Gabby." Her hand flew to her throat. Could this day get any worse? "What's happened to my sister?"

Diaz's voice softened fractionally. "It's not Gabriela."

Veranda twisted the phone cord through her fingers. "I don't understand."

"The girl said her name is Mia Pacheco. She has a fairly recent brand of a wolf's head on her chest. She was transported from the scene of a car crash at 8th and Watson. She was the passenger. The driver is an adult Hispanic male in his late twenties with a Villalobos tattoo over his heart. He's in surgery right now, but he's circling the drain. No seatbelt, airbag disconnected, lots of head and chest trauma. The girl was belted in though, so she's doing a lot better."

She reflexively flipped into detective mode. "Do you have an ID on the driver?"

"According to his license, his name is Felix Orteña."

She snapped her fingers. "I know that name. He's a coyote who doubles as a Villalobos enforcer. Huge son-of-a-bitch."

"The girl, Mia, says she's got important information about the raids and about the cartel, but she refuses to speak to anyone except you."

"But I don't know her."

"Well, she knows you. The rest of the task force is at the Fusion Center working on a new plan. Because of the media circus, Commander Webster is now running day-to-day operations on-site at the Center. He slotted Sam in as lead detective. That makes me redundant, so I was assigned to take you to the hospital and get this girl's statement."

"I'll be ready when you get here." She hung up and fished her house keys from a terra-cotta bowl on the hall table by the door, tossing them in her purse with the stack of business cards.

She watched from the window as Diaz pulled up a few minutes later, then punched in her alarm code and locked the door behind her before she strode to the Chrysler and got in.

As they drove to the hospital, she tried to make headway with Diaz. "I'm innocent, you know."

He kept his eyes on the road. "Detective, you've invoked. I can't discuss the case with you any further until we're in an official interview setting with your attorney present."

"I know, but I'm volunteering this on the record. No matter how it looks, I didn't betray my family, my department, and my country." She instilled every ounce of sincerity she possessed into the declaration. "I'd die first."

He said nothing, and they drove the rest of the way in stony silence.

Diaz pulled into one of the designated police parking spaces next to the emergency room entrance and threw a PPD placard on the dashboard. He badged their way past the hospital security personnel and checked the overhead boards for the ER patient list. The name "Mia Pacheco" was listed in bed seven.

Veranda had a growing sense of unease as they walked by the sequentially numbered treatment bays, separated by curtains draped from the ceiling. When they arrived at bed seven, Diaz pushed the curtain aside and walked straight in.

The area was empty. The gurney, gone.

Without waiting for Diaz, Veranda spun and ran to the bullpen in the center of the ER. "Where's the patient in bed seven?"

The ER nurses studiously ignored her, tapping on their computers and speaking to each other.

Frustration mounting, Veranda waylaid a passing orderly. "Where is Mia Pacheco?" she demanded, "She's supposed to be in room number seven."

Diaz stood next to her and held up his badge. A harried look on his face, the orderly huffed, marched to room seven, and snatched a chart from a hook on the door. "They took her to radiology for x-rays a couple of minutes ago."

Veranda released a relieved breath.

"Who's her treating physician?" Diaz asked. "We need to speak with him." He gave Veranda a sidelong look. "Or her."

The orderly's eyes drifted down the page. "Chart says it's Doctor Jones." He frowned. "We don't have a Doctor Jones. Must be some mistake."

Veranda and Diaz exchanged glances. "There's no mistake," Diaz said to the orderly. "The patient is a potential witness in a high-profile investigation."

Filled with profound dread, she voiced the inescapable conclusion. "Adolfo's got her."

31

VERANDA STIFLED THE URGE to punch the orderly when he put both hands up in the classic *don't blame me* sign.

"No one told us we needed to enact patient security protocols," he said. "Her name was listed right on the board. She should have been given an alias or admitted as a Jane Doe."

She was out of patience. "We can debate who's responsible later. Right now, we need to lock this hospital down until we find her. That girl is in grave danger." She lowered her voice. "If she's not already gone."

The orderly grabbed a white hospital phone and shouted a series of rapid-fire coded phrases into the receiver. Moments later, an alert blared through the intercom system and lights flashed on wall sconces.

An elderly security guard hustled toward them, radio squawking. He unsnapped it from the holder on his belt and listened. Over the din of the alarm, Veranda overheard a voice at the other end report a scuffle taking place between a patient and a nurse near the north side ER exit.

Without waiting for details, she pointed at the north hallway. "Let's go."

Diaz followed as she raced past the guard through a series of corridors toward the reported disturbance. She rounded a corner and spotted a petite teenaged girl standing barefoot in a hospital gown at the far end of a long hall. Next to her, a brawny male nurse grappled with a wiry Latino man in ripped jeans who sported a heavy beard. A wooden-handled hunting knife lay on the glossy tile floor between them.

"Police, don't move!" Diaz shouted, drawing his Glock.

Both men stopped fighting momentarily, their attention on Diaz's gun. The elderly guard, who had come up behind them, retreated down the corridor. She heard him holler into his radio to get backup and evacuate the area. Good, she didn't want anyone else coming down the hallway.

The girl seized the opportunity of a distraction. She grabbed the rails of a nearby gurney and rammed the bed into the bearded man's hip. He stumbled back from the impact, pivoted, and bolted through the exit door behind him.

Veranda called out to the male nurse, pointing at the girl. "Don't let her out of your sight."

Diaz stayed tight on her heels as she dodged around the gurney and rushed out the exit door, head swiveling in every direction. The bearded man had vanished. Diaz pulled a portable radio from his waist and broadcasted a lookout for the suspect.

When they came back into the hallway, the girl blinked up at them. Her slight body dwarfed by the hospital gown, she had dark circles under her sunken eyes that spoke of misery and suffering more eloquently than words ever could.

She wanted to wrap the girl up and take her home. Instead, she tilted her head down and spoke softly in Spanish. "It's okay, sweetie.

You're safe now." She hoped a bit of reassurance would help establish trust, because she had to step into her police persona and do her job.

She snatched a latex glove from a nearby wall dispenser. Not bothering to put it on, she draped it over her fingers and bent to pick up the hunting knife still lying on the floor. "Maybe we'll get lucky and his prints will be on this," she muttered, looking for something to use as a temporary evidence bag.

Mia trembled violently when Diaz holstered his weapon and strode toward her. Tall, muscular, and imposing, he towered over her.

"You're scaring her." Using her free hand, Veranda caught Diaz's arm. "Can we switch tasks, Lieutenant?" It wasn't her place to delegate an assignment to her supervisor, but the weapon had to be secured, and the girl seemed frightened of men.

Diaz gave her a curt nod and eased the knife from her grasp, using the glove as a barrier between his skin and the flat of the blade.

The male nurse held up a bright orange cardboard sleeve. "This is a portable sharps container. You can put the knife in and seal it."

"That's perfect." Diaz took the container. "And thank you for helping the victim before we arrived."

The nurse blushed to the roots of his auburn hair. "That dude hauled her off the gurney and tried to drag her out the door while she kicked and yelled. Saw him pull a knife on her." He spread his hands. "Couldn't just stand there and watch it happen."

"We'll need a statement," Diaz said, placing the container holding the knife on the gurney. "You'll be busy a while."

"I'll notify my supervisor." The nurse trotted down the hall. "Be back in five." He called over his shoulder.

Careful not to make any sudden movements, Veranda approached the girl slowly, as if she were a fawn lost in the woods. She gentled her voice. "Hey there. Are you hurt? Did he cut you anywhere?"

A silent shake of the head.

"Do you know who I am?"

The girl's eyes lit up. "You're Detective Veranda Cruz. I've seen you on TV … and I've seen pictures of you too."

"Then you know I'm here because you asked for me."

The girl peered around Veranda and flinched when she caught sight of Diaz again.

"Don't worry about him," Veranda said. "He looks big and scary, but he works for the police department like me. In fact, he's my boss, Lieutenant Richard Diaz. It's okay to talk in front of him. And he speaks Spanish like we do, so he'll understand what we're saying."

The girl nodded but still looked apprehensive.

Veranda reached out and gently took a small slender hand in hers. "Are you Mia?"

"Yes. Mia Pacheco. I have a twin sister named Sofia and she … she … " Mia burst into tears.

She pulled her into a tight embrace. "It's okay, you're safe here with us now. May I call you Mia?"

Mia nodded.

Having dealt with many crime victims, she had learned the importance of this simple gesture. Asking permission to use a person's name returned a sense of identity and control that had been stripped away. She found that affording this basic human right was often the first step in the healing process.

She waited for the sobs to subside to sniffles. "You must have something important to say. You were so brave to ask for me."

"I had to tell you what happened." Mia swiped the tears from her cheeks with the back of her hand. "I've been living with Señores Adolfo and Carlos Villalobos for almost two months. My mother brought Sofia and me here with their coyotes. They moved us around to three different houses since we arrived." Mia's words ceased. She lowered her head.

Guessing the reason the girl had abruptly stopped talking, Veranda stroked her hair. "It's okay, Mia. We're not concerned about your legal status."

Mia nodded, a nervous smile flitting across her delicate features. "My sister, Sofia, is the smart one. She was supposed to be in Arizona for a computer learning program, but the coyotes lied. They kept us. Said we owed them more money for our passage. They had promised us *Mamá* and I could work cleaning houses and offices, but that was a lie too. Instead, to earn money for them, they made us … made us … "

"You don't have to say," she whispered, pulling Mia back into her arms. She knew all too well what happened to female captives of the cartel. At some point, other detectives would interview Mia in detail about her time in Villalobos custody, but there was no need to drag her through it now.

Avoiding further emotional trauma, she guided Mia to a different part of the story. Taking a tissue from Diaz's outstretched hand, she offered it to the trembling girl. "Why did you need to speak to me personally?"

Mia's rapid breathing steadied. "Right after we got to Phoenix, Señor Carlos sent for Sofia. He told her she had to work on their computers. A guy named Nacho would supervise her. Nacho forced her to help him hack into the police department's computers."

At Veranda's raised eyebrows, Mia added, "That's how the cartel found out about the raids ahead of time. Sofia told me everything when we had time alone to talk. Nacho read your emails and got copies of plans showing where your team was about to search. He told Señor Adolfo, and he moved all of us into a warehouse that wasn't on your list. Then he and Señor Carlos and that horrible monster"—her frail body shuddered—"Salazar, flew to Mexico during the raids so they wouldn't be around."

Veranda felt a tremble. At first, she thought Mia was shaking with fear again. Then she realized her own body was vibrating with pent-up rage. Slowly, she turned her head to look at Diaz.

He stood stock still, mouth open, eyes wide.

Veranda dragged her attention back to Mia, who had started to speak again.

"While they were away in Mexico," she said, her voice tremulous, fixating exclusively on Veranda, "Sofia tried to send a message to your email, but Nacho caught her. So Señor Adolfo told me I had to die."

Veranda glanced at Diaz and caught a triumphant expression on his features that told her they had both arrived at the same conclusion. And it was a game changer. Mia had just given direct eyewitness testimony implicating Adolfo in an attempted murder. Coupled with the rest of the intelligence the task force had gathered, it would be enough to get an arrest warrant for Adolfo.

Mia wrung her hands. "That Felix guy I was in the car with, he was taking me out into the desert to kill me." She finished on a whisper. "So I crashed the car."

"I'm so sorry you had to go through that, sweetheart." Veranda hugged her briefly, mentally processing the new information.

Mia's voice grew stronger as she continued. "Sofia told me after Nacho hacked the police server, he figured out how to clone your cell phones. He got your team's numbers off the emails, and he cloned them all. He listens in on every phone call and reads every text you all send to anyone in your group." She scratched her head. "And he uses the phones track you. He's got all you guys color-coded on a display map. Sofia said he makes her help monitor everything."

Veranda locked eyes with Diaz, the pieces finally falling into place. "You called to tell me about the car crash. You said you were taking me to Phoenix General hospital." Her mind raced, making connections. "That's how they knew where Mia was. How they beat us here." She wrapped a protective arm around Mia. "That's how they almost got her."

Mia nodded, tangled tendrils of hair escaping from her messy ponytail as her head bobbed. "And now the coyote they sent here to take me will tell them you came. Señor Adolfo will know I've told you everything. He'll guess you'll go to his new location." She drew a deep breath, a slight smile turning up her lips. "Because I know where it is."

Veranda gripped Mia's thin shoulders. "You can tell me where Adolfo is now? Where he hid everything before the raids?" Veranda imagined a treasure trove of suspects, evidence, and contraband, all in one place.

Mia nodded. "You can't wait though. You should go now. Señor Adolfo has lots of people. They'll move everything out of there and hide it somewhere else."

Diaz signaled for Veranda to follow as he backed out of earshot. When she joined him, he spoke in a low voice. "There's no proof of any of this yet. We'll need computer forensics to check for traces of the hack, which could take days."

Veranda gritted her teeth and glared up at Diaz. "We don't have days, Lieutenant. We don't even have hours. You heard what Mia said."

He returned her glare. "We need corroboration. We've got nothing but the word of a teenage girl. Granted, she's very convincing, and I'm inclined to believe her, but we can't send our tactical team charging into a cartel stronghold without a search warrant. And a judge requires evidence." He put his hands on his hips. "At the very least, we've got to articulate exigent circumstances."

"If Mia's right, every scrap of evidence will disappear within the hour. If that isn't exigent, I don't know what is."

Silence stretched between them.

A tentative tap on her elbow caused Veranda to turn around.

Mia stood behind her. "There's more," she whispered. "I also know what happened to you last night."

32

IGNORING THE MEN BEHIND him lugging boxes and crates through the warehouse, Adolfo's finger tightened on the trigger. A fraction more pressure and Luis Patron's head would explode in a shower of brain matter and skull fragments. The .50-caliber round chambered in the hefty titanium-gold Desert Eagle Mark XIX semiautomatic pistol aimed at Patron's face would ensure he paid for his mistake.

An hour ago, Nacho intercepted a phone call from Lieutenant Diaz to Veranda Cruz. Apparently, Felix crashed and ended up in the hospital with the little *puta*, Mia. Adolfo immediately sent Patron to grab the girl before she could speak to Diaz and Cruz, who were on their way, according to Nacho. Patron called twenty minutes later to beg forgiveness for missing his chance. Worse yet, he'd seen Cruz with Mia before he escaped.

Adolfo wasn't sure the girl knew their location, but she'd proven resourceful in the past and he couldn't take any chances. Instead of celebrating Cruz's death as he'd planned, he was scrambling to relocate before she kicked down his door.

Three trucks, loaded with weapons and product, had already left for the border. Another stood waiting by the open bay doors as his men shuttled boxes into its cargo area. At the precipice of victory, defeat overtook him. And it could have been prevented, if the idiot quivering in front of him had managed to get that girl out of the hospital. He estimated he had about fifteen minutes before the police would find him, but he would make time to deal with his incompetent subordinate. In front of the others.

Tears streamed down Patron's hollow cheeks, dripping into his wiry beard. "P-please, *señor*, I got to the hospital as fast as I could. There was nothing I could do."

Adolfo scowled. "You could have done your job."

Carlos plopped a large cardboard box down and ambled over, a shark drawn to imminent bloodshed. He lifted a sardonic eyebrow. "Shooting the messenger, are we?"

After everything that had gone wrong, his men needed to know he could be every bit as ruthless as any member of his family. "I won't accept any more failure," he said.

A young girl's agonized shriek interrupted him. He turned to see Nacho marching Sofia, arm twisted behind her back, to the moving truck's front passenger cab. Sofia spun, jerked out of Nacho's grasp, and sprinted toward the main warehouse door.

Adolfo lowered his gun to watch as Carlos easily chased the girl down in a few strides. Clutching the nape of her neck, he pushed her down, forcing her to kneel on the cement floor. "Nacho, do you still need this *puta*, or do we kill her right here?" Carlos asked.

The very sight of her boiled Adolfo's blood. "That little bitch and her sister are the reason we're in this mess."

"I-I still need her," Nacho said, darting a glance at each of the two brothers in turn.

Adolfo longed to use the bullet he'd intended for Patron on the girl. "She must be punished."

"Don't worry about that." Carlos yanked her to her feet and shoved her into Nacho's arms. "When we get back to Mexico, she'll be branded, just like her mother and sister. Then I'll take my belt to her. When I'm finished, she will never dare to defy the Villalobos family again."

As Nacho led her into the vehicle, Sofia whimpered but didn't struggle.

Carlos turned to Adolfo. "Mention of her mother reminds me. What will we do with my women?" He pointed out the men, who had formed a brigade to pass crates into the truck's cargo area. "There's no more room in the vehicle with the equipment and our stash."

He had already made his decision. "We can't take the women."

Carlos gave a defiant huff. "We can't leave them here either."

He had no time for debate. "This truck is almost full. We only have one more vehicle coming, and it's a van. We can put the last few items in it, but there isn't room for any of the women."

"I'm not following."

He sighed, fighting for patience. Why did he have to spell it out? "When Detective Cruz arrives, all she will find is a burning warehouse."

Carlos frowned "And my women?"

"Will be inside."

He could see the moment comprehension dawned on his younger brother. Carlos dragged a hand through his hair. "Shit, Adolfo, that's my entire stable. They make good money for me."

"They can be replaced a lot easier than our computer equipment, our weapons, and our product."

"But—"

"Enough, Carlos. I've made up my mind." Closing the subject, he turned to face Patron, who looked as if he'd been trying to blend into the wall behind him. "I have other business to dispense with." He pointed the gun at the man's head again.

"Please," Patron pleaded. His entire body shook.

Adolfo hesitated. He despised meting out punishment. Especially when it involved a tremendous amount of blood and gore, as this execution undoubtedly would.

A deep voice echoed off the steadily emptying warehouse walls. "Either pull the trigger or put him to work moving boxes."

He looked over his shoulder to see Salazar saunter toward him. He'd canceled the order to terminate Veranda Cruz and called Salazar back to the warehouse to help with the expedited evacuation.

He lowered the gun and turned around completely to face Salazar. Stinging from the thinly veiled insult about his reluctance to kill in cold blood, he curled his lip as he responded. "Why don't you put those oversized muscles to use and let me do the thinking?" He nodded at the line of men hefting boxes.

Salazar bristled. "I'm not one of your coyotes and I'm not your servant, *pendejo*."

Adolfo's temper quickened. Salazar's very presence leeched authority away from him. He could not allow a subordinate to call him such a vulgar name in front of his men without retribution. Without further thought, he began to raise the pistol toward Salazar.

In a split second, Salazar closed the distance between them. Seizing the top of the slide to hold it in place, he effectively prevented the gun from firing. Then, with a practiced motion, Salazar twisted the weapon.

Adolfo's fingers were trapped in the trigger guard. As metal pressed against nerve and bone, his wrist bent at an unnatural angle.

"Damn you!" He rose up onto the balls of his feet as Salazar increased the pressure incrementally.

Out of the corner of his eye, he saw his men stop their work to watch the drama play out. Lightning whips of agony shot down his arm, holding him in place. The slightest movement brought him paroxysms of torment.

Salazar inched closer to him, his voice dropping to a barely audible rasp. "Never. Threaten. Me."

Locked in an oddly intimate embrace, his brain circuitry overloaded with messages from pain receptors to the point he could scarcely think. He did understand, however, that Salazar had spoken quietly so no one else could hear.

Eyes watering, he blinked at the chips of onyx that were Salazar's eyes and saw naked aggression. "You can't … talk to me … like that," he said, gasping. "Not in front … of my men."

"I will take your orders *if* you show me the proper respect." Salazar's voice was still deadly soft. "But know this, Adolfo." He gave the gun another fractional wrench and waited for the resulting stream of expletives to subside before he got so close their noses touched. "You are— what is it the Americans say?" Salazar switched to English. "A pussy."

He nearly passed out from the release of pain as blood rushed back into his hand when Salazar stepped back, pulling the gun from his nerveless fingers.

Gaze never leaving Adolfo's face, Salazar swung the pistol up and fired, point-blank, into Luis Patron's forehead. Without deigning to look at the body, now lying crumpled in a bloody heap against the wall, Salazar rounded on the stunned onlookers. "Everyone, get back to work. I have another bullet for anyone who is lazy." As the men hurried back to their tasks, he presented the gun, grip first, to Adolfo.

When he handed over a loaded weapon after humiliating him and taking over the discipline of his men, Salazar had emasculated him beyond repair.

Filled with impotent rage, Adolfo snatched his Desert Eagle and jammed it into the holster on his belt. Salazar could not have undermined him more thoroughly. His mind seethed with plots of revenge. First, he would wait for Salazar to kill Veranda Cruz, then he would find a way to feed him to *Diablo*.

A slow smile crept across his features as he pictured his father's ferocious black wolf enjoying an extra-large feast.

33

VERANDA BENT TO PEER directly into Mia's widened eyes. "What do you mean you know what happened to me last night?"

Shivering, Mia peeked at Diaz, then sidled closer to Veranda before she said, "Sofia heard them planning, and she told me everything. Señor Adolfo sent Salazar to your house last night. As soon as you opened the door, Salazar texted Nacho, and he called your cell phone using a blocked number. You were supposed to be distracted with the phone and the alarm when Salazar attacked you."

Veranda listened to the account in a detached way, as if taking a statement from a witness. She couldn't remember any of what Mia described. Even so, the hair on the back of her neck stood on end.

Salazar had been inside her home. With her.

"He injected you with something," Mia went on. "Then one of the cartel artists tattooed a wolf over your heart with a Villalobos family mark above it. They did it right there at your house."

Emotion clogged her throat. She had finally gotten some answers. Standing next to her, Diaz shuffled his feet, but she didn't look his way. She wondered if he still believed she was a traitor, then remembered her next question. "Did Sofia tell you anything about sending an email to the media?"

Mia bit her lip. "Sofia felt really bad about that. She said Nacho made her Photoshop a picture of you sitting at a table in the Villalobos family compound in Mexico. They took the picture with a drone they sent to your sister's *quinceañera*. In one of the pictures, you were sitting at a table, so you were in the right position."

Veranda hazarded a glance at Diaz. What would her supervisor, so keen to confiscate her badge, think of Mia's account? His dark eyes were riveted on hers, and she knew he had recalled the drone at the party.

Now that she'd started, Mia seemed anxious to continue. "But Sofia tricked Nacho. She messed up on purpose. There's a shadow on your body that doesn't line up with the ones around you. It's hard to tell, but it's there if someone's looking."

"What about the DNA results?" Even to her own ears, she sounded breathless.

"I don't know anything about that."

"I'm assuming those are genuine," Diaz said. "They wouldn't have given you the family tattoo otherwise. It's a point of honor. Even if it's part of a plan to set you up, only a true Villalobos would be allowed to wear that ink."

She considered his words. He was right. In that moment, she released the last vestiges of hope that the cartel had somehow faked the DNA results. "Why did they go to all the trouble to set me up? Why not just kill me?" She directed the questions at Mia.

"I heard them talking before they dragged me out. They wanted to make it look like you're a traitor. Señor Adolfo said everybody hates a spy."

Diaz stepped closer to Mia, his voice sharp enough to cut steel. "Why would he want everyone to think Detective Cruz was a spy?"

Mia quailed under his intense stare.

"For heaven's sake, Lieutenant," Veranda said, rubbing the girl's shoulder. "Dial it down."

Diaz stepped back but didn't ease the tension lining his features.

Mia turned to Veranda and swallowed. "Señor Adolfo said his plan worked and that you weren't a police officer anymore." She peered up briefly before looking down again. "Nacho found an email with an attachment that said you had to stay home. Señor Adolfo laughed and said you'd probably go to jail, except that … except that … "

"What?" Diaz and Veranda said in unison.

Mia twisted her fingers together. "Señor Adolfo sent Salazar to kill you. He's looking for you right now."

"That's it." Diaz's eyes left Mia's startled face to settle on Veranda. "You're going into lockdown."

"No way." She went from shock to antagonism in a nanosecond. "You heard what Mia said. Adolfo will vacate while you and the Feds try to scrounge enough evidence to secure a search warrant."

"There's more," Mia mumbled. When they turned, she cleared her throat. "My mother and sister are still at the warehouse where they moved all of their stuff. So are about thirty other women. They're captives. If Señor Adolfo has time, he'll take them so far away I'll never see them again." Tears pooled in her doe-brown eyes. "He might even kill my mother and sister for what I'm doing now … talking to you. He punished me every time Sofia tried to send you a message or get them caught." She appeared to gather her nerve and looked up at Diaz, then back at Veranda. "You have to leave right away to save them. If you wait, I'll never see them again."

Diaz's expression softened a fraction. Veranda needed no further invitation. "Lieutenant, the cartel had to empty all of their sites before the raids. Everything is consolidated in one location. Adolfo is there with all the evidence we need to send him away for life." She lifted a shoulder. "Hell, we might even have enough to shut the cartel down for good. It sounds like they've stockpiled their computers, data, personnel, weapons, drugs, *and* prisoners. That has never happened in the years I've investigated the cartel." She pleaded with Diaz, determined to make him understand. "We will never have an opportunity like this again. The very thing they did to save themselves is what we can use to take them down."

Mia turned beseeching eyes to Diaz. "Please don't wait, *Teniente* Diaz. Please go now."

Her heart pounded as she waited for Diaz's verdict. Mia had explained how the cartel had planted every incriminating item the media reported about her except the DNA results. She couldn't escape the truth. She was Hector's daughter. If Diaz trusted her, he would believe Mia's story. If he had doubts, nothing would convince him of her innocence.

Diaz tilted his head back and scrunched his eyes shut. After a long moment, he looked back down at them, resigned. "First, we need to safeguard Mia. I'll call for some uniforms to watch her and get the hospital to conceal her identity."

She released a breath she didn't realize she'd been holding. "Thank you, Lieutenant."

"That will take too long," Mia said, wringing her hands. "I'll find the security guard. I'll be fine. Just go!"

Veranda shook her head at Mia. "No, sweetie, we have to take care of you first, but I have an idea how we can make sure Adolfo doesn't slip through our fingers again while we get everything in place."

Diaz regarded her with suspicion. "I'm afraid to ask."

"After we make arrangements for Mia, I'll go to the cartel's warehouse and set up surveillance." When Diaz frowned and opened his mouth, she held up a finger. "I'm only going to watch from a distance. I'll make sure they can't identify me. Trust me. If they bug out, I'll follow from a discreet distance so I can see where they go. That should buy you time to get back to the Fusion Center and brief the task force." She paused. It cost her a great deal to admit the next part. "No one will believe anything I have to say, so you have to convince the task force."

Diaz looked skeptical. "I could use a hospital phone to call Sam."

"You can't," Veranda said. "They're monitoring Sam's cell phone, and there aren't any landlines at the Fusion Center. It's only a temporary location, so the techs never set up any infrastructure."

"Then I'll take you there with me. We'll convince them together."

Veranda did a mental head slap, frustrated they were wasting time debating the issue. "Lieutenant, Adolfo's probably packing up the warehouse as we speak."

"I don't want you going after the cartel alone, Veranda."

When he spoke before, she detected anger. Now, a deep ache infused his words. She was certain he didn't realize he'd used her first name, a rarity. She dropped her voice to a soothing tone. "I won't be alone for long. You'll bring backup." She had made her case. Now she waited in silence and fine-tuned her strategy.

He rubbed the back of his neck and shifted on his feet. Finally, he blew out a noisy sigh. "How will you get there and how will you stay in touch with us?"

Veranda barely managed to stifle a whoop. "I'm going to call someone who can give me a ride, a different cell phone, and a disguise. All in a matter of minutes." The final pieces of the plan coalesced in her mind as she spoke. "Once you're at the Center, get a new mobile and call me so I have your number. I'll update you then."

"How am I supposed to call you? I don't have your new cell number."

"Actually, you do." She grinned. "I'll explain the details before you leave."

Diaz shook his head. "I don't like this. You don't have a badge or a gun. And you're still suspended from duty."

"I won't take police action. Won't interact with anyone. Strictly recon. No one will even know I'm there." She decided to force the issue. "Lieutenant, it's time you made up your mind." She moved in close, tilting her head back to look him in the eye. "Are you a cop or a bureaucrat?"

A heavy silence surrounded them. Had she crossed a line? Then, with slow deliberate movements, Diaz brought his hands to his waist and unbuckled his belt.

Mia gasped and shrank back behind Veranda as he began to slide the belt through his pant loops.

Veranda blanched. "Lieutenant?"

"If you're going to do this, you'd better have some sort of defense," Diaz said. "Just in case." He pulled the belt the rest of the way out, deftly catching his duty weapon in its pancake holster when it fell free. Looking as if it caused him acute physical pain, he held the gun, holster and belt out to her.

She stared, transfixed. He'd just violated the most sacrosanct rule in the Regs book. An officer never gave up his weapon. If she fired it, Diaz would be held directly responsible for her actions. His career was on the line. This action, more than any words he could have spoken, demonstrated his trust in her.

"Take it," he said. "I'll get your Glock at the Fusion Center. Haven't had time to log it in at the Property Room yet." He tilted his head, eyes traveling over her. "The belt is too big, but you can find a way to wrap it around yourself so it holds the gun tight against your body."

When she still hesitated, he frowned down at her. "Veranda," he said softly, using her first name again. "I've only agreed to this insanity because I don't have a better plan. You'll need firepower if things go sideways, which tends to happen with those cartel bastards." He inhaled deeply and blew out a long, slow breath. "I want you back in one piece."

Seeing Diaz in a new light, she lifted the gun and leather belt from his outstretched hands.

34

VERANDA TURNED CHUY'S CELL phone over in her palm. "Screen's cracked."

Her cousin hooked a thumb into the waist of his motorcycle chaps. "I don't remember how the saying goes about beggars and choosers, but I think you're not supposed to be picky, *mi'jita*. The thing works. That's what matters."

Ten minutes after Diaz left for the Fusion Center, Chuy and Tiffany had arrived at the hospital. She'd asked them to hurry, and they had obviously taken her seriously.

Chuy's bald head gleamed under the fluorescent lights of the ER waiting room, bringing the tattoos covering his scalp into sharp relief. "You said you wanted us here fast, but you didn't say nothing about clothes."

With Veranda's personal car out of commission, she had asked Chuy to bring Tiffany and ride to the hospital on two bikes with an extra helmet. She hadn't, however, thought to tell him to tone down his girlfriend's usual attire.

She had gone to the ladies' room with Tiffany to exchange clothes. It took her five full minutes to wriggle into Tiffany's skintight black leather pants and matching bustier. The corseted top bared her shoulders and put her cleavage on full display. When she added Tiffany's thigh-high boots, the ensemble became full-on slut wear.

Now that she stood next to Chuy in the waiting room, she felt the stares of other hospital patrons. Men gawked and women sneered. She turned to Tiffany. "I don't know how you walk around like this. I look like Kinky South of the Border Barbie."

Tiffany motioned up and down her body, indicating Veranda's conservative pantsuit. "What about me?" She wrinkled her nose. "My estrogen levels are dropping every minute I have your monkey suit on."

"It's business attire." Veranda shrugged. "Not my favorite look either. I'd rather be wearing tactical gear."

Tiffany pouted. "This getup could be sold as passive birth control." She turned to Chuy and grimaced. "Don't look at me, *papi*—I'm hideous."

Chuckling, Veranda shot a mocking glare at Tiffany. "At least you're comfortable. "This outfit, on the other hand"—she pointed at herself—"could lead to medical complications."

Concern flitted across Chuy's face. "What are you talking about, *mi'jita?*"

Veranda quirked a brow. "I may need surgery to repair damage from this camel toe."

Tiffany bent to examine the formfitting pants clinging to Veranda's curves. "That's how they're supposed to fit."

Veranda stuck out her leg. "And thigh-high leather boots? Honestly, Tiff, how do you shift gears when you ride your bike?"

Tiffany scoffed. "Those heels are less than four inches. Practically flats. I ride in them all the time." She looked down at her feet, which were encased in Veranda's slip-on loafers. "These clod-hoppers, how-ever, look like the Buster Browns I wore as a kid."

Ignoring the commentary on her footwear, Veranda held up Chuy's cell phone. "And where am I supposed to put this? I couldn't even slide a credit card into these pockets."

"Same place I put my phone." Tiffany plucked it from Veranda's fingers and stuffed it into a small pouch sewn inside the top of the boot Veranda now wore. The phone rested against her thigh within easy reach.

Veranda gave Tiffany a slight nod. "Okay, I'll admit that's pretty cool, but still ... this outfit of yours leaves nothing to the imagination."

Chuy gave his girlfriend a lascivious grin. "It leaves plenty to *my* imagination."

Unfortunately, the bustier also exposed her new Villalobos cartel tattoo with the family mark, but there was nothing she could do about that now.

She turned to Chuy. "May as well complete my transformation to outlaw biker chic."

Grinning, Chuy tugged Diaz's leather belt and empty holster out from his vest. The lieutenant's duty weapon remained tucked into Chuy's waistband while she tried several configurations with the belt. Finally, she wrapped it once around her upper thigh, then crisscrossed it to circle her waist, buckling it at its farthest hole before sliding the holster in place.

She held her hand out to her cousin. "Gun."

He slapped the Glock into her open palm.

She pulled back the slide just enough to see that a round was chambered before easing it into place again. Next, she released the magazine, made sure it was topped off, then shoved it firmly back into the grip, listening for the *snick* that told her it was properly seated. Weapon check complete, she thrust the gun into its holster, where it hung low on her right hip.

Tiffany's eyes widened as she gave Veranda a long perusal. "You are a total badass." She turned to Chuy. "I want a gun like that. She looks fucking hot."

"I'm a convicted felon, *mamacita*. Can't have a firearm." He wrapped an arm around Tiffany's shoulders. "Nothing stopping you from buying one though." He considered Veranda. "Gotta say, it does look bitchin'."

Veranda rolled her eyes. "*Ay, yi, yi*. You've met your match, Chuy." She gave her head a small shake as Chuy pulled his girlfriend against him.

Tiffany playfully pushed away from Chuy, bent to scoop up a jet-black helmet from a nearby table, and held it out to her. "This is for you."

Veranda took it. "I'm glad you wear a full-face."

Tiffany nodded vehemently. "Fuckin' A. Going down once was enough for me to learn my lesson."

Her cousin's pierced brows drew together. "I don't know what you're doing, but I bet it's something completely *loco*. You want some backup?"

"No, Chuy, I can't involve you in this. You're a civilian. But thanks." She pulled the helmet over her head and flipped the black-tinted visor down. Reaching around to the back of her head, she draped her thick ponytail over her left shoulder, fanning the hair out to cover her tattoo. "No one will recognize me like this while we leave the hospital. Where did you park the bikes?"

"Follow me." Chuy and Tiffany led her through the maze of corridors to the ER's public parking area. Two customized Harley Fat Boys occupied a space. One was flat black with leering white skulls on each side. The other was silver with chrome pipes and a vivid green marijuana leaf airbrushed onto the gas tank.

Veranda put her hands on her hips. "Seriously, Chuy?"

He held out a key ring. "Just bought the weed one. Haven't had a chance to repaint it. The skull bike's better for, uh ... stealth mode."

She took the proffered key and slung a leg over the seat. She'd learned to ride when she was a teenager and a refurbished motorcycle was the only vehicle she could afford. After the engine caught, she looked over her shoulder to thank Chuy and Tiffany again as they clambered onto the marijuana bike. Tiffany made a face, pulling the legs of the pantsuit tight against her calves to keep them away from the pipes. Veranda thought she wasn't the only one who prayed not to be recognized as she watched Tiffany jam the spare helmet on and secure the chin strap.

Veranda shouted to Chuy over the din of his bike. "I owe you, Chuy."

He gave her a thumbs-up. "Keep the rubber side down, *mi'jita*."

Veranda sped onto the street, heading to the location Mia had given her for the warehouse. Earlier in her career, she'd worked patrol in the Maryvale precinct, which covered that part of West Phoenix. She knew the area well, and planned her approach to allow maximum cover. Accelerating onto the freeway, she thought about Diaz. He would have an uphill battle to convince the others she wasn't a traitor, a criminal, and a rogue cop.

As she neared the target area fifteen minutes later, she checked for the hundredth time to be sure no one followed her before she downshifted and turned onto a parallel street. When she thought she was close enough, she stopped in the empty parking lot of an abandoned factory, cut the engine, and dismounted, leaving her helmet on. She peeked around the corner at the building Mia had described, directly in front of her and across an alley, about thirty yards away.

Her heart skipped a beat, then went into overdrive when Adolfo stomped out of the warehouse, Carlos and Salazar on his heels. She edged out a bit farther from the crumbling corner of the paint-chipped factory wall to keep the trio in view.

Too far away to make out their words, she watched the men, who were apparently embroiled in an argument. Carlos waved his hands and gesticulated at the warehouse they had exited. Speaking rapidly, he jabbed a finger at a van parked nearby. There were no other vehicles in sight. Veranda observed their body language. Carlos pointed at the warehouse again and Adolfo shook his head.

If the rest of Mia's information was correct, crammed inside the building were at least thirty terrified women, information that would exonerate Veranda, and enough evidence to put Adolfo out of business for good. She prayed they hadn't been able to pack everything up in the time it took her to get here from the hospital. Her stomach clenched as she envisioned a fleet of moving trucks hauling contraband toward the border.

She slid Chuy's phone out of her boot and checked it. Diaz still hadn't called. He certainly knew Chuy's number, so that wasn't the reason for the delay. He must be getting a fresh phone. The cartel could listen in if she contacted anyone with the task force on their cell, so she resisted reaching out to her team. She stuffed the mobile back in its hidden pocket and forced herself to stay put and wait for Diaz to get in touch.

Carlos and Salazar both reentered the warehouse. Moments later, they emerged hefting large red plastic canisters with yellow corrugated nozzles protruding from the top. Veranda looked on in horror as they began splashing liquid from the canisters around the perimeter of the warehouse. The stench of gasoline wafted to her even at this distance. Muffled yells emanated from inside.

Her pulse kicked up. Those screams. The women were still in the building. Adolfo must have figured he didn't have enough time or vehicles to transport them in addition to his property. He had done the math and decided Carlos's captives could be more easily replaced than his cache of computers, weapons, money, and drugs.

Veranda yanked Chuy's phone out again and glanced at the screen. No calls. *Shit! What's keeping Diaz?* Her mind raced, searching for options.

She could call someone outside the task force and tell them to get to the Fusion Center to explain what was going on.

No good. First, her own department wouldn't trust her now, and second, even if it worked, SAU couldn't gear up and get to the warehouse fast enough from a cold start.

She could call 911 anonymously and tell dispatch to send officers out right away for a crime in progress.

She discarded the thought. Even if the dispatcher took her seriously as an anonymous caller, responding units would go completely unprepared into a situation involving armed suspects with incendiary devices. Officers and rescue personnel could get killed. And if she identified herself as Detective Cruz, the dispatcher wouldn't believe her. According to media reports, she was a criminal and a traitor.

Carlos and Salazar finished their circuit around the warehouse and returned to speak with Adolfo, who waited near the van. Adolfo jerked his chin at Carlos, who patted his pockets before pulling out something that fit in his palm. Veranda couldn't see what the object was, but tendrils of fear prickling the back of her neck gave her a clue. Then Carlos flicked his thumb, igniting a bright orange flame.

As Adolfo and Salazar watched, Carlos ambled toward the corner of the building, lighter in hand.

After several anguished seconds, a new plan formed in Veranda's mind. A desperate, insane, suicidal plan. She pulled her helmet off, laid it on the ground, and stepped out from behind cover.

35

VERANDA RECALLED HER TRAINING at the police range. First course of fire: shoot from behind a barricade at the twenty-five-yard line. She'd trained for this. Breathe in, breathe out. She drew a bead on her target and curled her index finger, smoothly squeezing the trigger.

Simultaneous with the report of her gun, Carlos's head snapped back and he collapsed in the gravel in front of the warehouse. The lighter dropped from his slackened hand, harmlessly extinguishing on the ground beside him. She had used the shot snipers took when an armed suspect held a hostage at gunpoint, aiming for a headshot to prevent his dying brain from sending a signal to his hand.

Adolfo raced to his brother's side as Salazar whipped a pistol out from his waistband and leveled it in her direction across the street. For a fraction of a second, their eyes met.

Cracks of gunfire rang out as the corner of the cement block factory wall exploded into pieces inches from her head. She ducked, whirled, and scurried along the side of the building.

Salazar's harsh command cut through the air as he barked at Adolfo in Spanish. "Drag Carlos into the van and torch the place. I'll deal with Cruz."

Heavy footsteps pounded in her direction. In seconds, Salazar would round the corner and shoot her in the back. She sprinted toward an open window and flung herself inside, tucking and rolling onto the cement floor. Using her momentum, she slid behind a wooden crate.

When Salazar peered through the window, she popped up and sprayed a rapid-fire barrage in his direction. *Shit.* She missed. Worse yet, she'd given away her position again.

Salazar's rich, deep voice called to her. "I went to find you earlier this morning, *hermosa*. Now you've found me. Why don't you come here?"

She couldn't help but admire his tactical prowess, taunting her while he zeroed in on her location.

Something scraped along the windowsill as he continued to goad her. "You're all alone too. No backup. Not for a disgraced cop and a member of the Villalobos family."

Anger blazed through her. The conscious part of her brain knew the emotion was unproductive at best, fatal at worst. She tried to turn the tables. "There's a whole SWAT team coming, Salazar."

"So, you know my name. I assume the *federales* told you about my special talent for eliminating problem cops. They call me *El Matador* because my kills are up close and personal." He let out a malevolent chuckle. "And I'll take my time with you, Detective Cruz. Or should I call you Veranda Villalobos?"

His words had their desired effect. She seethed with revulsion as a part of her mind processed the truth. That could have been her name. She realized he had used the distraction technique to approach the window as he spoke. Refocusing, she prepared to shoot another burst of rounds, waiting until he was silhouetted in the open frame.

He edged onto the sill, his bulky form momentarily backlit.

She loosed a fusillade of bullets, the staccato sound deafening in the enclosed space.

He thudded to the ground and she knew she'd hit him. His blasts of return fire told her the wound had not been fatal. A stream of Spanish expletives assailed her ears as she rushed for the side exit door. She peered over her shoulder to see him slumped on the floor, clutching his thigh. If she'd hit the femoral artery, he'd bleed out right there.

She tore out of the abandoned factory, doubling back to the cartel warehouse, scanning the parking lot. She couldn't see Carlos anywhere. A pool of blood saturated the ground where he'd dropped, and a dark red trail led to the waiting van. Fifteen yards away from her, Adolfo picked up the lighter and trotted toward the gasoline-soaked side of the warehouse.

She raised the Glock and took aim. "Stop!"

Adolfo flicked the lighter and glanced down at the gasoline sinking into the gravel by his feet. Eyes on Veranda, a sneer of contempt on his face, he gradually lowered the flame toward the liquid.

She tightened her index finger a fraction, taking the slack out of the trigger. "Don't do it, Adolfo!"

He bent at the waist, stretching his arm down farther.

She pulled the trigger.

No bang.

She tilted the pistol to examine it. The slide, partially locked back, exposed a round lodged at an angle in the chamber. During the shoot-out with Salazar, the magazine had double-fed, jamming the weapon.

While she began the clearing procedure, Adolfo crouched, touched the lighter's flame to the ground, and sprinted toward the idling van. Bright, hungry flames forked out, licking up the side of the warehouse.

Still unable to shoot, she raced after him, but Adolfo lunged into the driver's seat before she could get close. He accelerated and the vehicle fishtailed, tires spewing chunks of gravel in her face.

She flung her hands up and watched the van disappear. She assumed Adolfo moved his equipment and contraband before he fled. Now, every hope of recovering evidence to clear her name and arrest him had vanished. In the next second, her prey drive kicked in. She could jump on Chuy's bike and chase Adolfo down. No way could a van outrun a motorcycle. Adolfo behind bars. A huge chunk of the cartel's business shut down. Her gun and badge returned to her. She could make it all happen if she caught him.

The crackle of fire drew her attention to the warehouse. She turned and gaped at the outside wall, now completely engulfed in flames. Thick black smoke billowed into the sky. Still clutching the jammed gun, she finished the clearing procedure and shoved it in its holster before pulling out her cell phone to punch in 911. She had to call the fire department and let trained professionals handle the rescue.

When the dispatcher answered, Veranda blurted out the address. "There are about thirty people trapped inside. It's arson. They poured gasoline everywhere, so it's going up fast ... coordinate fireboard response with Lieutenant Richard Diaz of the PPD."

Keyboard keys clicked in the background as the dispatcher inputted more information. "What is your name?"

She ignored the question and told the dispatcher the arsonist had fled and gave a description of the van. "Hurry," she added. "The building's not going to hold up much longer." The dispatcher's response faded into the background as she considered her options. Without fire protection, she'd roast before getting anywhere near the victims in the building. Besides, firefighters were on the way. She was a cop. Her job was to arrest bad guys, not rescue people from burning buildings. She had done all she could for the women, and she still had a chance to catch Adolfo. But that window was closing fast.

Her eyes darted to the motorcycle parked next to the abandoned factory across the street. Time to decide. Try to help the women, or pursue Adolfo. She couldn't do both. Her adrenaline kicked in, ramping up for the chase.

Her mind cleared, and she made her decision.

Drawing a deep breath, she interrupted the dispatcher, who peppered her with more questions. "I'm going inside."

She disconnected before the dispatcher could ask any more questions or try to dissuade her. Almost immediately, the phone buzzed in her boot. The dispatcher, following protocol, attempting to reconnect with her. She ignored it and charged around to the rear of the structure.

As she drew near, waves of heat blasted her. Raising an arm to protect her face, she saw flames blanketing two sides of the warehouse. The back hadn't caught yet. Perhaps they ran out of gasoline before they could douse the entire perimeter. She heard a muffled crack, then a thunderous rumble shook the ground beneath her feet. It sounded like a section of the roof had given way.

The women were out of time. She pictured Gabby and her mother. If they were trapped inside, she would want someone to help. Even if it meant risking everything. She shut down her emotions and formulated a plan. Running to the back wall, she spotted a window and tried to push it open.

Locked.

Cupping her hands against the glass, she peered inside the room. Empty.

She drew the Glock, angled the gun to avoid blowback from shattered glass, turned her head aside, and fired. The window exploded into the room. She used the barrel to break out remaining shards jutting from the window frame.

Stuffing the gun back in its holster, she placed both hands on the sash and hoisted herself inside the room, which only contained long rectangular tables and office chairs. Photos of members of the task force covered the walls. *This must be the computer room Mia described.*

She reviewed the details in her mind, recalling the sketch of the warehouse Mia made while they waited for Chuy and Tiffany to arrive at the hospital. Diaz had taken the drawing with him to show the team. According to Mia's diagram, the women's quarters were nearby.

Heat washed over her when she opened the computer room door. Smoke gusted through a short corridor and shrieks filled the air. She followed the sound to a reinforced metal door. A sliding deadbolt secured the women inside. Veranda went to slide the bolt free and yanked her hand back when the metal burned her fingers. Her tight-fitting outfit offered no shirttails or sleeves to use as a barrier. She pulled out her gun and used the barrel to ease the bolt to the side. Gritting her teeth, she used her left hand to grasp the scorching metal doorknob and fling the door open.

Concerned the terrified women might flee in a panic, get lost in the haze and succumb to the smoke, she rushed inside to guide them to safety. Before she could get a word out, one of the women pointed at her and screamed, "Villalobos!"

A moment too late, Veranda realized how she must look. Dressed in black leather, covered in cuts and bruises, holding a gun, and sporting a cartel tattoo on her chest with a Villalobos family mark above it.

Something heavy slammed the side of her head. She staggered and dropped to her knees. The Glock clattered to the floor, and a young woman in a pink tank top kicked it away.

"No!" Veranda put her hands out to stave off a middle-aged woman in a blue dress wielding the base of a blender, swinging it by its cord as she approached.

"I'm trying to rescue you," Veranda blurted in Spanish. "The place is on fire. You all need to get out of here." She pointed over her shoulder. "There's a window in the computer room." She stayed on her knees, open palms raised, attempting not to look threatening. "I broke the glass out."

A deep male voice rumbled from the doorway behind her. "For which I am very grateful."

Still reeling from the blow, she turned her head to see Salazar, his gun trained on her.

"Stay right where you are." Covering the distance between them in one long stride, he bent down, placed the barrel against her temple, and cocked the hammer.

36

VERANDA THOUGHT BACK TO her first felony arrest. She'd forced the suspect to kneel with his hands up for a reason. The position put him at a complete disadvantage. Now Salazar held the position of strength. Any move she made would be telegraphed long before she could mount a counterattack. Heart slamming against her ribs, she calculated the odds of twisting out of the way before he could pull the trigger. Piss poor.

Salazar pushed the muzzle harder against her skull. "You can fight, *puta*, but you're no match for me. You made your choice, and now you will—"

A dull *thunk* reverberated through the room and the pressure from Salazar's gun lifted. Veranda spun to the side and jumped to her feet in a fighting stance. Before she could stop her, the same young woman in the pink tank top kicked Salazar's gun to a far corner.

Salazar teetered, and the woman with the blender delivered another vicious blow to his head. He went down in slow motion, sprawling on the floor.

The woman in the blue dress looked down at Salazar's inert form. "That was for Mia," she said. Tears glistened in her eyes as she glanced at Veranda. "An enemy of that *pendejo*, Salazar, is someone I will help."

Veranda's synapses began firing again. "You must be Mia's mother." At the woman's gasp, she added, "Don't worry, she's safe."

"What's going on?" Mia's mother said, frantic. "Who are you?"

"I don't have time to explain." She performed a quick mental inventory of the room. A kitchenette occupied one corner. The women must have been pressed into service to feed the men ... among their other duties.

She addressed Mia's mother, gesturing toward the terrified group of women huddled together as the crackling and popping from the encroaching fire increased. "Is this everyone?"

"Yes. They took my other daughter, Sofia, away with them." She stifled a sob.

Veranda decided her new ally was the best person to help. "You need to lead everybody out. Now."

Mia's mother hesitated, then seemed to come to a decision. "Here." She handed Veranda the blender base and motioned the others to follow as she darted from the room.

Veranda held the appliance up by its cord. It had been effective, but she needed to find both guns. Salazar appeared unconscious, maybe even dead, but she couldn't be sure and wanted firepower.

She spotted the Glock on the floor in the opposite corner and took a step in that direction when a muscular arm swept her legs out from under her. She landed hard on her back, knocking the air out of her lungs. Salazar rolled on top of her, pinning her under his bulk.

She swung the blender's base at his face, but he parried the blow, knocking the appliance from her grasp. He grabbed her hand, his other palm encircling her throat.

Aware she had only seconds before unconsciousness overtook her, Veranda scrabbled for the blender's cable with her free hand. She grasped it between her fingers, looped the cord around his neck, and pulled it tight. Salazar released her, fingers digging at his neck as he rolled off her body. As soon as his weight lifted, she raised her legs, jammed her feet into his side for leverage, and yanked the cable even tighter.

She leaned in to see Salazar's face turn purple and his eyes bulge. He clawed desperately at the plastic-coated cord, now biting deep into the flesh of his thick neck. She grunted as every muscle in her body tensed with effort. He gurgled and thrashed, but she held firm. A few moments later, he slumped.

She lessened her hold and panted with exhaustion, her thoughts warring as the room grew hotter.

She could flee to safety and leave Salazar to burn.

She could finish strangling him until he was dead.

She could use the cord to tie his hands and drag him out by his feet. Even if she couldn't lift him outside the broken window, rescuers would probably have enough time to extract him before the building was engulfed.

Whatever choice she made, no one would know. His life was in her hands.

She glanced down, noting the field dressing he'd made for his thigh to stanch the bleeding from the gunshot wound. His survival instincts were keen. He wanted to live. Despite that, he had entered a burning building to kill her. He would always want to kill her. But she could stop him, once and for all.

She looked down at his inert form. Was she a wolf? Or a guard dog protecting the flock, as Sam had claimed? According to her police training, she should render aid once a suspect no longer posed a threat.

Precious seconds passed. Tendrils of smoke curled through the doorway. She had to choose. Now.

She unwrapped the power cord from his neck and rolled him onto his chest. As he started to come around, coughing and wheezing, she used it to bind his wrists behind his back.

Cursing, she grabbed his ankles and dragged him into the short hallway. The heat beat at her. The ceiling above her creaked and popped, on the verge of collapse. She redoubled her efforts and pulled harder. Her strength waned. Moving Salazar cost her. Overheated air scorched her lungs. A thickening layer of smoke hovered overhead as time ran out.

Salazar let out a groan as she lugged him through the doorway into the computer room. The wail of sirens competed with the roar of the fire now that she neared the broken window. Would the fire crew check the back of the building soon enough? Would the women tell them she was inside or, afraid of authorities due to their illegal status, had they simply fled?

Veranda's muscles burned and fatigue set in. She couldn't lift him out of the window. The sound of grinding metal startled her. She looked up to see a support beam mounted in the ceiling bow ominously. She hunched over Salazar, covering his upper body as the ceiling gave way with an earsplitting crunch. Pieces of ceiling tile and building debris rained down on her back.

Fully conscious now, Salazar blinked up at her through the dust. "Untie me so I can get out."

She assumed he would try to kill her if she freed him. Completely spent, she had no strength left to fight him off. She gave him a shove. "Get up and walk to the window."

He struggled to his feet, unbalanced with his hands bound behind his back and the heavy blender base dangling from its cord around his wrists.

"Lean your chest and head through the window and I'll push you the rest of the way out."

"I could break my neck landing with my arms behind my back."

"Or, I could just leave you inside and let you burn. Your choice."

He swore and staggered to the window, forcing his head and torso through. He had to twist his upper body to get his broad shoulders through the opening. She bent down, wrapped her arms around his knees, and heaved with all her remaining strength. Salazar flopped out of the window and thudded to the ground.

Another piece of the ceiling buckled and fell, knocking her flat on the floor. The room shimmered and blurred. Consciousness ebbed.

As if from a great distance, her kickboxing instructor's voice reached her from the gathering darkness. *Get your ass up, Cruz!*

No one would get to her in time. She had to save herself. Physical reserves depleted, she called on her emotions to give her strength. For her, anger imparted power. And she knew exactly how to tap into her rage.

She glanced down at her chest, where the Villalobos family tattoo tainted her flesh. In this moment, she finally understood what Sam had tried to tell her. She had claws and fangs and a predator's instincts, but she was not part of the Villalobos pack. She had chosen to act as a protector, not as a predator. She had laid down her life to save the women—and even Salazar—as a true guardian would.

She may not be able to control her heritage, but her choices made her one of the sentinels who watched over her city. She belonged to no one, and she would not let *El Lobo* claim her. How dare he mark her as one of his own?

Fury now burning as hot as the fire around her, she forced her unsteady legs to stand, pitched forward, and clamped her hands on the window frame. With her last measure of strength, she hoisted her body through the window.

Slamming onto the ground in a heap, she coughed and gasped. Eyes stinging from smoke, she staggered to her feet and looked all around.

Salazar had fled.

37

TWO HOURS LATER AT police headquarters, Veranda hung back as Sam opened the greenroom door.

"Give us another five minutes, dammit," he said. "And she's not going out there until someone brings her a raid jacket." He shut the door in Sergeant Hearst's face and turned to her. "They can't wait to shove you in front of the cameras."

Still wearing Tiffany's biker-slut outfit, she tugged the bustier up to be sure nothing spilled out. "Yeah, I totally need that jacket. What's the rush with the news conference anyway?"

Shortly after falling through the warehouse window, she'd been grabbed by firefighters, who'd slapped an oxygen mask on her face and hustled her out to a waiting ambulance. During her checkup from the paramedics, she'd been interrogated by the entire task force and SAU. Every attempt to locate and apprehend anyone from the cartel failed.

Instead of being allowed to go home and clean up, Veranda and the team were ordered to headquarters after Chief Tobias informed them the mayor had called a news conference. Veranda had ridden Chuy's motorcycle, complete with police motor squad escort. She hadn't understood all the fuss at the time, and she wanted answers now.

"What aren't you telling me, Sam?"

He lowered his voice. "The mayor is out there in front of a pack of reporters right now telling them what a hero you are. You're about to be trotted out like a show pony."

"What? Please tell me you're joking." She swiped a hand across her nose in a vain attempt to clear the residue of smoke that continued to irritate her sinuses. "I thought I was headed for prison."

"Old news. Now, you're the police officer who saved more than thirty women from certain death while you singlehandedly took on a notorious drug cartel." His mustache twitched. "And it doesn't hurt that you were almost killed in the process."

She put her hands on her hips. "You can't be serious."

"The mayor stuck up for you after the multiple warrant service fiasco. He must've felt like a pair of cheeks when those photos came out making you look like you were in cahoots with the cartel because of blood ties."

She clenched her teeth at the mention of her public humiliation. She had vowed to keep the secret of her birth. Now she'd been exposed for all the world to see. But the world didn't know the true extent of her shame. The real victim was her mother, who had never asked for this fight. First Lorena's husband, then her eldest daughter, had dragged her into it. Veranda blinked and tried to catch up as Sam continued.

"Of course, I'm sure the mayor supported you based on a recommendation from Chief Tobias, who was about to lose his job this morning."

She cast her eyes to the floor. Yet another person who had paid a heavy price because of her. "I forgot about the chief."

"Now they both want vindication. They'll turn you from the goat into the hero and the mayor will be reelected while the chief stays in his comfy office on the fourth floor." He frowned. "Everybody's happy."

Cognizant of the edge in Sam's voice, she glanced back up. "Then why do you look upset?"

"Because you need to understand why you're suddenly the PPD poster child." He sighed. "It's politics. Also, I don't like it because they're going to make you get in front of those microphones and make a speech. And *El Lobo* will see it. The target on your back will be bigger than ever."

"In case you forgot, I blew Carlos's brains out and neutralized Adolfo, who's now a fugitive with outstanding warrants and can't operate freely in the US anymore. His house and all of his properties in Phoenix will be seized." She lifted a shoulder. "Hector can't want me any deader than he already did."

"But seeing you on camera. That'll drive the point home like nothing else."

"Fuck him."

Sam gave a bark of laughter. "There's the attitude that's made you so popular with *El Lobo*."

"You mean my father."

All traces of amusement fled Sam's rugged face. "The decisions you made at the warehouse prove where your heart is. Remember our conversation a few days ago when you felt bad about chasing Roberto Bernal instead of stopping to help Castillo?"

"Yes," Veranda said quietly. She lowered her head to study Tiffany's ash-covered boots.

"This morning at the warehouse, you could've chased after Adolfo. You called the fire department to rescue the women. No one would blame you for not running into a burning building before help arrived." He frowned. "In fact, Diaz is still furious you put yourself in harm's way instead of waiting for the firemen to show up."

"I had to do something."

"Exactly." He grew animated, voice rising as he continued. "You watched it all go. Every scrap of evidence that could exonerate you, the cartel's contraband, and the computer-hacking equipment. Worst of all, Adolfo himself." He paused. "You let him walk in order to rescue the women. Hell, you even saved Salazar."

She owed him the truth. She met his intense gaze and said, "I almost didn't."

"When it counted, you proved you were a guardian. You protected the flock."

"Yeah, well I didn't mention during my after-action debriefing that I actually enjoyed choking out Salazar. When I thought of all the people he's hurt and killed …" She hesitated a moment, deliberating whether to tell him the rest. "I seriously considered leaving him to burn."

Sam placed a hand on her shoulder. "But you didn't *do* it. We all have dark thoughts at times. Our actions are what define us." He dropped his arm. "And thank the good Lord for that, because if I was tried for every criminal thought that passed through my mind, I'd be a lifer."

She gave him a wry smile. "Say what you want, Sam, but I don't feel respectable enough to be a guardian. I'm too much of a wolf. Sometimes I feel like two sides of me are at war."

He studied her, as if reflecting on her words. "If you're a wolf, then you're a breed apart from the rest of the Villalobos clan. I don't care what your DNA report says."

A different breed of wolf. She turned the concept over in her mind.

The door banged open and the entire task force trooped into the greenroom. Diaz carried her raid jacket. His dark eyes lingered over her curves, accentuated by Tiffany's getup, as he handed it to her.

Marci gave her an appreciative look. "Just for the record, I freakin' love that outfit. You totally rock the whole dominatrix Latina biker chick thing. Personally, I think you should wear it out there with your tattoo on full display." She waved her hand indifferently. "Tell them all to kiss your ass if they can't handle it. Never apologize for who you are, Veranda." She looked around as if daring anyone to contradict her. "I sure as hell don't."

She cracked a smile. "You're awesome, Marci."

"I know, right?" Marci winked. "Smart. Sexy. Sassy. I've got it all going on."

A chuckle went around the room as Veranda snapped on the blue nylon windbreaker with the PPD logo embroidered on the upper left chest, directly over the tattoo. With HOMICIDE stenciled in bright yellow letters on the back, the jacket covered her from neck to mid-thigh, and she felt the police department cloaking her blemish.

Agent Rios inclined his head at Veranda. "Agent Lopez and I will fly out tomorrow. We will search for Adolfo, Salazar, and Sofia Pacheco in Mexico. I do not believe they will kill the girl. According to her twin sister and her mother, they never injured Sofia because she is too valuable to them."

"What about Mia and her mother?" Diaz wanted to know.

Lopez responded. "They are both anxious to return to their home in Mexico as soon as possible, as are all the other women. We delayed our flight back so we could personally escort them after they give statements. They understand they may be needed for a trial."

Sam snorted. "Doesn't look like that'll happen anytime soon. Every single suspect's either dead or in the wind. We've got warrants out, but..." He spread his hands in futility. "We wanted to get evidence against *El Lobo*'s daughter Daria as well, but apparently she never had anything to do with the human trafficking operation, so the women don't know much about her."

Agent Gates stepped forward and extended her hand. "Detective Cruz, I apologize for blaming you for the failure of the raids. The leaks in the computer system were so pervasive nothing we did would have succeeded, no matter how much time we took to plan the takedown."

Veranda returned her handshake. "You were trying to make the operation a success. All of us were caught off guard."

Agent Tanner, ears reddening, bobbed his head in agreement. "We all share the same goal, Detective. No hard feelings."

Veranda willed herself not to roll her eyes. Agents Flag and Wallace snickered behind Tanner's back as Gates grimaced.

Agent Lopez crossed the room to face Veranda. "Detective Cruz," he said in his accented tones. "I have never met anyone who crossed Salazar and lived. You must be as brave as everyone says. I will admit, at first I was afraid the Villalobos cartel had infiltrated the Phoenix Police as they have my own agency. Those pictures of you on the news, they were... Anyway, I know now that you are your mother's daughter. It doesn't matter who your father was."

Thoughts of her mother pained her. She pictured Lorena locked inside her house, too ashamed to show her face in public. At that moment, Veranda decided she would do something about it.

Diaz tugged out his buzzing cell phone to glance at the screen. "The mayor just finished his statement to the media. Chief Tobias is about to introduce you, Detective." He nodded in her direction. "You're up."

Sam leaned down to whisper in her ear, "They're looking for a hero. And they've chosen you. Go with it."

"I'm not the one who deserves admiration." Determination welled inside her as she marched toward the greenroom door. "And everyone will know it by the time I'm done talking."

38

VERANDA ENTERED THE MEDIA briefing room through the rear stage door. At the sight of her, reporters erupted with a volley of questions and cameras flashed. She stood mutely on the stage behind him while the chief raised his hands for the horde to settle, then spoke into a bank of microphones. "Detective Cruz is a hero who put her life on the line to rescue thirty-two women who would have perished in a deadly blaze if not for her intervention."

The more he expounded on her courage, the hotter her face burned with embarrassment. At first, she had trouble identifying the emotion making her insides squirm. It wasn't pride. Or satisfaction. Then it struck her: guilt. The suffering she'd brought upon her family had molded itself into a leaden lump and sank down to her gut.

Chief Tobias announced her name, pulling her from her reverie. Her nylon jacket crinkled as she trudged to the lectern. A hush descended over the mass of reporters and camera crews while she adjusted the microphone.

Grasping both sides of the lectern, she cleared her throat. "Thank you, Chief, but let me be clear ... I'm no hero. I did what I'm trained to do." Looking out at the hushed audience, aware of all the eyes upon her, she forged ahead. "The true hero is my mother, Lorena Cruz-Hidalgo-Gomez. She has remained silent about her ordeal for decades, but now everyone knows—or thinks they know—her story. I will use this opportunity to set the record straight in the hope that she can reclaim her life. Ever since my DNA results were leaked to the news, my mother shut herself away from the community she loves." She narrowed her eyes. "And she deserves better."

No one spoke. No one moved. She sensed the tension in the room as they waited for her to continue. Even Kiki Lowell, sitting near the front on the edge of her seat, leaned forward in rapt attention.

Telling her mother's story would forever change both of their lives, but she was finished keeping secrets. "When my face was splashed all over the news as the daughter of *El Lobo*, many people jumped to the conclusion that my mother had an affair with a notorious criminal back in Mexico while she was married. Nothing could be further from the truth."

The moment had arrived. Her mother might never forgive her, but she had to advocate for her anyway. She raised her chin and spoke in a clear, carrying voice, "Hector Villalobos raped my mother."

A murmur went around the room.

"More than thirty years ago, Hector murdered my mother's first husband, Ernesto Hidalgo, an honorable federal police agent working in Mexico City. After he killed Ernesto, Hector broke into my mother's home and forced himself on her." Her fingers tightened on the lectern's wooden edges. "She barely escaped with her life."

She directed her next comments at the cameras in the room, speaking directly to the public. "My mother is a Christian woman, devoted to her husband. She's devastated by the gossip and whispers. Her private nightmare has become public. No rape victim should ever go through that."

Some of the reporters fidgeted in their seats, others became interested in their notepads.

"To make matters worse, she didn't discover she was pregnant with me until she arrived in Phoenix. She didn't know if my father was her husband, or his killer. She always hoped I was her husband's child." Veranda's voice caught. "And she held onto that dream until early this morning, when she learned the truth from watching the news. Now she won't come out of her house or speak to anyone because she's ashamed." Veranda paused to rein in her emotions. "My mother is a victim. No ... a survivor. And she shouldn't feel any disgrace, but she does."

Kiki Lowell tentatively raised her hand.

Veranda ignored her and went on. "I'm grateful every day that my mother took a chance on me. She raised me and helped shape the person I am." She straightened. "I can't change who my biological father is, and some may hold it against me. But know this: I will fight Hector Villalobos with every ounce of strength I have. I won't stop until there is justice."

Kiki got to her feet, waving her arm to attract Veranda's attention. An older reporter sitting next to her reached up, clutched her elbow, and yanked Kiki back down into her seat. She quailed under his withering glare.

Veranda released her white-knuckled grip on the lectern and spread her hands wide. "Six weeks ago, the Villalobos cartel burned down our family's restaurant. But a new one is under construction. And it will rise from the ashes like a phoenix. A few days ago, I stopped by the construction site and saw my mother bringing Red Bird of

Paradise bushes there to plant. She chose them because they make her think of phoenix fire and of renewal."

She paused, debating her next words. She'd chosen a course of action, but should she make it public? Knowing her mother would see the broadcast and might be too angry to see her again, Veranda realized this may be her only chance to communicate.

She pictured her mother's soft hazel eyes, came to a decision, and plowed on. "As soon as I leave this building, I'll plant a Red Bird of Paradise bush beside the restaurant construction site next to my mother's."

She hadn't originally intended to disclose her plans, but was desperate to reach out to her mother. She would go to *Mamá*, beg her forgiveness for telling the world her secret, then ask her to help plant the new bush. "I want her to know she will get past this. *We* will get past this."

Veranda raised her voice, letting her passion fill the space around her. "My mother suffered in silence for decades, kept her misery and humiliation to herself while she helped and supported everyone around her. Family, friends, her community, strangers in need—it didn't matter." Veranda slammed her fist on the podium. "The secrets and lies are over, and Lorena Cruz-Hidalgo-Gomez should be able to go out into her community with her head held high. Because of this courageous woman, I am a better person. And our city is a better place."

Without another word, Veranda pivoted and strode from the dais, reporters shouting questions at her retreating back.

39

Villalobos family
compound, Mexico

ADOLFO SHRANK DEEPER INTO the plush leather chair in his father's office. He noted the vein pulsing in *El Lobo*'s temple as he raised the television's remote and clicked off the live newsfeed from Phoenix. When the screen went black, absolute silence pervaded the space.

Three sets of hostile eyes turned on him. Adolfo knew an attack could come from anywhere around the mahogany table. Daria and Salazar didn't trouble to hide their contempt, and his father's cold glare chilled him to his core.

He mentally reviewed the series of events after he set fire to the warehouse. He'd driven the van to his penthouse suite in downtown Phoenix when Salazar called his cell phone. Unwilling to double back to pick him up, he sent one of his men to collect Salazar in an alley a few blocks from the burning warehouse.

The magnitude of his situation set in when he phoned Daria, instructing her to be at the helipad on the rooftop of his luxury high-rise in fifteen minutes or he would leave without her. Salazar was last to arrive, the propeller blades already churning as he dived into the chopper, crashing into Carlos's blood-spattered corpse on the floor. They had flown straight to Mexico, where he now faced his father's judgment.

Accusation lit Hector's eyes when he finally spoke to Adolfo. "Why are two of my sons dead when Veranda Cruz is still alive?"

Adolfo offered the only satisfactory reply. "I accept responsibility, *Papá*."

Daria and Salazar remained conspicuously silent. He was sure they enjoyed watching him feel his father's wrath.

Hector glowered from his position at the head of the table. "You asked to be in charge. I trusted you. Now our business is in shambles, our suppliers are looking for other markets, and our distribution network is crumbling. The convoy of vehicles and equipment you packed up in Phoenix are currently traveling to the border. Let us hope they arrive here safely."

Adolfo's pulse, already racing, kicked into overdrive. There would be consequences. He struggled to find purchase in the shifting sands of blame. "I had everything under control. I didn't foresee the girl escaping. If she hadn't gotten away—"

"The girl escaped from one of your brother's coyotes. Are you accusing Carlos of incompetence?" Hector asked in his softest, most deadly voice.

The question concealed a trap. Adolfo had already accepted responsibility. If he tried to foist blame on his younger brother, he appeared deceptive. On the other hand, if he continued to shoulder all of the blame, he could end up a scapegoat. He traversed a field of landmines, any of which could explode in his face without warning.

"No, sir." Adolfo responded quickly. "I was in charge. I'm just explaining how—"

"How you didn't oversee every aspect of your operation. That is one of the hallmarks of effective leadership." Hector placed his palms on the table. Nostrils flaring, he lowered his voice to a whisper—more menacing than any shout. "You must always know what is going on. You must hold your people accountable. You must only delegate responsibility to those capable of handling it."

Adolfo did his best not to flinch at the end of each declaration. "What's going to happen now?" His father's overblown speech about leadership surely preceded a lesson for him. And *El Lobo* was a brutal teacher.

Before Hector answered, Daria spoke up. "You failed, Adolfo. Now it's my turn. I already have a plan to regain our control of the narcotics market and expand it into a new area." She turned her attention to her father. "Opioids. Everyone is getting hooked on prescription pain killers. The US government is taking steps to limit legal consumption, which opens a whole new market for us. All of those people won't be able to quit, they can't get their pills legally, and they're not comfortable with shooting up." She bestowed *El Lobo* with her most winning smile. "Perfect sales opportunity for us. Not only will we recover our losses from Adolfo's disaster, we will be bigger than ever."

Hector's demeanor shifted, taking on the air of a corporate raider scouting a potential conquest. "As I mentioned before, our chain has been severely compromised. I'm sure we can make the product, but how can we deliver it to customers?"

"We will divert our distribution," Daria said. "I already have networks in place for weapon sales. It's easy to convert my arms dealers to drugs. Unlike my dear brother"—she shot him a disdainful look—"I can still travel freely across the border and take charge of our main hub in Phoenix."

Red hot coals scorched Adolfo's belly. Daria had made her power play. Constantly undermining him, she'd made it clear she intended to take the reins of the family business.

"Interesting." Hector steepled his fingers. "Adolfo had big dreams of dominating the world markets, but he failed to take care of the details. And look what happened."

"I am not Adolfo." She spat his name out like spoiled meat. "I solve problems. And the first one on my list is that bitch, Veranda Cruz. Bartolo is dead because of her, and now she killed Carlos. Now not only will she die … she will suffer until she begs for death. I will see to it personally. Then I will take my place as your successor when you retire, *Papá*."

Hector tilted his head, a thoughtful expression on his face. "Actually, I have other plans. You may run the US distribution network, but Salazar will run all divisions of the business outside of the States. He will also see to the development of our new opioid manufacturing division."

"What?" Daria lurched forward in her seat. "That's most of our organization. And the pills were my idea."

Hector appeared unfazed by her display. "Salazar has proven his loyalty, and his skill, many times over."

Adolfo resented Daria, but he would choose her over the interloper his father had somehow come to trust above his own flesh and blood.

Apparently anxious to take Salazar down a notch, Daria directed a question to her father. "Didn't you task Salazar with killing Veranda Cruz?"

Salazar, occupying the chair to Adolfo's right, mustered a defense. "And I would have done it. Except that Adolfo canceled the hit and called me back to the warehouse after that *cabrón* Felix let the girl escape."

Daria's hairstyle, a French twist high on the back of her head, revealed the scald creeping up her graceful neck. "What is it with Salazar? Why are you turning over the majority of our family business to him?" She flung out an arm. "He's just a ... a ... foot soldier."

For once, Adolfo agreed with Daria and opened his mouth to join her protest.

"Silence." Hector stood and paced to the imposing family crest mounted on the wall. "Do you recall when I told you about my days as a Federal Judicial Police agent working with Ernesto Hidalgo?"

"Yes," Adolfo answered, noting that Daria dared to cross her arms and set her jaw without responding. *El Lobo* had always granted her more leeway, but Adolfo sensed she grew perilously close to the edge of his tolerance.

Hector clasped his hands behind his back and studied the intricately worked shield featuring two black wolves standing on their hind legs against a gold background. "I explained how I was tipped off before Ernesto could arrest me, but I never said who gave me the inside information."

His father often went off on tangents, but Adolfo found this turn of conversation bizarre. Why had his father referenced an incident from over thirty years ago in response to a question about Salazar? The man was close to his own age. He couldn't possibly have been his father's source. Adolfo cut his eyes to Salazar, who wore his usual inscrutable mask.

Hector pivoted to face them. "Our agency chief at the time was an older man with a much younger wife. She was quite beautiful, and I sensed a woman like her would likely be … unfulfilled in such a marriage." A humorless smile crossed his features, then disappeared. "I flirted with her at every official function. Eventually we had an affair." He shrugged. "She had no interest in leaving her husband and, at the time, I wasn't looking for a wife. We had strong feelings for each other though, and when she overheard her husband talking about my impending arrest, she told me all about Ernesto's investigation and the charges he would place. I made my move that very night."

From his father's previous stories, Adolfo knew his move had been to kill Ernesto and burn the evidence. Hector still had to leave the force, but he'd thwarted any potential prosecution against himself. Not only had he never been arrested, he had never even been charged with Ernesto's murder. Information about the chief's disloyal wife was new to Adolfo, but unrelated to their current situation. Perplexed, he studied his father, who appeared to select his next words with considerable care.

"When the chief's wife turned out to be pregnant a few months later, she convinced him the baby was his. I suspect he may have had his doubts, but he never mentioned them as far as I know."

Adolfo looked at Salazar with dawning comprehension. Shock gave way to rage.

Hector stood his ground, gazing down at Adolfo and Daria in turn. "Of course, I knew the child was mine, and you each know how I feel about our noble bloodline."

Adolfo seethed. *The fucking bloodline.* His father's religion. Preached to them from the time they were old enough to understand. *El Lobo*, born into poverty, sought to elevate his position in society. He justified his atrocities with references to his birthright. He traced his ancestry through the conquistadors back to Spain, when his family held vast wealth and power. Now it appeared his father had expanded the gene pool. Again.

Either unaware or unconcerned about the impact of his revelation, Hector plowed on. "When the boy came of age, I introduced myself. I must confess I was impressed with how he'd turned out. He only needed a bit of prompting to understand how he could prosper working for me. The only caveat was that he would have to prove himself without using my name. He would rise or fall in the Villalobos organization on his own merit. He also couldn't use his old last name anymore." Hector scowled. "He had grown up with the last name of his mother's husband, that *pendejo* chief of police, who wasn't even his real father. With my help, he created a new identity using his mother's maiden name as his surname before joining the military. By the time he got out, he had become known simply as Salazar, the fierce warrior. Only after he joined my organization did he become *El Matador*. Very few people outside this room are aware of his true background."

Adolfo glanced at Daria, who looked like she wanted to hit something. She had obviously come to the same conclusion he had.

"There is another important point to this story I haven't mentioned yet." Hector stroked his silver and black goatee. "I promised the chief's wife I would wait until our son turned eighteen to introduce myself and I would never mention our relationship to anyone else. In exchange for my silence, and for allowing my son to bear another man's last name, I chose the child's first name and she convinced her husband it was her idea."

Adolfo's mind reeled. He struggled to keep up with the revelations, sensing another one barreling directly at him.

With grim satisfaction lighting his eyes, Hector continued. "From the time I was young, I decided to name my children alphabetically, and I already knew what my first son would be called."

Adolfo finally found his voice. "Your chief's wife's maiden name was Salazar." He made it a statement.

Hector nodded silently, apparently waiting for Adolfo to arrive at the inexorable conclusion.

Adolfo swallowed the bile in his throat and directed his next question at Salazar. "What … is your first name?"

Salazar's ebony eyes were trained on Hector. His father. He did not acknowledge Adolfo's question with even a glance.

"Salazar's first name is Adelmo." Hector's eyes shone with pride as he returned *El Matador's* gaze with obvious affection. "Which means noble and strong."

Adolfo heard his voice crack with strain as the final piece clicked into place. "If you named all of your children alphabetically … "

"Yes, Adolfo. Salazar is my true firstborn son."

Daria shot to her feet and stomped across the room to confront her father. "But he is a bastard!"

Hector moved so fast Daria had no time to react. He backhanded his daughter across the face, the *smack* as loud as a gunshot. The blow knocked her off her feet, sending her sprawling onto the thick Persian rug.

Eyes wide, she laid a quivering hand on her cheek. She slowly withdrew it and stared at the blood on her fingertips caused by her father's ornate family crest ring.

316

Nostrils flared, eyes narrowed to slits, *El Lobo* spoke to her in a lethal undertone. "Never call him that again."

Daria gazed up at her father, mouth working, no words coming out.

Adolfo sensed the power shift in the room. The world had tilted on its axis, as Salazar usurped his *and* Daria's place in the pack. This brutal display made his father's choice clear. He and his sister had been shunted aside, while Adelmo Salazar would be groomed to take over the family empire.

He looked down at his sister, still on the floor. Perhaps she would finally ally with him against the outsider. He extended a hand to her.

She turned to him, her eyes full of molten fury. "I don't need a fucking hand from you, *pendejo*."

Adolfo lowered his arm as Daria got to her feet. As always, he was on his own.

Hector chuckled as if Daria were a precocious child who had said something cute. Smiling, he smoothed his lapel and looked at his daughter. "I know you want to take over someday, *mi'ja*, but I am simply not prepared to accept a female as leader of the family business."

Daria bristled. "Women have led entire nations, *Papá*. Let me show you what a female can do." She pointed at Adolfo. "As I predicted, Adolfo disgraced himself, but I have done nothing wrong."

Adolfo clenched his hands into tight fists. He would tolerate insults from his father, but not his sister. Aware he could do nothing at the moment, he buried the seeds of revenge in a fertile corner of his mind to germinate, silently vowing they would bear fruit.

Hector scrutinized his daughter. "I will give you a critical assignment, *mi'ja*. If you succeed, I will reconsider your position in the future."

Daria shot Salazar a venomous glare before turning back to her father. "Name it."

Hector sneered in his direction. "Adolfo brought me Carlos's body, and now I must bury a son." He turned to Daria. "You will bring me Veranda Cruz's body, and I will also bury a daughter."

40

VERANDA PULLED HER DARK sunglasses from the Tahoe's console and shoved them on to block the late afternoon sun as she cruised down the street to her family's cluster of casitas at South Mountain. After hours of questions from detectives and a second debriefing with the task force, Diaz had reinstated her to full duty.

She sighed as she recalled his parting instructions. She was to report to the Professional Standards Bureau first thing tomorrow morning. The department would conduct a full investigation into all circumstances surrounding her suspension and the shooting of Carlos Villalobos. She doubted the blood sample they had taken would still contain any residue of whatever Salazar had injected her with, but no one questioned her claim of memory loss any longer.

The Tahoe's oversized tires crunched on the gravel driveway when she pulled up to the largest house in the center of the family property. She'd called ahead and asked Chuy and Tiffany to meet her here, intending to put her own clothes back on, then convince *Mamá* to go to the construction site of the restaurant with her to plant the Red Bird of Paradise bush.

Chuy had apparently told the whole family she was coming, because she'd been forced to navigate around several familiar cars on her way down the long driveway. The skull motorcycle leaned on its kickstand next to the mailbox, and she was relieved Chuy had picked it up from headquarters.

After coming to a stop, she adjusted the rearview mirror to check the cargo area. She smiled at the dense bush, secured in place with twine, its fiery blossoms topping slender sprigs jutting from verdant foliage.

She pushed the SUV's door open, swung down from the driver's seat, and started for *Mamá*'s front door. Doubt crept in and she hesitated, looking down at her PPD raid jacket, snapped up all the way to her throat. Marci's words came back to her. *Never apologize for who you are.* Wasn't she about to tell her mother not to be ashamed anymore? The cartel had tried to humiliate her by permanently marking her and exposing the truth about her birth. Veranda couldn't change her past. Neither could Lorena.

A few weeks ago, her mother had finally stopped wearing the heavy silver choker that covered the scar left by Hector's knife the night he raped her. Veranda had celebrated that victory. Now what would it say if she hid her tattoo as her mother had concealed the wound on her neck for years? The tattoo, like the scar, had been inflicted by the Villalobos family. She drew a deep breath and yanked the jacket open, pulling the snaps apart with a series of pops. She shrugged out of it and tossed the nylon windbreaker into the open driver's door window. She would greet her family with the Villalobos body art fully visible. She would own it.

She strode to the door and knocked.

Tío Rico answered. His eyes traveled from her face to the tattoo on her chest above the bustier. His expression clouded as he looked back up at her. "Come in, Veranda."

She walked into the living room, crowded with family. Her *tíos* and *tías* and *primos* were all there. They took in the tattoo, and the smiles slid from their faces.

She looked around. "Where's *Mamá*?"

Lorena made her way to the front of the group and stopped short. She looked her daughter up and down, eyes brimming with unshed tears. "Gabriela used her laptop to show me your speech on TV. *Ay, mi'ja.*" She shook her head. "I've been a fool hiding in my house."

"Oh, *Mamá*." Veranda rushed to her mother and swept her into a tight hug. She felt the warmth of a muscular chest against her back as Chuy joined their embrace, his ink-covered arms wrapped around both of them. One by one, the rest of the family gathered around, squeezing together to form a group hug. Somebody sniffled, and Veranda fought to maintain her composure.

Finally, they broke apart, Lorena dabbing her eyes with a tissue.

A tremendous weight lifted from Veranda's heart as she gave her mother's hand a squeeze. "Since you saw the news conference, you know I have a Red Bird of Paradise bush in the car. I'd like to drive you to the restaurant site to plant it now, before sunset."

"We'll all go," Chuy said. "Tiffany brought your clothes if you want to change first."

Tiffany strutted toward her in an electric blue tube top, a micro miniskirt, and spike stiletto sandals. She held out a paper grocery bag. "Everything's in here. No offense, but I couldn't stand wearing that hideous pantsuit a minute longer." She shuddered.

Veranda took the bag. She looked around the room at her family. They had accepted her back into the fold. They knew who she was, what she was, but loved her anyway. Suddenly, getting back into her police persona didn't seem so urgent. Something more important took precedence. She slowly set the bag on the floor. "Let's go now."

Everyone piled into various vehicles. Lorena sat next to Veranda in the front passenger seat of the Tahoe. Her stepfather sat directly behind her in the seat next to Gabby, who cuddled the quivering little Chihuahua puppy.

"I named him Randy," Gabby said. "You know, like the boy version of Veranda." She scratched his tiny head. "He's my best friend, and he's teaching me to be brave … like you."

"I'm honored." Veranda smiled as she led the caravan of vehicles from the driveway and onto the street toward the restaurant.

There had been moments the past few hours when she'd felt like a Chihuahua snarling at a Pit Bull. She'd dared to stand up to the cartel. She'd even taken a bite out of them. And no doubt, they would strike back soon.

Her thoughts continued along this dark vein as they rode in silence. Within a few minutes, she turned onto the street where the restaurant was under construction. Her uncles' food truck squatted next to a cluster of card tables under a tarp in the parking lot, concealing much of the building. Cars lined the street, and Veranda assumed her stepfather, Miguel, had his crew working into the evening to speed up the project.

She wove the Tahoe around the various cars and trucks, searching for a place to park, when her mother gasped. Veranda stomped the brake pedal, alert for signs of danger. Her eyes found the construction zone. Scores of people milled around carrying Red Bird of Paradise bushes in their arms. She recognized friends and neighbors from the community chatting as they used shovels from the site to dig holes a few feet from the building's foundation. Camera crews were shooting footage of the event. Kiki Lowell held out her microphone, interviewing someone in front of a local nursery truck, loaded with bushes, parked nearby.

Lorena began to sob. She covered her face with her calloused hands and tears gushed between her fingers. Veranda stretched an arm around her mother's shoulders. "They're here for you," she whispered. "The whole community came out to support you, *Mamá*."

Then it was Veranda's turn to gasp. Sam walked into her line of sight from around a corner, directing members of the task force toward an empty patch of ground with freshly dug soil.

Agent Gates trudged toward the makeshift plot holding two bushes in her arms. Agents Lopez and Rios followed in her wake with more plants, while Sergeant Jackson and her Homicide squad carried shovels. Her mouth fell open when Lieutenant Diaz, Commander Webster, and Chief Tobias rounded the corner pushing wheelbarrows filled with bags of potting soil.

Unable to hold back any longer, Veranda allowed the tears to flow down her cheeks. The community had come out to support her mother, and her police family had come out for her as well. They had accepted her.

And she would learn to do the same.

Acknowledgments

Every day, law enforcement officers (LEOs) guard the flock, keeping the wolves at bay. Ever vigilant, they stand ready to sacrifice all. As someone who spent 22 years carrying a gun and badge, I have a special connection with the characters in my stories. Through fiction, I hope to shed light on the very real personal and professional struggles LEOs—and those who love them—endure.

Over the past year, I attended many book-related events. Spouses, partners, friends, and children of other authors—along with my own—helped bright-eyed writers spread the word about the latest book. For the "roadies" in our lives, it's a labor of love. For the author, it's a debt that can never be repaid. A special thank you to my roadies, Michael and Max, for making the journey fun.

No story would make it onto the shelves of bookstores, libraries, and other venues without a team of professionals working hard behind the scenes. Terri Bischoff, Acquiring Editor for Midnight Ink, is one of those heroes in the industry who has devoted her life to shepherding books and authors through the arduous journey to publication and beyond.

Every so often, you meet someone with such dynamic positive energy that you must take notice. When that person also shares your vision, the universe must take notice. My amazing and talented agent, Liza Fleissig of the Liza Royce Agency in New York, is that kind of person.

A special thank you to professional organizations for writers such as Sisters in Crime, International Thriller Writers, and Mystery Writers of America. Every year, they help aspiring writers learn the craft, and established authors connect with readers. Their encouragement, support and wisdom make all the difference.

I am blessed with a wonderful family, whether blood-related or bound by love. Their acceptance of me, with my many foibles, warms my heart as nothing else can. First and foremost are my husband, Michael, who encourages my dreams, and my son, Max, who inspires me every day. In addition to relatives and in-laws, I consider some of my closest friends to be family. One of those dear individuals is Deborah J Ledford. Words cannot express my gratitude for your love and support over the years.

Finally, I would like to thank readers of crime fiction. I have so much fun meeting people who are excited to discover a new voice and a new story. I love engaging with readers. After all, they are the reason I write.

SkipStyle Photography

About the Author

Before her foray into the world of crime fiction, Isabella Maldonado wore a gun and badge in real life. She retired as a captain after over two decades on the Fairfax County Police Department and moved to the Phoenix area, where her uniform now consists of tank tops and yoga pants.

During her tenure on the department, she was a patrol officer, hostage negotiator, spokesperson, and recruit instructor at the police academy. After being promoted, she worked as a patrol sergeant and lieutenant before heading the Public Information Office. Finally, as a captain, she served as Gang Council Coordinator and oversaw a patrol district station before her final assignment as the Commander of the Special Investigations and Forensics Division (since renamed the Investigative Support Division).

She graduated from the FBI National Academy in Quantico in 2008 after eleven weeks of physically and mentally challenging study for 220 law enforcement executives from around the world. She is proud to have earned her "yellow brick" for completing the famous FBI obstacle course.

Now her activities involve chasing around her young son and enjoying her family when she's not handcuffed to her computer.

Ms. Maldonado is a member of the FBI National Academy Associates, Fairfax County Police Association, International Thriller Writers, Mystery Writers of America, and Sisters in Crime, where she served as president of the Desert Sleuths Chapter in Phoenix in 2015 and currently sits on the board.

www.MidnightInkBooks.com

From the gritty streets of New York City to sacred tombs in the Middle East, it's always midnight somewhere. Join us online at any hour for fresh new voices in mystery fiction.

At midnightinkbooks.com you'll also find our author blog, new and upcoming books, events, book club questions, excerpts, mystery resources, and more.

MIDNIGHT
INK

MIDNIGHT INK ORDERING INFORMATION

 ### Order Online:
- Visit our website www.midnightinkbooks.com, select your books, and order them on our secure server.

 ### Order by Phone:
- Call toll-free within the U.S. and Canada at
  1-888-NITE-INK (1-888-648-3465)
- We accept VISA, MasterCard, American Express and Discover.
- Canadian customers must use credit cards.

 ### Order by Mail:
Send the full price of your order (MN residents add 6.875% sales tax) in U.S. funds, plus postage & handling to:

> Midnight Ink
> 2143 Wooddale Drive
> Woodbury, MN 55125-2989

Postage & Handling:

Standard (U.S.). If your order is:
$30.00 and under, add $6.00
$30.01 and over, FREE STANDARD SHIPPING

International Orders (Including Canada):
$16.00 for one book plus $3.00 for each additional book

Orders are processed within 12 business days. Please allow for normal shipping time.
Postage and handling rates subject to change.